DRAGON SCHOOL
EPISODES 6 - 10
Sarah K. L. Wilson

For all who love truth in a world of lies
and love hope in a world of despair,
this book is for you.

This is a work of fiction. Similarities to real people, places, or events are entirely coincidental.

DRAGON SCHOOL: EPISODES 6-10

First edition. June 7, 2018.

Copyright © 2018 Sarah K. L. Wilson.

Written by Sarah K. L. Wilson.

Dragon School: Dusk Covenant

Map

For a downloadable map, please visit www.sarahklwilson.com.

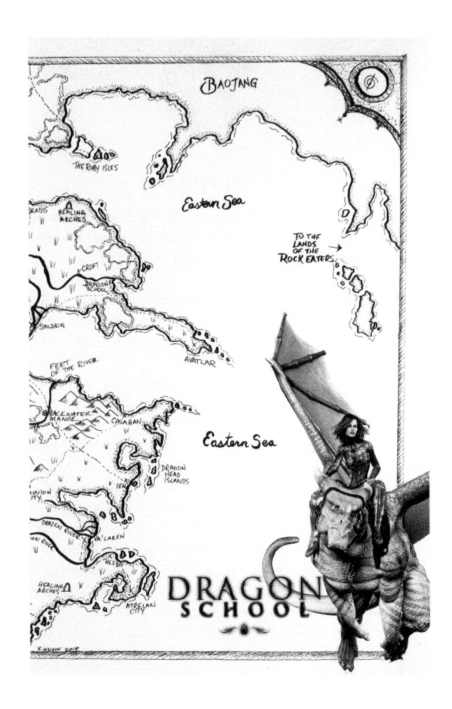

Chapter One

A deafening roar filled my ears as we fell away from the edge of the sky city Vanika. Kyrowat banked to the left, letting the blast of magic hit him on the belly, blocking us from the worst of it.

Hold tight.

His command in my head was so powerful that I found myself obeying before he'd finished the order. We corkscrewed through the air and my world was a blur of orange fire, rending steel and a force so powerful that it was all I could do to cling to his back. Hubric bucked and twisted in the saddle in front of me, his wiry frame moved almost fluidly despite the chaos, as if this was far from the first time he'd weathered such storms.

Are you safe?

Raolcan's thoughts had an edge of anxiety. He didn't need to be worried about me. I was more worried about the city behind us. The Dusk Covenant was destroying it one piece at a time. Sad enough that they were ruining such a mind-blowing structure and center of culture, even worse that there were thousands of innocent people within the city who didn't have the time or means to get out. Not everyone could fly away on dragon-back.

Kyrowat's spin ended and I gathered my balance enough to look out across the afternoon vista. The sun was dipping toward the horizon and soon it would be nightfall. Where would we go? The city was in flames and filled with our enemies. We had no supplies, and already I felt the cold biting through my leathers. How would Rakturan feel, being carried in the mouth of a dragon?

He's not fond of my breath and he thinks I'm drooling too much. Does he have any idea how hard it is to fly with your mouth open and not drool? He should try it!

He should just be glad Raolcan was purple or he'd probably have been chomped in two by now.

It's a favor to you – and to Savette. She likes him for some reason.

I hadn't expected Raolcan to do Savette a favor.

I'm growing fond of her. She might be cold and distant, but it's a shell around a very sensitive interior.

I felt a pang of jealousy. Raolcan and I – our bond was supposed to be special.

So, I can't be friends with anyone else?

My cheeks felt hot despite the freezing cold. He could feel my jealousy! But how did you keep from feeling fear when it just welled up on its own? I'd saved Savette, and now I'd risked the one thing I had – his friendship.

Two things: First, she saved you this time, so you're probably even. Second, you haven't lost my friendship. I can be her friend and yours at the same time. I'm a pretty amazing dragon that way. And just so you know, we have a bond that no one else can have. It doesn't matter who I am friends with, it won't lessen that.

There was no one as good as Raolcan. Chastened, I watched where we were going and tried to push aside my embarrassment at being so foolish. Ephretti led us toward the mountain foothills to the north-east like she had a place in mind. She was angling to a point where the forest cleared and a river ran through the snow, unfrozen so early into winter.

I risked a look behind us. Dragons bubbled out of the sky city like a pot boiling over and all around the perimeter, ropes and cables extended to the ground. We were too far by now to see the colors of the dragons that swirled around the city or the contents of the baskets and boxes being lowered to the ground. I fought a roiling belly as I thought of the panic that must fill those busy streets and the fear in the hearts of the people there. I should be there helping them. It wasn't fair that I was safe when so many others weren't.

I'm glad you're safe. It's why I came for you. We can only do what we can.

Maybe we could go back and ferry people to safety.

Then what of Savette? She's still too full of magic. What about Rakturan? Your comrades will happily kill him if you don't stop them. What about Hubric? Did you not swear to him? None of us can do everything, spider. Crushing yourself under responsibilities that aren't yours is not wise.

We sped toward the forest floor. I could make out a small farm along the bank of the river. Smoke billowed from a chimney and there were cleared animal pens – although I saw no animals. Someone stood in the farmyard looking up at us, as if waiting for us to land. Ephretti descended first with her two dragons and Lenora's.

Her dragons are twins. They can't bear to be separated. One of them should be carrying this foul-tasting prince!

How had Raolcan brought them all in time to save us? I still didn't understand that.

I was listening to Savette's thoughts while you were gone. Chaotic. Yellow and black and white. She was worried about magic she sensed in the city. She could feel it like wells being tapped all around her with golden streams flowing upwards. They were drawing too much. Too much. It was filling her up, too. She didn't want it, but she couldn't stop. The Magika – Zavin – who was helping her didn't believe it when she tried to warn him – but I did. I could feel it was real.

He must have been scared.

I knew I had to act. I spoke to the boy – Aldeen – and he saddled us all and opened the doors. He took Dashira's dragon. We were preparing to leave when I could sense conflict above. Dashira was up there and Zavin and two others – enemies, maybe. Their thoughts were chaotic. There was golden light and a feeling of power and then Savette came running down the steps to us and leapt on my back. I didn't wait. I could feel she was terrified. As we launched through the door, power surged behind us ripping the place apart. We barely made it out alive. Enkenay has an injured leg.

How could Aldeen ride Dashiva's dragon?

She's his mother. Dragons respect blood. Even Whites.

He's a trainee?

Too young for that.

And now without a mother.

We don't know that. We don't know anything except that we are alive. Hold on to that, spider. If my senses are right, this is only the beginning.

Chapter Two

He touched down on the grassy field before the farmhouse moments before we did. I held on tight as Kyrowat skidded to a stop beside Raolcan. Beside us, Ephretti and Lenora were already leaping off Bellrued's back while Raolcan spat Rakturan out with the force of someone dispelling phlegm.

Rakturan rolled across the snowy ground and spun up to a ready stance, on one knee with his sword held ready before him.

I need a drink. Anything to wash the taste of him out of my mouth.

Raolcan flared fire off in a safe direction. Maybe that would burn the taste away.

Hubric held his hands up. "No need to begin fighting all over again. We're here now and we'll deal with things as they stand."

"You were going to leave me to die." Rakturan's features stood out on his beautiful face as if anger intensified them. "How do I know you won't kill me now?"

"I'm a Dragon Rider of the Purple, boy."

"That means nothing to me!" Was that fear he was hiding in his voice?

"It means lies don't suit me. You should know that. If you don't, then you shouldn't be in the Dominion."

"I am a foreigner in this land, come in peace to marry one of your own, and *this* is how you treat me!"

Hubric cleared his throat, but there was a warning in the action. Kyrowat flamed dramatically to the side, as if to remind Rakturan that he was a dragon, too.

"A message is not as important as your life."

"I will be the judge of that."

We broke through the narrow supply corridor and into an open room beyond. The man with the authoritative voice had his back to us, and two other men, rough, bloody, and wearing dented armor, stood in front of him. Were they dragoons?

"As you say, of course, my liege," one of them said, but worry etched deep lines across his forehead.

The man with his back to us turned and I gasped when I saw the mask that covered his face. The Dominar! He was alive!

Chapter Four

We dropped to our knees, but the Dominar waved a dismissive hand. "No time for that."

Hubric stood, and I fought my way back up to standing.

"It's good that you're here, Dragon Riders. I have need of you." It would be easier to tell what the Dominar thought if he didn't wear the mask. "Grim are the circumstances and dire the need."

"We are your servants," Hubric said, fist to heart. We all joined him in the salute. I glanced at Lenora and her eyes were wide when they met mine. Were we really here? Helping the Dominar in the middle of an insurrection?

"A message must be delivered to Comard Eaglespring, General of the Spire, Lord of War in Dominion City. I demand your service, Purple rider, and that of your Sworn apprentice."

"Of course, Dominar." Hubric – always focused and ready to spring – seemed even more intense as he replied.

"The boy says you brought with you another man and a Magika. Is she fully trained?"

Hubric shook his head. "The girl is Savette High Castelan of Leedris. She is no trained Magika but came into her power during torture by enemies. She may overcome her bounds and perish in the aftermath."

The look on the dragoons faces was grim and one spoke so quickly his words tumbled over each other. "Please, my liege, do not allow her near you. We can not bear another attack today."

"She'll find better help in Dominion City than where we are headed." The Dominar's words were firm.

"Your message could be lost if she loses control," the dragoon said.

"You would prefer her with us, then?"

The dragoon looked away and the Dominar said, "It is done. Now, there was another, a fighting man?"

"The Baojang prince," Hubric said.

The dragoons straightened at his words, swords rasping as they were drawn hurriedly from sheaths. "You brought him here? Why?"

Hubric bowed. "My deepest apologies. We did not expect our Dominar – long my he reign – to be at our safehouse. We came here to regroup."

"You were unaware of the secret passages to this farm on the trolley beneath the earth?" the dragoon asked.

"Very aware, but we had no suspicion that they would be used by you."

"Enough. We have barely enough time to plan for the future without second guessing the past," the Dominar said. "We require you, Green Dragon Rider, your apprentice and the lad who greeted us here to bear us to safety to the mountain hold of Gerdath. Have you the ability to bear Baojang with us as well?"

"Yes," Ephretti said firmly. "It is an honor to serve."

"Then so be it," the Dominar said. "Gather the supplies immediately and prepare the dragons while I write the message for the Purples to carry." He motioned to me and Hubric gently pushed me forward.

I hobbled to the side of the Dominar and he led me to a small table beside an open fireplace. A fire was set but not lit, and in the cold afternoon it felt very bleak.

"This is your first message, Sworn?" His tone was kind.

"Yes, my liege."

"Then let's make it memorable, hmm?"

"I don't think that will be difficult, Lord Dominar."

He laughed. "I suppose not."

Chapter Five

If I had ever, in a fit of fancy, imagined what it was like to be with the Dominar – the great ruler over our vast land – I think I would have imagined bowing Castelans, fascinating subjects on bended knee, guards with flashing armor, and a sense of awe over everyone. What I wouldn't have imagined was a man in a cold farmhouse sitting at the farmer's table on a hand-hewn wooden chair. He worked a stub of pencil across paper, carefully writing out his note in a florid hand.

He must have brought the writing supplies with him. They were hardly the things farmers might have. The only thing that made him still look like a ruler was his ostentatious clothing and the fanciful mask that covered his face. In this weather, it must sting with cold. Was it my imagination, or did his head droop under the weight now that the attention and pomp were past?

He rubbed the mask over his forehead and I noticed it was more polished at that point as if this was his habit. Was he anxious? Was he broken-hearted over the loss of his dragoons and friends? What a strange time we lived in where tragedy and uncertainty swept up common people like me and the most uncommon person in the world in the same moment.

Tragedy and uncertainty are both things of which no one is immune. Not even dragons.

When he was done, he pulled a white cylinder from his waistband, rolled up the note, slid it into the cylinder and then pulled out a pouch with balls of wax and sealed either end with wax.

"Usually, I'd put my seal on the missive, but I'm afraid it was lost in transit," he said, turning to me. What would it be like to relate to the whole world through that mask? "Amel Leafbrought, Sworn of the Purple, accept this missive from the hand of your Dominar and give it to none other than its recipient, Comard Eaglespring, General of the Spire, Lord of War. Or, if he has fallen, to his rightful heir. Swear this by the Truth which is all you have."

I'd never done this before. I glanced around, but Hubric had disappeared. Had he gone to gather supplies? I'd have to do my best.

"I swear it by the Truth which is all I have. I'll deliver the message."

"Then fly like the wind, Sworn. Let nothing hinder you until you reach your destination."

I bowed. It felt right under the circumstances. As I straightened, he placed the message cylinder in my hand and I shivered at the touch of his glove against my skin. Who would have thought that I would ever brush up against royalty? It was beyond belief. I'd better be sure not to disappoint him. It was time to fly.

Always ready for that!

My first mission! My first chance to really be a purple Dragon Rider.

Don't get too excited yet. Bow again and get out of the Dominar's view before you dance with joy.

I hastily bowed and tucked the cylinder into my leathers before I hobbled away. The Dominar's dragoons watched the back door and windows, their movements twitchy.

"Tell your Green rider to hurry," one of them said to me as if a trainee would say such a thing to a full Dragon Rider.

I tried to offer him a calm expression with a nod, but his face grew thunderous. Wrong move, Amel. I hurried out of the room and back into the corridor of supplies.

"Amel. You have the message?" Hubric had eight large leather satchels around him. They bulged with whatever he had packed in them. Food, I hoped, and other supplies. On top of the heap, he'd thrown three fur cloaks, leather gloves, and woolen cowls. They wouldn't be enough in this weather, but they would have to do. Some sort of fur with lacings was thrown there as well – over-boots perhaps?

"Yes, master."

"Good. A first message is a very important moment for any Purple Dragon Rider. The Dominar gave you a great honor by singling you out for it. He probably doesn't realize that usually we would wait many months before you were given one of your own, but you will do fine. I'll be with you every step of the way."

I smiled timidly.

"First rule to delivering messages?" His question was so fast that I wasn't sure what to say. I hadn't been taught this! He clapped a hand on my shoulder. "The first rule is: don't lose it. It's not like we can put magical beacons on them to find them if they are lost. Keep it on you. Keep it safe. Check often that you have not lost it."

I nodded, gravely.

"Now," he said. "Let's get this gear loaded up. It will take a few trips, but we need to be gone as soon as we are able. Ephretti is almost ready to leave and we all must leave at once or we risk showing our location to our enemies. By now they may have regrouped enough to watch the skies."

I slung one of the satchels over my shoulder and followed after him, glad the crutch he'd given me was rugged enough for the terrain. Things were uncertain and tragic and yet in the middle of it all, a little orange flicker of hope was on my horizon, bright and lively. I was going to chase that for as long as I could.

Chapter Six

Hubric was right about Ephretti. As we pushed through the doors and out into the dusk, I could see she had all her dragons lined up in a row. Lenora and Aldeen were loading them with gear. Lenora dropped hers and rushed over to me.

"Amel! Your first message! That's so exciting."

I smiled in return, pleased but not sure what to say.

"Listen," she said, not waiting for me to respond. "We're going to be split up for a while. But you and I are rising through the ranks fast. We're going to see each other again. I want you to swear that we'll stay friends." She looked both directions like someone was going to overhear us, but everyone else was too busy with their own tasks. "Things are getting dangerous and chaotic so quickly and we Castelans have our alliances, our masters have our vows, but you aren't a Castelan and you'll need friends again. So, swear we'll stay friends. Swear you'll call on me when you need help. I swear that I'll be there for you."

I nodded, blinking back tears. "I swear."

"And stay out of trouble! Especially if you run into Leng Shardson! That man is going to cause you trouble!"

She hugged me, smiled quickly, and ran back to her task, leaving me lightheaded as I hobbled toward Raolcan. I had another friend. It made me feel all soft and sweet.

I told you that more people would see your value. Just keep persevering and one day you'll have more friends than you can fit on my back. Speaking of which, you might need to help Savette right now.

As I drew closer, I saw what he meant. Hubric and Ephretti were crouched over Savette and Rakturan. She was curled in a ball on the ground, her too-light cloak wrapped around her. Both her hands gripped one of Rakturan's.

I dropped the satchel and hobbled over. Hubric looked up at me, concern on his face.

"She won't let go of him."

Ephretti looked up, too, her sharp, beautiful features etched with condemnation.

"We need to load Baojang with us. Those are our orders."

"You shouldn't separate us," Rakturan said. His voice was tender, and one of his hands gently stroked her back.

Ephretti turned to him, frustration emanating from her face. "You shouldn't be holding her like that. You've no more rights to her. You are promised to someone else."

Rakturan flushed but his words were bold. "Your Dominar is still considering my request to return my troth to Savette Leedris. She needs my protection – especially now."

"You can see her power as well as I can," Ephretti hissed. "You want it for yourself and for your nation. This isn't love, it's a power play."

"It's not." He shook his head, but now the blood drained from his face as Ephretti crossed her arms. "We leave in five minutes and by order, you fly with us."

"By whose order?" He swallowed.

Hubric laid a hand on his arm. "Prince, we're not friends, but stop for a moment while I talk to you like we are. I'd rather just knock you to the ground and throw you over Ephretti's dragon, but I'm feeling gracious right now. Look at the girl. She clearly needs help. The sky city is in uproar and she won't get it here. If you really care for her, you'll let us take her to Dominion City to see the best Magikas there."

Rakturan's expression was torn, his hand shook in Savette's.

"You want what's best for her?" Hubric asked.

"Yes." It sounded like a vow.

"Then let us take her to Dominion City."

"Why can't I go with her?" His eyes looked desperate. Why? Did he really care this much – could that be possible when he knew so little of her? – or was Ephretti right and it was all an act to get power?

"Orders." Ephretti drew her blade. "And no, I won't tell you whose. Not yet. You're a prince of Baojang. Act like it. There is a war that needs to be prevented and you and I need to do that. You can't chase after a girl when you have a nation to defend."

He looked like he was being ripped in two and then he swore violently. I thought that I saw tears in his eyes as he stood, disentangling his hand from Savette's grip. Was it a trick of my imagination? She reached toward him and I stepped forward and took her hand in my own, dropping to the ground to croon in her ear.

"It will be okay, Savette. I will keep you safe."

"Stay with her and I'll load the dragons," Hubric said. "We'll load her last. She'll go with you on Raolcan?"

I nodded.

"Good. Best for everyone that way."

He strode off and I rubbed Savette's back like Rakturan had before. For a moment, I thought I was hearing things, but no. Raolcan was singing us both a dragon lullaby in our minds.

Towering, white in field of blue,
Soft and gentle as we flew,
Through the golden sunlight bright,
Dream of never-ending flight.

Chapter Seven

We flew through the night, the icy wind biting at us through the fur cloaks and woolen scarves.

How do you think I feel? I could use one of those cloaks.

For a wonder, Savette slept through most of the night, leaning against my back. Her gentle snores could be heard any time the wind quieted enough to hear anything.

She needs the sleep, poor girl. She hadn't had a good sleep in a long time.

As if sleeping against my back as we rode Raolcan was any kind of rest.

It is compared to what she's been through.

Did he know what that was?

Some secrets leak out, but I'll guard them safe for her. She's one of us now – broken.

Broken and yet terrifyingly powerful. If those blasts of magic back in Vanika were just little bits of her power overflowing, what more could she be capable of?

If it doesn't consume her first.

The hours passed slowly, made slower by my anxiety about Savette and the intense cold. When had I last slept? I was tired enough to sleep for a week curled in a fur blanket with Raolcan on one side and a raging fire at the other...

Wake up. I don't need you to guide me, but you do need to be awake when we fly.

Why? Wouldn't the straps hold us in place?

Would you want me to fall asleep? If I fall, I might not wake up before we hit the ground. I'd be fine, but what about you two?

Was he teasing me? Whether he was or not, I worked to stay awake, wiggling my toes in my good foot and the fingers in both hands to try to keep the blood flowing. I had so much to think about, but in the cold, my thoughts just circled around and around on each other. Savette – cold – message – cold – Rakturan – cold – Savette – cold –

It makes for boring mental conversation.

Get me warm and I'll be as interesting as you like!

Look! Dawn breaks.

To my left, the sky was lightening. Moments later, a ring of gold curved around the horizon. He was right. Day had come. My heart soared at the thought of the sun on me, warming my face, warming my back, warming...

Not yet, I'm afraid.

In front of us, Hubric and Kyrowat leaned into a dive. We followed them, tight on their heels. Plunging through the clouds, I saw the tops of the trees of the forest below us and a long cliff face. Kyrowat was aiming at the spot where the trees met the cliff face. We followed and then he turned, unexpectedly, and ducked into a cave on the cliff face, higher than the tops of the trees, but hidden by the curve of the rock. Raolcan followed him and the rising sun was eclipsed by the dark of the cave. It must have been massive to hold two dragons.

It's going to be tight.

A light flared ahead and then Hubric strode forward with a lantern in hand. The cave was very tight. With both dragons pressed against the walls, there was only a tiny space in the middle. Already, I felt it warming up with the heat of our bodies.

We will keep warm enough in such a tight space. Two dragons can really heat things up.

Hubric helped me ease Savette down and then he spoke.

"We need some sleep, or we'll drop out of the sky. Should be warm enough here for a few hours. Then we'll mount up again and find an inn before nightfall. No need to stand watch. The dragons will know if anyone comes."

I nodded, sleepily. I didn't need convincing. We'd laid Savette against Raolcan to keep her warm and I lay down next to her, curling up in my cloak, making sure that as much of me as possible was against the side of my dragon.

Sleep well, spider.

Food and drink and other necessities could wait. For now, it was sleep, sweet, sweet sleep...

Chapter Eight

"He was trying to help me to form a channel to let off the magic. It filled me up – too much, he said. It will overwhelm me if I can't let it off, but it keeps building, building, building." Savette's voice was thin and shaky as she spoke. I woke to her words.

She's speaking to Hubric. Stay resting for now.

"Magikas draw power from set wells throughout the land and they can contain it within themselves for a time. Too much and it overwhelms them."

"I know that from my studies. But it's not like that for me. I feel it in everything and I just keep drawing, drawing, drawing on it."

"And is it letting off?"

"It did when I blasted Magika Hectorus. It did when I blasted those men trying to kill you."

"And the explosion?"

Her words came through chattering teeth. "I felt him outside. I could tell he was full of magic. He was going to do something ... I didn't know what. I warned the dragons. I rushed towards them down the steps. Magika Zavin and Ephretti Oakboon called to me to stop, but they hadn't expected me to run. I screamed at them to follow, but they just stood there. We escaped. Just in time. The explosion – that's what will happen to me if I don't learn to control this."

"We'll find you help." Hubric's voice was full of confidence.

"No one can help."

"And one will come from the north, burning, burning,
Judgment and Wisdom borne by the flow of spirit to spirit
Do not speak to us of the times that follow,

For they shall be as a dream of death as a nightmare walking,"

Hubric was quoting again, but it was Savette who finished his quote: *"The dusk shall vanquish all but the covenant until the dawn of the tide."*

How many of these prophesies were there?

Hundreds. They speak of a day of desolation that will come and of the key to the rebirth of the whole world.

You know about them, too, Raolcan?

We dragons learn them by rote, just as your Castelans do.

I shivered in the dark of the cave. I didn't like these prophecies. It wasn't good to dwell on hard times coming. It made it harder to grow strong now.

And yet, without them how would we hope? How would we know what to do when disaster strikes?

With our own wits and good judgment?

Have you met people? How many of them have good judgment? And what about when two wise people disagree?

They were good points, but I'd still rather live without prophecy.

I think Savette would rather live without it, too. But she's stuck with it now. What's happening to her isn't normal. Hubric is right to quote the prophesies. Who knows if there may be a key there?

Who made these prophecies in the first place?

They come to us from beyond, but they were mostly written down by Ibrenicus and others like him.

"You awake over there, Amel?" Hubric asked. I sat up and rubbed my eyes. "We should eat, drink and take care of anything necessary before we fly again. We'll stop at an inn for tonight, but we need to put a hard day of flying in first. We slept longer than we planned to. It's almost noon."

He looked worried.

"Will a few hours make so great a difference? It will take days to get to Dominion City."

"Days? Ha! Try weeks."

"Even flying?"

"The Empire is vast, Sworn. It is both our security and our frailty."

I nodded and turned to Savette. "Do you need anything?"

Her white, glowing stare made me swallow. "I've been taken care of."

What were we going to do about those eyes when we got near people? Those were sure to draw attention.

Hubric handed me a white silk scarf. "When we get close to a town, you'll need to bind her eyes with that. You won't mind, will you, Savette?"

"No," she said, distantly.

"Better that people think she's blind than that they see what really has happened to her."

Chapter Nine

There's something special about a hamlet town on the edge of a mountain range. Maybe it's the way that the farms nearby seem to be placed on the top of every rolling hill with their sheep and crops planted out around them like roots to a great tree. Maybe it's the way the people's gaits seem more playful and less purposeful. It gives the entire place a feeling of home and family and happiness. We arrived in Linsc, setting our dragons down in the town square.

People arrived so quickly that it was like mosquitos at night – our mere presence attracted them without any need to do or say more.

"Have you come from Vanika, Dragon Riders?" The man who spoke looked like he was the mayor. He wore a thick band of cloth around his belly, an emblem stitched onto the front in careful needlework.

"You've heard news of Vanika then?" Hubric asked.

"Horses came through an hour ago. On their way to Dominion City. They said terrible things. Things that can't be true." Around him the gathering crown nodded, grim expression on their faces.

"Such as?" Hubric seemed undisturbed by their stares and I was glad we'd thought to bind the scarf around Savette's eyes. These people were touchy. Who knows what they would do if they saw her white glowing eyes right now.

"They said the city was devastated by Magikas," one man said.

"Said refuges are flooding the surrounding towns. Said they'd be here by tomorrow or the next day. How are we supposed to take care of refugees? We can barely keep our own farms profitable with the Dominion's new taxes and trade to Baojang tariffed like it is!"

The mayor held up a hand. "The riders said that the Dominar is dead. Do you know if that is true?"

"Sounds like tall tales and stories to me," Hubric said, drawing a thin stick out of a pocket and chewing on the end of it. "And while I love a good story as much as the next man, what I really need is a couple of rooms for the night."

"A couple?" a robust man beside the mayor asked. He wore the white apron of an innkeeper.

Hubric held up two fingers. "Two rooms. Hot food. A bath if you have it."

"Two silver each," the man with the apron said.

"You rob me blind."

"If you want hot baths you pay hot bath price."

Hubric scratched his chin and pulled a face before saying. "Two it is then."

"So, there are no refugees?" the mayor asked. "Vanika has not fallen?"

"She stood where she always has when I left her," Hubric said, "but as to refugees, I don't know. There was chaos in the city when we left."

The crowd stiffened at his words. This wasn't what they wanted to hear.

"Shouldn't you have stayed to fight?" a little boy asked before being hushed by his mother.

"We're purples, boy," Hubric said. "Our game is the delivery of messages."

"And are you delivering one?"

Hubric winked. "Always. Come here."

The boy ran forward and Hubric extracted a candy from his pocket and gave it to the boy. "I have a message for you: candy makes life sweeter."

The boy laughed, and tension dissolved in the ring of people.

"Well, come on then. Daylight's wasting," the innkeeper said. "There's room in the stableyard for the dragons as we've no horses at present. It's up to you to tend them, though. I won't lose an arm to one of them, I can tell you!"

I wouldn't eat his arm if we were out of supplies and facing down a dinner of grass and shoots.

I was looking forward to the bath, but at the same time worry filled me. What would these little towns and hamlets do with the refugees who were on their way? It was this very thing we had wanted to prevent all along and now it was happening anyway. I felt raw inside thinking about it.

Chapter Ten

*W*ake up! *Wake up!*

I woke with a start. Savette snored in the bed next to me. We'd both bathed the night before and our hair was wet, but she'd insisted that I leave the scarf over her eyes. She'd produced a pair of tiny silver scissors and cut the frazzled ends off my burnt hair without cutting my skin, so she must have been able to see somehow – and to still be in the real world enough to offer an act of kindness to me.

"Get up Savette. We need to dress," I said, pulling my leathers back on. There was a pounding on my door. I shoved my boots on my feet, grabbed my crutch and hobbled to the door.

The pounding began again, as I unbarred the door, opening it quickly. Hubric rushed through, nearly knocking me down.

"Close it up again. Are you packed?"

He helped me swing the door closed and bar it. I worked quickly to strap my crutch to my arm.

"I put all our things away before we went to bed."

"Good," he said, snatching up our satchel and helping Savette up. She was fully dressed but struggling with her fur cloak. I scrambled to help her despite Hubric's desperate expression. "We need to leave. Now."

"What happened?" I asked. I still felt groggy. How long was it until dawn?

"Chaos. Other travelers arrived throughout the night. They are trying to seize our dragons." He flung the shutters open and, in the yard, I saw a ring of men – at least thirty. They were armed, but their clothing and helms were unpolished and unmatched. Who could they be?

Ruffians from the countryside around Vanika. They think they can take us as mounts.

Were they crazy? I watched as one man ran toward Kyrowat, axe in hand. The dragon gouted flames, lighting him up like a torch. A dark figure pulled back from the ring into the shadows. There was something familiar about him...

Definitely crazy.

"Up on the window ledge," Hubric said, pulling us forward. "Here, take the bag, Amel. I have Savette."

I slung the satchel over my shoulder and Hubric helped Savette climb up onto the sill. Kyrowat launched into the air, flying toward the inn. Hubric and Savette leapt at the same time and Kyrowat caught them on his back, bouncing with their sudden weight and then pushing hard with his massive wings to gain height. Maybe this was why they made us practice so many leaping maneuvers as trainees.

I scrambled up onto the ledge, swaying there. The bag was heavy, and my dead leg felt like lead. All the muscles around it ached after yesterday's icy ride. I felt sweat forming just from my climb up to the ledge.

There was a new pounding at the door and this time I couldn't be Hubric. In the yard, Raolcan spread his flame out thick as snow as the ring of men focused on their solitary target. Could he hold out on his own? There were so many! Fortunately, they seemed to fear the flame, attacking only in little bursts.

There was a splintering sound from the door. Raolcan launched into the air, his wings sweeping a half-dozen men aside as he gained height. I clung to the window ledge waiting for him. More splintering met my ears and the sound of something heavy hitting the door.

"You might as well open up!" a voice called.

Fear shot through me. Hurry, Raolcan!

The door burst open and the room filled with angry people and gleaming weapons at the same time that Raolcan shouted, *Jump!*

I leapt, sobbing with relief as he caught me. Fingertips had brushed my arm as I leapt. It was that close. Why would they try to take Raolcan and Kyrowat? Did they have a death wish?

People do strange things when fear grips them.

We rose above the cloud layer and pulled in tight to Kyrowat who snapped half-heartedly at Raolcan. My heart jumped.

Don't take it seriously. He's riled up from the fight below. He won't hurt you.

I signaled 'What now?' to Hubric in Dragon Rider sign.

"No more inns," he mouthed to me.

I nodded. It looked like we would have another cold night flying. At least the moon was bright above the cloud cover and Raolcan seemed energetic.

I need to eat soon. A sheep would be nice.

We'd have to tend to that when dawn came. How could I ask Hubric in a respectful way?

Don't worry, Kyrowat is complaining about it incessantly. He will relent.

I could almost feel Raolcan's mouth watering.

Chapter Eleven

Hunting went well for the dragons – or sheep-stealing perhaps, but I tried not to think about that. It was a serious crime in our village. A hanging crime.

I'd like to watch them try to hang me. They don't have enough rope or a high enough gallows.

I shuddered. I didn't want to think about that. Hubric and Savette and I sat on a grassy knoll eating our own lunch of dried sausages, hard cheese, and crusty bread. Hubric had the foresight to stock up on supplies at the inn but if we weren't going to another soon we would have to ration the food.

"So, no more inns," I said.

"Definitely not," Hubric said. "When we need supplies, we'll barter with individual farms. When we get farther south the chaos should reduce. Refugees will only go so far, I'm sure. They'll be waiting for the dragoons to come and restore order in Vanika."

"And will they restore order?"

"As soon as they can get there."

I turned to Savette. "Do you need anything? You could take your blind-fold off."

She shook her head. She seemed to prefer it and it didn't hinder her at all from moving freely as if she could see through it. Maybe she could.

"Are you finding a way to harness your magic?"

She shook her head again.

"Let her be, Amel," Hubric commanded. "It's her fight, not yours. All we can do is be good friends to her right now." He cleared his throat awkwardly. "In the meantime, there's something we need to rectify about your education."

Had I failed in some way? I felt my heart speed up, my face growing hot.

"Oh, calm down. You're too conscientious, girl. Here's the thing: you're a cripple, but that doesn't mean you can't fight. It will be harder because you're slow and you can't maneuver or balance as well, but it isn't impossible. I think it would be best for you to use a reach-type weapon like a quarterstaff. It gives you something to lean on and you can use it to maneuver between strikes and defenses. It's why I gave you that crutch."

I looked at my crutch curiously. Other than being beautiful and metal, there was nothing weapon-like about it.

"Here, pass it to me." Hubric held out his hand and I unbuckled the crutch from my forearm and handed it to him.

He took the crutch in expert hands and twisted the carvings just below the handgrip. The top of the handgrip popped open and Hubric flicked the crutch forward and an inner shaft slid out, doubling the length of the crutch and locking in place. The forearm grip was still there, but the shaft was long now.

"I'll teach you the basics, and we'll work together on how to adapt the moves to your capabilities. I won't always be around, and we can't send you out there defenseless. You saw how quickly things can go sideways."

"Thank you," I said, and I meant it. Raolcan was always there for me, but sometimes he wouldn't be close enough to help.

"Okay, let's start with a simple pivot and see how we can adapt it for you. Watch me."

Over the next three days, I both loved and hated our practice drills. I loved learning the new skill and dreaming about mastering it. In just three days, Hubric taught me to pivot and spin using the staff like a crutch. He taught me two simple strikes from a position where I balanced on my good leg and one simple block. I hated it because my good leg was sore and tired, aching almost as much as the bad one now that we were pushing it so hard.

"It will hurt less as you grow stronger," Hubric promised, but that was poor consolation during fitful nights of aching sleep.

Savette remained mostly silent; sleeping when we slept and eating when we ate. She liked to stay close to Hubric or me and slept next to Raolcan. He didn't seem to mind.

I like her mind, even when it's turbulent and wrestling the great snake of magic that threatens to choke it out.

I was surprised to see that Hubric slept against Kyrowat, too.

"Only a fool passes up extra warmth on a winter's night," he said when he noticed me watching, but I thought it was more than that. They were as close as Raolcan and I were.

All purples are close to their riders. He and Kyrowat share a mind like we do and like Leng and Ahlskibi do. It's one reason we are solitary. We don't need or want many others around.

It made a lot of sense.

On the third day, I woke to see Savette standing on an outcropping close to where we were camped. She held her arms up as if reaching for the rising sun and I could have sworn that her whole body was glowing, though it might have just been an effect of the dawn and my own tired eyes.

"In the dawn glows the chosen,
Bringer of our enemies' downfall.
Light the only companion,
On journey to the heart."

Hubric had woken, too, and as always, he had a prophecy to quote.

"Do you think your prophecies are about Savette?" I asked, quietly.

He shrugged.

"If you don't think they are, then why do you always quote them?"

"Habit," he snapped, but I thought it was more than that. I thought he believed them and that he thought they were being fulfilled in Savette.

I watched them carefully that morning, certain that I saw him showing her deference in his decisions. Was it just the compassion of an old man for a pretty young woman, or was it something more? Did he think Savette was the chosen one of prophecy?

Chapter Twelve

We found a farm that night and paid the farmer for a place to sleep in his barn. His wife offered some roasted vegetables at a hefty price and a pair of sheep for the dragons. Hubric paid them the full price without haggling over it. Hot food was a luxury and it was nice to know the sheep wouldn't be stolen as we left the farmhouse for the barn. The farmhouse door closed with a bang and I saw the farmer's wife closing the curtains with a frown on her face. Profit or not, she wasn't happy with us sleeping in her barn. We'd left Savette with the dragons, so it wasn't like she'd even seen the things most likely to spook her.

"We want to come and go as easily as we can," Hubric said, by way of explanation. "Haggling arouses interest. You saw their faces. They want as little to do with us as possible, so we accept the dry barn on a wet night and the hot meal with grace and move on. It's the Dragon Rider way."

It was certainly wet. Yesterday we had left the snow-covered ground and entered a world of gray skies and constant rain. I was looking forward to somewhere dry to sleep for the night.

"Perhaps we could try an inn again tomorrow," I suggested. The price for the barn and vegetables had been as steep as any inn would be.

"No more inns," Hubric said.

"How do you get coin, Hubric?" I asked. It wasn't like there was time to make money on the side when you were busy flying the Dominion's messages from place to place.

He chuckled. "Dragon Riders are issued yearly funding from the Dominar. We are his vassals. The Council of Sky People divides the funds amongst the school and the Colors to meet our needs. The Color issues us a monthly stipend."

"We have our own governing body? A council?"

He laughed again. "You really didn't get very far in your training, did you? Of course, we do. Someone has to deal with all the boring politics and administration. Now, enough about this. We have hungry people to feed – me especially, and then you need to train with your staff, and when you're too tired to move I'm going to teach you cards."

"Is that essential to my training?"

"It's essential to my sanity. It's been more than a week since I played and I'm feeling an itch." His grin was infectious, and I laughed. I didn't usually have much energy left after practicing with my staff, but this sounded like it would be more mental than physical.

Raolcan and Kyrowat were already lying outside the barn in the dripping rain. They couldn't fit through the barn door.

We don't mind sleeping in the rain. At least it isn't snow. That's a relief!

And at least Hubric had a pair of sheep for them.

It will tide us over until we can get a real meal, although we've been given strict warnings to eat them over that hill in the distance so we don't terrify the farmer.

"Get Savette settled inside with some food. I'll bring the sheep over to Kyrowat and Raolcan. They can't eat them so close to the farm," Hubric said. He shoved the pot of roasted vegetables at me and strode away.

I found Savette next to Raolcan. She was caressing his wing absently, her face tilted up to the sky as if she didn't care that her blindfold was getting wet. I could see a faint glow behind it. Was the light in her eyes getting brighter, or was it just because the cloth was wet?

"Come inside the barn, Savette. We can dry out and eat something hot."

She didn't answer, so I hobbled closer and touched her shoulder, balancing so I could still hold our dinner at the same time.

"Savette?"

"Mmm?"

"Come into the barn with me for the night. The dragons will be fine."

"Someone is coming." Her voice was far away.

I spun around, peering into the fading light in every direction. There was no sign of anyone but us.

"Let's deal with that when they get here."

"He's having trouble finding us."

"Can you follow me?" I still couldn't believe that she could move around with her eyes completely covered. It made me nervous. What else could she do now?

Without answering, Savette turned to me and when I began to hobble toward the barn, she followed me.

"Who do you think we really are, Amel? Are we oppressors because we harness dragons and ride them when they should be free?"

"Perhaps," I said. I didn't like the idea of dragons being bound to dragon riders any more than she did.

"Or are we the best defense our people have? Where should our priorities lie? Should I be trying to learn more power to defend my people, or should I forsake it and refuse to participate in protest for what they do to dragons? Should I seek to fulfill Hubric's prophesies or wait to watch someone else leap in and fulfill them? Should I let this magical self merge with this shadow of who I used to be, or should I hold them apart to keep them both safe?" She sounded so torn, like she'd lost her inner source of guidance.

"I think you should ask someone wiser than me," I said. I was shivering, and not just from the rain.

"Who is wiser than you, sweet Amel?"

"Hubric? Ephretti? Raolcan. There are many people wiser than I am."

She laughed. "Modesty is a lovely trait, but it's not entirely honest right now. I think your words are exactly the ones I need right now."

I swung the barn door open. The hay was stale, and mildew tinged the air. We walked in together and I scrambled to drag an old barrel out of a corner for Savette to sit on as I rummaged through the barn for supplies. There. An empty crate I could flip over and use as a table. I set to work.

"I know nothing about magic, Savette," I said as I worked. I didn't have much to offer her, but if she wanted my words, I should think of something to help. "But I think I know you a bit. You're honorable and deep. You want to serve your family and the Dominion and you don't want to hurt the people around you or be boxed in. The best way to do that isn't to fight this power. It's to channel it somehow into good. Don't let it eat up who you are. Don't get blinded by ambition or greed. Find ways to make it serve you instead of you serving it."

Her arms hugged her and I heard her muttering, "Let it serve me."

Hubric entered the barn, banging the door shut behind him. "Well, it's a good night to have a roof over our heads. It's only drizzling now, but it will be howling soon enough out there. I brought our things inside."

He carried the satchels full of our gear into the barn and looked over the food I'd laid out. "Eat first, fire second. We need to dry out the fur cloaks and our clothing. No one wants saddle chap, do they?"

I shook my head. He nodded briskly and handed around the food and we ate in silence, enjoying something hot for a change.

Sheep's not bad, either ... for something domesticated.

I could almost feel that he was over the hill instead of right outside the barn door. I was getting better at sensing him.

I was just finishing the chores after dinner, hanging the last of the wet things up around the flickering fire I'd built over the grate when the door opened again with another bang. Hubric had gone out to scrounge more wood. He needed to be more careful with that door or we'd be paying for that, too. Savette leapt to her feet. Startled, I turned to look at the door.

Hubric stood on tiptoes as a man shoved him forward into the barn, a knife to his neck. On either side, two pairs of intruders spread out on either side to surround us. I gasped.

"These are the ones we're looking for, alright," said a slight woman with a long scar on her face. There was something familiar about her. No, not her. It was her cheek. She had a symbol tattooed on it that I'd seen before. The sign of a spiral with a line slashed through it. I'd seen one just like it on Magika Hectorus' robes.

Chapter Thirteen

My eyes ran over our attackers. The man holding Hubric was huge, but he was only holding the knife and no other weapons. I knew by now that Hubric could have fought him if he wasn't ambushed. They must have caught him by surprise when he stepped out of the barn.

The weedy woman and the man beside her held swords, but they stood in dramatic poses, not with their feet well balanced beneath them. Hubric had taught me to stand properly to fight. It was clear that these two were untaught.

On the other side of the room, was a young man in Magika robes and a woman holding a quarterstaff. Their clothing and weapons didn't match the others. They'd been pulled together from what was available. Did that mean they were Dusk Covenant? And didn't they know that we had dragons?

They know.

Had they sent men out to attack out dragons? There was a roar from outside the barn and a flash of brightness like one of them had flamed. What was going on?

Four Magikas. We rushed back when they grabbed Hubric and found them here. They work against us and we don't dare flame your barn.

My heart was in my throat. The woman nearest me took a step forward and I shuffled my foot to the position Hubric had taught me, flicking my crutch into a quarterstaff with practiced skill. Five to two in here and four to two out there. It was time to put my lessons to work, even if it made my stomach churn just to think of it.

"This one has teeth!" the woman in front of me laughed. She braced her quarterstaff like she meant to attack.

43

"The cripple?" The man beside her frowned. "You're worried about a cripple, a blind girl, and an old man?"

"I'm not worried," the woman said, taking a second step forward. That quarterstaff was looking dangerous.

Colorful flares and gouts of flames showed through the cracks in the barn walls, but I didn't dare worry about Raolcan. I had my own problems here. My palms were slick with sweat at the thought of my first fight.

You're ready. Do exactly what you were taught. And don't worry about us. Kyrowat is wily and I am Raolcan!

My opponent jabbed at me and I pivoted out of the way, turning my pivot into a block just as Hubric had taught me. From the corner of my eye, I saw him slip out of the grasp of the man holding him while they were all distracted by my fight. I didn't have time to watch more. My enemy's quarterstaff came whistling toward my head. I dropped to one knee, using my own staff to jab at her. She barely blocked the jab and then I was pulling myself up on the staff and using it to pivot out of her reach again.

I spun to where Savette was in view. She threw up her hands, spread wide and forward like she was about to launch something into the air. Wind whipped up around her, billowing her long silvery hair out in every direction. Her hands filled with light that focused into a beam shooting out from her hand. As it left her palms she crumpled to the ground like a dropped doll. What -?

I felt the crack of my opponent's staff to my ribs. I shouldn't have let myself get distracted! Frustrated, I barely got my staff up to defend myself from the follow-up. My ribs ached, my eyes burned with the afterglow of Savette's magic, and pain seared through my head.

As I spun out of the way of another attack I saw Savette's beam had found its mark. The Magika was nothing but a pair of velvet boots smoking on the floor and a black char mark all around where they lay. I gasped and spun. I needed to get out of this defensive stance or I'd be no help to anyone! The other woman – the one with the tattoo on her face – was closing on me from my weak side. If two of them engaged me at once, then all was lost.

I jabbed toward my original opponent, following that up with a wide, two-handed strike toward her head. Bewildered by my sudden attack, she missed the block on the second blow and staggered. I took my opening and struck her knee. It must hurt so much to get hit there! Why was I doing this to her? I needed to stop and think about my actions!

Stop second guessing yourself and strike or they'll kill us all!

I obeyed. First, I hit her with the end of my staff, a hard jab to the midsection and then a second whack to the ribs. She fell to the floor, but a moment later, I fell, too, my quarterstaff knocked out from under me, and with it, my balance. The tattooed woman leapt on top of me, straddling me and pinning me to the ground.

"I have the other girl!" she yelled. "Which one are we supposed to take alive?"

"The blonde," the thick, muscle-bound man yelled, and the woman suddenly had a wicked glimmer in her eye. I heard a cry and the thick sound of something heavy hitting meat. "Don't think you can get me that way, old man."

I twisted, looking for Hubric. He was kneeling on the ground, one man dead and bleeding beside him and the man with the knife leaning over him, pulling his knife from Hubric's arm. We were outmatched and beaten. Was there anyone to rescue us?

These Magikas are tough. We still have two more to dispatch. We can't flame the barn without hurting you, too.

What would we do? I squirmed under the tattooed woman and she smacked me in the face. My head rang with pain and I tasted blood. I coughed and sputtered on it.

"Not so high and mighty now, are we, girl?" she asked, sword raised. She was watching me like she wanted to see something on my face before she finished me.

Help comes!

Raolcan! Always there for me!

Not me.

The door opened, once more with a crash. Could no one treat that door with respect? Through the smoke and dust with moonlight outlining him from behind, the silhouette of a man rushed forward. One swipe of his curving sword and the head of the large thug was severed. He toppled forward as Hubric dove out of the way. Two more steps and the figure leapt forward.

His plucked my attacker off me and flung her to the side. She hit a beam and fell senseless to the floor.

A hand grabbed mine, pulling me up. I was shaking from top to bottom when I finally met his eye. Rakturan.

Chapter Fourteen

"You shouldn't have left me behind if you couldn't protect her," he said, letting go of me and rushing to Savette's fallen form. "What have they done to her?"

"Nothing," Hubric said with a cough. His hand felt at the wound on his arm gingerly. "She did it to herself. Her magic is too strong. She needs help. And right now, she needs time to recover."

"She needs healing arches," Rakturan said. He lifted her up, clutching her close to his chest as he stood. She looked small in his arms. And what were healing arches?

Magical healing. They're a magical place of healing. Don't ask me how it works, only that strange things happen. It amplifies some things and minimizes others. Supposedly, they eat magic and dispel magical ailments.

How did Raolcan know everything?

I'm a lot older than you and I listen. Besides, I'm good at everything, even eating Magikas.

He was kidding, wasn't he? He wouldn't actually eat them.

You don't need to worry about them anymore. We finished them just before your prince arrived. He brought other problems with him, though.

"We're under orders to bring her to Dominion City." Hubric's stance changed slightly, like he was preparing to fight once again.

"In Baojang we have healing arches. I could arrive there in a week at most and then she could be healed." Rakturan's expression was hard as a stone.

"A week? It would take us longer to get to the border of Baojang by dragon! How do you..." Hubric's voice faded off.

He came on a dragon.

"You came here on a dragon?" Hubric clenched his fist, his face flushing as he spun and stormed out the barn door. Had Rakturan stolen a dragon?

Rakturan carried Savette over to a stack of loose hay on the corner of the barn and laid her down, taking off his rain-soaked cloak and laying it over her.

"Don't do that," I said. "You'll give her a chill. Here." I limped over to our own cloaks where they were drying by the fire. The ones closest to the flames were dry. I gathered one up and brought it to him. "Use this."

He frowned, but he placed the dry cloak over her instead. He reached for the blindfold over her eyes.

"She likes it there," I said.

His hand hovered over it, as if uncertain whether to believe me or over-rule me. Before he could decide, Hubric arrived with another bang of the door. I clenched my jaw. Seriously? Could no one open or close that door without pulling the whole barn down behind them?

"You brought Enkenay?" he boomed.

Enkenay? Wasn't that Dashira's dragon? The white one that Aldeen rode?

Yes. What he does is wrong.

Why would she let him ride her?

Baojang has tricks we did not know about.

But you couldn't just steal a dragon. It didn't work that way.

"I did what I needed to do," Rakturan said. "She needs protection and it's clear that the two of you aren't up for the job. If I hadn't arrived, you'd both be dead."

"Our pact is clear." Hubric's words were hard as flint and he spat each one out like he could dent Rakturan with them. "A dragon must bear one rider. One! When his rider dies he dies, too. When a dragon's rider dies, we release him to die in peace. It's wrong to ensnare him again!"

I hobbled to the door and peeked out into the driving rain. Raolcan and Kyrowat stood with their backs to me, as if they were guarding the barn. In the rain before them, a white dragon crouched. He was larger than the other two, but his wings were ragged, and he was painfully thin, sores like the black bubbles that infected Leng after Magika Hectorus' attack spotted his white hide. I gasped and stepped back, letting the door bang closed.

"It's wrong to let him rot beneath you as you enslave him for your own goals." Hubric looked like he might explode. "We have a pact with them."

"I don't," Rakturan said, "and your pact is terrible. There is no reason for that animal to die."

"They aren't animals," I said at the same time that Hubric spoke.

"He's already dying! Can't you use your eyes!"

"He needs the healing arches. Just like she does," Rakturan said.

Hubric drew himself up as if he was going to reply but instead he snorted. "Help me clear these bodies, Amel. We'll decide what to do with the Dark Prince after that."

"Decide what to do with me?" Rakturan laughed as we made our way to the first body.

Hubric searched the pockets, pulling out a map, a flint, and a few coins. He opened the map and saw our course plotted out along it. These people had followed us from the beginning. A few of the towns along the way were marked with the spiral with a line through it that I'd seen before.

"Dusk Covenant," Hubric said to me, pointing to the spiral. "Their motto is 'a way through chaos.' The spiral is the chaos, the line the way through." I nodded and he turned to Rakturan. "The girl stays with us, prince. So, yes, if you want to be near her, then it is for us to decide what to do with her."

Hubric pocketed the things he found and motioned to me to search the others.

"It's better if she comes with me now," Rakturan argued. "Only Baojang can save her. We can offer her the healing arches. What can you do? Watch it wear her away to nothing but an echo?"

"Why do you care, Baojang?" Hubric asked. "You barely know this girl."

I searched through the pockets of the woman I'd knocked out. She moaned and Hubric rushed over to bind her hands. She had nothing of significance in her possession except a medallion bearing the Dusk Covenant mark.

"In our lands, the prophesies say:

'Offered then denied,
Bride of Morning,
Dark's only hope of peace.
A deal with death he strikes,

And from his mouth springs truth
To save the morning light.'
I'm certain it means she is the key to peace."

"We have our own prophecies," Hubric grunted.

"And do they say things about Savette Leedris?" Rakturan asked, folding his arms over his chest.

I searched the tattooed woman as Hubric finished with her hands. She had a handful of small things, but nothing that seemed to matter to our purposes except for a letter.

"Perhaps."

"Than you know that we must bring her to the arches," Rakturan said, triumphantly.

"We have our own arches, prince. You are not the only nation with culture and power." Hubric lashed the last living enemy and grabbed the feet of the huge man Rakturan beheaded, dragging him toward the door. He was surprisingly strong for someone so old. Rakturan joined him, grabbing the other leg to pull him outside.

"Then you know we must bring her to one. Where is the closest healing arch?"

I opened the letter and began to read as they finished pulling the dead out of the barn. I didn't know how they were going to bury them in this rain, and I didn't want to think about it.

Dragons flame. Flame equals pyre. There will be no burial.

He sounded like he didn't care.

They tried to kill you. The living ones are lucky Hubric doesn't bring them out here for the same fate.

I shivered and opened the note.

"Gather all who are sworn to the Dusk in your region and follow Hubric Duneshifter, Purple Dragon Rider. He is flying between Vanika and Dominion City. Kill the Dragon Rider and the dark-haired girl with him but spare the girl with light hair. She is to be brought – alive – to Shadowboon Grove among the Spires before the Upheaval.

Send any fast riders you have to Abrechda. Our plans for Leng Shardson did not go as planned, but he remains a thorn to the Covenant and has been placed on the roll of the Hammer. A reward is offered for his head."

I shivered.

On the back of the note was a sketch in charcoal of a large man, buried in the ground up to his waist. Around him swirled the spiral of the Dusk Covenant.

Chapter Fifteen

"What did you find?" Hubric asked, snatching the note from my hand. I couldn't speak, couldn't quite breathe. They'd come looking for us on purpose. They wanted us dead and Leng, too. It was ... I knew they were my enemies ... it was just ... I knew that when you fought evil people they fought back ... I

Calm. Calm. Breathe. They are no match for us, spider. Do you think Ahlskibi will let them hurt Leng? His flame is more powerful than my own. He'll snap their bones in his teeth.

But they'd come for us tonight and they'd almost succeeded. If Rakturan hadn't arrived when he did, the woman would have sunk her sword into my throat.

Calm. Easy. It did not happen and it will not happen again. We won't let it.

You couldn't guess these things would happen, so you couldn't prevent them.

We were relaxed and lazy. They took us unawares. That won't happen again, I promise you. We will set watches. We will stay focused. No one will take you from my care, spider. No one!

I drew a huge breath and let it out, leaning into the feeling of relaxation that came with the exhale. I focused on that and on the presence of Raolcan in my mind, always there, always loving me, so different – so dragon – and yet so mine.

Yours, spider. Always yours.

"So, they are hunting us now," Hubric said, in the same tone he might use to state the price of eggs. He fished into a pocket and produced a small leather pouch, opening it and taking out a needle and thread. He carefully threaded the needle.

"They almost killed us. Leng-"

"Is able to look after himself." Hubric's frown quelled any objection I might have. He unfastened his leather shirt and shrugged out of it. His grizzled body was still bound with wiry muscles and the wound in his arm spread red blood over his skin. "And we will look after ourselves, too."

"What have they drawn on that letter?" Rakturan asked, pointing to the backside of the note where the dark figure was drawn. "It looks like an Ifrit."

"Don't be a fool," Hubric said, gritting his teeth and pausing as he put a neat stitch into his own arm. I grimaced in sympathy. "It's just a poor job of drawing. These people weren't exactly prime specimens, if you know what I mean."

I glanced to the people tied on the ground. No one was conscious to take offense.

"Can I read the letter?" Rakturan held out a hand.

Hubric grunted and nodded to where the letter sat beside his sewing kit. He put another stitch in place with a grunt. "I suppose we're stuck with you now until we reach Dominion City, aren't we?"

"Look!" Rakturan pointed at the note. "It says 'Upheaval' with a capital 'U.'"

"Fascinating. Let's study the exact wording and really parse it out." He punctuated the word 'out' with another stitch.

"No, it means the magical act of Upheaval, where they pull ancient creatures out of the ground – Ifrits."

"I don't believe in Baojang legends," Hubric said, tying off the final stitch before putting the needle and thread away.

"But do they believe in you?" Rakturan looked up, his golden eyes glowing in the light of the fire and I couldn't help but wrap my arm around myself protectively. In the dark, minutes after an attack, anything felt possible and I felt incredibly vulnerable. "Where is this Shadowboon Grove?"

"Close by." Hubric shrugged back into the leather shirt without bothering to clean the blood off his arm or wrap a bandage over the wound. "If we left now we could make it there by late afternoon. But we are not going there. It's not on the way to Dominion City."

"We're going to the Healing Arches," Rakturan said. "What do you call them here?"

"Spires," Hubric said quietly.

"Then we know where we need to go," Rakturan said.

"I know that I need to go to Dominion City to deliver the message entrusted to me." It seemed very silent when I was finished.

"A message. You'd risk your friend for a message." Rakturan's eyes turned in judgment on me.

"There are healers in Dominion City and they will take good care of her," I said, swallowing.

It felt too much like last time. Last time I'd had a message entrusted to me – an important one. Last time, Savette had pled with me to break that trust for the sake of our friendship and I'd refused. What should I do now? I'd sworn to deliver the message with haste. I'd also promised Savette that I would take care of her. How in the world could I choose between them?

Chapter Sixteen

I looked to Hubric. After all, he was my master. What did he think? He opened his mouth to speak, but at that moment, Savette groaned. Rakturan rushed to her side, leaving us where we stood, watching him. He gathered her into his arms.

"You're safe now, I'm here."

"Rakturan?"

"Yes. I'll protect you. I swear by my blade and my crown that I will not abandon you."

She clung to him. "It's alive. Alive and wild within me. I have no control. I can't hold it in much longer."

"What you wrestle is like a great anaconda. If you stop fighting it will turn and squeeze the life out of you. You can't give in. Keep fighting."

"I'm so tired." She sounded like a small child. "I need rest."

"I'm going to get you rest." He turned and glared at me with burning golden eyes.

It was too much. I looked away and hobbled to the door, let it slam open – again – and limped out into the night. I didn't care that it was raining, didn't care that it was dark. I needed Raolcan.

He stood like a massive stone carving, guarding our door and I found his face in the dark and wrapped my arms around him. What should I do?

Loyalties are always hard. Where does your strongest loyalty lie?

"To you."

I sensed his satisfaction through our connection.

But what after that?

"I don't know. I promised I would take care fo Savette, but I also promised I would deliver the message. To do one might delay the other. I swore to the Dominar, and I can't just go back on that, but Savette is my friend. Personal isn't the same thing as important."

True. Personal always trumps important. You have no power over the great things of this world. Even delivering that message is a small thing. Your responsibility to a friend is something else entirely. She only has you.

"And Rakturan."

Yes. But without your agreement she has nothing.

"So, you're saying I should make her struggle a higher priority than the Dominar's message."

The Shadowboon Grove is out of our way. It will make us turn from our path to Dominion City and then, when we do go back to delivering the message, we will approach the city from a different direction.

Fascinating, but hardly important at a time like this when I felt torn in two!

You miss my point. We are being hunted. If we change directions, it will throw our enemies off our trail.

That was a good point. But what about Leng? I ran a hand over my wet face. I was worried about him. They wanted him dead, too.

Leng can take care of himself, and so can Ahlskibi. Don't worry about them.

I heard a cough behind me and turned to see Hubric holding a lantern.

"It's never easy when you are carrying a message. The message always has to come first," he said. When he stopped it looked like he was chewing his cheek.

"But?"

"But what?"

"You look like you're about to say 'but.'"

He laughed. "But this new information about an Ifrit – that's important enough for a Dragon Rider to investigate. It has the potential to threaten the Dominion. We are allowed to deviate from our course if we think the Dominion is in potential danger and that we can prevent it or report on it. It's one of two exceptions to the rule of delivering messages first."

"What's the other exception?"

"Defense of the innocent. In this case, I'd say you could argue both."

"I thought you didn't believe that was a picture of an Ifrit."

"I don't like the Dark Prince and I don't like giving him the benefit of my trust."

I laughed. We were on the same page there. I didn't much care for Rakturan either – even if I owed him my life now.

"I think you want to go there because of the prophecies," I said, mildly.

"Good guess. I don't like stupid trainees. I'm glad that you aren't stupid."

"So, which is it? Imminent danger to the Dominion or curiosity about the prophesies?" It took all my courage to say something so bold to an authority figure, but this was my first message. I had to make the right choice.

"Or even protection of an innocent being consumed by magic?" Hubric asked, his eyes twinkling in the lantern light. "Who says it can't be all those things? Life is complicated. It doesn't fit in tidy rows or measure perfectly by rule. The easier you are with that, the more good you'll do."

"So, you think we should go to Shadowboon Grove. Raolcan thinks we should go. Rakturan thinks we should go. Why am I the only one who is worried about getting this message delivered on time?"

"Because you're the only one here who is a trainee. Wisdom is acquired, not granted – or at least, rarely granted. The story of Mamoda the Wise being an exception, of course."

"Who?" I was beginning to think that I was very uneducated.

He shook his head and sighed. "We'll work on reading the classics after we deliver the message."

"And we'll deliver the message after we go to Shadowboon Grove," I said, my voice trembling and my palms sweating as I spoke. Was I making the right decision? If I was, then why was my belly so knotted up?

"Good choice," Hubric said with a smile. "Now, let's get to work. We have lots to do before we leave and no time to rest."

Chapter Seventeen

Re-packing the dry things and re-saddling the dragons was easy enough. Dealing with the captives less so.

"If we tie them to the central beam, the farmer will find them in the morning," Hubric said.

"How do you know?" I asked. "I don't want them to freeze or starve."

They were conscious now and one of the girls gave me a terrified look.

"Are you kidding me? He'll want to be sure we are gone and that if we aren't we pay for another night. Trust me. He sees us as a potential for money and he won't want to lose a coin of it."

"Even after the magical battle here last night?"

"Common people usually pretend not to see those things. They don't want to look ignorant, so they pretend that kind of thing is normal unless you tell them it isn't. Works in our favor."

"So, he'll release them when he finds them?"

"Most likely. Maybe for a fee."

"That's a problem," Rakturan said from where he was guiding Savette up on her feet. She clung to him and he caressed her back or shoulders with his free hand, like calming a wild animal. "If they are freed they will continue to hunt us."

"What alternative is there?" Hubric shrugged.

"The same option we had with the dead."

"We aren't barbarians," Hubric said, crossing his arms over his chest. Rakturan looked like he was going to challenge the decision, but then Savette tripped and he scrambled to steady her, cooing gently to her. I hoped I never looked so foolish if I ever fell in love.

Trust me. You and Leng are already almost that bad.

Raolcan was just jealous.

Jealous of a bald-headed boy who keeps on flying away from you when he should be flying to you? I don't think so.

"I think that for someone getting his own way, you sure complain a lot," Hubric grumbled. "Just be glad we're heading to the Spires. That *is* what you wanted, isn't it?"

"I'm worried about Enkenay," Rakturan said, not for the first time since we explained our decision to him. "How do we know that he'll be okay."

"He'll go home to die. It's the right thing," Hubric said, but his grumble had turned to sincerity. "It's good that you're worried about him, but you should never have taken him."

"He agreed to take *me*. I think he's connected to me somehow."

We emerged into the yard where Raolcan and Kyrowat were already saddled and ready to leave. It was still cool, but the rain had stopped, leaving everything smelling fresh and new. Enkenay stood in the same place he'd been since he arrived, but he lifted his nose when he saw Rakturan, as if he were happy to see him.

He is happy. He wouldn't have gone with Rakturan if he didn't want to. His rider is dead, and he is dying, but he's formed some kind of connection to Rakturan.

"Help Savette onto Raolcan with Amel and you will ride with me, Dark Prince," Hubric said.

"I think it should be the other way around," Rakturan objected. "Savette deserves the best rider to carry her."

I ignored him and so did Hubric. Rakturan helped Savette onto Raolcan and I helped him strap her in place. She was drifting in her own world again, but as I cinched the last strap, Rakturan leaned in and placed a gentle kiss on her lips. Her eyes flared so brightly that the light shone through the scarf and he startled, pulling back.

"Was it magical?" I asked, dryly.

"What?" his voice sounded hoarse.

"Nothing." I mounted Raolcan and settled my crutch at his side, trying not to grin.

Nice burn. There's hope for you yet.

Rakturan strode over to Kyrowat looking dazed and took Hubric's hand to be pulled up into the seat. The moment their hands met, Enkenay snapped at Kyrowat. Kyrowat snapped back, scrambling forward, but Enkenay reared up on his hind legs, neck extended and mouth open, roaring in Kyrowat's face.

Kyrowat shifted his weight, dodging to the side of the roar, and Rakturan was thrown clear. He rolled to the side, scrambling back up on his feet. Were they really fighting? What was going on?

Interesting. Enkenay is not finished with Rakturan. I thought it might be so.

Kyrowat spun and despite a shout from Hubric, he clamped his jaw around Enkenay's neck, forcing him into the dirt and pinning him there.

"Well, I see you have a loyal ally here," Hubric called over the scuffling sounds of one dragon trying to twist out of the grasp of the other. "It seems Enkenay is not finished with you, Dark Prince."

"Does that mean Savette and I can ride him together?" Rakturan was balanced on his heels, squatting slightly and holding his hands out to either side like he was prepared to leap aside or attack at a moment's notice.

"It means *you* can ride him – because he says you can and I won't argue with his free will over it. If he attacks Kyrowat again, he'll see what a mistake that is, though."

"And Savette?"

"Don't push your luck."

Rakturan nodded and Kyrowat let Enkenay up, dodging aside when he did, as if to prevent a further attack. Rakturan took Enkenay's saddle from where he'd stashed it and started to saddle the decomposing dragon. Oddly enough, the White stood still as he worked, as if he and Rakturan had worked together for weeks.

Don't forget. We are people, too. Enkenay makes his own choice in this.

I hadn't forgotten. I respected dragons rights as individuals.

Just one of many things I love about you.

"It's strange," Savette said from behind me, her voice otherworldly and distant. "He looks like he is dying, but within him, I sense so much life. If I could just draw it back..."

I shifted nervously. "I think you should worry about yourself right now, Savette. We need to get you well before you go messing with life and death."

She started to hum a faraway tune and her tune carried on as we lifted off into the sky, following Kyrowat toward Shadowboon Grove and whatever healing or terror might lie there.

Chapter Eighteen

The area around Shadowboon Grove looked like the earth had knotted and tangled in on itself. There were rolls and ripples that led to hills and valleys so sudden that there was more vertical land than horizontal. Good thing I was riding Raolcan and not a horse! A horse would take weeks to get through the space we flew over in a few minutes – maybe even longer.

You wouldn't like horses. They smell funny. They have bad attitudes. They're lazy.

They don't bite their riders' arms off or flame people they don't like.

Like I said, they're lazy. Anyone with ambition tries to flame their enemies from time to time. Besides, they eat grass. Grass! It's incredibly gross.

At first, the land had been bare and tangled but now it was tree-covered and tangled. It made for an interesting sight, visually, but there was nowhere to set down for a break and my leg was sore and lower back aching. I needed a bathroom stop and a chance to get a fresh drink.

Agreed on all counts.

Hopefully, Hubric was right and we would be at our destination soon. The hills were a little higher ahead and the dragons had to climb higher into puffs of cloud to cross over them. We raced upward and then swooped down over the other side as my breath caught.

I still wasn't entirely used to the feeling of nothing between me and the ground. It made my stomach rock when he did things like that but that wasn't the only reason I felt ill. Beneath us was a dish-shaped valley.

At one end, a circle of spires and open arches stood, open to the sky, the floor between them made of a cracked marble that once had been a massive mosaic picturing a stylized dragon. Around the spires and arches and creeping over the marble floor, the forest had grown up. Trees pushed their way upward, roots buried in the cracks, widening them and finding purchase wherever they could. Vines covered portions of the arches, hiding them completely. Most could still be seen, the white stone sticking up like teeth from a lower jaw.

We circled around the spires, looking for a spot to land. What was that happening on the other end of the valley? Was that-?

The ground bubbled and spat like a cauldron on that end of the valley, as if it were made of liquid and not of rock. I thought I could make out tiny figures centered around the roiling mass, but it was hard to tell in the corrugated landscape. They could just as easily be standing rocks and burned out tree hulls as people. Something about the place felt strange, as if I could tell we were not meant to enter.

Nowhere is off limits for dragons.

No one said anything about off limits. I was much more worried about the bad feeling tingling down my spine. The one that screamed danger.

All I feel is excitement.

Savette's hands reached from behind me, gripping me so tightly that I could hardly breathe.

"No, no, no," she said.

I tried to signal to Hubric that we shouldn't land, but he wasn't watching my hand signals. Kyrowat dove into a spiraling landing, aiming for a spot right in front of the arches, Enkenay dove next, and Raolcan followed.

"I don't think we should land!" I yelled.

It's fine.

Savette's hands were shaking and sobs ripped through her. I tried to pat her hand with mine, but I wasn't going to be much comfort. I had a terrible feeling about this place.

Chapter Nineteen

Rakturan leapt off Enkenay while we were still landing.

"Healing Arches! Here! This is incredible. The ancients built these, infusing them with magic from self-perpetuating pockets that they say reach to the very center of the earth. If you put someone with magic in them near these they can do incredible things – heal the whole world!"

"Has that ever happened before?" I asked. Savette's grip on me was making me nervous. She was more agitated than ever, and she almost felt as hot as Raolcan. That couldn't be good.

"Don't you people know anything in the Dominion? Need I tell you the stories of Ash and Harika, Jasper the Golden, Brave Kajisha and the five heads of Landeran?"

"Yes?" I'd certainly never heard those tales. They must be from Baojang.

Hubric's eyes traced the arches as he spoke:

"Born high on the mountain,
Blazing bright under the sun's demise,
Twice blind but still seeing,
The only bulwark against the dark
Watch as the arches proclaim
Dominion of Light."

"We know of the Ibrenicus Prophecies, too," Prince Rakturan said, walking towards me. "They speak of the Chosen One who will save the world, though they are very vague."

Prophesies always are. No one believes it's a prophesy if you say, 'The soup will be too salty on Tuesday.' It's just too specific and too boring. People like prophecies to sing.

I just wanted to get out of this valley alive. I had the creepy feeling that something was watching me. As Rakturan lifted Savette down from behind me, I turned to watch the shadows behind us. Dusk had descended, and the light was of that certain quality that was almost harder to see through than the black of night. I could hardly tell shadow from object or movement from stillness. A creeping sensation ran up my back and then down again.

Steady, spider. Steady.

I shivered.

"See something, Amel?" Hubric asked.

"Why did the ground on the other side of the valley look like it was boiling?" I asked.

"Boiling? I didn't see that. Did you look properly or were you dizzy from the descent?"

I hadn't been dizzy – or at least not enough to throw off my vision. Something had been going on there.

"What about the Dusk Covenant? Weren't they supposed to be here?"

"Thankfully it seems to be just us," Rakturan said, helping Savette toward the arches. "Would you like the blindfold off, High Castelan? Perhaps you'd see better."

"Overwhelmed," Savette said, her hands clutching at him like they had at me.

"Save your strength." He lifted her, carrying her toward the wide arches. There was no door, or rather, each arch was one. Why build a structure with no roof or proper door? It could never serve as shelter or defense. Never be practical in any way at all. I needed some sort of defense right now.

"Did you see something, Amel, or are you just worried?" Hubric asked. He was half in the saddle like he was going to decide whether to get down or not based on my words.

"I thought I saw something. The ground boiling and shadows that could have been people."

"Or could they have been shadows?"

I shrugged.

"Dismount and help us get Savette into the Spires. It's common to jump at shadows on your first delivery. Don't worry about it."

I scrambled to obey, clutching Raolcan for a moment too long as I dismounted. Anxiety rippled through me, spiky and sharp.

I'm here. I won't let anything hurt you.

I strapped the crutch to my arm and hobbled after them, carrying a waterskin. We were all thirsty after such a long flight. Savette would need a drink. Would the dragons be fine?

We are always capable of looking after ourselves.

I noticed Enkenay easing himself through one of the arches into the large courtyard beyond. I didn't like looking at him for long. He seemed to be decaying before my very eyes with nothing that I could do about it. Maybe if I was White...

No one can cure death.

But just to ease his pain would be good. It was funny that he was so taken with Rakturan – of all people! – that he would go with him here.

Everyone needs a purpose. Even the dying. Don't take his from him.

Hubric lit a lantern but it was almost unnecessary. Savette stood in the center of the circle, glowing as bright and white as the moon. The bandage around her eyes fell and white light flared from her eyes, lit her face, and haloed her whole body. I stared at her, stunned, then looked for Hubric, catching his eye as he shared my moment of awe.

"Rakturan?" she said. "Are you close?"

"I'm right here."

"Can I trust you?"

"Yes." He seemed to be trembling beside her and their words were pitched so low that it felt like eavesdropping to listen to them.

"In this place and at this time, can I trust you?"

"I swear."

"I was meant to be your bride. A price to prevent war. An object to be traded from one man to another. You know that. And you also know you didn't want me. You wanted someone less noble, less loyal, less pure. You wanted someone you could control and use. And when you saw my new power you wanted that, too." She sounded so clear, like she was actually with us this time instead of half-floating out in her other world.

"Why are you saying all of this?"

"I want to know if it is true." She took his hands in hers and looked up at him, her face so vulnerable, but so bright that it lit his, too. "I don't think you can lie here. I don't think anyone can." Savette turned to me. "What did you think of me when you first met me, Amel?"

The answer sprang to my lips before I could speak it. "I thought you were arrogant."

"And yet you loyally help me. Why is that?"

"You're my friend." Again, I hardly thought before the answer as in my tongue.

"See? The truth." Savette turned back to Rakturan. "And now I want it from you. Why are you here?"

"I've fallen in love with you."

"So quickly?"

"I didn't ask for it. It just happened and now," he paused, shaking his head. "Now nothing is too great to give you. No risk too much to take, no price too much to pay for your safety. I want you whole and well and happy."

"Then I can trust you?"

"Above all others." It was a vow.

"Good." She took his face in her hands. "I need help. I need someone to help me walk through this. I can almost feel what I need to do, but I need someone to remind me what is true. Will you stay here with me?"

"Of course," he breathed, leaning in close.

I looked away. The moment felt too private to watch. My eyes struggled with the dark behind me after the bright of Savette. I kept blinking away purple ghosts in my vision.

Wait. Did I see someone creeping up to where the dragons rested? Was that a form? Or was it only the purple light? I squinted, staring into the darkness. Behind me, a strange buzzing sound at the edge of my hearing began. I shook my head to try to clear it, but it was no use. I'd lost track of the shape. Wait. Was that another? I was almost sure it was...

Thunk! A crossbow bolt buried itself in the ground beside me.

"Enemies! Enemies are here!" I shouted.

Hubric cursed and I heard the sound of glass breaking as his lantern went out. No time to wonder why. I raced to Raolcan as fast as I could on my crutch, but before I was even there he let loose a stream of flame in the opposite direction. In the light of the flame, dozens of figures raced toward us, weapons in their shadowy hands.

Chapter Twenty

R aolcan took a step backward and I dodged his foot just in time.
Climb up quickly, spider.

I grabbed the saddle, scrambling up, frustrated as my dead leg weighed me down and held me back. The seconds dragged out like hours as my fumbling movements finally pulled me into the saddle.

You'll have to strap in while we launch.

It was all the warning he gave before leaping into the sky. I clutched the saddle tightly with one hand, fumbling with the other to attach the waistband.

Hold on with both hands this is about to get interesting.

I cinched the belt into place, but the thigh and shoulder straps dangled loose. No time to strap them in. I shoved my crutch into its spot on the saddle and hung on with both hands. Raolcan swooped around the healing arches, flying low as he circled back to where we had been standing. This would have been easier for him without me on his back.

Then how would I keep you safe?

Dark figures rushed toward the arches, weapons raised and a yell in every throat. How many of them were there? The ground seemed to be crawling with them.

Raolcan dove low, belching fire at them as he passed. Clothing and people lit up like torches and I clenched my teeth against the horror of it. Raolcan pulled upward as we shot past the horde on the ground, wheeling up into a tight circle again.

As we turned, I saw Kyrowat behind us, rushing down a parallel path to the one that Raolcan had just taken, spitting his own gouts of flame as he went.

Hubric gave me a signal, a loop motion of one forearm rolling over the other – again. He didn't even need to order it. Raolcan was already completing his circle and coming back around for another pass. I hated this. I didn't like seeing people burst into flame, didn't want to hear their shouts, didn't –

Would you rather watch them kill your friends in the circle? Savette who you have worked so hard to save?

So far no one had made it past the arches. Raolcan and Kyrowat had scorched everyone close, but another wave brought our enemies rushing toward the arches. I held my breath. I didn't want to see Savette butchered in there, or Rakturan who had saved my life, or Enkenay - even if he was dying.

Evil is powerful. It infects people – and dragons - but they also feed it. They choose to embrace it and then we have our own choice to make.

We dove low just as the front of the wave was pushing into the arches. Raolcan blasted them with fire and inside the arches Rakturan spun, sword in hand, to dispatch two who had escaped the flames. What choice did Raolcan mean?

The choice to defend what's worth protecting or, in faithlessness, to let it be slaughtered by evil.

That didn't' sound like much of a choice.

That's why I'm not shy about flaming our enemies. They would rip you to pieces if they could. I will not allow that.

The attack broke with Kyrowat's next burst of flame. Rather than running into the inferno, the black wave of shadow fell back. I looked to Hubric who made two pointing motions that meant pursuit. Raolcan pulled in next to Kyrowat and we flew after them. What did you do when they fled? It seemed wrong to flame them when they were running away.

And let them regroup? You'd have to fight the same battle twice.

I looked nervously over my shoulder at the healing arches. Savette stood within, Rakturan in front of her his sword held high. Her glow had grown faintly blue and now wisps of light floated out from her, like vines spreading out from their root. They formed a mandala pattern of light over the ground, spreading outward one layer at a time.

There's something strange about our enemies. It's almost as if they are luring us out from the-

Raolcan roared and reared backward mid-flight. I screamed, clutching the saddle, just trying to stay in place. What was happening? I gripped the saddle as Raolcan arced to the side. Beside us, a dark force hit Kyrowat, sending him spinning end over end until he crashed into the ground. I felt the reverberation of his crash in the air. What would it have felt like on the ground?

Ifrit! Raolcan's tone felt frightened, and no wonder.

As we curved around, I finally got a good look at our enemy. My own heart stuttered in my chest.

A dark figure of wispy, ever-moving shadow stood before us. When the shadows moved too far apart, a red glow of fire shone through from the heart of the creature. Shadow bubbled the ground around him, swallowing up any of the human enemies that got too close. There were still hundreds of them, but worse, much worse, was the figure bubbling up from the ground behind him.

Inside a ring of Magikas, a second Ifrit was rising from the earth.

Chapter Twenty-One

Raolcan reared up again. This time spurting flame at the towering Ifrit. The flames were so close that they felt hot against my skin and hair. I held on tight, terrified as the Ifrit swiped at us. Raolcan dove, sweeping to the side as he circled around the Ifrit, flames spurting out as he attacked.

Across the valley, Kyrowat recovered himself and leapt back into the sky, but the Ifrit was fast. He spun to face us and flung something in his hand toward Raolcan and me. Raolcan flamed, but the shadowy mass he threw at us was impervious to the flame.

It hit us, darkness surrounding us. I had the feeling of tumbling over and over, but no reason to think it was really happening. I couldn't see, couldn't hear, couldn't feel. Terror filled me. I'd never expected to fight a demon from the back of a dragon. I'd never even expected to be on the back of a dragon while he spat flame at an enemy. My legs and arms were trembling so much that I couldn't get them to stop. My heart was racing too fast. I couldn't catch my breath. I bit my lip hard, tasting blood.

Something jarred me, shaking my grip loose on the saddle. I clutched the safety belt with both hands, hoping and praying that the leather straps would hold. My vision cleared suddenly, and once again the moon and stars were visible. I tried to still my breathing, tried to see what had happened. Raolcan crouched on the ground, and I dangled at his side, held in place by the safety straps.

We were on the steps of the arches. We must have been flung by the Ifrit all the way across the valley. Somehow, in the chaos, the army of human shadows had surged forward again. They were minutes from overtaking us. In the air, Hubric and Kyrowat wheeled and dove, spitting fire as they attacked the

Ifrit again and again. Kyrowat favored his left side, only making right turns. Was he injured from his fall?

Yes.

"Raolcan?" I asked, pulling myself back up on the saddle. "Are you hurt?"

Yes.

I gasped, loosening my safety straps and grabbing my crutch before dismounting, awkwardly. How badly was he hurt? I stepped back, looking him over. One of his wings was crumpled to his side. At my thought, he pulled it in, protectively. Blood leaked from his mouth and nose and he trembled like a leaf in the wind.

"Raolcan! No!" I ran to his face, wrapping my arms around his head. "Can you fly?"

No. I could tell he was holding back pain. That's why he didn't say more.

"Can you get inside the arches?" I asked, anxiously.

Our enemies rushed across the landscape, the Ifrit at their head. Kyrowat's flames did nothing to stop him.

I'll try.

Raolcan pulled himself forward on his forelegs. His right wing fighting to help pull him. His back legs dangled uselessly behind him. I knew that feeling. I knew how helpless it felt. I tried to make my thoughts strong and hopeful to help him. After all, this place was called the 'healing arches' that must mean there would be healing here, right?

What were we going to do? Our dragon's fire couldn't stop the Ifrits. Our enemies were on their way. We had one warrior who could wield a sword and one girl with magic who had no idea what she was doing. I chewed my lip and tried not to think about it. I tried not to think about how afraid I would be when men with weapons rushed into where we were. I tried not to think about what it would feel like to die. Tried not to think about what it would feel like to watch Raolcan die.

It was impossible. It was all I could think of as Raolcan finally pulled himself through the arches and took a place next to Enkenay within. At least we'd die together.

Worth it. You've been worth everything.

So had he.

Chapter Twenty-Two

Savette flared like a candle lit in a dark room. Her light increased suddenly and powerfully and the mandala around her began to spin as it spread. She rose in the air, her hands thrown outward to either side and her blank face lifted upward, hovering above the ground. She was a vision of purity and light, but tears tracked down her face, flowing constantly. Was she hurt, too?

It hurts her.

I thought it was supposed to heal her. What was it doing to her?

Exposing the truth. Truth is very painful and goodness flares violently in the presence of evil.

Was she reacting to the coming Ifrit? Was she trembling?

"Can your dragon fly?" Rakturan yelled to me as I hobbled under the arches and took a place between Savette and Raolcan. I was worried about them both.

"No. Can Enkenay?"

"I don't think so. He tried to fly when you were fighting, but he couldn't get into the air."

The Ifrit outside roared and Rakturan cursed. "If Hubric would just come back, we could flee aboard his dragon. Do you think he can carry four people?"

I didn't bother answering. I wouldn't leave Raolcan. Hubric wouldn't ask me to. I knew that without having to ask. I had a feeling that Hubric wouldn't leave me, either. He'd sworn protection over me.

The Ifrit hit Kyrowat with the same shadowy ball he'd flung at Raolcan. Kyrowat was flung across the valley, encased in a sphere of darkness. The first wave of our enemies hit the arches at the same time, rushing up the steps toward us. I braced with my crutch quarterstaff and beside me, Rakturan leapt forward, sword slashing across the chest of the first man to dart through an arch.

Savette screamed as a wave of white burst from her, growing wider as it raced outward. Everyone in its path disappeared as the wave hit – but not the Ifrit. He roared, his huge hand grabbing the arch in front of us and pulling it up from the ground. Soil and rock fell from its base as he flung it aside. Savette hit him with blast after blast, keening in pain as she fought.

I flinched at the sound, but I had my own work to do. A few members of the Dusk Covenant snuck around the sides of the Ifrit, coming at us from either side. Raolcan blasted the ones that came his way with scorching fire, but his head was leaning on the ground now. His strength fading. He seemed too dazed to even think clearly.

Amel?

I'm here, Raolcan. I'm here. I moved to shelter him, fighting off a stray attacker until he walked into the path of Raolcan's fire. Raolcan blasted him away.

On the other side, Rakturan fought, sword carving through his enemies.

The Ifrit leaned forward and took a step into the healing arches. Savette screamed, "Rakturan!"

And Rakturan darted away from his still living opponents, rushing to put himself between her and the Ifrit.

The Ifrit lunged for him and he dodged, tripping and falling backward, his sword falling out of his grasp. Savette caught him, clinging to him from behind and above him. She was rising further off the ground, tears pouring from her eyes and the light so bright that her skin was translucent, her hair a mass of silvery wisps lit with blue-white light. She wrapped her arms around Rakturan's dark chest, leaned her head on his shoulder, and closed her bright eyes. Rakturan's shut, too, as if he were drinking her embrace in, one last time.

I held my breath. If only hopes could save. If only wanting something could hold back evil. I hoped with all my heart, but even as I hoped I was certain I was watching her last living moment.

The Ifrit leaned down so that his wild face was inches from theirs. His mouth opened, roiling lava moving within. On his head were ten horns, made of dancing smoke and his eyes were pits of fire. His lips moved as if he were forming a word.

And then, as if they were one person, Savette and Rakturan opened their eyes.

White light flared so brightly that I couldn't see. I was thrown off my feet, landing hard on the ground and smacking my head. Everything was gone in a moment of pain and light. I coughed and gasped, my fingers reaching out but finding nothing but the cold forest floor. Blinding pain filled my head and purple after-images clouded my vision. I pulled myself up on hands and knees, shaking my head to try to clear it.

Thank you, Hubric, for a crutch that stays attached. By the time I pulled myself to my feet, my vision had cleared enough to see. The Ifrit was gone. The attackers before us were gone. I'd been thrown out of the arches. I hobbled, stiffly, back to them.

Savette and Rakturan were on their knees, holding each other in a tight embrace. Savette's glow had reduced again, but her eyes were still white as the center of the sun.

"Raolcan?" I looked, to where I'd seen him last. He lifted his head, stood, and shook out his wings. "Your wing!"

The look he gave me was the closest thing I'd ever seen to a dragon smile. He leaned forward and rubbed his cheek against me.

You're alive!

Me? He was the one I'd been worried about!

We're all alive.

Beside him, Enkenay stood and shook like a dog, his wings unfurling. Far from the patchy, broken thing he'd been just moments before, he was completely whole, his white scales shining in the moonlight.

"They really are healing arches," I said in wonder.

A tiny prick of pain filled me as I realized I'd been thrown from the arches at just the wrong time. If I'd been in there, like the dragons had, when the flare of Savette's power peaked, would I be able to walk on two legs now? I pushed the thought aside. This wasn't the time. Raolcan and Enkenay were healed. Savette and Rakturan were still alive, murmuring to one another. What about Hubric? Where was he?

Let's look. Come on.

I hobbled to Raolcan, climbed onto his back and held on tight as he leapt into the air. The cool air of night seemed so fresh and calm for a place filled with such violence. Where was Hubric?

There! Kyrowat emerged from the night, Hubric on his back with a grim expression on his face. He was dirty and tired looking, but whole. He motioned for me to follow and we landed outside the arches.

"Can everyone still fly?" he asked, but it wasn't to me. I could tell because Kyrowat cocked his head as if he were answering mentally.

Hubric turned to me, "We need to go. Now." I opened my mouth but he silenced me with a single motion. "The ones who live fled. They had a second Ifrit with them. Tired as we are, we don't dare stay here. We can talk all about this later. Tonight, we flee."

"Of course."

"Rakturan," Hubric called. "Bring Savette. We must flee! Not a moment to spare!"

Rakturan and Savette emerged from the arches, but it was not Rakturan leading Savette. She led him.

Rakturan's eyes were blazing with white fire - just like hers.

Dragon School: First Message

Chapter One

We fled, in the black of night, from those spine-shivering terrors. If it had taken all the magic Savette could draw to demolish one Ifrit, what could we do if the other one found us? Hubric and Kyrowat led us and Raolcan and I brought up the rear. Between us, Enkenay bore Savette and the Dark Prince. They'd bound their eyes with scarves again and they clung to one another like survivors pulled from the wreckage of a ship. I watched them as much as I watched the horizon, scanning, scanning, scanning for any sight of a creature made of smoke and fire with ten horns on his head.

Fear fuelled me, keeping my tired eyes from closing. My bad leg throbbed incessantly – it had twisted in the battle and while it wasn't broken, I was sure it must be a mass of bruises under my leathers. I wasn't going to think about how it could have been healed if I had just landed inches closer to the arches. No, I wasn't going to think about that. I didn't think about it through the long hours of flight. I didn't think about it as the sun came up – finally – on the horizon, bathing me in gold and hope. I didn't think of it when Hubric signaled a weary stop and we landed exhaustedly next to a pond in a rolling field of grass.

Stop thinking about it. Seriously. You're driving me crazy.

But honestly, how did you stop thinking about something like that? I'd been so close to having something I'd wanted all my life. I'd been so close to getting what I didn't even believe was possible. Now that I knew it could happen, how could I stop longing for it?

You're going to eat yourself alive. Like Draakuna who bit off his own tail, and finding that he tasted very good, quickly devoured the rest of himself.

I really hoped that was some sort of dragon legend and not something true. It sounded awful.

No more awful than what you're doing to yourself. Set it aside. Raise your chin high. You are Amel Leafbrought, rider of Raolcan the Purple. Your value does not lie in your leg.

He was right ... of course.

I'm always right. It's exhausting.

Hubric dismounted. Stumbling for a moment before easing into a crouch. Kyrowat slumped beside him. Were they injured? I dismounted and hobbled over to him. Every step was heavy. Had I ever been so tired?

"Hubric? Are you hurt?" I squatted down beside him.

"No," he grunted. "Tired. Kyrowat also tires. We need an hour to rest. Make that two hours. One for me, and one for you. The dragons need to sleep through both or we'll fly them to death."

He has a point. That healing left me worn out.

"Can you take the first watch?" Hubric asked me, rubbing his face tiredly.

"Yes," I said. How did you take a watch?

Sit on my back while I sleep so you are up high and watch all the horizons. We're in a wide field. No one can sneak up on us if you watch carefully.

"Thank you." Hubric didn't even bother to pull out a bedroll or blanket. He slumped against Kyrowat, closed his eyes and was snoring before I stood.

Beside Enkenay, Savette and Rakturan lay in the long grass, their arms entangled around each other. It was going to be hard not to sleep myself, but I needed to stay awake to keep them all safe. I climbed onto Raolcan's back again and sat up in the saddle, scanning the horizon through a yawn. Raolcan's breath grew long and deep as he fell into sleep. Good. He deserved it. They all did.

I needed to think about something other than sleep to stay awake. My leg. No. Raolcan told me not to think about that. Savette and Rakturan? Something had passed between them that I didn't understand. Some bond that formed with the change of Rakturan's eyes. Could all those strange prophecies Hubric was fond of quoting be about them after all?

I scanned the horizon carefully in every direction. The mountain and hill country had sloped into these rolling plains of grasses nearly as high as I was. From dragon-back I could see over them, but not with my feet on the ground. I'd heard tales of these plains – the heart of the Dominion where crops grew twice in a summer and herds ate their fill, guided by migrating families. There was a peacefulness in the way the wind waved the heads of the long grasses to and fro, in the patterns they formed and the whorls of air on grass. With nothing but grass and sky, the sky felt very close, like I could reach out a hand to touch the wispy ribbons of cloud above. I'd never been in such a place before.

I'd been looking too long in one direction. I turned slowly to look behind me. The grass was moving in a straight line towards us. This time, it wasn't the wind moving it.

Chapter Two

"Raolcan! Hubric!" I called. "There's something in the grass!"

What was it? All I saw was the grass rippling and rolling like something was on the way. Raolcan's head arched up and his gaze followed the rippling grass.

Up, up, up!

Kyrowat leapt up, leaving Hubric to fall to the grass, his head spun to follow Raolcan's gaze. Hubric scrambled to his feet, calling to Savette and Rakturan.

"On your dragon, now! Now!"

I still couldn't see what it was. Was it so small that it was disguised by the tall grass?

Strap in! Secure your crutch and our baggage. Hurry!

I scrambled to obey, tightening and fitting straps in place.

Launching!

I was still fumbling with my waist strap when Raolcan leapt into the air. Beside us, Enkenay surged upward. I leaned to the side, straining to see what was below me, and then Raolcan spun suddenly to the side with an angry cry. I held my waist strap in both hands, clinging to it as he snapped in one direction and then the other. Heat flared over me, leaving me hot and afraid. Had one of the dragons flamed?

Kyrowat.

Why would he let off flame so close?

He fights for us.

We were flung to the side so suddenly that I fell from the saddle, only my safety belt holding me. I reached for the saddle and clung to it, as Raolcan flew in a wide curve, arcing upward. My heart hammered in my chest while wind whipped through my hair and around my legs. Only my hands clinging to the saddle and the leather of my safety strap held me.

Free! Thanks to Kyrowat.

Now that the arc was predictable, I was able to catch one of the stirrups with my good foot and scramble back into the saddle. Below me, in a green field of waving grass the Ifrit stood with hands raised high, flames swirled in his mouth and the smoke of his horns flickered and flared in time with it. Between he and us was Kyrowat, swooping in a second time to flame at the Ifrit, but I noticed he kept a wide space between them. He wasn't taking any more risks.

That was close.

Where was Enkenay?

Above us. He launched when we did, but the Ifrit grabbed my tail. I couldn't get free until Kyrowat flamed him.

I swallowed. He'd had Raolcan's tail! It was the Ifrit who had shaken me loose! My head was spinning. My vision darkened.

Come back to me, Amel. Don't spiral out of control. All is well, spider. He cannot reach us here. He is bound to the earth.

Enkenay dropped to our level and we drew up beside him. I signaled greeting to Savette who held his reins with Rakturan behind her. Enkenay must have agreed to let her be his rider, too.

He owes nothing to Dragon School anymore. His bonds broke when he died.

He died?

Just before Savette healed him. He is a free dragon now. But he's adopted those two.

Kyrowat pulled in between us, looking unhurt, though Hubric's expression was grim. He signed to follow and for me to take the rear as he sped ahead of us. There would be no rest for me tonight, and no more rest for anyone else.

We will be fine. Dragons are made of tough materials. See Enkenay? He's not even flagging, and he was dead not even a day ago.

I thought Raolcan hated White dragons, but he seemed to be taking to this one.

Enkenay is different. He's more than a normal dragon now.

Good. Because we were going to need more than normal the way things were headed. We were going to need everyone to be extraordinary.

Chapter Three

I slumped over Raolcan's back, fingers tingling as I clutched the saddle and tried to keep my drooping eyes open. I'd been nodding in and out of sleep. I didn't even know how long. It was our third day of flying. We stopped every four hours to refill waterskins, let the dragons drink, and do other necessary tasks, but Hubric only allowed ten minutes each stop and none for sleeping. I still couldn't believe that the dragons were flying without stop all this time.

I am growing very weary. Hubric presses us too hard.

The moon was nothing but a slender crescent tonight, but with no clouds in the sky, I could still make out the velvety landscapes below. The constant grasses had morphed slowly into fields interspersed with rock formations and ahead was a single, slender, pillar-like formation of rock, rising high above the landscape. What would have caused such a thing to exist? It was formed almost as if human hands had carved it and then it had slowly crumbled – far too regular for the fashioning of wind and rain, but such a thing was impossible.

My mind drifted, imagining giant people with hammer and chisel carving this pillar in certain strokes. I startled. What was that?

We're landing. Oh, my wings ache! I hope he lets us sleep.

I could barely open my eyes to see us land with a bump on the top of the pillar.

The needle. Humans call it that.

Hubric was already dismounting and Enkenay was settling onto the narrow top of the pillar. There was room for three dragons and four people and not much else.

"We can see everything from here," Hubric said. "And even our enemies must sleep sometimes. We need to stop or the Dragons will not recover."

I couldn't imagine a safer spot to choose. No humans could reach us here.

"I'll take first watch," Hubric said and I didn't bother to wait to hear the rest of his words - if there were any. I loosened the belt around my waist and fell asleep in the saddle, across Raolcan's back.

When I woke, stiff and sore, the sun was up and Hubric squatted over a tiny fire, a kettle and mugs prepared.

"Is that tea?" I asked thickly, sleep still heavy in my body.

"Better than tea," Hubric said with a tired smile. "It's caf. It will put a jolt in your blood and keep you going days past when you should."

"Do you have enough for two?"

He grinned as he poured out a second mug.

"I let you sleep through both watches," he said. "We'll give the others a little more time and then we fly again."

"Is it always like this on the road?" I asked, sipping the black bitter drink. It was harsh on my tongue but the feeling of it as it filled me was like drinking pure sunlight.

"Sleeping in strange places with Ifrits chasing you, enemies in every town, and powerful people along for the ride?" he asked, gesturing to Rakturan and Savette. "Yep. Pretty much. The Dragon Rider life isn't ever boring."

I took a long sip of caf. The bitterness was growing on me. Hubric pulled a battered book from a pocket in his leathers and flipped through it until he found what he was looking for. I sat down on the ground near the fire, enjoying the warmth of it on my face and hands as I sipped my caf. I still felt bone-weary, but at least I could keep my eyes open.

"Twice blind," Hubric muttered.

"What?"

"Twice blind but still seeing,
The only bulwark against the dark
Watch as the arches proclaim
Dominion of Light." His eyes were far away as he spoke – not even looking at the book.

"That's those prophecies again, isn't it? I thought you had them memorized."

"Some." He turned to look at Savette and Rakturan. Did he still think the prophecies were about her when there were two of them now with glowing eyes? "Twice blind..."

Oh. Now that I looked at them, too, I saw what he meant. Twice blind – two of them blind? And that part about the arches ... we'd been inside a ring of arches. Maybe he had a point.

I looked up to find him staring at me.

"You see it, too. Don't you?" He sipped his caf, never looking away from me. "You see it's her. It's a good thing that you pulled her along with you, Amel. She needs to be guarded. If the Dusk Covenant knew about her – although I suppose they know a little now – they'd never let her survive."

"They weren't going to let her survive before. They stole her and held her captive."

He looked at the horizon. "They didn't know who she was or they'd never have kept her alive. She is everything they fear."

"Who are they?" I asked. "It doesn't make sense to start a secret society to destroy your own country. There must be something else to it."

"There's always layers with people, Amel. Layers of wants and which layer makes the decision is always a question. Some swear to the Dusk because they do hate the Dominion. The Dominar has enemies and there are people who abhor our way of life and the systems that hold us together. It becomes worse if someone they love is hurt or killed in the middle of that system. Those are the true believers – people who aren't much different than you or I, but they've lost everything but that one desire – the desire to right one particular wrong or make someone pay for what happened. It eats away everything but that one thing and they lose any conscience about how their actions might affect others. All they see is their goal."

I shivered. "That was what Magika Hectorus was like. But it wasn't what Corrigan was like."

"Like I said, there are layers. People might agree with the principles but there's more to it. Maybe they finally find a place with the true believers – a place they never had before with anyone else. Maybe the ideals, while not that important to them, open up paths to success or honor that weren't open to them before. Maybe they get power they didn't have. Maybe it just makes them feel good to rub other people's faces in the dirt or feel like they're somehow in the right or cleverer than their neighbors, or to rebel – not against anything, just to rebel in general. People are strange. In that buzz of thoughts and wants any one thing could be the controlling impulse that launches them down a path you can't turn back from."

It made a lot of sense. After all, I'd joined Dragon School with a lot of layers. I'd wanted to keep my family safe from the burden of my care and I'd wanted to go out in a flame instead of just rotting slowly over the years.

"What about your secret society?" I asked. "The Lightbringers? I know nothing about them."

Hubric coughed. "You shouldn't know *anything* about us. That's the point of secrecy. But Ephretti had a loose tongue and no surprise. She's been smitten with Leng Shardson for years. She isn't taking a rival very well."

I felt my cheeks growing hot. I looked at my mug of caf instead of Hubric's piercing eyes. He saw too much.

"But now that you know, you need to either swear secrecy and agree to be an agent of the Lightbringers or join us yourself."

"What does an agent do?"

"You keep our secret and report information about the Dusk Covenant so that we may counter their actions."

That seemed simple enough. I wanted the Dusk Covenant eliminated, not just countered.

Hubric coughed and I looked up at him again. His eagle eyes were trying to stare right through me. "I'd rather you joined, apprentice. Although that's ultimately up to you."

"What does it mean to join?"

"Lightbringers protect the light. We stand for truth and right. We do not tolerate lies or evil. It's not about protecting the Dominion – although we do that, often. It's about the prophecies. We believe they will come true at the time we most need them, and we do what we can to protect and promote them."

He offered me the book in his hands and I took it. It was thinner than I'd thought, but the words in it were small, densely packed on the page in a tight, spiky handwriting. The leather cover was old and battered, crumbling at the edges.

"That's my copy," Hubric said. "If you join, you'll be expected to copy it into your own book and keep that book on your person, memorizing as much as you can of it and being faithful to keep the words of the prophecies to the best of your ability."

"It sounds like it takes up a lot of time. I mean, I'm still learning to be a Dragon Rider. I'm not sure I'm ready to have my whole life controlled by prophecies I don't even believe."

"Don't you believe them?" he asked, looking meaningfully to Savette.

I swallowed, nervously. Maybe I did. I wasn't sure. It was certainly strange to watch her and Rakturan sleep, their glowing eyes shining through where the blindfolds had slipped.

"Think on it," Hubric said.

"I will," I promised. It seemed like a heavy promise – like a decision that was going to affect my whole life, and I wasn't sure that I cared enough to want it, but it sure seemed to matter a lot to Hubric.

I forced a smile for his sake, but inside I felt suddenly unsteady.

Chapter Four

A *Lightbringer, hmmm? Look at you getting these lofty invitations,* Raolcan said as we flew toward Dominion City. Hubric assured us when we left the pillar –called "the needle" by locals – that we'd be there in only a few hours.

I didn't ask for lofty invitations. I wasn't even sure what to make of this one. How could it be lofty if it were secret? How could it be worth it if it required that I live my life by a book Hubric had written out in cramped handwriting? I'd given him back the book before we left, but I'd need to read it myself before I decided.

Maybe you should copy it. Just in case.

Was he suggesting that I should join them?

If you join, I will have to as well.

And what did that mean for a dragon? He couldn't exactly write out his own prophecy book.

The Lightbringers do more than study their prophecies. The legends of them – while unclear and difficult to find – are incredible. They do acts of great power together for the preservation of humans and dragons. They're older than the Dominion. And some of what they do involves us, too.

And they thought Savette was promised in their prophecy? Shouldn't someone else have come along a lot sooner than her?

Hubric thinks that. He doesn't represent all of them.

Interesting. I would want to meet more of them, first. I hadn't liked Ephretti.

But that's just jealousy.

And I hadn't liked Dashira.

But she's a White and Purples are opposed to Whites.

Which was something I still didn't understand.

We believe truth is the most important thing. They believe healing and peace are. Those things come into conflict from time to time.

How? Truth brought healing. There could be no true peace without it.

Spoken like a true Purple. They see things otherwise.

Well, I'd still need to meet more Lightbringers. And I'd need to read this book.

In the distance, two mountains rose over the rolling plains beneath us. It was hard to make them out in the haze of the sun, but they had a strange shape.

I've seen them before, they're the twin cities. Dominion City and Sky City. The first sky cities of the Dominion.

Really? They were huge.

Bigger even than you imagine. It will still be hours before we reach them.

Ahead of us, a wall loomed with towers placed regularly along its length. The sides of the wall were smooth and the towers were great spires rising in the air and allowing no purchase for a dragon who might want to land on one. I saw lights flicker in the spires. Someone was up there watching.

The city spreads to the ground as well and both the base cities and the sky cities require a wall of defense. It is no help against dragons, but helpful against all else. The lights you see are mirrors. They use them to signal to one another and to the guards in the sky cities.

Would it be enough against Ifrits?

Doubtful.

Hubric signaled follow as we drew near the wall. He rolled Kyrowat into a dive toward the gatehouse stationed over the main road leading into the city. The road was packed with people and animals, queued up to enter the area surrounding the cities. It felt so strange to see them all constrained to the breadth of the road after I'd known no limits but the sky for this long.

It's my gift to you. The closest thing we mortals get to real freedom.

Enkenay followed Kyrowat in his dive as Savette and Rakturan adjusted the scarves over their eyes. Despite their distance and bright-eyed blindness, they seemed to be following what was happening around them.

We brought up the rear, diving to swoop low over the ground parallel to the road just like the other two dragons. I couldn't help but smile as I looked at the people lining the road, gasping and pointing at our dragons as we passed. It must be astonishing to them to see such glorious creatures so close. Only weeks ago, I would have felt the same. So much had happened since then to put me – in the brown leathers of the Sworn – on the back of a dragon flying past people who were just like me.

I wondered, suddenly, about Savette's dragon. He couldn't be dead if she were still alive, could he? After all, if he died, wouldn't she die, too?

Something strange is happening to her. It was enough to heal death in Enkenay and set him free of his bonds. Perhaps it is the same for her.

There was so much I didn't know, and I longed to know it all.

Even the long life of a dragon is not enough to teach everything that is. Be content with what you have while always learning anything you are offered.

Kyrowat landed just outside the gatehouse in front of the wall. Enkenay and Raolcan quickly joined him. I felt my heart speed up as I saw a cluster of guards in black ride out from the side of the gate on black horses, white and silver banners swirling around them. Dust rose as they hurried toward us, their leader wearing a fur cloak and carrying a massive, silver hammer.

The gate guard. This is how they receive enemies.

But we weren't enemies!

Something has changed to make them think that you are.

Chapter Five

Hubric called down from his perch just as the leader drew his horse to a dusty stop. "Castelan Gendrin Cabridis. Lieutenant of the Silver Cord. It has been some time since last I saw you at your father's table."

Now that the soldiers were closer, I was surprised to see that the lieutenant was hardly older than I was. There were two grizzled faces in the riders behind his back, but just as many fresh and young. Shouldn't a position as important as guarding a gate be for someone older?

Shouldn't a job as important as delivering the Dominar's messages be for someone older?

Ouch.

"No time for pleasantries, Hubric Duneshifter," the Lieutenant said, his expression grim. His eyes scanned us, nervously and he drew back in his saddle when he saw Savette and Rakturan, their eyes bound with white cloth. In the bright sun, it was hard to tell if any of their light was escaping through the blindfolds. "Word has reached us of turmoil in the north and the twin cities are filled with anxiety. Twice now, we've had Purple Dragon Riders assaulted in the streets by citizens demanding information they didn't even have. All Dragon Riders are required to be escorted directly to General of the Spire, Comard Eaglespring regardless of where you are bound. This is for your own protection and the defense of Dominion City and Sky City."

Hubric nodded. "Of course."

My heart was beating quicker now that I heard him say the General's name. It was almost time to deliver my message. My hand felt for the pocket in my leathers where I kept it safe. It was still there – a hard object under the leather.

"We ask that you wait for a proper escort on the other side of the wall," the Lieutenant said. He looked nervous now and his horse shifted, whickering as it did. "The city guard and the Blacks will come to escort you. Until they do, you can book rooms at the inn."

He gripped the haft of his hammer, rolling his shoulder.

Hubric tilted his head slightly to the side. I was beginning to understand what that meant from him. He saw something that I didn't in those words.

"When was the last escort sent?"

The Lieutenant jutted his chin forward as he spoke. "Four days ago."

I sucked in a quick breath. We didn't have time to waste!

"Our message is urgent," Hubric said. "We need to deliver it as soon as possible."

"I'm under orders to enforce these procedures with all necessary force."

That's why he looked so nervous and gripped his weapon so hard! He was afraid he'd have to attack our dragons to make us obey.

He should be afraid! Little gnat. I'll squash him like a bug.

Hubric threw up a hand as if he were warding off the dragons and I noticed Kyrowat and Raolcan exchange a look. What were they planning?

We have your backs whatever you decide.

"Our message is for General Comard Eaglespring himself," Hubric said. "Perhaps if you could send word to him directly that we wait here."

The Lieutenant frowned, his other hand finding the haft of the hammer. I could almost see a 'no' forming on his face when Enkenay reared up suddenly. As soon as he was in the air, he smashed back down on the ground, his fore-feet hitting with a boom.

Enkenay has no patience.

The horses whinnied and one at the back reared before his rider brought him under control. Even the Lieutenant's mount rolled her eyes nervously. Shrieks and the sounds of nervous animals came from the nearby road.

"Word will be sent," the Lieutenant said. His young face looked drawn. Was that sweat in his light-colored hair? "And I need your word of honor that you will wait for your escort. It may come sooner than you think. We await an important arrival and I've been told the escorts will arrive around the same time. That arrival must not be delayed."

"We have other news. News for whoever is the ranking officer of this gatehouse."

"I'll take your news."

"You are the ranking officer here?" Hubric asked. He sounded disbelieving.

The Lieutenant flushed. "At present."

Hubric frowned, but he gave the message. "An Ifrit follows us. Its wrath is terrible."

"A legend?"

"An Ifrit. Alive and deadly. You must take necessary precautions."

The expression on the man's face was cynical. He didn't believe us. I felt a spike of fear shoot down my spine. We'd come to the greatest city in the Dominion and this was the best we could find to relay our news to?

"Let me escort you to the waiting area," the Lieutenant said.

Chapter Six

The waiting area was right inside the walls, like Lieutenant Cabradis told us. He'd insisted that instead of flying over the walls, the dragons crawl through the gates. He'd backed up the muttering crowd, making us about a hundred enemies in the process, and then stood well back as we squeezed through the gates. Kyrowat had sneezed during the process, leaving a black soot mark on the wall. I was certain it was on purpose, though Raolcan wouldn't tell me if it was.

Serves them right. Those soft humans scrubbing soot off walls might be our only entertainment for a while – until the Ifrit shows up and kills them all.

Inside the wall, there were a barracks, guardhouse, stables, tavern, and inn. Cabridis asked us curtly not to leave the area until our escort arrived. He did not send out a messenger, but he did send two guards who followed us as we found a place in the shade behind the inn for the dragons. I wondered if there were sheep here to feed them.

Horses make a great substitute.

I hoped he was joking.

I'm not.

He really did push jokes too far!

"Time to see if the inn has any rooms empty," Hubric said as I helped Savette and Rakturan down from their dragon. Savette clutched my hand and Rakturan held hers. He'd been as silent and otherworldly as she had and I was starting to get worried about them. One Magika about to explode was bad enough. Now we had two.

We followed Hubric to the front of the inn where a wide front porch was shielded from the sun by the overhanging roof. An old man slept on a chair on the porch, an equally old dog sleeping at his feet. An array of other chairs stood empty, each one a different size and shape. I didn't have a long history of staying at inns, but this one seemed more bedraggled than the others I'd seen.

As we stepped inside there was a bark from behind us and a cough. I spun to see the old man stand. "Looking for rooms?"

"Yes," Hubric said.

"Four?"

"Two."

The old man nodded. His face was rutted with lines and his eyes tired. "I'm the innkeep here. Not much business despite the traffic. Get a small pittance from the Dominar to keep the place up for travelers and the like. It's a penny a room per night, meals extra, no baths."

"What if I just pay you for food right now?" Hubric asked.

"Penny a room per night, meals extra, no bath."

Hubric's eyebrows rose but he produced two pennies and handed them to the man.

The old man gave a gappy toothed grin and held up a bottle. "Liquor is free if you play cards."

A smile spread across Hubric's face. "Then consider that bottle empty already."

"What rooms are ours?" I asked. Clearly, I was the one who would have to find our rooms and set Savette and Rakturan up. The promise of cards had Hubric lit up like a torch.

"Pick any one you like that's not already occupied," the old man said. I hobbled forward, still leading Savette and Rakturan but paused when the man spoke again. "You should consider playing a hand or two with us when you're through. We had word that an entourage is on it's way. Could be interesting."

"We didn't see an entourage while we were flying. Just the usual farmers and merchants," Hubric said, sitting in the chair beside the old man.

"They'll be flying and have to go through the gate as you did. One of the guards told me that. From the north. There's some sort of important High Castelan with them. Our tribute bride to Baojang. A girl named Starie Atrelan."

Beside me, Savette and Rakturan gasped and I cleared my throat to try to disguise it. "Of course, I'd like to see that. I'll be back as soon as we're settled here."

Hopefully, he didn't notice how tight my smile was or how quickly I led Savette and Rakturan into the dim inn, holding my breath until the door banged shut behind us.

Chapter Seven

S tarie was coming here! If she saw us, then any hope of going unnoticed would be lost. Especially if she saw her promised groom here with Savette, a white scarf over his eyes. I was breathing too quickly, my thoughts tumbling over each other. I needed to calm down and think. A hand clamped over my shoulder and I jumped with a squeak.

"It's just me," Rakturan whispered. "Get us to our room as quickly as you can, Amel."

Who said that he and Savette would share a room? Savette would bunk with me and he could stay with Hubric.

The inside of the inn was cleaner than I'd expected from the outside, though empty. The outside door opened into a common room filled with tables, chairs and a long bar. All of them made of wood and polished to a gleam. Above the bar, a symbol was burned into the wood – a sun rising over a single hill. There was something familiar about that.

We crossed to the wide staircase at one side of the room and climbed to the second floor. I fought not to think how nice it would have been if my leg had been healed. No point dwelling constantly on what wasn't. Better to deal with what was.

I tried the first three doors, finding them locked and opened the fourth with a sigh of relief. Two simple cots were set up with grey woolen blankets and pillows. Simple, but good enough. There was a single window and a stand with a bowl and pitcher. I crossed to the window and checked to make sure it was secure. The view out the window was of our dragons.

We could be unsaddled if this is going to be a long wait. We're all tired and hungry, so if you see any horses unattended...

Ha. Ha. Very funny.

"I think you'd better stay in the room," I said to Rakturan and Savette. Rakturan was already closing the door as Savette sat down on a cot. "I'll bring our gear up. Can you manage to find what you need without me?"

"We aren't blind," Savette said. "Not really. We just see two worlds, this one and another and sometimes it's hard to focus on just this one. We see ... more ... and what we see is more focused, but it means sometimes we miss details in this world."

"So, you're safe if I leave you here?"

"Of course." She smiled serenely.

"I'll help you find the second room, Dark Prince."

He sat down beside Savette. "I'm not going anywhere."

I coughed. "It might be more-"

"I couldn't leave her if I wanted to. We're connected by what was done at the healing arches," he said. "And I'm worried for her safety. I heard what you heard. Starie Atrelan is on her way. She could recognize us and likely she is bearing word from Baojang. They will not be pleased that I abandoned my duty there. It would have been different if I had returned with my original bride, but now... You must keep our identities hidden."

He was so difficult for me to understand. At first, he'd been a mystery. I still didn't know what he was doing so far off course when I met him, or why he seemed to be conspiring against the Dominion. Then he'd seemed like a typical enemy, working to find our vulnerabilities for his advantage. But he'd surprised me by chasing Savette when she was kidnapped. Had he done it purely for love, or was it also to aid his nation? And how had he fallen in love so quickly? We still didn't know how he had escaped from Ephretti and taken Enkenay.

"Maybe it's time you explained yourself, Dark Prince," I said, crossing my arms over my chest. "If I'm going to keep your secrets then I think it's time that you shared them with me."

He pulled the blindfold off his eyes and light flooded the room. I hurried to close the shutters, clucking my tongue.

"Do you want the whole world to see?"

"See my eyes, you mean? There's nothing I can do to stop it. I'm filled now with Savette's magic, bound to her."

"That's your magic, Savette, not his?"

"I don't know," she admitted, leaning her head on Rakturan's shoulder. "I'm not sure about anything anymore. I need time to keep trying things to figure out what is happening."

"So, the arches didn't heal you?"

"I'm not at risk of exploding anymore, but the arches changed Rakturan, too. Together, we have a balance."

I shook my head. This was a lot to consider.

"In the Ruby Isles, you wanted anything but the Dark Prince."

"That was so long ago." Her voice sounded small.

"It was less than a fortnight ago!"

"Was it?"

I sighed. "And you, Dark Prince, you were all full of plots to overthrow the Dominion and anger that you'd been stuck with the noble High Castelan Savette Leedris."

"I won't deny it," he said, his bright eyes turning on me so that I had to look away. "I was plotting to conquer your lands and Baojang continues to plot without me. When I realized what was happening – that someone from my home had begun to infiltrate even my guards in an attempt to remove me from the succession– I knew I had to choose someone to ally with who had the power to help me. The obvious choice was Savette. I hadn't planned to fall in love with her, and certainly not so quickly. It wasn't until she was stolen away that I realized ... I realized I didn't care about the plotting anymore, I just wanted her back." He ran a hand through his hair and began to refold the blindfold. "When she came to save us – actually scooped me from death with the mouth of her dragon -"

Hey, that was me! Of course, he doesn't give me any credit.

Rakturan couldn't hear his objection. "I'll never be my own man again. I'm hers for life. They took me to that fortress with the Dominar, but they didn't expect that a dragon would let me steal away with him. Enkenay was a life saver. Without him, I wouldn't have escaped, wouldn't have arrived in time to save you, wouldn't be able to channel the extra power from Savette. She has my full allegiance now."

"So, I'm supposed to just trust you then?" I asked. I was worried. I'd been certain that I understood him, but this loving, devoted side was so unexpected. "If you are so trustworthy, why do they call you the Dark Prince?"

"For the same reason that they call Baojang the dark country," Savette said, her voice far away. "They are full of mystery. Baojang honors the night."

That was probably something I would have known if I'd had proper Dragon School training.

"Accept it," Rakturan said. "I am different than the man you first met."

"So quickly?"

"What is time? A thousand years can pass in a single day."

I was just supposed to accept that and change my mind about him? I didn't like thinking I could have been wrong about something ... or someone.

"I'm going to get our things," I said as Rakturan re-bandaged his eyes. "You should stay out of sight so that no one asks questions. I'll bring you whatever you need."

"If we are going to help Savette then you need to learn to trust me, Amel."

"I don't trust easily, Dark Prince."

He still made me nervous. Could I really believe his words?

"And if you want us to remain incognito, you might want to stop calling me 'Dark Prince.'"

"And what should I call you then?" I asked, crossing to the door. I already had my hand on the handle, ready to leave when he answered.

"How about Rak?"

"Fine."

Chapter Eight

I hobbled down the steps and out to where Hubric and the old man were playing cards.

"Two knaves on your mountain spire," Hubric said, laying his card down. I watched the steady stream of travelers walking by the inn, or riding horses, or pulling carts. None stopped now that they were through the gates. Would they make it to the cities by nightfall? We would already be close if we hadn't been delayed.

I tapped my foot irritably. I needed to go and get the baggage but watching all these people walk by just made me want to join them instead of staying here. The message in my pocket felt like a heavy lead weight. How long would we be grounded here? We'd been stuck at this inn for less than an hour and I already felt like a prisoner. A prisoner waiting with the sure knowledge that an Ifrit approached.

You're getting more dragon-like all the time! Now you know how I feel when they make me sit in an alcove.

He was right. He'd learned patience and endurance. Maybe I could, too. But it felt so difficult to sit here knowing there was an Ifrit out there somewhere doing who-knew-what and that I had a message from the Dominar waiting to be delivered.

"How long do you think they'll keep us here?" I asked aloud.

"As long as it takes," Hubric said before laying down another card.

"One White Queen?" The old man laid his own card with a gleam in his eye. They'd found a deck and a rickety table from somewhere.

"Is there anything we can do to speed things up?"

"Not unless you have a way to trump a General's orders." Hubric seemed almost as distant as Savette as he thumbed through his cards.

"Three swords," he said, laying down seven single sword cards.

The old man cursed and gathered up those that were left. "You win that hand."

"Barely, and there are so many more hands to this game." Hubric took a sip from the wooden cup in front of him.

"Hubric?" I said, impatiently.

"Mmmm?" He was sorting through his cards now. In the distance, I heard shouting and the flow of people passing in front of us slowed.

"It's just that the message is important and we're just sitting here. Can't we hurry this up somehow?"

Hubric's gaze shot up to mine, the deadly stern expression on his face silencing me. What had I done wrong? He looked at me like I'd suggested killing someone!

"I'm happy playing cards, apprentice. Is the baggage taken care of yet?" His eyes were back on his cards, his tone easy going.

"No, master."

"Then let that be your first priority." His words were so clearly a dismissal that my eyes widened. Hubric had never treated me like this before.

Frustrated, I hobbled to the back of the inn, unsaddled the dragons and made sure their water troughs were full. Would they be fine in what was essentially a stable yard?

I don't like it any more than you do, but yes, we'll be fine.

"Can I leave the non-essential baggage and saddles with you here?"

I'm not going anywhere. It's better than you carrying them up and down the stairs.

"Thank you."

I gathered up our personal satchels and one that had dried foods and waterskins and hung them over my shoulder, so I could limp back to the front of the building. I was getting quicker on the crutch. There were some advantages to a physical lifestyle.

"Four mountains," the old man said as I climbed the last stair onto the wide porch. Cards! How could that possibly be important compared to the message we'd been sent to deliver?

By the time I'd reached our room again and deposited the gear there, Savette was asleep on the bed and Rakturan sat on the other bed, his head in his hands.

"There's food in the satchel," I said, placing it on the bed beside him and stowing the other bags. There was a small access door to the adjoining room. I opened it and looked back and forth. Hubric would have to take this one. It was identical to ours in every way.

"Thank you," Rakturan said as I returned, looking up at me through the blindfold – or so I supposed. The way they did that was creepy. "You have to believe me that I'd do anything for her now. She's like a ship that sailed by and I got tangled around her anchor rope. I can never go back to where I was before. There's just something about her that I need to protect and nurture and without that ... without that there's nothing."

I watched him for a long moment. He looked so sincere. "If that's true, then tell me why you were sailing so far south."

The minutes hung between us before he said, "There are those in your nation who want the downfall of the Dominion and they are more than happy to conspire with a foreign prince to make it happen."

Chills shuddered down my spine. "People like who?"

"People you know."

The blood drained from my face as I thought about who he could mean. Outside, another trumpet blast sounded.

"Amel!" Hubric called from below. "Apprentice!"

"I have to go," I told Rakturan. "But later, you need to tell me more."

I hobbled out the door and down the steps to find Hubric below waving at me. "The Innkeep says there's food behind the bar. Be a good apprentice and go get it, would you?"

I frowned. What had happened to him? This wasn't the Hubric I knew. With a frustrated sigh, I went back into the inn and found the bread and cheese behind the bar. I looked again at the ostentatious wood carving behind the bar. Someone had taken a lot of time to burn that sun into the wood with a small iron.

I was just negotiating my way through the door when the first dragon crawled through the gate. He was green and muscled and walking beside him was Artis. Artis! Here! Behind her, Grandis Elfar strode, her own dragon in tow.

My mouth fell open at the same moment that the old man said, "You'd think she'd never seen a dragon before."

"Give us the food, Amel. Five nations to your one queen," Hubric said, and I stumbled forward, starting to place their food on the table, my eyes still riveted to the gate. The next dragon to walk through was Asteven, his Gold head held high. On his back, leaning forward to press down on his back, rode High Castelan Starie Atrelan dressed in the strange hard-shell clothing the Castelans had worn at the ball on the Ruby Isles. Around her eyes was a black cloth. Her head turned toward me as she rode through the arch, but the stonework caught on her scarf, pulling it down from her eyes.

I gasped as the scarf revealed two eyes black as Savette's were white. Just as hers shone with light, these ones seemed to eat the light nearby, clouding Starie's face in shadow.

Chapter Nine

There was a clatter as I dropped the tray on the table, and my gaze finally pulled away from Starie to the mess I'd made. I opened my mouth to apologize at the same moment that Hubric grabbed my elbow and pulled me down to whisper in my ear.

"Enemies. All. Don't say a word, just go back upstairs and keep your wits about you."

He shoved me aside and said more loudly, "Enough help, apprentice, if this is the best you can do. Take yourself back to the rooms."

I hobbled inside and back up the stairs feeling bewildered. First Hubric started acting like a fool over cards and ordering me around and now ... this. What had I seen? Were Starie's eyes really black with light-eating darkness? And what was she doing here with Grandis Elfar and Artis? I shivered. Something wasn't right about this. To get those eyes, Savette had suffered horribly. What had happened to Starie to get hers?

I flung open the door to our room and hobbled in. Rakturan was asleep next to Savette on a single cot, their hands intertwined affectionately. We'd need to find them a wedding chapel before long.

I bolted the door and checked the shutters on the window. Everything was secure. All I had to do was wait. I took some time to wash at the basin and to straighten my hair, combing out the inevitable tangles from a life of constant flight. I oiled my crutch so that the quarterstaff top could pop out easily and then, finally, I lay down on the bed and drifted into an uneasy sleep.

I woke with a start when a knock sounded on the door, hurrying to open it. Rakturan was already standing, sword in hand, his blindfold over his eyes.

"I have your back," he whispered.

I unbarred the door, but before I could open it, Hubric pushed through, nearly knocking me over. The old innkeeper was behind him. They shut the door behind them barring it again and the old man produced two huge leather sacks.

"I think they're big enough," he said.

"For what?" I asked.

"We have permission to move on," Hubric said. "But we are to accompany the Dragon Rider procession that just arrived."

I felt lightheaded. If Starie knew that Savette was with us – or worse, Rakturan! – there was no telling what she would do.

"We can't do that. If they see Savette or Rakturan-"

I was interrupted by Savette. "There is evil out there as powerful as the Ifrit. Whatever it is must be avoided at all cost."

"Not all evil can be avoided," Hubric said, his face grim. "Sometimes it must be deceived."

The old man shook out one of the leather sacks and laid it on the cot. "In the sack, pretty lady."

Savette and I gasped at the same time and Hubric looked a bit chagrined. "We need to keep you and Rakturan safe. That means, these folks can't know about you. We need to keep you hidden until we arrive somewhere safe. You can keep a waterskin and some food in there and you'll be tied to Raolcan and Kyrowat so there should be no problems."

"Why not Enkenay?" Rakturan asked. He looked wary even with a blindfold obscuring most of his expression.

"Enkenay's White. He can't read your mind like the Purples can. He definitely can't talk to you in it. We need dragons who can. Enkenay will have to carry the baggage."

"They can speak into your minds?" Rakturan looked shocked.

"No time for that," Hubric said, taking the second sack from the old man and spreading it over the other bed. "Get in the sack. We have just a few minutes to gather our things and saddle up before we are expected to join the entourage.

Rakturan kissed Savette goodbye – so intimately that I blushed – and then helped her into her sack.

"You trust the innkeeper?" I whispered to Hubric.

He snorted. "Didn't you look above the bar? Why do you think I sent you in there? I'm not in the habit of treating apprentices like servants."

The wood burned sign above the bar! It had been there all along. The sign of the Lightbringers! I looked up to see the old man grinning at me.

"And the cards?"

"You don't get to learn the language of the cards until you join us officially," Hubric said, handing Savette a waterskin and small parcel of food and then tying up her sack. On the other bed, the old man did the same for Rakturan. "Now, gather up the baggage again. Corbin and I will have enough to do carrying these two down to the dragons."

I obeyed quickly, gathering up the baggage again and slinging it all around me by the straps. I was getting sick of playing mule, but I didn't envy Hubric and the old man as they slung Savette up onto the old man's shoulder – could he even carry her? – and Rakturan onto Hubric's. He was already sweating as we opened the door and walked down the stairs.

"There's a back door," the old man said, leading us through the kitchens to the stableyard. His voice was tense with exertion.

In the stableyard, the dragons were ready, heads up and alert. I dropped the baggage and hurried to saddle Raolcan. The old man laid Savette across the back of his saddle, strapping her into place with the baggage straps.

"Are you okay, Savette?" I asked.

"It's uncomfortable, but I can manage."

We saddled the others, securing Rakturan and the gear. The old man circled our dragons, adding some sheepskins to the leather sacks to obscure Savette and Rakturan's forms.

"Still okay? I asked her as I strapped in. I had a rein for Enkenay to attach to the saddle, giving the impression that he was being led by us.

"Yes. It actually helps a bit to feel the straps holding me."

We mounted up and Hubric whispered a thank you to the old man with the words, "Honor to the Light and to all who bear the name. Defend and protect what was trusted to you."

The old man whispered the same and then we were marching out in a line, Kyrowat in the front and Enkenay bringing up the rear. He snapped lazily at Raolcan's tail.

Just what I need. An irritated dragon on my six. We need to get his rider back to him as soon as we can.

I wasn't worried about Enkenay. He wasn't the one with eyes like the black of death.

Chapter Ten

I was already craning my neck trying to see out in front of Kyrowat as he walked around the building. At least twenty Dragon Riders were mounted and waiting in front of the inn, having just come through the gate. In the distance, a formation of dragons was flying towards us. From the city. Apparently, there was no additional inconvenience if the dragon rider waiting was Starie. As usual, the world bent backward to please her.

And that's not at all a bitter thought.

How could you fight bitterness? It just crept up in response to the seemly endless injustice of the world.

Oh, I'm not judging. I'm as bitter as anyone. I just know how it gnarls a person, twisting them into something hard.

Did I want to be hard? Or did I want to be tender, to feel the pain of the world and be sensitive to the needs of others? That sounded good, right up until the moment that you felt all the pain that people were willing to lash at you.

The first face I saw clearly was Grandis Elfar's and when she saw me her expression went from shocked to furious in the space of a second. She leapt off her dragon and stormed across the dusty street to me.

"Amel Leafbrought, the runaway! And wearing brown leathers, too! Get down off that dragon. You have lost every right to ride."

Hubric coughed. Kyrowat coughed. Grandis Elfar spun around as fire burst in a tiny ball right behind her.

"Are you speaking about my apprentice, Elfar?"

"Hubric Duneshifter!" She looked affronted and stood a little taller, crossing her arms over her chest. Hubric, on the other hand, looked unconcerned as he pulled a deck of cards from his pocket, shuffling them in his hands. "You've turned up again, I see, and still just as interested in other people's business."

"It's my business now, Anda."

Anda? He called her by her first name? I could feel my eyes growing wide.

"And how is it your business if I drag this runaway off her dragon, tan her disobedient hide and draft her into the servant ranks?"

"She's my new apprentice," he said casually, offering her the deck. "Pick a card."

"I will not be picking a card!" Grandis Elfar sputtered. "Explain yourself this moment."

"Well, I found her wandering the streets in Vanika," Hubric said with a raised eyebrow. "You'd think we'd employ a Dragon School Grandis to keep that from happening, but no matter. I took her in hand, and discovering she was Purple, took her on as an apprentice, oath and all. Since the Dominar was there, we made it all official and had her swear before him. You know me, Anda. I always do things by the book."

"Hardly! I don't know what game you're playing Hubric-"

"-and you won't until you pick a card-"

"-but I assure you that it ends now. I am here in an official capacity, escorting the future Bride of Baojang to the Capitol on orders from Grandis Dantriet."

"Here's the thing, Anda," Hubric said, putting the cards away. "I don't much care what you are up to as long as you aren't tearing apart the fabric of reality, bothering my apprentices, or winning at a card game I'm playing. Do what you please. Now, if you don't mind, our escort is almost here, and I have a message burning a hole in my pocket." He gestured to me. "Come along Amel and keep a tight reign on the White."

I watched Grandis Elfar with wide eyes as we rode by. She sniffed but didn't look in my direction. I felt almost giddy at Hubric's defense until I saw Starie sitting gloriously on her Gold dragon, four full Dragon Riders surrounding her on matching Gold, heads high, leathers polished, and weapons in hand. She had a full honor guard. Her bandaged eyes followed me as I rode by and little stabs of terror ran through me. She was like a counter for

Savette. Black to white. Good to evil. Innocent to guilty. What did that say about those who rode with her?

I peeked a glance at Artis who bit her lip as she watched me, like she was worried both for me and about me. That's what you got when you were set on always obeying authority no matter what that authority said. You got yourself into murky waters.

A good lesson to see someone else learn so that you don't have to. Some authority must be followed for honor or because they represent what is right, but there are times when another path is vital. Like when you went off to save Savette. And when I chose you.

Wait. Was he supposed to choose someone else? Was that what he was saying? Had he bucked authority by choosing me? Raolcan?

Those spooky gazes were still on us as Hubric chose a place for us at the end of the line.

Smart. Keep your enemies in your sights.

Did he choose me against orders somehow?

I fly my own arc, spider. You should know that by now. No regrets.

I couldn't help the surge of affection I felt for him at those words. No regrets. But I also couldn't help but wonder who the dragon community had wanted him to choose. Could it have been Starie up there on Asteven with her eyes bound in black?

Beneath me, Raolcan shivered, a full-body quiver that made me queasy.

Don't say freaky things and I won't shiver like that.

Deal.

Even as we found our place at the back of the line, Starie's face was turned to us. I hoped we didn't stop anywhere along the way. The sooner we got away from her the better.

I think our paths will cross hers many times. And we will regret it every time they do.

Chapter Eleven

We flew three hours before the first break was called just outside a bustling town along the Dragontail River. I was amazed how populated this area within the walls was, and how large. The wall must have taken decades to build.

Two centuries, if I recall correctly. This is the heart of the Dominion. The place of artisans, Magikas, and soldiers. The home of nobility, philosophy, and religion. Our visit here will give you little more than the briefest taste of it.

Despite the weighty message in my pocket and the friend I was hiding in a sack behind my saddle, I was desperate to see more of it. This town, alone, was almost as populated as Dragon School. There were three mills on the river, their wheels turning endlessly as they ground out flour. I felt jittery at the thought of entering the town and watching the people at work there. They were dressed with large white placards made of stiff cloth hanging from their necks and tied around their waists that were worn on top of their other clothes. The clothing they wore was of fine, even cloth with rich blue tones I'd never seen in the dyes of the north.

Indigo. It grows here. It makes a lovely dye, but too expensive for many in the north.

The placards had symbols and designs embroidered on them in colored thread. I was fascinated by how each was subtly different.

They denote the place they are from, their families, and trades. See the one where crossed axes are interwoven in the design? He and his family harvest wood.

What would my placard look like if I lived here?

There would be a very handsome purple dragon on it, obviously.

Hubric set us down a little way away from the others in the clump of trees, stationing the dragons so they could drink from the river but also shield us from view with their bodies.

"We need to be quick but subtle here," he told me as we dismounted. "The dragons need water but our 'cargo' also needs to stretch and take care of necessities. Keep watch while I help them."

I stood on the side of the dragons closest to the other Dragon Riders, watching as the Blacks tended to their dragons with military precision and trying to look nonchalant as I checked Enkenay's straps. Good thing the Blacks were between us and Starie's entourage. I was still certain that she could see me through that blindfold – and that she meant me no good. I'd threatened her the last time I'd seen her and even now I was keeping her ticket to royalty from her.

I was worried enough that every movement towards us made me more alert. Was that someone looking at us? No. He was watching the diving bird in the river bringing up silver fish. Was that someone walking this way? No, he only wanted to check his dragon's hackles. How about that dark figure skirting the Blacks in a billowing cloak? I held my breath as I recognized her. Artis.

She was, indeed, walking toward us. I coughed loudly, trying to signal to Hubric.

"If you have a cough you must wait two minutes for me to get you a drink, apprentice," he called. Two minutes. She was closer than that. I couldn't afford to have her find us in the act of stashing Savette and Rakturan back into their sacks.

I hobbled forward. If I met her halfway, maybe that would keep her far enough away. We met halfway between the Blacks and my dragons. She looked nervous, looking this way and that, her eyebrows knitting together and her hands twisting in her cloak.

"Amel! It's really you. I thought you were dead in Vanika. We heard word that the city was attacked by some unknown force and thrown into chaos. How did you escape?"

"You betrayed us," I said. Who cared about my escape compared to that?

"I was helping you!" Her eyes pled to be understood. "You were sinking your own futures! I had to tell someone before you all became servants forever! And thank goodness I did! Olla and Orra were forgiven and they are with a Green Dragon Rider now who is training a knot of Green Initiates. That would never have happened if I hadn't alerted the proper authorities!"

"And what about you?" I asked. "Did you get some sort of reward for it? A promotion?"

She flushed. "I've been assigned some extra tasks, but they are secret and I can't discuss them."

I frowned.

"Don't look like that, Amel. I deserved some sort of recognition for what I did! I followed you all through the mountains and brought you to an inn to keep you safe."

That wasn't how I remembered it. I sighed. Maybe I needed to give her the benefit of the doubt.

"Do you need something that I can give you, Artis?"

"I just..." she looked away, her cheeks flushing. "I just want to be sure that there are no hard feelings."

Did I have hard feelings? If she and the others had been there would we have saved Savette any better than Lenora and I ended up saving her? Probably not. I took a deep breath.

There is honor in forgiving an offense.

"I forgive you, Artis," I said.

She smiled. "Starie Atrelan wants to see you, too. She says she has so much to say!"

I bet she did. I was saved having to reply by the call to saddle up. We were off again. Hubric looked nervous as I remounted Raolcan, leaning in to whisper.

"Next stop is the Garrison. Your message must be delivered immediately. We have no more time to lose."

Chapter Twelve

The Garrison was a massive, sprawling heap of buildings, pavilions, archery ranges, fencing rings, stables and dragon cotes. Approaching it from the air, I felt a stab of terror. It lay across the plain in the area between the two sky cities. Their massive construction hung above us, dwarfing even dragons into inconsequential specks.

Hardly inconsequential.

I'd been staring and staring at the sky cities for the past hour, barely wanting to blink there was so much to see. Roads led to the towers beneath the sky cities where baskets hauled a steady stream of traffic up and down. Dragons flew in a continuous ring round the cities, a black mass of defenders in motion as constant as heavenly bodies, speckled occasionally by fleets of Reds, pods of Greens or Golds, and the occasional solitary White. I saw no other Purples.

I told you we are rare. You're lucky to have met three of us.

The Garrison was like the black shadow under the sky cities, merging on the edges with the other cities below the sky cities, but separate from them. It must have housed thousands of soldiers, officers, and Dragon Riders.

Tens of thousands.

Black and Red dragons moved to and fro from the Towering cotes on the south side. Someone had built ragged towers on the four corners of the Garrison. They were spiky with men and weapons, the berms built between them carried a steady circling of men on watch. At the center of the Garrison, a massive black spire rose into the air.

I'd never been so nervous about entering a place before – not the sky city of Vanika or even Dragon School. There wasn't a single person down there who couldn't kill me in an instant.

And if they try, I'll slaughter them by the thousand.

I thought he'd said there were tens of thousands.

Well, even I have limits on how much carnage I can make.

We banked down towards a huge open square in the center of the Garrison, the Black Dragon Riders who escorted us leading the way. As we landed, the buildings swelled in my view to full size. On one end of the square, a set of steps led up to what looked like a small palace. Behind it was the black spire I'd noticed before, a twisting mass of woven metal or something like it. I couldn't tell if it was hollow or solid. There were no visible windows on the sides of it. Long white buildings laced with arches stood to our left and right, roads weaving between them and meeting here in the cobbled square. This place was old and well-used. How long had the Dominion kept a garrison here?

A few hundred years. This place is steeped in tradition. Try not to set a foot wrong.

We landed, and the Blacks dismounted at a stunningly quick pace, fanning out across the steps with weapons in proper display. The garrison here must have been used to frequent dragon landings in the square. The people along the edges of it continued with their work as if nothing was happening. One column of men was marching along the edge of one of the white arched buildings while another group of men in drab clothing worked to repair the stonework on the other. A squad of men in drabs were at work sweeping by the barracks, too far away to see clearly. On the steps of the palace, men in white and silver were arrayed with pikes held out and gazes forward like they were on guard duty.

Which, of course, they are. No pomp is too much for the Palace of War.

The what?

Where the generals are housed and meet to plan and campaign. It's an official part of the Garrison at Dominion City.

I'd expected smoky tents and dirty, bloody weaponry.

We aren't at war in the Capitol. Not yet.

The doors to the palace opened and a man walked through with a segmented coat like those I'd come to associate with High Castelans and the Dominar. He wore a helm formed to look like a dragon head in black, inlaid with silver. A bright white cloak flapped in the wind behind him and he was flanked by five rows of two men each. They descended the stairs with an air of authority. Hubric dismounted quickly, and I followed suit.

He hurried over to me while I was still adjusting my crutch.

"We need to deliver the message immediately. Our other 'cargo' will have to wait. Kyrowat will ensure it is safe."

I nodded. I noticed that Grandis Elfar's party had also dismounted - all but Starie. Their honor guard fanning out around her perch on the golden dragon.

"I am Castelan Jagrud Tedris," the man in the dragon helm said. Up close he was middle-aged, still fit and powerful with white streaks in his beard. "Keeper of the Garrison. All visitors riding dragons are required to report here before continuing on to your destinations by order of Comard Eaglespring General of the Spire, Lord of War. Please state your intended destination so that we may prioritize you."

"We come bearing a message for Comard Eaglespring General of the Spire," Hubric said loudly.

"Noted." Castelan Tedris turned his level gaze to Hubric and gave him a slight nod – one professional guardian of our dominion to another. I appreciated that. Hubric deserved respect. He turned to Grandis Elfar. "And you?"

"I am Grandis Elfar of Dragon School, leading the retinue of High Castelan Starie Atrelan, promised Bride of Baojang. We come to speak to the Council of Castelans in Dominion City and to show them this." She nodded to Starie who removed her black blindfold. Gasps filled the courtyard and there was a clatter as one of the guards on duty dropped his pike.

"That man is on report!" the Keeper said.

Grandis Elfar raised her voice above the noise. "High Castelan Starie Atrelan is the promised one of the Ibrenicus Prophesies and our rightful ruler."

The Keeper's face went white as his cloak.

Chapter Thirteen

"Silence!" Castelan Jagred Tedris said, his voice resounding over the courtyard. "Silence!"

"You will not silence me," Grandis Elfar said, her shoulders thrown back and her head high. "You haven't the right or the rank."

"But perhaps I have the wisdom," Tedris said, a scowl on his face, "not to throw words like that around where just anyone can hear them." He scanned the courtyard. "All of you leave your dragons here. My men will watch that no one disturbs them."

"All of us?" Grandis Elfar asked looking at Hubric and me.

"Are you deaf? Put the blindfold back on the girl. We'll wait for the General to decide on this matter." He looked shaken, despite his scowl and hard words. Who wouldn't be when confronted with Starie's black stare? "And until then, I'd rather confine the witnesses to where I can watch them. Lieutenant Heighthopper?"

"Sir?" A guard stepped crisply out from behind him.

"Get a detail of fresh guards to watch these dragons and the entrance. Once they are stationed here, gather your watch and these Black Dragon Riders and bring them to the green gallery to receive further orders. Until that time, no man is to speak. Not about this or anything else or by the heavens I will see you discharged."

"Yes, sir!" Heighthopper marched away crisply and Castelan Tedris turned back to us.

"Follow me."

Hubric stationed himself at my right, between the Grandis and her party and me. I appreciated the gesture, as if he could guard me by his mere presence, but I was more worried about Savette on Raolcan's back. How would she stay still for so long while we were gone - in the confines of a tight bag, no less?

She's asleep. The magic wears her out. Rakturan, too. Don't fear. Kyrowat and I will keep them still or do what is necessary to keep them from being found.

They were going to be afraid when they woke.

We will speak to their minds and comfort them. There was a pause. *Okay, I will, since Lord High and Mighty Dragon Kyrowat says that's beneath him.*

I tried not to snort out my laughter and judging from Hubric's expression he was doing the same thing.

Not everyone is willing to break the rules and customs like I am. But I say that customs are made to serve us, we are not made to serve customs.

But if everyone thought that way there would be lawlessness.

I'd flame anyone else who disobeyed our customs. That's only for me.

I had to stop talking to him or I really would laugh out loud, which would be ridiculous since we were following an officer who looked like he might spontaneously combust from anger and a Grandis so haughty that it was amazing her feet even touched the ground while she walked.

We were falling behind the others, my limp always a problem and even more so on the long flight of stairs. I gave Hubric an apologetic glance.

"Easier to see what's happening from here anyway," he said, his eyes never leaving Grandis Elfar and Starie.

A pair of guards flanked us, but they were still far enough back that they wouldn't hear a whisper.

"Do you doubt your interpretations of the prophecies?" I whispered.

"Hardly. Listen to this one:

'*The imposter arises, opposite the good,*

Proclaims a new era

Stands where good once stood

A reign of the terra.'"

"That means nothing to me," I whispered back. "What's a reign of terra? Should that be 'reign of terror?'"

"You would know what it said if you were copying your own text. And terra means earth. But exactly what it means is yet to be discovered."

"But you think it's about Starie?"

"I'd be shocked if it wasn't. The prophecies fulfill themselves before our eyes."

If terra meant earth, did it have something to do with the Ifrit that rose from the earth? What if Starie had been in a place like we had, but instead of finding healing arches she'd been found by an Ifrit? Would that be enough to give her black, light-sucking eyes?

"What can we do?" I whispered. Someone needed to stop her. Someone needed to prevent this 'reign of terra.'

"For now, stay quiet, watch, and deliver your message. We Purples stand for truth. When we have a chance to give it, we will. Until then, we wait."

I wasn't sure that waiting and watching were good enough, not with the anxiety that was brewing inside me right now.

Chapter Fourteen

I would have expected a palace – even one clearly owned by the military - to have some comforts. I would have been wrong about this one. The halls were clean and bright with lantern light, but few decorations lined the walls and what there was consisted of weaponry, maps, or illustrated campaigns. Guards were stationed at most of the doors, standing tall and straight with weapons ready. We were hustled through the halls to the center of the palace at a pace that I couldn't keep up with. Fortunately, Hubric lingered back with me, his eyes constantly watching Grandis Elfar and Starie, narrowing whenever they spoke or whispered together.

Despite the spartan décor of the palace, it was still beautifully built. When, at last, we came to a pair of large doors carved with inlaid golden lions, the Castelan leaned in close and whispering to the guard. The guard disappeared into the room and then returned moments later, whispering to the Castelan before retaking his station.

"Come with me," Castelan Tedris said, his lips thinning as he compressed them when he looked at the Grandis. She hadn't made a friend there.

We followed him through the doors. I was awed by the architecture here. Dragon heads were inlaid in the marble floors, arches lined the room beyond, and dozens of lit chandeliers hanging from a ceiling so high that I couldn't see it in the dark above.

At the center, a ring of older officers, muscled but grizzled with age, gathered around a long table. Maps were spread across it with stacks of lists between them. A separate table, filled with sand and small glass figurines, stood to the side. Five scribes sat at their own small desks writing furiously and younger men and women, that I guessed were under-officers, worked at the map table and moved figures in the large sand table. The entire room bubbled with orders, replies, and questions like a human beehive, vibrating with pent-up excitement and purpose.

The older officers – generals, I thought – were certainly impressive. Their ornate armor - segmented and elaborate like that worn by the Dominar - was complimented both with Dominion colors and unique patterns inlaid across the breast. I was beginning to understand from our travels that this must designate their position and origins, like the placards on the commoners did.

Castelan Jagrud Tedris marched us straight to the ring of generals and snapped an elaborate salute, fist to heart. The generals grew silent, turning to us. There were four present – all male, though otherwise very different.

I scanned them, wondering which one was Comard Eaglespring. Was he the hulking man with flowing white hair and skin as black as night? Or the narrow, swarthy man with a nose like an axe? Or the one whose pink skin was over-flushed in the heat of the busy room? Or the one with impressive white wings of hair on either side of his head and a forked beard? They all shared one thing beyond the armor in common: they stood as if they owned not just this palace, but the entire world.

"Audiences were not granted to outsiders today, Jagrud Tedris," the one with flowing white hair said.

"No, General Honorspur, Lord of Cities."

"Then why have you brought travelers here? There is a time and a place for them beyond bothering generals at the strategy table."

Castelan Tedris looked stalwart, like he expected to be attacked and ordered not to defend himself, he looked toward Hubric almost desperately. "This Purple Dragon Rider has a message for General Eaglespring, Lord of Spires."

"Does he now?" the one with white wings in his hair said, there was a slight smile buried in his beard.

"Protocol for that is to send a messenger to the General directly, Castelan," General Honorspur said. "It's not like you to require reminders about protocol."

"No, sir," Tedris said, drawing in a long breath. "I'm afraid news was shared in the courtyard that required me to bring all those present to a secure room under your supervision, Generals."

General Honorspur turned to Hubric. "You violated oaths in revealing a secret message in public?"

The general with the pink skin pulled irritably at his collar. He seemed more interested in it than what was being said.

"I did not," Hubric said.

"Enough of this!" Grandis Elfar stepped past Castelan Tedris, her face haughty. "We've waited long enough. The Purple's message is of little consequence compared to the news I bring. I have found the Chosen One of the Ibrenicus Prophesies and I am here to present her to the Council of Castelans. I will be heard. Immediately."

"Dragon School is respected here, Grandis, but you should remember that you are not a General of the Dominion. You don't have the right to make ridiculous proclamations without backing up your words," General Honorspur said.

"That's not a problem," Grandis Elfar said smugly. She motioned to Starie who stepped forward, despite her black blindfold, and then ripped the blindfold from her face.

Gasps filled the room and the pink-faced general collapsed in a heap on the floor.

"Best to put the blindfold back on," the General with the white wings in his hair said, his eyes riveted to Starie's life-eating eyes. Under-officers scrambled to help the fallen general, but this one didn't pay them a moment of attention. "And then you can finish explaining yourselves."

Chapter Fifteen

"It was after Baojang disappeared that we noticed something strange had taken over. She was listless, like her mind was somewhere else," Grandis Elfar said to the general. Hubric stood beside me, tense like he was ready to spring, one hand on my upper arm as if he feared I would lunge forward, too. "We thought perhaps she was simply disappointed or worried about what had happened to her groom. We brought her to the healing arches."

That was exactly like how things had been with Savette – except for the bright light in her eyes and the magic.

Remember not to trust your enemies. Their relationship with truth is only passing. Who can say if what she says is true?

But if it wasn't, how would she know exactly what had happened to Savette?

The men working on the fallen general whispered frantically to each other and a moment later one of them ran out. Around us, the scribes, secretaries, officers and everyone else were on their feet, faces grim as they watched. I bit my lip. The officer taking care of the general on the floor was sweating, a worried look on his face. Had Starie's single glance killed him? Could she kill in the same way that Savette had healed? Suddenly, and accidentally?

I felt Hubric shifting at my side, as concerned as I was, though his iron hand stayed riveted on my arm.

"It was there that her eyes grew dark," Grandis Elfar said. "And those of us with her saw visions of mighty beings rising from the earth."

Ifrits! There had been Ifrits there, too, but the Grandis said nothing of the Dusk Covenant, and hadn't we been the ones at the nearest healing arches?

If she arrived here straight from the Ruby Isles she would have taken a different path than we did and that would bring them near to other arches.

"It was exactly as the prophecies foretold. You've heard them yourself:
Offered then denied,
Bride of Morning,
Dark's only hope of peace." She looked dramatically around the room. "Starie Atrelan was to be the bride of the prince of Baojang, offered to him at the Ruby Isles, but he denied her, leaving secretly. She is the hope of peace, sent by the dark. You need only look at her eyes to see it. They are even spoken of elsewhere in the prophecies,
Blazing bright under the sun's demise,
Twice blind but still seeing.

"Starie Atrelan," the Grandis continued, "is blind, but more than that, her eyes are black. How else could you interpret 'twice blind?'"

"And so, you brought her here," the general said, his head tilted to the side as he listened intently.

I felt like I had caterpillars in my belly. Those prophecies were not about Starie! Even I could see that, and I didn't believe in them! Savette was the one with the bright glowing eyes. Hadn't those prophecies said a bunch of things about the light? They hadn't mentioned the dark, had they? Or at least not the parts that Hubric had quoted to me. But how did I know if I didn't read them myself?

You really should read them. Then you would know for sure.

Was anything sure when it came to prophecies? Grandis Elfar's explanation about the dark eyes meaning 'twice blind' sounded awfully compelling.

Unless you know about Rakturan and Savette – together, they are 'twice blind.'

But were they? Technically, they could still both sort of see. They could get around on their own.

So can Starie. I saw how she was looking at us.

It had seemed like nonsense to copy out a book of prophecies before, but that was before someone tried to say that Starie Atrelan was some kind of

Chosen One. That was before she was clearly a counterfeit, and no one would ever know the difference!

"We need to show her to the Council and declare the prophecies to be fulfilled." Grandis Elfar's voice rang through the cavernous room.

I couldn't stay silent and listen to these lies! "The prophecies can't be about Starie."

Grandis Elfar's head whipped around and she fixed me with a poisonous look.

Hubric's grip tightened on my arm. That hurt! "The girl doesn't know what she's saying. She's in shock. All of us are."

I thought we were going to speak the truth when the time came!

Not in a room full of enemies with the real Chosen One vulnerable and tied to my saddle! You'll get her killed!

The general cleared his throat. "I've heard enough. We'll alert the Council that you are here, Grandis. Until then, please accept my hospitality. I will attend you as soon as this mess is sorted out." His arm swept across the room, including Hubric, me, and the fallen General in his comment. He turned quickly to an under-officer. "Lieutenant, please show them to my private study until I can attend them in person."

Grandis Elfar's smug expression as she walked by made me want to try out one of Hubric's curses. Starie and her retinue followed, and I cringed as I saw Artis at the back, sneaking a look at me. Artis only ever wanted to do what was right. How had she ended up in this mess?

We each make our own decisions and we stand or fall by the truth of them.

Chapter Sixteen

"How is General Bagden?" the white-winged general asked as a man dressed in white arrived.

He checked the fallen general and then shook his head. "Dead, General Eaglespring."

Comard Eaglespring! He was the one I needed to deliver the message to, but now I was worried. He seemed open to Starie as "the Chosen One" and dismissive of Hubric and me. Would he accept our message?

"Then take him for burial preparations," General Eaglespring said impatiently. "We've not the time to wait for the dead to resurrect. Our Dominar is missing and girls are popping out of the woodwork claiming to be the Chosen One."

Hubric coughed.

"I'll get to you, Dragon Rider," the General said, curtly. "The rest of you get back to work. Except for you, Envoy Endrey. We'll need you." He turned to us. "Follow me."

"You heard the General," General Honorspur barked as we followed Eaglespring out of the room. Behind us, the stunned people turned back to their tasks as if nothing had happened. Had General Bagden been important? Did no one care about his death?

I think you'll find that military people do care enormously, but they are trained not to let it affect their ability to operate. They'll have someone bumped up to General by the end of the day and taking over wherever that man left off. And can you hurry it up? Savette is awake and she needs to get out of this sack.

I could try. I would try. No promises, though. I'd never delivered a message before and I didn't know how long it would take.

We followed Comard Eaglespring through a small door into a room with a roaring fire, a wide black desk and sparse, but functional, furnishings all painted black or white. It was clearly a room for meetings. Eaglespring leaned against the desk, arms folded over his chest and a frown on his face.

"Thank you for joining us, Envoy."

The Envoy nodded solemnly. He wore Imperial livery and his bald head gleamed in the firelight. He was the age of my grandfather and he kept his hands buried in a roll of leather that hung from a strap around his neck. Perhaps he kept messages or notations there?

Envoys are like stationary Purple Dragon Riders – only not nearly as amazing as us. They handle the dispersal of Dominion communications within cities and large compounds.

Hmmm. That sounded boring compared to carrying messages over distances.

Of course it's boring! They may as well be chained to a desk, but they have the power of lions. They are not people to be trifled with. One wink from him and four people could try to kill you before you found your bed tonight.

I shuddered.

"You have a message for me?" Comard Eaglespring asked Hubric, his hand outstretched to receive it.

Hubric stepped aside, motioning to me. "My apprentice carries your message."

"And who sends it?" The General's gaze was on me now, his fierce face lined with suspicion.

"The Dominar, long may he reign, General Eaglespring," I said, fumbling in my pocket before finally producing the white cylinder. I held it out to him and Hubric signed for me to kneel. I knelt hastily, and the general took the message from me, slipping the message out from the cylinder.

"It remains unread?" he asked.

Hubric sucked in a breath.

"Of course," I said. "I have followed the Dominar's instructions to the letter."

"As we always do." Hubric's tone chastised him.

The general shrugged, shaking his head. "My apologies. Today has been full of unwelcome surprises and this ... " he tapped his finger on the message as he read it again. "This changes everything."

He ran a hand over his face, tension filling every feature, before turning to the desk and scribbling a note to hand to the Envoy.

"Ensure the Council receives this as soon as possible," he told the Envoy before turning back to us. "I'll have a message to send back within a few hours. I'm sure Envoy Endrey will as well. I'll leave him to pass on whatever he needs. I hate to say this, but we'll need to ask you to sleep in the cotes with your dragons. I'll have you provisioned, but as soon as I finish drafting a response I'll expect you to leave. There won't be time for cushy beds or places by the fire."

"One more thing," Hubric said.

The general raised an eyebrow, clearly irritated by the addition.

"An Ifrit is loose north of the cities. It chased us from the healing arches to the Needle. I haven't seen it since."

"Ifrit?" The general snorted. "You've been out on your dragon too long, old man."

"My hand to the truth, we saw it close up. It's a threat to the cities here and all the citizens under your protection." He just said it like he didn't even care that Eaglespring thought he was crazy. I felt warm in my chest. Would I be that courageous someday?

"I'll make a note of it," Eaglespring said wryly.

I hoped he really did. Without Savette, we would be dead at the hands of those things. What would an Ifrit on the loose do to a village or a farm, or a city full of people?

"And now I'll leave you to the Envoy. When you're finished together, Castelan Tedris will take you to the cotes."

Hubric bowed and I followed his lead. When we straightened, the door was closing and the general was gone. The Envoy turned to me with a smile.

"You wouldn't be Amel Leafbrought, would you?"

"Yes?"

His smile widened. "I thought there was unlikely to be two girls with a crutch riding dragons. I have a message that was left with me for you some time ago and one that was left with me yesterday. You're a popular girl."

Chapter Seventeen

The Envoy opened his large pouch and produced two slender white rolls, handing them to me. "Receive these messages from my hand whole and delivered to their recipient." I took the messages as he turned to Hubric. "I have at least a dozen messages headed back to the Dominar, long may he reign. He opened his pouch and began to carefully sort through the rolls within, assembling a small pile on the desk and giving them to Hubric with his ritual words. I wasn't listening. I'd already opened the first message, sliding a small silver ring off the outside of the message before reading it.

It read:

Amel Leafbrought, Dragon Rider Initiate,

I suspect that you will come through Dominion City much sooner than anyone would think. Hubric never stays anywhere for long. I hope you are well and not in trouble. Trouble finds you far too often.

I can't stop thinking of the way you look over your shoulder at me, the way your head tilts to the side when you are thinking, the way that long hair of yours hangs over one eye while you bite your lip, as if it can shield you from all the troubles of the world.

Ahlskibi is sick of my thoughts. He says that if I don't find something else to think about, he will leave me and fly the messages on his own. He's never been in love.

I spoke to Ashana Willowspring, head of Purple Dragon Riders on my way through Dominion City. She has not yet given me permission to seek a life with you, but she allowed me to present you with my davari. I hope you will wear it with affection until I can find a way to offer you more.

You have my heart in your palms,

Leng Shardson of the Purple Dragon Riders.

What was a davari?

It looks like a silver ring.

I looked at the silver ring in my hand. It was very small – a tiny dragon biting his own tail. I slipped it on my finger. What a strange ornament.

It's not just an ornament. It has special significance to Dragon Riders. It's the symbol of a promise not yet fulfilled.

I felt tingly at the thought. What promise did this little ring signify?

Maybe the promise that he would give you all that you deserve.

We didn't do those sorts of things in common villages. I thought Leng was born a commoner, too. This seemed like Castelan behavior.

It's Dragon Rider behavior. Dragon Riders take oaths and promises seriously. You still don't realize how serious they are about a promise. Leng made you a promise. This is the physical token of that promise.

He'd also said that kisses were promises. I would have rather he'd given me more of those.

Stop whining and enjoy the ring.

"Amel," Hubric said to me, pulling me out of my thoughts. "Let's go. I'm sure the dragons are anxious for us to return."

His tone suggested that it wasn't just the dragons waiting. Of course, it wasn't. I was being selfish musing on the letter when there were more important things to think about. I tucked it into my pocket, smiling to the Envoy and then following Hubric out of the room.

Even with the note hidden, I couldn't stop thinking about it. As we followed Castelan Tedris through the palace, past armed guard after armed guard and through one weapon-laden hallway after another, all I thought of was a slender man on a purple dragon flying messages in the cold and wet. He was thinking of me out there. Me. He'd given me this ring-

A davari.

-to remind me of his promise.

I didn't even listen as Castelan Tedris apologized to Hubric for having to house us in the dragon cotes. My cheeks felt hot at the thought of the precious letter in my pocket. While he explained that he'd already had his men lead our dragons there and provide cots, resupply, and a hot dinner waiting, my mind was imagining the next time I saw Leng. He'd see this davari on my

finger. He'd know that I'd accepted his promise. I didn't care about the dark outside. My heart felt light.

Even Hubric must have felt lighter with our messages delivered. He was asking the Castelan where he could find a card game as we passed into the tall tower that served as dragon cotes for the garrison. Most of the alcoves were filled with Reds and Blacks, but as we climbed up to the third floor where we'd been given alcoves side by side, I saw a few other colors.

"Your dragons are touchy, aren't they?" Castelan Tedris said as he showed us the alcoves. "One nearly bit my man when he tried to unload them. I'm afraid you'll need to unsaddle and unburden them yourselves."

"Only nearly?" Hubric said. "The dragons must have really liked him."

"Ha!" Castelan Tedris said. "As soon as we have messages from the General, I'll send for you. Don't stray too far playing cards. I think he means for you to leave the moment he's done. That might be only a few hours from now." He looked out at the black sky, speckled with stars. "I'm glad I didn't' join the Dragon Riders! Your hours are terrible."

"But our chances of being impaled on a sword are significantly lower," Hubric countered.

"Indeed!" The Castelan was still laughing while he left.

Hubric looked around the outside of the cotes and I joined him. There were no other dragons housed near ours and although there was a spiraling staircase around the open outer wall, there was little traffic. The soldiers had left us cots and food as promised and even curtained off the back of our alcoves to make make-shift rooms for us to sleep in.

"And now we must hurry," Hubric whispered to me. "Our cargo needs to stretch their legs before we fly again."

Chapter Eighteen

We worked quickly to free Savette and Rakturan from their sacks, stashing them behind the curtains.

"And now what?" I asked Hubric, exhaustedly as we sat huddled on the cot and stool they'd placed for me behind a curtain in Raolcan's alcove. We'd already split the hot food into four portions and were hungrily eating our shares. "Shouldn't we be bringing Savette before that same Council if she's the real Chosen One?"

"So, you believe now," he said, quietly. "You believe because you saw the opposite was falsehood so this must be truth. Is that it?"

"I don't know," I said. "I just think you make a lot more sense than they do. They twisted those prophecies of yours though. They know them as well as you do."

"Know them?" He snorted. "Of course, they know them. Or at least enough to use them for their own ends. Trust me, their allegiance to the prophecies goes no further than the moment the prophecies say something they don't like. Their true allegiance is to their own cause."

"And what is that?" I asked, scraping my dish to get the last of the food out. Splitting two portions among four people didn't quite leave enough to fill everyone.

"Power. A vision for the future of the Dominion that puts them at the top and everyone else out into the cold – or worse."

"Don't people object?" I asked.

"It's not like they phrase it that way."

Rakturan cleared his throat and I found myself startled by the sound. "We have our own factions in Baojang who agree, and it has long been my

135

suspicion that they are working with your Dusk Covenant. They plan to overthrow the governments of both nations and install their own. That can't be allowed to happen. Nor can we allow them to install their own Hasa'leen in Savette's place."

"Hasa'leen?" I asked.

"We have the prophecies, too. They just say slightly different things to us. Our name for the one you call the Chosen One is 'Hasa'leen' – bringer of light."

"Fitting," Hubric said. "And you agree with me that Savette is the Chosen One?"

"She gave me this new sight. How could she do that if she was not?" His tone was almost worshipful as his fingers interwove with hers. Savette looked placid beside the passion on his face. "She is bringing something new and I'm the first part of that. It can't be stopped. Mustn't be stopped."

"Then promise me that you are done working for Baojang," Hubric pressed. "Done working for your own position. Don't give me your drivel about being in love. Just tell me your loyalty is to Savette – the Chosen One - and swear a bonding oath."

"Wait-" I began. Should they really be swearing oaths right now?

"I swear by the Light and the Truth - which is all I have - to uphold the person, safety, honor, and sanctity of the Chosen One, Savette Leedris of the Light." He said it so suddenly, so intensely that I felt myself physically drawing back, my eyebrows rising. I didn't even notice that my spoon fell to the floor until I heard it clatter. So much in that promise. So soon.

Life is short. Especially for humans. There's no time for hesitating.

But it was only weeks ago that he was her enemy, determined to bring her down and destroy our Dominion. And then he said he was in love – and he probably was – and now this? Could any person authentically change so suddenly?

No one knows the heart of a man except for that man. People change. Sometimes they change in an instant.

I swallowed. I hoped I wouldn't change like that.

"And what about you, Savette?" Hubric pressed. "Do you understand what I am saying about you?"

"I know of the Lightbringers, Hubric Duneshifter," Savette said, calmly. "I don't know what you expect me to say. I didn't plan for any of this. It's happening now, no matter what I do."

"I suppose that will have to be enough for now," Hubric said. "We will protect you as you try to find your way."

"We must hurry, whatever we do," she said. "Darkness is growing. I feel it expanding, like a cloud of dust. There are not enough of us to hold it back. We must fight against it."

"We will."

She bit her lip. "But will we be enough?"

Hubric looked at me. What did he expect me to say?

"I can tell by what you've said and done that you believe, Amel. The only person who doesn't know where you stand is you."

Did he expect me to make a rash vow like Rakturan?

"It's time to choose, Amel. I need to ask you to do Lightbringer business, but I can't unless you are a part of us. If you can't be, or won't be, then it's best that I leave you here and go on alone."

"Are you saying that I have to commit to believing this whole prophecy business or I'm out of your apprenticeship?" I asked. My words were tight, filled with anxiety and suspicion.

"You've already been protecting Savette. You've already been fighting to show the truth. You've already fought against the dark. I just want you to admit it – to yourself more than to anyone else."

The silent minutes dragged out as I fought with my own emotions. I didn't want to say it out loud. My belief – what there was – was too fragile to say. I didn't want to have to admit that their crazy beliefs might be right. But what was the alternative? Starie? Absolutely not! The Dusk Covenant? I'd rather go back to my tiny village and leave this new life forever. Ifrits hunting the innocent in the dark? Someone had to stop that!

"Fine," I said, eventually. "I admit it."

Chapter Nineteen

Hubric let out a long breath, like he'd been nervous waiting for my answer.

"Good. Yes, that's very good. We don't have much time. I'll attend to the dragons and to Savette and Rakturan. I need you to go to a card game."

"What?" Was he crazy?

"It can't be me. I need to be here for when the message comes from the general, but one of us needs to go to the game. There will be vital information there, both for us to give and for us to receive."

"Like the card game with the innkeeper?"

"Exactly." He fished into his pocket and pulled out a small purse. "Take this. It will be just enough - probably."

"But I don't know the language of the game!"

"You don't need to. The game is being played in the dry store room inside the south servant's entrance in the palace. No one will stop you from going in that entrance and the card game is informal. Tell them your mother sent you."

"What?"

"It's the password. Then, when they place the first bet, wait for someone to say 'three silver' but only lay down two. That's the contact. You listen carefully to everything he says – the exact words, mind you! – and report those back to me. And on one hand, you need to play a single black knave, but when you lay him down, call him a prince. That's all. Can you do it?"

"Yes ... I think."

"Good. The game begins at the top of the hour, so you'd better get going. What did your note say?"

"What?" I should have known that he'd see my reaction to the note.

"Ah. From Leng. Understood. What about the other one?"

In the excitement, I'd forgotten about the other one.

Hubric chuckled. "Forgot about it, did you? Well, it's easy to forget things when you see generals die from a single stare and then you get inducted into the Order that will be saving the world. Read it when you get a chance and tell me if it's important. Now, run along."

I hurried out and down the stairs to the south entrance to the palace, my heart pounding in my chest. I needed to read that message, but first I needed to get to the game and remember it all. Could I remember that much? Without taking notes? If only I had a pencil and notebook!

No time to fret.

The servant's entrance was busy despite the late hour and I had to stand aside as a group moving large crates left through the door. Eventually the last of them left and I walked through into a wide storeroom. At the back of the room, a man stood with his burly arms crossed over his chest. Behind him, I saw a fire burning and a table set up nearby surrounded by hunched figures. The card game.

I hobbled forward but as I did I saw a figure in a dark cloak enter from a door on the other side of the room.

She was faster than I was and drew up to the man with crossed arms just as I was arriving. Flinging back her hood she said hurriedly, "My mother sent me."

It was Artis.

Chapter Twenty

What was she doing here?

She's playing cards.

But she wasn't a Lightbringer!

Obviously. But other people play cards. I bet even the Dusk Covenant plays cards.

He had a point. When the burly guard turned to me I felt my cheeks grow hot.

"My mother sent me," I said.

"There seems to be a lot of that going around right now." He winked at me. Did that mean something?

I hurried past and took a seat at the table.

"Buy-in is two silver. Pay up or leave," a man in fine clothing said. He was clearly a Castelan.

All the classes were represented around the table from Castelans to servants, but silver was produced by all and the card play was fast and furious. I scrambled to produce my two silver and saw Artis offering hers in a dignified manner.

A woman with a wide scar on her cheek led the first round. "Two Dragon Rider trainees. Isn't that a privilege."

The laughter around the table made me think that wasn't a compliment.

"Sick of the skies, girls?"

"Of course not," Artis said with a nervous giggle.

I ignored the comment, looking at my hand.

"Two silver," the scarred woman said, throwing her coins into the center of the table.

"Two silver." Artis followed her.

My turn was next. I put my coins in.

"Quiet, aren't you, girl?" The woman said to me.

"I'm just here to play cards." What did she expect? That we'd braid each other's hair and whisper secrets?

She chuckled and the next in line threw his silver in the center. He wore plain clothes with white dust on them. A baker. After him was another soldier, deep in his cups already, his eyes red-rimmed.

"Three silver," he slurred, throwing in two coins.

My contact! I tried not to look as excited as I felt.

"We're still on two, Cord," the scarred woman said with a sneer.

The last two players – Castelans in fine clothing – placed their blind in the center of the table and the game began.

"Pair of Queens," the scarred woman said, laying her cards down.

"Five black arches." Artis had a sparkle in her eye as she laid down her cards. Was it possible that she was communicating with someone just like I was?

"Nice," the woman complimented her.

I didn't even know enough of the game to know what a winning play was. Not even enough to know what I was allowed to lay down. Maybe Artis's choice was a genius move. No one else seemed as impressed, though.

I laid down my own card exactly as Hubric had instructed. "Black prince."

"A fool's move," Cord mumbled.

"Who cares? If she can't play, then we get all her money," the baker laughed. On the other side of the burly guard, the sound of voices grew louder. People were filtering into the storehouse. "Let's clean these novices out of coin to make way for some more experienced blood. Pair of Dragons."

"Pair of knives," Cord said, laying his cards down.

"You're one to talk about fools! Wasting knives in a pair like that," the baker scoffed.

I was so desperately trying to remember his words for Hubric that I missed the other players turns. The baker took the money from the middle and Artis dealt the next hand, waiting as we all bought in again.

"Four generals," she said, laying her cards in a row to whistles of appreciation.

"She means business, boys and girls!" Cord's drunken comment was slurred.

We each took our turn. I didn't bother trying to win. I didn't know the game anyway. I placed three dragons down.

"Again, with the foolhardy moves," Cord scoffed. "It's like you've never played. Don't you know that a hand like that should be saved for a Dominar run? This isn't Backwater Manor."

I felt my face heating. "I'm so sorry."

Was he going to stop playing? I needed to watch and report to Hubric.

Stop panicking. That man knows this business better than you do. Just listen and remember.

"Don't worry about her," the baker said. "She's out of coin. This is her last round. Hopefully, she got a taste of what she was looking for."

I bit my lip. If this was my last round, then this was my last chance to receive a message from my contact.

Cord hummed a tune as he thumbed through his cards.

"Full army," he said, at last, shoving all his cards into the center.

"And you called her the fool," the scarred woman laughed. "Put your money where your mouth is."

"Gladly," he said, dumping a huge pile of silver into the middle of the table.

"You shouldn't play drunk, Cord," the baker said. "What makes you think you'd win on a hand like that?"

"I'll be fine as long as no one has the Dominar."

One of the Castelan's laughed, placing a card with a silver crown and mask on the table. "I do. Game's over, chump."

"There's always hope," Cord said, standing and stumbling towards the door.

I stood as well.

"Learn to play cards better before you come back," the baker laughed, but I'd seen all I needed and I was anxious to return to the dragons. Maybe Hubric could make sense of the game. I certainly couldn't!

I hurried out of the storehouse and out into the night, hobbling to the dragon cotes and opening the door into the darkened building. As I was stepping onto the stairs, I heard it creak open behind me.

Chapter Twenty-One

I climbed the stairs, looking over my shoulder frequently. The cotes were empty except for the dragons bedded down there and those of us with Hubric who had to wait for a message. That meant that no one had bothered to light the staircase or the interior of the cotes.

I could see well enough to climb. After all, as the circular staircase went upward, spiraling in the center of the tower, there were exits into individual alcoves every couple of steps. The light from the moon shone through the alcoves and into the interior of the tower, but only in tiny pools of light between thick shadows.

I didn't need to be worried about falling into the center of the tower – not with a waist-high railing keeping me in the staircase, but I couldn't make out who was following me in the dappled light.

I could hear them, though. Two sets of footsteps – or at least, that's how it sounded. Maybe there were more. I wasn't a tracker who could pick out the exact number of people following me.

What's happening?

I was being followed up a dark staircase with who knew how many people behind me. Could Raolcan send Hubric to help?

He was called to the General just after you left for the card game. He's getting the final message. He hid Savette and Rakturan in the luggage again before he went so that no one would find them. They're tied into the bags.

So, there would be no help from Hubric.

I'll ask Kyrowat if he can get word to Hubric.

Too late. Unless he was very close, they would be on me before he could come to my aid. I pushed harder, stumbling slightly in my haste and slipping on the stone steps. I fell, banging my shin against the stone step and falling backward on my bottom. It took a moment for me to stop my tumble and haul myself back onto my feet. I couldn't afford to do that again. Slow and steady. That was the key. If only I could get my heart to obey that order. It was pounding faster than horses' feet over a flat shoreline.

Hubric comes, but he is still in the palace. It will take time. Where are you?

I was about one more floor beneath Raolcan, if my memory was correct. Steady, Amel. Steady.

Can you get to the outer staircase? I can do nothing for you there in the center. I can't fit through the inner door and if I just flame randomly I will hurt you.

The footsteps behind me sounded so close. I rushed into the next alcove, pulling up short when I realized it was occupied by a black dragon. If I took a step inside, I'd be in his range of attack.

"Don't bother trying to hide, Amel," Artis' voice said right behind me. "We saw you duck into that alcove. And you're far to slow to outrun us."

"What do you want?" I asked. I hated that my voice trembled. I didn't want her to know I was afraid.

"We can't have you running loose, little Dragon Rider," a deeper voice said. Was that the woman with the scarred face? "The Grandis says you know things you shouldn't."

What did I know?

You know Starie was working with the Dusk Covenant. You know they have a plan for her. The Grandis knows that you know – after all, you tried to tell her about it many times. You refused to stop trying to warn her no matter how much she ordered you to stop.

Oh. That.

Artis stepped into the alcove and I slid with my back to the wall, trying to stay as far away from the strange dragon as possible. If only he were purple and could understand my mind!

He's not listening to me. He's cranky that you're there.

"So, you want me to come with you?" I asked my pursuers.

The scarred woman's laugh was ominous. "Sure. That's what we want."

"It didn't have to be this way," Artis said, her voice filled with sadness. "I tried to tell you just to leave things alone and do what was required. Why couldn't you have listened?"

"Why can't you think for yourself?" I countered, but the bold words were lost behind the chattering of my teeth as I slid further into the dragon's alcove. His great yellow eye was half open and watching me. "Why do you let other people tell you what right and wrong is?"

"I'm not the fool walking into a strange dragon's alcove," she said. I glanced back and saw her and scar-face standing in the doorway. Neither one had stepped into the room yet.

"Enough playing around," Scar-face said, drawing a sword and stepping into the alcove.

Watch out!

I spun to see the black dragon rear up. In the glitter of his golden eye, I saw myself reflected. He lunged at me at the same moment that Raolcan yelled.

Smack him hard on the nose!

The Black dragon snapped at me, and I clenched my jaw, drawing in all my courage not to close my eyes. As his jaw came close, I punched him as hard as I could on the nose. It was like hitting a wall. Tears filled my eyes, blinding me. My hand hurt like I'd broken all the knuckles in it. I cried out in pain, but the dragon reared back, surprised.

Run!

I rushed past him as fast as I could, making it to the outer staircase outside his alcove just as he snapped again, this time at my heels. I was already climbing the steps again, in a daze, but fighting to keep my wits about me.

I was lucky to be alive. There would be time to celebrate later. I struggled up the steps. Just a few more and I would be at Raolcan's alcove. Come on, Amel! There was his entrance! I saw his worried face poking out, looking at me.

Relief filled our connection and I started to smile. Too soon. A hand gripped my ankle, pulling me backward. I fell, smacking my face against the stone step and seeing stars. Pain blossomed in my face.

Use your crutch to hit back. Turn. Now.

I fought my pounding head and the blackening of my vision, twisting to obey his order.

Jab with your crutch!

I grabbed it with both hands, jabbing it toward Artis who had my ankle. I hit her in the mouth, bloodying her lip. She yelled but released my foot.

Crawl up the steps. Crawl!

Desperately, I pulled myself up the steps on hands and knee. It was like his voice in my mind was a lifeline. I fought to obey.

I made it up two steps. I was so close to the alcove.

Keep climbing! Climb past me.

I climbed, kicking out when I felt a foot connect with my bad leg.

Cover your head with your arms.

Sobbing in desperation, I wrapped my arms around my head.

"They won't stop my sword, girl," Scar-face said. She was right above me. I could almost feel her cold sword piercing me through and leaking my life onto the stone beneath.

Heat seared across me, a roar filling my ears. My tears, pouring out in my terror, dried instantly.

Get up! Get up and move.

I could barely catch my breath as I pulled myself up on my crutch and stumbled over the charred black stone around me to the next step. Behind me, I heard tears and quavering breath as Artis kept following me.

"Go back, Artis," I said, my voice breathy through adrenaline and exhaustion. "You don't need to die for this."

"You don't understand," she said. "I don't have a choice and neither do you."

"What do you mean?"

She was level with Raolcan's alcove now, in the exact spot that her ally had been burnt to char and blown off the side of the tower. I was three steps higher, quavering from the exertion.

"You haven't read that note yet, have you? So, you don't know that they have him. They'll kill him if you don't obey. Just like they'll kill my family."

The note. I'd forgotten about it again in all the excitement and danger.

"You don't need to tell them. Say that we left. Say there was nothing you could do."

She shook her head. "Sorry."

As she raised a hand, the dagger in it flashing in the moonlight, Raolcan's flame engulfed her, throwing her, alight, over the side of the stairs and out into the night. Her scream filled the night.

I dropped to the steps, shaking, losing my dinner over the side of the tower.

Deep breaths. Deep breaths, spider.

You didn't have to kill her,

I will never let anyone take your life, Amel.

There had to have been another way. I wasn't even sure she was going to kill me. Maybe she just wanted to capture me.

I could hear her thoughts. This was a mercy for her.

I reached into my pocket, shakily pulling out the other note and unrolling it. Despite the moonlight, I had to squint to make out the large, bold words.

It read:

We have Leng Shardson. Deliver Savette Leedris to Dominion City in exchange for his life before the next moon or he dies. Slowly.

Dragon School: Warring Promises

.

Chapter One

"I leave for one moment and you kill two people." Hubric grabbed me before I fell. My head felt light, but my fingers clung to the scrap of paper like keeping it safe could prevent it from coming true. "What's that?"

He took the paper from me and pushed his shoulder under mine to help me limp back into the Raolcan's cote.

Steady now, spider, Raolcan told me. *They lie. That's what evil people do.*

They'd had Leng before. They'd tortured him and tried to kill him before and now this paper said they would do it again unless I gave them Savette - the Chosen One – or at least according to Hubric.

"Let's take a look at that note." Hubric held it up to the moonlight, cursed and then lit a candle in a wall bracket. I already knew what it said:

We have Leng Shardson. Deliver Savette Leedris to Dominion City in exchange for his life before the next moon or he dies. Slowly.

My head was clearing enough to stand on my own, but I still felt sick. Leng and Savette were in danger and Raolcan had just flamed Artis.

She had it coming.

She'd been a friend. She said she was in a bad situation, being blackmailed.

So she turned around and did the same to us? What did she think would happen? Compassion is good, but I don't pity those who choose to do evil. You can't be responsible for the actions of another, but you are responsible for your own actions. Don't let anyone tell you otherwise. Don't let them say "you made me do it." No one can make you do anything unless you want it more than the alternative.

Quite the speech. It didn't help.

Hubric whistled. "So, they have Leng Shardson."

"We need to find a way to save him," I said.

He met my gaze with his flint-hard eyes. "Are you suggesting we give them what they are asking for?"

"Of course not."

He nodded. "Good. Savette Leedris is the Chosen One. I will defend her with my dying breath – and so will you. Never forget, you are sworn to the Dominar, sworn to me, sworn to your dragon and soon you will swear to the Lightbringers. Whatever your personal feelings, those allegiances always come first."

My voice felt shaky with tension as I forced my words out. "Are you saying I should just leave Leng out there to die? They said they'd make him die slowly."

"We don't know how much of that is true."

"No," my voice rose. "We don't. It could all be true. Who knows how long this message has been waiting for me? He could already be dead!"

"Calm down." His words were like ice. "Before you fly off the handle, let's talk calmly."

I ran a hand through my mussed hair, blinking back tears. "Okay."

"I have a message to deliver and orders to immediately fly north to deliver it to the hands of the Dominar."

That was expected. I nodded my understanding.

"And you should have some messages for us from the game. Did you find your contact?"

I nodded as he drew close, looking around as if he were afraid of being overheard.

As if Kyrowat and I wouldn't tell you there were strange minds listening.

A gout of flame from Kyrowat's stall punctuated his words.

"Fine," Hubric said over his shoulder to his dragon. "I trust you. I won't doubt you again." He turned back to me. "Tell me everything he said."

"Ummm," I thought back. It felt like ages ago even though it was less than an hour ago.

"Quickly. Or do you think no one will notice that our dragons turned two women into piles of charcoal?"

"I played the Prince and he said it was a fool's move."

"Sometimes a fool's move is the only one you have. I'd say Rakturan is definitely that. Go on."

"He played a pair of knives."

"That was those two assassins Raolcan just killed."

"Really?" I felt a tingle in my chest. If I had known the code I would have expected them. "When one of those assassins played four generals he said that she meant business."

Hubric grunted. "I was worried that was true. Four of those generals we met tonight are with the Dusk Covenant."

"How can that be true? Are the Dusk Covenant everywhere?"

"Their influence spreads. Even more among the rich and powerful." He leaned against the wall. "What else?"

I was looking at the moon. So big. So silver. Was Leng looking at that moon? Was he held somewhere against his will hoping against hope to be freed?

"Amel? What else?"

I snapped back to our conversation. "I played something at random. I don't know how to play cards. He said that a hand like that's for a Dominar run. What's that? And something about Backwater Manor."

"What did you play?" he looked tense.

"I don't remember."

"Think, girl!" His eyes were so intense that I swallowed. What had I played? It hadn't seemed to matter. At the time.

You played three dragons.

"Three dragons."

Hubric cursed. "We have to leave tonight for the north, Amel. We have no other choice."

"Leng needs us." I turned my back to him. I didn't know what to do about Leng. I didn't know where he was or even where to start looking and of course I wouldn't trade Savette for him, but I couldn't fly in the opposite direction!

We'll figure something out, Amel.

"Did he say anything else?" Hubric asked from behind me.

"He played a full army."

"A bold move." I heard shuffling, like he was picking something up. His tone was light and friendly.

"That's what the others said. He just said it didn't matter as long as none of the rest of us had the Dominar."

"In the end that's what matters," Hubric said. His tone now was so regretful that I started to turn to look at him. "It all rests on who has the Dominar."

There was a pain in my head and the world went dark.

Chapter Two

I felt something cool on my forehead.

"Are you awake, Amel?" Savette asked gently. She was bathing my forehead with a cool cloth. I sat up. "You shouldn't get up too quickly. Hubric said you'd have a knot on the back of your head and a splitting headache."

He was right about the headache. Where were we?

A field near a pond approximately two hours north of the wall around Dominion City. Hubric didn't waste any time.

I needed to get up and get going. If we'd flown two hours north of the wall, it would probably take me about four hours to go back to the city.

And say what at the wall? You have no message and they aren't letting Purples through on their own.

I'd have to think of something. I swayed as the pain hit me like a hammer flattening pot-iron.

"Lean on me. I'll help you drink something," Savette said kindly. She was still so distant, but before this magical change, she'd never been so kind. "Suffering focuses the mind."

Had she heard my thoughts?

No. She's just very perceptive now.

And wait. How did I get here unless Raolcan carried me?

Of course I carried you.

Against my will? When he knew I wanted to find a way to save Leng?

Sometimes the best thing I can do for you is to stop you from getting yourself in trouble. Running off to try to find Leng on your own, against orders, when you have no idea if he's even in danger? That's a fool's move.

Was he joking? He thought he'd done the right thing? He'd betrayed me. He hadn't been on my side. He'd been with Hubric who hit me over the head and loaded me onto Raolcan without my permission!

I sputtered as Savette gave me a sip of water just a bit too quickly.

"Hubric will be back in a few minutes and then we'll need to fly again," she said. "It will be dawn in an hour and he says he has a place in mind with real beds for tomorrow night."

Dawn? I'd been unconscious for hours! Well, I wasn't wasting any more time.

"Thank you for the drink, Savette."

"Of course." She smiled in the dim light of the nearby smoldering fire. "We're friends, Amel. You usually have to help me, but I'll help you, too, whenever I can."

Her words almost made me feel guilty about leaving before Hubric got back.

Going where?

Back to Dominion City.

No.

Wait. What? He was flat out refusing to go?

I'm a dragon, not a horse. You can't just kick me with spurs and make me run. I'm staying right here until Hubric returns, and when he does, we're going with him.

My mouth was open. I knew it was, but I was too stunned to shut it. He meant it. He wasn't going to go with me. That gave me two options. I could go with him in the direction I didn't want to go, or I could try to hobble across the landscape on my own.

It's days on foot from here to the nearest town. And you'd have to carry your own food and water. And you have no idea where you are.

Frustration and betrayal filled me.

You can't always call the shots, Amel. I'm your dragon. I will back you up into the face of death, but every once in a while I'm going to say no to your ideas.

I closed my mouth with a click, too angry and hurt to say anything. What could I do? I had no options.

"Good. She's awake. Time to get airborne," Hubric emerged from the shadows, drinking from a mug. Caf, no doubt.

"You hit me on the head and conspired with my dragon to bring me here against my will!"

"And you're going to pout like a child about it? We both know you were in a jam. You couldn't leave me and Savette and you couldn't walk willingly away from saving your sweetheart. I did you a favor and didn't make you choose."

"It was my choice to make," I said quietly.

"Trust me. You'll thank me later. Now, mount up. If we fly hard all day we'll be at our destination by late afternoon and finally get a hot meal, a soft bed, and some friendly discussion. It's been a while since we slept without fleeing."

"What about the Ifrit?" Savette asked quietly. I felt a chill wash over me. The Ifrit. I'd forgotten about him. And Starie. And Artis' death. I bit my lip as sadness washed over me.

"What about him?" Hubric asked, casually.

"I saw the wall when we left. Something attacked the gatehouse and lit it on fire. There were people everywhere trying to put it out. I felt him there."

Hubric shifted, sipping from his mug before answering. "You were in that sack. I didn't think you saw."

"I see everything, Hubric." Savette sounded so calm, but also like she was far away. "I felt him watching us and I felt him turn to follow."

"Why would he do that?" Hubric asked quietly.

"Because he wants Savette," Rakturan said, emerging from the shadows. "And he will hunt her until he kills her or is killed in return. We can't flee from him forever."

Hubric cleared his throat. "I'm not sure what else you expect from me. I'm doing my best to keep you safe."

"I think we take him to the Feet of the River," Savette said quietly.

"Even in Baojang, we know about that place." Rakturan crossed his arms over his chest, staring at Hubric through his bandaged eyes.

Hubric ran a hand over his weary face. "See Amel? This is why you need your head screwed on straight. These people want to go to a place where nine out of ten men die and you're pining over a man who's probably sleeping in a soft bed somewhere."

"Why do nine out of ten men die there?" I asked.

"Because they go there looking for magic. Don't ever look for something you don't want to find."

"We have no other choice," Savette said.

The silence stretched out long and deep.

"It's two days before we'd have to turn in that direction or miss our chance," Hubric said eventually. "Give me until then to decide. And if you feel that thing watching, do me a favor next time and let me know."

Chapter Three

D awn was long past and so was noon. Raolcan flew without pause and if
he listened to my thoughts that was his business, but I wasn't directing
them at him. I'd thought loyalty meant he'd always be on my side. I hadn't expected that he'd have his own opinion – or at least, that his opinion would be
different from mine. After all, I was clearly right. How could an intelligent
dragon fail to see that?

It was probably a good thing that he wasn't answering my silent accusa-
tions. I wanted to fight with him. I wanted to convince him to be on my side.
His silence cut me. It reminded me of how lonely my mind was without him
and how desperate I was to patch things up. The problem was, I wasn't quite
desperate enough yet to admit I'd been wrong.

I leaned back in the saddle to speak to Savette. Hubric had her riding
with me even though he'd allowed Rakturan to ride on Enkenay. He'd said it
was because he was worried about my head injury. I was pretty sure he just
wanted added insurance that I wouldn't fly away. As if having Raolcan on his
side wasn't enough already.

"Can you feel the Ifrit out there?" I almost shivered at my own words.
Imagine being able to sense those horrifying creatures?

"Always. But exactly where is the real question."

"How do you feel him?"

"He's evil. A thing made of evil desire and the twisting of human power
and authority. He's everything that the light is not and now that I'm filled
with the light, I can feel those things of evil. They repulse me – I don't mean
they make me sick, although I guess they do. I mean like a lodestone pulls

metal in but can push another lodestone away, in that same way they push at me. We repel one another."

What would it be like to have such a relationship with dark and light?

"And Rakturan?"

"Rak pulls me closer. I feel him always, drawing me closer and closer."

I blushed. "I think you two should be married."

"Have you seen any wedding chapels?"

"Maybe we'll find one on our way." And how strange would that be? Their wedding was meant to have been two royals uniting two lands in what would have been a massive display of pomp and wealth. Instead, they would be two people hiding and running for their lives with a pair of dusty Dragon Riders and three dragons.

"If we do, then Rak and I won't pass it without saying our vows and pledging our futures."

"You seem so sure. He was an enemy not long ago."

"Now he is heart of my heart and soul of my soul. The light that fills me links us. We've become two halves of one whole."

Such a strange thought. "What is the light, exactly, Savette? Is it the magic that Magika's pull from the ground."

"I used to think so. Now I doubt it. This isn't Magika magic. I can't make fireballs or strike with lightning. I can't bind or loosen dragons. I just ... I know *good*. I know truth. I feel the truth of something and sometimes I can make that truth real."

"Ummm... what?"

"Like, I knew that Ifrit was nothing but dust and hate. When I was so full of the light that I could barely breathe, I pushed that truth back at him and he became what he always was – nothing but dust and hate."

"And Enkenay? He was dead!"

"He had loved his rider, Dashira. He loved Rakturan. I showed him the truth – that his heart was full of a new rider and he had every reason to live again – and he lived."

What a beautiful way to do magic. Transformation through complete truth. What if I asked her to show me my truth? Would it heal me, or would I be nothing but dust like the Ifrit? I should ask. No! I shouldn't. What if I was wrong and I... better not to think about it.

I hope you're done sulking and ready to be friends again because this silence is killing me.

Was that an apology from Raolcan?

What do you think?

Probably not, but at least we were still friends and I didn't have the heart to keep him away anymore.

I love you, too, spider.

I felt his relief and affection intermix with my own. It had been quiet for too long in my mind.

I'm glad you're back. We've got trouble up ahead.

Trouble?

Three riders on horseback. Two of the horses have large bundles – man-shaped bundles. They ride full-speed on the North Road and bear no emblems.

What did that mean?

Likely bandits or some other unsavory people. The kind who might kidnap someone and stuff them in a sack. We'll overtake them in just a few more minutes.

Already, my lesser, human eyes could see the horse galloping ahead. Would Hubric stop for them?

Kyrowat's already getting excited. It's been a while since he had a nice horse dinner.

Seriously, he was pushing that myth too far. Soon, I was going to believe that they really ate horses and that was just plain ridiculous.

Chapter Four

A cloud of dust followed the horses. If we'd been chasing them on the ground it might have obscured them from our view. As it was, it only helped us see them more clearly.

Kyrowat started his descent first, talons out and feet reaching forward. The horses sped, flecks of sweat flying from them as they ran.

They're running them to death. Why?

The horse in the lead stumbled as Kyrowat descended before him. He tumbled into an awkward roll over the dirt and stone. Raolcan and I swooped low over the road, parallel to the horses, while Enkenay landed behind them, rearing up to signal there would be no retreat.

Raolcan's landing was more of a skid than a proper landing, coating Savette and me with dust. I spat, trying to clear my eyes as the wafting smell of sulfur and a burst of heat told me he'd flamed someone.

When the dust cleared, a horse was screaming, and another was running, riderless, into the surrounding grassland. The horse that fell writhed on the ground, his rider pinned under him and a large sack thrown clear. Another sack lay beside a long black soot mark and two bodies lay on the ground as if they had been dropped there.

I gasped at the sudden carnage.

It's a warning to all not to mess with dragons.

We didn't even know who they were.

Hubric suspects he does.

I dismounted, helping Savette off.

"Stay back," Rakturan called as he moved to the lame horse. He stood so that his back was to us, hiding the injured horse's head from view. A moment later the thrashing stopped. I didn't look closely. I didn't want to know what had been done.

Steady, spider.

Instead, I limped to where the first sack had been thrown clear. I heard coughing from within. It lay in the dust, worn leather but clearly man-shaped. I reached with trembling hands to my belt and produced a small knife. There was no way that these shaking hands could untie those knots. They were stretched and tight as if someone had been straining against them.

Carefully, I cut the leather thong holding the back closed and then hobbled backward, flicking my crutch into a quarterstaff just in case.

"This one is dead," Rakturan called from behind me. He must have meant the man pinned under the horse. I didn't want to know if he was dead before Rakturan got there.

"They're Dusk Covenant," Hubric called. He was near the fallen men on the ground, examining their bodies. "What were they hurrying off to, I wonder?"

From the bag I'd opened, an arm emerged and with more coughing, a man followed it. He spat and black fluid hit the ground. Horror filled me. What had we done in scaring his captors? Had we hurt him somehow and damaged him inside?

He was young but grizzled like he lived outdoors in tough circumstances. He coughed and spat again. Were those Dragon Rider leathers? His gaze met mine, so familiar and yet so different. He reminded me of Leng.

"You need some scarves girl. It's impossible to tell what Color you are without them."

"I'm Sworn," I said, eyes wide as he coughed and spat again. "I'm not allowed to wear the Colors." His own scarves were purple but tattered and dirty. "What did they do to you?"

"Killed my dragon. Cut poor Darshh's head right off in front of me while his big trusting eyes looked at me. Hollowed me to the core. They killed Uhynmal and Nonoloes with him – Whites, not that I hold that against them. They had a group of Magikas to hold our dragons in place. They're collecting us – Purple Dragon Riders, I mean."

"What can I do for you?" I felt like crying watching him cough up black fluid while he spoke of his dead friends.

"A little water would be nice. Is that Hubric Duneshifter over there?"

"Yes," I said as Savette brought him a flask.

"I'm saved by a legend," he laughed, but his laughter quickly turned to coughing. "Duneshifter!"

Hubric joined us, helping a limping young man with him. This one wasn't a Dragon Rider. He wore armor, but his face was bashed and bloody.

"They shouldn't have tried to outrun us," Hubric said.

"They're in a hurry," the Purple said. "Are you okay Findar?"

"I'll live," the soldier said thickly. He was leaning hard on Hubric.

"Why the hurry, Talsan Woodcarver?" Hubric asked.

The Purple – Talsan – smiled and then burst into a fit of coughing.

"We don't know," Findar said. One of his eyelids drooped over a puffy eye. "They took Casaban on the coast and before they'd finished sacking the city they stuffed Talsan and me into bags and rode away."

"Casaban?" Savette's tone was horrified. "Who sacked Casaban?"

"Baojang." Findar's voice was grim. "It was a fleet of ships from Baojang, but they weren't alone. Someone in the city opened the gates to them and our own Magikas turned on us. Casaban should have been impregnable. I watched our own Magikas throw balls of fire at the Blacks who swarmed to defend us against the ships. I watched them call something dark and fiery from the ground. It ripped the keep apart with its bare hands." His eyes were faraway, pain etching his face. "I fought with the others, retreating as we needed to. We'd been pushed back as far as the dragon cotes when the Magikas came. I was hit hard and lost consciousness and woke up a captive with Talsan."

"The fools thought he was a Purple Dragon Rider, too," Talsan said between coughs. "They're rounding up every Purple they can find and bringing them to the Feet of the River."

Chapter Five

"Why would they be hunting Purples?" I asked as we sipped caf together. I'd lit a fire and boiled the water with Savette while Hubric and Rakturan dragged the dead to the side and constructed pyres. With dragons on hand, lighting a hot enough fire was never a problem, although the dragons were gone right now, dealing with their own needs. Raolcan wouldn't get more specific than that.

We're eating. That's all you need to know.

"I don't know," Talsan said. "But I know that's why they took me and why they took Findar. They thought he was a Purple because he was fighting in the cotes and he passed out in front of a purple dragon's cote. They took another Purple, too, but the groups holding us split up and the other group had him."

"Was he sick, too?" I asked gently, pouring a little more caf in his mug. He smiled gently at me before suppressing a cough.

"Dying, you mean? Don't look shocked. I know what's happening here. I had a tight bond with Darshh. It's fitting that I won't outlive him by very long. No, he wasn't dying. His dragon had escaped somehow. I don't know how they were separated. I asked, but I was cuffed for speaking and they dragged him away. The next time I saw him he was being stuffed into a bag just like me. Poor kid. Wasn't very old to be a full Dragon Rider. Spine of steel, though. Proper Purple."

Hubric's expression was grave. He reached for Talsan's hand gripping it in one fist and saluting with the other – hand to heart. "As are you, son. Thank you for your faithfulness."

Talsan gripped Hubric's hand and then waved him away. "I'm more dragon than man these days. Doesn't feel right to be so alone in my head. What do we do now?"

"We fly to Backwater Manor. There are people there who will help both of you heal."

"Not to the Feet of the River?" Talsan looked worried. "That other Purple needs our help."

Hubric took a final sip of caf and handed me his mug. "My messages are too important. I can't stop for a rescue mission. Maybe the people of Backwater can help."

"I don't think I know that place," Findar said. His words were still slurred and I was starting to wonder if some of his teeth were broken. He wasn't much older than I was.

"It's not far," Hubric said. "They'll have soft beds and medicine for both of you."

Talsan looked down the road with a worried expression. Was he thinking of walking on his own to get to these Feet of the River?

"Savette, you ride with Rak," Hubric said. "Amel can take Talsan and I'll take Findar. It's a short hop from here to Backwater Manor."

His tone said it was settled. I dumped the kettle over the fire, and gathered up the mugs, wrapping them in the basket that kept them safe. The kettle would be cool enough to wrap in wool and leather in a minute and then we could leave.

"Thank you for saving us," Findar said to Hubric.

"Think nothing of it." Hubric's tone was rough but I could tell he was touched by the gratitude.

"Did you catch the name of the other Purple they captured?" I asked Talsan. It wasn't like I'd know who it was. I didn't know any other Purples except Leng and Hubric, but I felt like he should be remembered.

"I did not," Talsan said. He ran a hand through dusty hair. He looked so tired that I just wanted to let him sleep for a while. If Hubric was right, then there would be a place for him to rest when we arrived at Backwater Manor. He coughed, spitting black phlegm up from his disintegrating lungs. How long did he have left?

When his fit subsided he said, "He mentioned his dragon by name, though. Ahlskibi."

I felt like someone had hit me in the belly.

Chapter Six

"I told you he was in danger!" Why did my chest feel so tight? "They captured him just like they said they did, Hubric!"

Hubric was in front of me so quickly, taking the hot kettle and basket from my hands that I hardly blinked before they were gone. He set them on the ground and grabbed me by the upper arms, looking into my eyes with a gaze full of compassion and sincerity.

"Think for a moment, Amel. Stop and think. What does this tell you?"

"That he really was captured by the Dusk Covenant!"

"When did they take you?" he asked Talsan.

"Three days ago. They fled with us on horseback that night."

"Were there Dragon Riders with them?"

He shook his head. "Magikas. Many Magikas, but no Dragon Riders."

Hubric's eyes were on mine again, tenderness filling them. "There is no way that they knew he'd been captured when they wrote you that demand letter. It was a ruse. A fake. If you had returned to the city, if - skies forbid - you had brought them what they wanted, it would have done nothing to keep him safe. They lied to you."

"But they have him now."

"They don't have Ahlskibi."

"Hubric." My voice sounded so small. "Now that we know where he is. Now that we know. We can't fly in the other direction."

"We can and must, my friend. Our oaths to the Dominar demand it."

A sob caught in my throat.

"Come. We'll find help at Backwater Manor. There may even be those who can go after your friend."

I nodded, my vision swimming with tears.

"If I could do both I would. Last time was different. Last time I was saving you from making a mistake. This time, I feel as torn as you do. I feel as much pull as you do to fly after him, but what can we do, Amel? We must fulfill our vows. We are duty bound."

I bit my lip. The tears were running fast down my face. Without Hubric's hands around my arms, I'd be sagging against my crutch. I felt like someone had thrown my heart on the ground and stomped all over it. I just didn't have the heart to fly in the other direction.

"Look at me," Hubric said. I looked at him. His smile was gentle and brave. "I'm known everywhere for being a trickster and a bit of a magician when it comes to getting what I want. There will be a way to save Leng. I will find it without risking our messages. Do you understand?"

I nodded.

"Do you trust me?"

Did I? I was still mad about before.

He was looking out for you then. He looks out for you now. As do I. We will find a way to honor our obligations and rescue Leng, too. Likely, Ahskibi is already working to free him.

But where was Ahlskibi when he was captured? It didn't make sense that they could be separated.

We don't know. All we know is that we are in this together. Give Hubric the gift of your trust. He has been nothing but kind to you.

"I trust you," I said, hoping Hubric understood how hard this was for me.

"Then let's fly."

Chapter Seven

"Was Leng hurt when you saw him?" I asked Talsan. We'd flown in silence except for his coughing, but the question wouldn't go away. It seared through my mind like a hot poker.

"Yes. I'm not sure how badly." Talsan said between coughs. "He was hunched over. Favoring his right side."

The good thing about Purple Dragon Riders was that they told the truth.

You're eating a hole inside yourself with worry and anger. You're not helping anyone with that.

But what other alternative was there? I couldn't shut off anger like you turned a spigot. I couldn't stop worrying any more than you could stop the rain.

Focus on what you can do.

What could I do sitting on the back of a dragon? Maybe, I could help Talsan.

"What are you thinking about, Talsan?"

He coughed, laughed and then coughed again, his breath coming in wheezy spasms. "I was wondering how soon my death approaches, Sworn."

How did you comfort someone who was dying and couldn't be saved?

"I just keep feeling like there is something more I need to do before I go. Maybe it's saving this Purple rider. Leng, did you say his name was?"

"Yes."

"And you are friends?"

I nodded.

He slumped to one side coughing.

"Do you need help, Talsan?"

When his coughing subsided, he spoke again. "No. I'll be fine. No one can help me now, though I hope there will be a hand to help lead me over the chasm to the next world."

I shivered.

"Don't fear death, Sworn. It comes for us all."

"You're not afraid?"

"I didn't say that." He coughed.

Was that smoke I smelled? Wood smoke? The smell was getting more powerful by the moment. I scanned the ground, but it was hard to see anything beneath the blanket of thick trees. They stood high and broad so that their canopy blocked a clear view of the ground beneath it. Up ahead was a river winding through the trees.

There! There's a dark patch along the river.

So there was. Hubric angled Kyrowat toward the dark patch and we all followed, but there was fear in my bones as we descended. Hubric had spoken of Backwater Manor – a place of allies and warm dinners. Was that where the smoke was rising?

What Hubric didn't say because others were listening is that it is also an outpost of the Lightbringers. I just caught that in Kyrowat's thoughts. A safe-house of theirs like the farm where you met the Dominar and received his message. It's manned all year round.

Someone had lost their home down there.

Worse. It's not just smoke I smell. There are dead people below.

As we descended lower, we finally broke the canopy of the high trees, flying beneath their branches along the winding river. The dark patch drew closer. Savette was signaling anxiously from Enkenay's back. Something down there disturbed her. Her signals weren't clear. Was she simply alerting us?

Perhaps it was Dusk Covenant on their way to the Feet of the River.

Was that near here?

Maybe you should have paid more attention to your lessons. If someone launched a boat from here, the river would take them as far as the Feet of the River by morning.

That was fast. Nearly as fast as a dragon could fly.

It's a mighty river – the Great Drake River.

It figured that it would be named for a male dragon. I'd never seen anything faster than Raolcan – except the Ifrit.

Now that we were closer, I saw the charred foundations of several small buildings and one long building up the hill from the water. The smaller ones looked to be the size of cabins – perhaps a dozen of them. The larger one was four times the size. Perhaps a storehouse or Great Hall of sorts. The smell of smoke was thick, but there was very little smoke left. Tiny tufts of white swirled up from the wreckage.

The fire is out now. All that remains is whatever didn't burn.

A boathouse stood untouched with a pair of long riverboats tied to the dock. Whatever lit this place ablaze must have burned fast and quick. It hadn't destroyed every building.

My hand went to my mouth involuntarily when I saw the first heap of burnt clothing on the ground between the buildings. My other hand joined it when I saw the second. There were at least a dozen people strewn in the ashes and three dead horses.

Skies send mercy. Rain of mercy. Sun send warmth to bring us back from the edge of death.

Behind me, Talsan cursed between his coughs. There would be no help for him or Findar here.

Chapter Eight

"We'll gather the dead and bury them properly," Hubric said as we landed.

"No, we can't stay," Savette said. Her head whipped wildly from one side to the other like she was looking for something.

"They're my friends," Hubric said, wearily. "Lightbringers. That's Tessa Goodhearth there on the ground." He pointed to one of the figures. "Why would we not stay to properly care for her body?"

"There's something in the air ... something not right..." her voice faded out.

Hubric rubbed his forehead, looking, for the first time since I met him, his full age. "Of course, there is. It's the smell of my friend's burning flesh."

I swallowed. What a horrifying thought.

"They deserve to be decently and respectfully laid to rest. Can you give me a solid reason not to do that? Do you feel some sort of enemy around? We saw no one from the air. Whoever did this is gone."

Savette shook her head. "It's just a feeling. A terrible, terrible feeling."

"Do you feel the Ifrit here?" Hubric was already climbing off Kyrowat. He did not expect her to say yes.

"I feel evil just like his ... but I don't feel him. It's like an echo of him. Usually, you can feel him in the earth since he is made of earth."

"But not right now?"

"No..." she seemed uncertain.

"Then let's get to work." Hubric strode over to his fallen friend and I got down from Raolcan, helping Talsan to do the same.

"Who is the girl with the bandaged eyes? The one who can feel evil?" he asked.

"Savette Leedris." What point was there in lying? He wouldn't live out the week.

"A Castelan?"

"High Castelan," I corrected, but I was just distracting myself. I'd never dealt with so many dead bodies as there were today. I wasn't sure I could handle more.

Talsan bent double in a fit of coughs, spewing black all over the ground. He spat, wiped his mouth and then turned back to me. Was there anything I could do to ease his pain? No one should die like this.

"It's worth it," he said when he caught my eye. "Darshh was the best of dragons and my very best friend. I'm dying now because we were so close that our souls intermingled. There isn't one without the other anymore, but it was worth it."

That was something I understood. I felt the same way about Raolcan.

You know you are my life.

"Come on," he said, gesturing for me to follow. "We'll gather up the poor souls who ran toward the docks."

I followed him, grateful that he walked slowly enough that I could keep pace with him.

"I'm glad to see you're a Purple. All the best of us are Purples," he said.

I glanced behind my shoulder. Raolcan leaned gently over a body Hubric had laid out. I knew he was about to honor the dead with his flame. Hubric and Findar had already moved to another fallen victim but Savette clung to Enkenay, shaking from head to foot while Rakturan tried to console her. Was her magic affecting her again? I hadn't seen her so affected since the night at the healing arches. It set my teeth on edge.

"I've met more than my share of Purples, or so Hubric says."

"Oh, we're rare alright. Don't even know each other half the time, if we didn't go to school together. It's a lonely life and even our council are taciturn and prefer to be alone. It's a good life, though. None of the competitive brutality of the reds or the sycophantic words of the golds. I never could see the attraction to that. Healing is good, but it was clear pretty soon why Whites are our enemies. You can't get a straight answer out of one of them. Blacks are stuck. Stuck in one place forever like a planted tree. Who chooses that? If I wanted to be stuck I would have stayed on my parents' farm."

"You left out the Greens," I teased. It was too bad Talsan was leaving this world. It was better for having him in it.

"Thick headed fools who rush to conclusions without thinking. You'll learn that if you run into them often."

I already did know it, but I still missed Lenora, Olla, and Orra. I honestly hoped to see them again. I wouldn't even mind seeing Ephretti if she rode in here with a plan to save Leng.

We leaned down to gather up an elderly man whose prone form was half-charred. A tear slid down my face. He'd had friends and maybe family. Who had done this to him? He had no weapon marks or arrows on him.

"Never seen a man die like this," Talsan said, sadly. He took the man's long belt knife and put it in his own belt before helping me lift him.

I tried to follow his lead and grip the poor soul under the shoulder, but he was heavier than I thought, and I lost my grip, dropping him and even losing my balance so I fell to the ground. Embarrassed, I struggled to stand again.

"I'm so so-"

"Down!" Talsan seemed panicked.

I looked up to see a figure rising up from the river. Water poured off his enormous body, sliding away to reveal a massive, towering form of smoke and fire. A steam-like hiss erupted from his open, cavernous mouth.

Behind me, I heard Savette scream at the same moment that the Ifrit lunged toward me.

Roll to the side!

I obeyed without questioning Raolcan, rolling to the side and then planting my crutch and heaving myself back on my feet. I wasn't fast enough. The Ifrit lunged towards me again. He was about to knock me off my feet. To kill me, as he'd likely killed the old man I'd been trying to respect. I couldn't run fast enough, couldn't dodge, couldn't even fight such a massive creature. I clenched my jaw and squinted my eyes. At the last possible second, Talsan leapt between us with an ululating cry. The Ifrit scooped him up and threw him, dashing him against the ground. I fled toward Raolcan. He darted past me, clearly on the warpath.

Faster than even my dragon, a bolt of light sprang from the hands of Rak-turan and Savette. It sped past Raolcan and towards the Ifrit. Together, Rak-turan and Savette screamed, lifting off the ground like they were being drawn up by ropes, their hands clasped together.

The bolt struck the Ifrit and he went white and then the white light flared out from him in a wave toward us, knocking first Raolcan and then me off our feet and throwing us backward to the ground. My head rang and my vision doubled, purple images filling what little clear vision I had.

By the time my vision cleared, there was no more Ifrit in sight.

Chapter Nine

A re you hurt?

My ears were ringing. Purple images danced across my vision. But no, I wasn't hurt. I pulled myself up on my crutch. My leg and hands were shaking. He'd been waiting for us. Lurking under the river like a horror of the deep. Was Raolcan hurt?

No.

I limped over to Talsan. His body was twisted in a way that bodies weren't meant to be twisted, like a wrung-out rag. Behind me, I heard Hubric's voice raised. His pitch was too high, like his own ears were ringing, or perhaps emotion was simply overpowering him.

"I thought you said you couldn't sense it here?"

I stumbled to my knees beside Talsan. Black fluid leaked from the corner of his mouth.

Savette's voice countered Hubric's. "It must have been the river. It cloaks the earth beneath it. I didn't feel him because he was hiding under the water."

Talsan's breath was gone. I closed his eyes. That he was dying already didn't change the deep sadness blossoming in my heart. He'd been one of us. A Purple. And he'd been desperate to save Leng, just like me.

"You should have mentioned that you couldn't feel him under water!" Hubric sounded as desperate as I felt.

"Leave her alone." Rakturan's words were almost a hiss. "Didn't you see her blow the Ifrit away? You aren't her sworn master like you are Amel's. Finding Savette doesn't make her your keeper."

"I'm so sorry, Talsan," I said. I searched his message pockets. I didn't expect there to be one. Wouldn't he have mentioned it if there was? All there was in his message pockets was a battered deck of cards and a small, palm-sized leather-bound book, tied with leather lashings. I unbound it and began to read.

Ibrenicus Prophecies
Copy penned by Talsan Woodcarver

He'd had his own book of prophecy, just like Hubric. Did that mean he was a Lightbringer? I tucked the book in my own empty message pocket and the deck of cards in the other and took the long knife he'd removed from the old man and put it in my belt. I didn't want to forget Talsan. He'd saved my life. He'd given his for it, instead. And these things had mattered to him. I'd use them and remember him.

The argument behind me was getting louder. I stood up. I didn't think I could drag Talsan to a pyre on my own.

Let me take care of him and the old man. I think the other humans need your help.

I swallowed back a lump in my throat, not even bothering to blink away my hot tears. Talsan shouldn't have had to die like that.

He was right, though. He did have one more thing to do before he died. His death was noble. We will remember him among dragons, even as we remember Darshh, his companion.

Those last words sounded formal.

They are dragon funeral rites.

I glanced at Raolcan. His eyes looked glassy, too.

"We aren't bound to you, Hubric. We don't have to stay with you and we don't care about your Lightbringers!" Rakturan's voice was louder.

I spun and headed towards them, trusting Raolcan to do his work for Talsan. Hubric stood with his arms crossed and Kyrowat's head right behind him, like he was backing Hubric up. Rakturan and Savette stood opposite to him, their own arms crossed, their bright eyes penetrating the scarves wrapped around them.

Off to one side, Findar coughed miserably, looking from one group to the next. If we'd hoped to keep our identities quiet, we hadn't succeeded.

"And where would you like to go?" Hubric's voice was icy, his eyebrows raised as he spoke.

"The Feet of the River," Savette said. "There is something there – don't ask me what – something that we need."

"Leng is there," I said. "Or will be soon."

"What could you possibly need at the Feet of the River?" Hubric asked, frustrated.

"Read your prophecies," Savette shot back. "You know exactly what I'm talking about:

The light brightens and grows
Crown to toes
But fragile lies
Our key to the skies
And only the arrow
Shot from the bow
Can steel us for
Coming war. "

"It's an obscure passage," Hubric said angrily. His hoary eyebrows knit together as he peered at her, but I noticed Kyrowat back up a bit and begin to look toward Raolcan. He was no longer as certain as his master. "And it doesn't mention the Feet of the River."

"Where there are feet there are toes," Savette said triumphantly.

"Ridiculous!"

"Whether it means that or not," Rakturan said, quietly, "tomorrow we will fly east with Enkenay and follow the Great Drake River to its Feet. We'll find out for ourselves."

"Come with us!" Savette pleaded.

"I cannot." Hubric hung his head, clearly torn. "My messages are too important."

"Important enough to leave Savette with no one but me to protect her?" Rakturan asked.

"They could stop a war. They could keep our Dominion whole," Hubric said, his words as heavy as stones. Each one laid down carefully. "I dare not break my vow."

I dared. I realized in that moment that I dared to defy Hubric and break my vows to go after Leng. Perhaps, in the morning, I would fly east with Savette and Enkenay.

Hubric's head whipped toward me. "Did you like watching Talsan die slowly? Did you like watching him cough up his life?"

"Of course not!" I was horrified he would suggest such a thing.

"Vow magic is real, Amel. Leave with them tomorrow, and that will be you. You might live long enough to save the boy, but not much beyond that. And Raolcan would die with you."

Could that really be true?

He's right about the Dragon Rider vow magic. You know it keeps us within our alcoves when we are in training. You know it can bind a rider to their dragon so that their lives are intertwined. Trust me, he is likely correct when he says we will die that way.

I thought Hubric was on my side.

Hubric is on the side of the Lightbringers and the Dominion. You are his vassal. In his mind, it is your job to plant yourself firmly on his side.

"The dragons are exhausted. Our enemy is vanquished. Let's finish honoring the dead, clean up, and set up camp. There is nowhere else nearby to go. We might as well camp here." Hubric's tone was so sorrowful that I almost thought he might be sad to have to fight with Savette and threaten me.

If you don't know how torn up he is, you still have some growing up to do.

Chapter Ten

By the time we'd honored the dead, built camp and cooked dinner, none of us were speaking anymore. We all knew who wanted what. Savette, Rakturan and I all wanted to go to the Feet of the River and Hubric wanted to deliver his message to the Dominar. I couldn't leave Hubric. He didn't want to leave the Chosen One.

At one point - I didn't even hear what prompted it - Rakturan said, "What are you going to do to stop us?"

After that, there was nothing but bitter silence and cold anger between us all. Hubric searched the rubble and found a bottle of something, but he didn't offer to share it. He sat and drank in front of the fire as the shadows grew into the dark of night.

Rakturan and Savette set up one of our tents and hid themselves within. I heard the susurration of whispers when I passed it, as if they were in deep discussion. Would they decide to go on without us like they were planning? If they did, they would be on their own and impossible to hide from prying eyes. They'd also have no one else to help if it turned out the Feet of the River were already crawling with Dusk Covenant. If I couldn't go with them, then they should at least wait for us.

I helped Findar get comfortable, sharing our blankets with him. I'd be a bit colder tonight without the extra blanket, but at least I had Raolcan. I was worried about Findar. His injuries seemed severe and he winced often with pain.

"Do you think you can sleep like this?" I asked, leaving him close to the fire.

"I'll be fine," he said, his words tight and his eyes on Hubric. Even someone outside our party could feel the tension between us.

With a sigh, I left him, finished tidying the campsite, and curled up in my other blanket against Raolcan. With the Ifrit gone, we didn't need to watch the camp so carefully. We knew who had destroyed this place and he was gone now.

Enkenay says he will keep watch for the first stretch. Raolcan was as tired as I was – more, perhaps. He and Kyrowat had seen little sleep in the past week.

I'm so tired I will sleep for a week if you don't wake me. Tell me if there's any trouble. We should be safe here.

My own feelings and thoughts were tangled knots. I didn't want to think about the decisions that would be faced tomorrow morning. Would I have to choose Hubric over Savette and Leng? I refused to dwell on it, forcing the thoughts from my mind. There would be enough heartache tomorrow morning.

Just sleep...

I thought I heard Raolcan's thoughts fade seconds before sleep found me, too.

Everything was silent when I woke, stretching in the dim light of early morning. My blanket had fallen off and the fire was out. Shivering, I nuzzled against Raolcan, feeling his snore vibrate through his entire body. At least he was warm. I tried to get comfortable again, but I couldn't. There was something about the quiet that troubled me. Had there been crickets last night that were gone now? Was that it? Or some other sound that was missing now? I stood up, letting the blanket fall to the ground. Across from the dead fire, Kyrowat snored, his breathing matching Raolcan's. Good thing Enkenay was keeping watch.

Hubric was sprawled by the fire, without a blanket, arms and legs spread outward. Who slept like that? It was as if he had nothing troubling him at all, while I was plagued with worry. I swallowed down irritation and walked around Raolcan's sleeping form to check on Savette and Rakturan.

Their tent was gone. So was Enkenay. I glanced down the river in one direction and then the other, my heart pounding. It must be a mistake. Maybe they went for a walk. Maybe they needed some time alone for a few minutes. Maybe they decided to fish.

The boats at the dock were gone, too. That must be it. They'd gone fishing. I hobbled down to the dock, looking up and down the Great Drake River for as far as I could see. There was no sign of a boat. No sign of a dragon. Nothing but water, waving reeds, and the occasional diving bird.

Heart thudding, I raced back to the campsite. In my sudden clarity, I saw that Findar was also gone. He'd taken my extra blanket with him. Behind me, the sun rose in the sky, shining its golden beams across the ground, painting it gold and black in the tiger stripes of dawn. A long black shadow stretched out from Hubric's prone form, but in the golden light, I saw something I hadn't noticed earlier.

Blood.

I hurried toward him, dropping to the ground.

"Hubric! Hubric, are you okay?"

At his groan, I almost sobbed with relief. His hand went to his head and I pushed it away, studying the gash on the back of his skull. It was shallow, I thought, already crusting over.

"What happened?" he asked.

"They're gone," I said, and I could hear the panic in my voice.

"Savette, Rakturan, Enkenay, and Findar. All gone. The boats and the tent and my blanket and everything they had."

"Slow down." He stood, shakily, hand still clutching his head, while the other hand patted his Dragon Rider leathers urgently.

"Gone where?"

"I don't know! I woke up and they weren't here! What are you looking for?"

"My messages," he said, a look of absolute horror on his face. "They're all gone, too."

Chapter Eleven

"Someone must have hit you over the head," I said, reaching for the healing kit in his baggage nearby. With the wound already healing, it was easy enough to bandage it. "Hold still."

"Not Savette. She wouldn't have hit me."

No, she wouldn't have. "I don't think Rakturan would, either. They probably slipped away so that they wouldn't have to say goodbye and fight with us about going."

"Findar." Hubric cursed. "What did we really know about him?"

"We knew he was hurt. And we found him in a sack, carried by our enemies."

Hubric batted my hands away as I finished the knot. "Enough with that. We haven't the time. What if Findar hit Savette and Rakturan over the head and hauled them off, too?"

"Enkenay would never have flown them."

The dragons snored on. Why didn't they wake? Hubric followed my gaze and snorted.

"My fault," he said. "Dragons can enter a deep sleep to replenish what was lost in prior days. It's why they can fly for days on end without a proper sleep. I told these two they could enter it and replenish. I thought that with the Ifrit defeated and Savette and Rakrturan on our side..."

I nodded. It made perfect sense.

"Both boats are missing," I said.

"So, he could have loaded them into the boats..."

"I think you're upset, Hubric."

His eagle-eyed gaze locked onto mine. He shook his head and began to stuff loose items into his bags, scanning the burnt-out husks of the buildings.

I tried again. "If Findar had kidnapped Savette and Rakturan, then Enkenay would still be here. I think that they left first on Enkenay. Probably to go to the Feet of the River and probably as soon as we were asleep. I think that after that, Findar saw his chance, stole your messages and hit you over the head to keep you from chasing after him. It makes sense that he'd take a boat. It's fast. Raolcan said it would take you to the Feet of the River in a single day."

"And the other boat?"

"Maybe he didn't want us following."

We looked toward the river and then Hubric said, "Come on."

I followed him to the dock, looking down the river with him, a second time. This time, I saw the second boat stuck in the reeds, so far down the river that it was almost out of sight.

"Your theory holds up," Hubric said.

"Findar must think that your messages would be valuable to the Dusk Covenant."

"Of course, they are!"

"Can you deliver them without the physical copies?"

He sighed. "We don't read the messages. I don't know what they say."

"That seems like a bad policy in this situation."

"It's been our policy for the last hundred years."

"Age doesn't confer brilliance."

His laugh was so bitter that I flinched.

"Oh, don't flinch like that, girl." He sighed and raked a hand through his hair. The lines on his face looked deeper. "You didn't leave me, Amel. You didn't sneak off into the night even though I know you wanted to."

"No, I didn't." I felt overwhelmed with an emotion I couldn't explain. It brought tears to my eyes. Hubric's own eyes were glassy.

"You stayed with me. You kept your vow."

I nodded, unable to speak at the emotion. I didn't know what I was feeling – because it was just a flood of feelings. Frustration and relief. Loyalty and anger. Affection and bitterness. It was a toxic, roiling mix of it all because

I wasn't sure if I should be proud or ashamed, if I should feel cherished or captive. I felt like a big hot mess.

"That means something to me, girl. I know you didn't just stay to save your own skin. You chose to stay. Now we are in the pot together, about to get cooked. But we're not alone. We're together and I'm just grateful to have you."

I couldn't hold back tears. Especially when he hugged me. He was the prickliest person I'd ever met. He was like a second father. He drove me crazy. I thought maybe he understood me.

"We'd better wake the dragons," he said when he was done hugging me. "It will take them a few minutes to wake up fully. Can you re-saddle them while I take a gander around?"

"Sure," I said.

Raolcan was incredibly difficult to awaken. In the end, I pushed one of his eyelids open with two hands while shouting "Wake up!" in his face.

It took him about thirty seconds to glean the situation from my brain as I saddled him and loaded the gear we had left.

We're in big trouble.

Understatement.

Something is different between you and Hubric.

Hubric and I were friends. I moved to saddle Kyrowat. He let me, but the look in his eyes was suspicious and he burped once into the trees, lighting a small one ablaze, as if to remind me that I was a human and he was a dragon.

You were always friends.

A different kind of friends. Like me and Raolcan.

That's called 'family.'

Like Savette.

That's family, too.

We needed to find her and to find Leng and to make them safe, but there were fewer of us now. What could two Purple dragons and two Purple Dragon Riders do?

Just about anything.

"There was nothing left in any of the buildings. Nothing of value and nothing that says this was a safehouse of the Lightbringers." Hubric came up from behind me. "We have no reason to stay. Best to mount up and leave. I have a plan."

"A plan?" That was more than I had.

"We'll go up as high as we can and look for allies. We need those messages back and we need to protect the Chosen One. We can't do this alone. Follow my lead and mind the signals."

I nodded, although we both knew that since we were Purples, it was the dragons who would be doing the flying – and most of the communicating.

Aren't you glad we're here? You'd be lost without us.

Chapter Twelve

W e spiraled upward slowly, following Kyrowat.

The trick is to get as high as we can. It's a clear day. No cloud cover. If we get high enough, we might see other dragons.

How far would they be when we found them?

They could be very far. Days away, even.

Would we see the Feet of the River?

Sort of. Everything will look very small to you. We'll mostly be scanning for movement, and by "we" I mean Kyrowat and me, of course.

Of course. Sometimes I wondered why dragons ever agreed to let humans ride them. We seemed to get all the advantages.

A long time ago, long before the Dominion, dragons were free and roamed the land without human interference. There were few humans then and those that there were lived mostly to the north of here. In those days, volcanoes were frequent things and tremors shook the lands. And in those days, the Ancients of Baoqueea – the nation that existed before Baojang – brought up Ifrits to exercise dominion over their enemies. Nations lay in ruins and people were shredded like stalks of wheat in the harvest.

We dragons suffered, too. We were unorganized and scattered. We were hunted down and destroyed by Ifrits. All but Haz'drazen, Queen of Dragons and her brood. She sought a new land for us to increase and find safety in the south where the red of volcanoes bloom in the skies.

It was there that she found a man – Haz, the first of the Dominars. Haz and his small nation made a truce with Haz'drazen- it's how she received her name because she was just 'Drazen' before but when she adopted him she became 'Haz'drazen' or 'Dragon of Haz' - and together they routed the Ifrits and drove back Baoqueea. It was on that day that dragons and the Dominion swore one to another that we would forever be bound to the prosperity of the other. You give of your young and healthy and we of ours to form the dragons and Dragon Riders that defend the Dominion - and with it the safety of our shared lands.

As much as it pains me to admit it, there are some things that humans do better than dragons.

Such as?

I said I'd admit it, not that I'd elaborate.

I couldn't help but laugh at that.

There. Hubric signals to us.

His signal said we'd be heading north by northeast two hours. I couldn't see a thing except for the ground below laid out like a tiny carpet. I could barely make out the track of the winding river or see where it flowed into the gray sea beyond. The air felt too thin. It made it hard to concentrate.

Heading lower. Hold on.

We dove, following Kyrowat's swooping trajectory and I was grateful when the air began to thicken again. What had Kyrowat seen?

I saw them, too. A group of about twenty Reds. They fly toward the coast – east - and south. Perhaps they have heard of the fall of Casaban and fly to her aid.

Perhaps. It didn't seem like enough to take back a city, but what did I know of war?

We'll know soon enough. We will intercept them in about two hours. Rest and be patient.

Patience had never been my strongest point, but I had something to occupy me. As we flew, I took out the small book of Ibrenicus Prophecies I'd found in Talsan's pocket and began to read.

These are the prophecies collected by Ibrenicus of Haz, son of dragons.

For the time comes soon in which these prophecies will be needed so that the world is not broken by a war between the earth and the sky. For long years we have fought, but peace is brokered, and we lay down arms. We shall grow sleepy in comfort and one day our children will have forgotten the grim battles fought for the peace they think they hold in their palms.

We know it is never so. No man owns peace. No man may hold it tightly and forbid its theft. We may only respond when war is brought to our gates and pray we respond rightly, for truth is often mocked and lies win hearts faster than flames consume a forest. Who can stand when men give way on every side to the force of their desires twisted against them?

It is for the wise that I collect these words and store them up in this book. That when the Chosen One arrives you will recognize what you see. When your salvation is near, you may lay hold of it. Do not wait. Do not doubt. Seize life while you still have breath and peace before it has dissolved like snow.

Eerie words. Ibrenicus was quite the optimist.

And yet, Raolcan reminded me, *you have seen what the Dusk Covenant can do. You have seen the Ifrits they have raised up. Does a battle between the sky and the ground really seem so strange?*

Some of my worst enemies were in the sky, too. Wasn't it obvious that Starie and Mistress Elfar were bent on their own purposes?

Haz'drazen will never permit Ifrits. Perhaps it doesn't mean every dragon and every creature of the land. Perhaps it means the heads of them will be at war.

I wasn't very good at this speculation.

I have a bad feeling that you will need to learn it. We are the only ones who can keep Savette safe, and I grow certain she is the one of that prophecy.

Him, too! Was he planning on joining the Lightbringers?

You joined. That means I did, too. Though Hubric needs to make your joining formal. I think he planned to do that at Backwater Manor with others of the Order, but that didn't happen. He was as troubled to delay your formal entry as he was by Findar's betrayal.

It mattered a lot to him.

I have a bad feeling that this coming war will be a close one. Every soul on one side or the other counts. Every choice will mean death for someone down the line. We must be so careful to be wise in what we do.

I bit my lip. I was anything but wise. I'd wrestled with each decision along the way; often not certain I was making the right one. Why was so much on my shoulders? Weren't there better people for this job? Hopefully, there really would be wisdom in this little book I carried. If there wasn't, the consequences could be deadly.

Chapter Thirteen

We met the Reds as they landed beside a tributary of the Great Drake River. They landed in formation and crisply dismounted like it was a military drill – which I supposed it was. I noticed that though they wore leathers and scarves like regular Dragon Riders, they also had badges and insignia on their leathers and their dragons' saddles prickled with weapons. Polearms, swords, shields, bows, and arrows – they were like flying armories. The scales of the Reds looked thicker, tougher, more gnarled that that of our Purples.

Are you saying they look more masculine?

Actually, they looked more like someone had left them in the ocean and they'd developed a barnacle crust. Raolcan's mental laughter made me smile. So, he didn't like thinking some other dragon was more masculine, did he?

There's nothing tender about me, Amel. Not even my ego.

Liar.

Fine. I'll admit it. I wish I had a thicker crust.

If he wasn't careful, I'd be the one laughing and now was a bad time for that. Kyrowat landed in front of the Reds seconds before we did. The closest Red snapped at him and Kyrowat reared up, flaming the grass beneath the Red's feet. A blaze of grass fire rushed through the group of Reds accompanied by loud curses and shouts.

"Hubric Duneshifter," the rider of the Red dragon said as he strode forward. "I see your Purple is as touchy as ever. Well met, friend."

"And you, Cynos Vineplanter. Is that still Mionshc? He looks more crusted than ever."

"Don't say that too loud, or your friend won't be the only one lighting grass fires!" Cynos laughed heartily.

He was heavyset for a Dragon Rider – almost as thick as a warrior was – with thick black hair and stubble across his brown chin. Knives and short swords were strapped all over the outside of his leathers. Was it possible that I could wear those even though I was Purple? They made him look so intimidating.

Only if you learn to use them. Otherwise, someone will grab one from your belt and stab you with it.

I didn't want that.

"Do you fly to Casaban?" Hubric asked, stamping out the fires as he dismounted Kyrowat. Was that a smirk on Kyrowat's face?

Cynos nodded. "We were headed to the Capitol when we received word of the fall of Casaban and we set out that very hour. I wish I had more dragons, but we were off on guard duty watching the back of a traveling High Castelan and he required no more protection than this."

"I have also heard of Casaban. The situation is dire – but what will you do with only twenty dragons?"

Cynos frowned. "Hold them back, I suppose. Keep them from taking more territory until we are joined by others. Only a week ago we received news of the fall of Vanika – a sky city! – and now this. These are dire times, Hubric. Do you carry messages to the north?"

"I did."

"Did?"

Hubric looked uncomfortable, his eyes wandering over the Reds as they cared for their dragons and took care of necessities. I took the moment to dismount and secure my crutch.

"We rescued two men captured by our enemies in the fall of Casaban," Hubric said eventually. I could tell he was ashamed to admit it. "In the night, one of them stole my messages and fled."

"And how did he outrun Dragon Riders? Are Purples as slow as people say?" Was he teasing, or mocking? It was hard to say.

"He had a boat and the river is fast."

Cynos nodded.

"So, you go with your apprentice to recover the messages."

Hubric nodded. "But I have a small problem."

Cynos smiled cynically. "Would a Purple talk to people if they didn't need help? You would have let us pass without ever knowing you were here if you had the choice."

"Don't take it personally."

"Trust me, I don't. The rest of us are very happy without your company."

This time it was Hubric who frowned. "The Dusk Covenant gathers at the Feet of the River. We heard news that they stole Purple Dragon Riders at the fall of Casaban and brought them there. That's where our messages are heading. We don't have the strength to recover them on our own."

"The Dusk Covenant? They're the stuff of stories. No more real than unicorns or machines that replace horses." Cynos shook his head, reaching into his dragon's saddlebag to pull out a water skin.

"Who do you think was responsible for the fall of Vanika?"

"Baojang."

"Alone? We were there. We saw what happened. Baojang may have led the charge against the Dominar – long may he reign – but it was the Dusk Covenant that felled the city."

Cynos swallowed, worry etching lines in his forehead. "You were there, you say?"

"Yes," Hubric said. "I bore messages from the Dominar to Dominion City. Now, I am on my way back – but I can't bear messages that I don't have. Please. Please, Cynos. Reds are our allies. Help us to recover the messages and our captive brothers. A few days will not make a difference to Casaban."

"It could. You know what a raided city is like. You know how badly we need to take her back and bring safety to her people again."

Hubric ran his hand over his face. "You know how important our messages are. They mean the difference between men moving or stationary, supplies sent or people starving, war or peace. Please, Cynos. Please help me recover them."

Cynos stood a long time looking at the burnt grass at his feet while behind him the other Reds bustled around making the most of their temporary stop. Eventually, he looked up at me.

"You took a cripple as an apprentice?"

"Yes," Hubric said. I liked that he felt no need to explain himself.

Cynos gave me a long look. I clenched my jaw and looked back with a steady, level gaze. He didn't know me. He didn't know that my leg made no real difference at all.

"You see things others don't, Hubric Duneshifter. If you say these messages come first over Casaban – well, maybe you see something I don't."

His mouth twisted like he was going to say no to us anyway. He couldn't. If we didn't have his help, who else would help us? They would kill Leng. Kill Savette and Rakturan when they arrived. Destroy the messages or use them against the Dominar. I didn't know everything that they'd do, but I knew the Dusk Covenant well enough to know that they'd use anything they could to destroy us all.

"This is a matter of war or peace, of life or death for us all, Cynos Vineplanter," I said, keeping my expression hard as a rock. He must see how desperate this was! He must.

He stared at me with wide eyes, like he hadn't expected me to speak, but after a moment he nodded.

"We fly with you," he said and then turned to Hubric. "Three days. No more."

Chapter Fourteen

"There they are," Hubric said. "The Feet of the River."

What had I expected from that name? Maybe I'd linked it to "foot of the river" in my mind, like the foot of a mountain. Maybe I had thought it would just be where the water poured into the sea.

That would be the mouth of the river.

And of course, this was that, too.

We were perched low on the rise of a hill about a mile away, our dragons hiding on the other side of the huge outcropping. Hubric and Cynos had insisted that we climb to the top – with his lieutenants – and watch the Feet of the River from this vantage point. They'd produced a number of small telescopes and were carefully scanning the entire area with constant warnings to me to avoid making a "profile" by getting too high.

That was how I came to be lying on my belly, in the dirt, looking out over a panoramic landscape where the rushing Great Drake River rolled in muddy turbulence into the greeny-blue tide of the Eastern Sea. I wished I had a telescope like the Reds did. They had a lot of very interesting equipment that we should really consider.

Don't turn traitor on me just to get great gear!

No one said anything about being a traitor. That glass was just extremely handy.

"Let your apprentice take a look," Cynos said handing Hubric the glass.

Hubric handed the glass to me with an indulgent smile. "What do you think, Amel?"

"Where can we get one?" I asked, raising it to my eye and studying the river banks hungrily. I'd been longing for a closer look at these.

"See, she should have been Red," Cynos said, but I barely heard him.

Along the river bank, were a series of statues – or at least, they had been statues at one time. And when they had been, they must have been almost as tall as a sky city. Now, what must have been hundreds of years later, they were rubble – huge white stone chunks of rubble-strewn along the river bank, larger than houses or even guard towers, in some cases. All that was left of what had once been statues of twenty people on each side of the river bank, was twenty pairs of feet, broken off at the knees, or ankles, or in a few cases the thighs. Where their sandaled toes met the river, the water lapped around them, rounding the feet off so that they were blocky and worn compared to the exquisite detail of the ankles and knees above them.

"Reds aren't known for their acceptance of physical difficulty," Hubric said, diffidently.

"I saw no difficulty when she scrambled up the hill. The girl is fit," Cynos said. I would have preened under his praise a month ago. Now, I had more important things to think about.

"Who were they?" I asked.

"The statues?"

"Yes," I said.

"No one knows anymore," Cynos said. "They guarded the Great Drake River from our enemies who might come this way."

"By means of the river?"

"Or the sea, I suppose," he said.

Reds don't talk to their riders. That's why he doesn't know the truth but look at Hubric. I bet he looks bemused.

He did.

It's because we know there wasn't always a river here.

There wasn't?

In the days when dragonkind were young, this was a split in the earth, and from it, our enemies drew up the Ifrits. We – the people of the Dominion and the dragons - fought them long and hard and when they were banished from this earth, we built the statues to remind us always to stay on guard against them. But that was long ago in the days of the First Dominar. And people forget things too quickly.

But dragons remembered.

We have long memories. Even those of us who live short lives tied to humans.

I'd forgotten about that. I had the terrible feeling of all the air being sucked out of my lungs at once. Because of me, his life would be shorter. Because of me, he would die young. He would die in battle or die like Enkenay was going to before Savette saved him and there was nothing I could do about it, because even if I lived a long life – for a human – it would be a short life for him.

Don't spiral away, Amel. It will be as it is. I made a choice.

But he hadn't chosen life as a dragon bonded to a human.

I did choose to live it with you.

He did. And his explanation of this being a big deep pit of Ifrits didn't explain the river.

When we drove the Ifrits away, the ancients rerouted the river to flow down this path instead. It was a great feat, accomplished by humans and dragonkind working together to move the earth and rocks to do our bidding. We filled the pit with water to keep away any thought of bringing Ifrits back to this land.

That was all well and good, but I suddenly had a terrible feeling of foreboding. After all, Savette – who could usually sense Ifrits - had not sensed the Ifrit beneath the water. What if there were hundreds of them waiting beneath that river. Waiting in their pit. Gathering one upon another. Until one day, they broke free.

Down in the rubble around the Feet, I saw something stir. I peered through the glass at it, uncertain about what I was looking at. A group of people walked out from behind one of the statues. The bottom half of their faces were stained red, like someone had painted half of their faces, and their hair stuck up a hand-width into the air. I'd never seen anyone like them before.

"Who are they?" I asked Hubric handing him the glass.

He peered through and then his face went white and he handed it urgently back to Cynos.

"Rock Eaters are here."

Chapter Fifteen

"Rock Eaters," Cynos said, his tone full of horror. "There! Just past the wave breaks. Three ships flying black flags."

"What does that mean?" I whispered to Hubric.

"They come from the dark continent," he whispered back.

"Baojang?"

"Baojang is on the dark continent, certainly. The Rock Eaters lie deeper within. They don't speak a language we know. We have sent emissaries to them in the past. They kill our people ruthlessly and without warning. What little information about them that has trickled back worries us. Their customs make no sense to us. We cannot seem to communicate, and they have no mercy."

"There are men of Baojang here, too. I see their saffron pennants. Perhaps a hundred mill around the Feet close to the sea. I think I see tents. They are camped here."

It was hard to see anything between mounds of rubble, but Cynos was expert with his glass.

"Any sign of Dragon Riders?" Hubric asked, scanning the ground.

"See that hilltop between us and the sea?" Cynos asked. I peered towards it. The land jutted upward, ending abruptly in front of the Feet and the river. Had it been carved by water or by the hands of man and dragon before the monuments were set in place?

"I see it," Hubric said, squinting.

"Take the glass again."

Hubric lifted the telescope up and grunted. "I see them. Four Purple Dragon Riders in heavy stocks. There must be twenty magikas around them, meditating – or something – and a dozen large tents."

"Do you see Leng?" I asked, anxiously. I wanted to see through the glass myself, but Cynos already had it back, peering through it at the hills.

"Maybe," Hubric told me. "I can't see faces clearly."

Cynos ran a hand through his hair. "But where are the messages you lost? In that camp, or the one on the beach, or somewhere else?"

"Wherever they are, those Dragon Riders need to be freed."

"Agreed," Cynos said. "But what are they doing to them there?"

Hubric knows. Kyrowat is a very clever dragon.

"They are using them – using their ability to speak to dragons – but amplifying and extending it with magic. They are using it to keep dragons and men of the Dominion far from here."

"What are you talking about? What ability to speak to dragons?" Cynos looked mystified.

"It's a Color secret," Hubric said, looking uncomfortable. "One we are sworn to keep quiet about. But right now, you need to know this. Purple dragons – so elusive and strange to the rest of you – can speak into the minds of man. When they choose their rider-"

"*They* choose?"

"Listen. Don't interrupt. When *they* choose their rider, they start to speak so frequently that the rider also develops the ability to stretch out with their mind – at first it just results in greater range between the dragon and the rider. Then, it moves to sensing little things about people – things they can't quite explain. In the end, we can start to read thoughts, too. Who knows how far it could go? Most Purples don't live as long as I have."

Cynos' face was pale. "I don't think I like the sound of that. Tell me you aren't reading my mind."

"Your mind?" Hubric laughed. "I wouldn't dare. Who knows what filth you have in there? It would be like eating garlic and tasting it on your breath for a week."

Cynos laughed but I could tell he was relieved. "Let's go back down the hill so we can talk freely.

We climbed back down the hill as carefully as possible, working not to make a sound or cause a rock to tumble or fall. We didn't dare alert our enemies to our presence. At the bottom of the hill, in a cluster of tall trees, Cynos motioned us to form a tight ring and Hubric spoke again.

"Kyrowat thinks that they are using the Dragon Riders as a mental shield to hide what they are doing here. Perhaps they fog the mind of those passing so that they do not notice those gathering here. Perhaps they plant within them the idea to go elsewhere. All of it would have to be amplified by magic – but there are plenty of Magikas on that hill..."

Cynos grunted again. "Then they'll use it on us when we venture close."

"We'll need to be prepared for that."

Cynos gave Hubric a long look and then cleared his throat. "Us, but not you, my friend. You are hereby charged to fly directly to the Dominar and tell him of what has transpired here."

"Charged by who? You're no master of me!" Hubric looked put out, his face flushing with his words.

Cynos shook his head. "You know this as well as I do, Hubric. As long as we were only recovering your messages, you led. Now that there are enemies invading the Dominion, this is Red territory and we have dominance here. This battle is mine to fight. And I will fight it without you."

Hubric leaned in close and I thought he was trying to keep his voice from carrying to me or the lieutenants, but I could hear him just fine. "This is suicide, Cynos. You see our enemies out there. Any attack on them is sure to be met with more force than we can possibly handle. You need every dragon and rider. Don't deprive yourself of two Purples."

"One Purple." Cynos was so calm. And yet, Hubric's words about suicide hadn't even made him blink. Did he already expect to die?

Yes. As soon as they saw the assembled forces they knew they would have to fight – and die – for the Dominion. Their dragons also understand.

"Then let's send the girl, my apprentice. She's already delivered her first message. She's ready to carry word to the Dominar on our behalf. She met him in person. She's ready."

Why did it sound like he was pleading?

Cynos shook his head grimly.

"I know why you ask, Hubric." He laid a hand on Hubric's shoulder. "I'd give you this if I could, but I can't. I need every dragon I can get. I must have hers. But not yours. This message could mean the life or death of our Dominion and you are a full Dragon Rider, fully mature and ready. We can't possibly send a half-baked Purple to deliver this message when we have a full Purple to do it. I'm sorry, friend, but the answer is no. You will fly away and tell the Dominion of this threat and we will stand and fight. If the girl survives the battle, she will be free to return to your side. Now, I'll give you a moment to say your goodbyes while I discuss strategy with my men. I hold you on oath to do as promised, Hubric. Don't try to trick me or to swap places with her. Your word compels you."

Hubric looked slightly chagrined, as if he was planning to do exactly that, but then he nodded and put his fist to his heart.

"By my word and the truth, which is all I have, I will deliver your words to the Dominar – long may he reign."

Cynos nodded briskly and turned away and Hubric rounded on me.

"I can't get out of this one, Amel. He has me by the word and there's no getting out of it. I'm bound as sure as magic."

He looked so agitated that I laid a hand on his arm. "It will be okay, Hubric. I have Raolcan."

He nodded jerkily, like he was holding back tears and pulled his neck scarf off to retrieve a leather cord. He pulled it free and gently placed it over my head. On the end, a message cylinder dangled.

"There's directions and a map in there to a place I know north of here. It's coded, but you're a smart girl and you'll figure it out. If. When. If..." He coughed. "I don't know what I'm saying. *When* you get out of there with Savette and Leng, you're to follow that map to the hidden place and wait for me. I will be as fast as a cat caught on the feast table and I'll get right over there to retrieve you. Understand?"

I nodded. But how could I promise anything? After all, we weren't supposed to part ways, but his previous obligations bound him. And I was just as bound in so many ways. How could I know what promises I could keep and which ones would unravel me?

Hubric took a silver ring from an inner pocket and handed it to me. "It's my davari to you, Amel Leafbrought."

Like the one Leng gave me? My eyebrows knit together.

"It's not like that one from Leng. It's not a romantic gesture. It's a promise. My promise to you. I'll come back for you. I promise."

I took the ring and when I looked up there were silver trails on the old man's face. He frowned and looked away, not wanting me to see him cry.

"I believe you, Hubric. Be safe." On an impulse, I hugged him. He patted my back awkwardly.

"I'll be back for you, girl. Don't let me down, now."

"How would I do that?" Our hug broke and I swayed backward on my crutch.

"By dying. That's how. Don't die."

I laughed, relieved that it was all he was asking, but he seemed serious when he patted my shoulder and strode away. I wished - as I watched him walking so quickly in the other direction - that there were stronger things than words to communicate how you felt. Mine just never felt substantial enough.

Chapter Sixteen

"Over here, girl," Cynos said, gesturing to me. I joined the circle that now had all twenty of the Red Dragon Riders. "Remind us of your name?"

"Amel Leafbrought." I tried to make my voice strong, but it was hard with Hubric leaving. I hadn't realized how much I'd grown to depend on him. Out of the corner of my eye, I saw him checking Kyrowat's straps and then whispering something to Raolcan before he mounted up again.

"And you have this wonderous gift of being able to speak to your dragon, Amel?"

I felt my cheeks heating. "Yes."

Cynos nodded, briskly. "Then this is our plan. The Magikas may be Dominion citizens, but if they are fogging the minds of those who come close for the sake of our enemies, then they are enemies, too. They have forfeited their rights to our protection. Understood?"

The men in the ring nodded and I added my nod. Obviously, anyone working with the Dusk Covenant was my enemy. I didn't need reminding of that. Behind the group, Kyrowat leapt in the air and Hubric gave a sign of farewell.

Cynos keep his voice low but he spoke briskly. "We'll fly straight to the hilltop where they have the Purple Riders. If they are using them to fog minds, we need that to stop first or we won't be able to route our enemies or even engage them. The Magikas holding the Dragon Riders are our first target and freeing them is our first priority. Amel, as a Purple trainee with the ability to speak to your dragon, your job it to keep us focused and clear. That means asking your dragon to remind ours why we are flying toward that hill. Understood?"

I nodded.

"We will chant to ourselves why we are here. 'Fly to the hill. Free the Purples.' Over and over as we fly, we will say these words. Understood?"

There were fist to heart salutes all around and I hurriedly added my own.

Cynos nodded, satisfied. "Formation D seven with Amel tucked on our six. She is an honored guest and to be treated so. She is unfamiliar with our maneuvers, so expect that." He turned to me. "Watch for the signals. Some will be unfamiliar to you, but some are standard signals. Do your best to keep up. Once your task of keeping us alert is complete you will join us in freeing the Dragon Riders and await further orders." He turned back to the group. "Rock Eaters and Baojang invade our lands in this place. We know our duty. We know our Color. With our blood and lives we will defend the Dominion. We will repel her enemies. We will lay havoc to her plans. Defend the Dominion."

"Defend the Dominion," they chorused back.

Cynos gave us a hard smile and saluted. "Mount up!"

I followed the others toward Raolcan. My heart hurt that Hubric wasn't with him and my hands were shaking at the prospect of a battle my allies were certain we would lose.

Hold onto courage, Amel. We will free Leng and help Savette. Have I let you down yet?

Never.

Then don't doubt me now!

When I joined him, hunkered low in the grass, I couldn't help but give him a hug around the neck.

Let's go get your friends.

His straps were secure and load safe. Hopefully, Hubric had taken whatever he needed from my pouches.

He left you a medical kit.

I mounted up and stowed my crutch, settling into the straps. As I tightened the last one, Cynos signaled launch and shot into the air. Behind him, the Reds launching in waves, and we were last, launching into a stiff breeze with our minds set on our task.

"Fly to the hill. Free the Purples," I said. Would Raolcan remind the Reds?

I'll be like a bee in their ears. Finally, a chance to annoy Reds without any chance of fall-out. You have no idea how they set themselves up for it.

They did?

Trust me, those gnarled Red giants take themselves way too seriously.

At that moment, we crested the top of the hill and flew up over it and for the first time, I saw exactly what we were dealing with all in one wide dragon-view.

Chapter Seventeen

O ur first target was to our right, the tall hill crawling with ant-like creatures – Magikas and Purples- as Hubric and Cynos had seen in the glass. There were many of them. Enough that I felt a hard lump forming in my belly at the thought of sweeping into all those Magikas bent on taking back my friend.

"Fly to the hill. Free the Purples." I chanted.

Down. Closer to the water I could see the other camps, and out in the bay were the ships they'd seen. It might be a small group - as far as invading armies were concerned – but it was large enough that my head felt light and I thought I might lose my lunch.

Standing on a rocky outcrop over the river, stood Rakturan and Savette with Enkenay behind them. Their blindfolds were off, and light flooded the area all around them. Rakturan stood straight and something – magic? – amplified his voice so that I could hear it even this far away.

"Men of Baojang," he said. "I am your prince - Rakturan. Come to me. Rejoin your prince."

There was a stir in the ranks of Baojang and a matching stir in the ranks of the Rock Eaters. What had Savette and Rakturan gotten themselves into? They were powerful, but powerful enough to take on an army? I didn't think so.

One thing at a time. Focusing on everything will make it seem too large and you will crumble. Pick one thing and focus on that first. Until the ward keeping us away is down we can't help, and neither can anyone else.

"Fly to the hill. Free the Purples," I said aloud.

In front of Savette and Rakturan, the waters of the river parted suddenly and an Ifrit rose up out of the water. Behind him, a second one began to emerge. That was too many! They couldn't handle more than one. We'd seen what one could do alone. There was just no way that they could fight two at once.

A third Ifrit emerged from the depths as the Rock Eaters began to form ranks behind them. The men of Baojang moved purposefully toward Rakturan. Were they going to join him as he'd asked, or were they also bent on his death?

Confusion hit me like a wall. Why was I here? I suddenly didn't know. Were we going the wrong way? Weren't we supposed to be heading west? There had been something about a ward? No, that wasn't right. I was flying a message to the Dominar. I should be doing that right now.

"Fly to the hill. Free the Purples," I said. It sounded ridiculous. What hill? What purples?

Ahead of me, I noticed the Red formation growing ragged as dragons swooped in loops to turn instead of flying forward. Raolcan? Were we supposed to do something about that? For some reason, it felt like I was supposed to...

Hold fast. Keep saying the words. I'm ordering the Reds back around.

His mind felt focused. He knew what we were supposed to do.

"Fly to the hill. Free the Purples."

At the front of the formation, Cynos began to sign an order to wheel the formation. Raolcan! Could he stop Cynos' dragon?

Mionshc. He's a stubborn one, but I am under his skin. He won't wheel.

Two dragons at the far left of the line fell out of formation but quickly settled and returned.

Seiddet and Lekwbeh. They have weak minds. I must keep an eye on them.

We were close enough now that I could see the Magikas scrambling into formation on the hill. There were two lines of them, encircling their prisoners, arms in the air and ready to attack us. The frantic feel to their movements was a welcome sight – at least they hadn't planned for this. But what could our dragons do with the captives at the center? If we attacked the Magikas we would flame the prisoners for sure.

No wonder Hubric had found it difficult to pick out Leng. I couldn't see faces clearly even now. The prisoners were arranged in what looked like stocks. Their heads and hands locked into a series of long boards that formed a ring on the top of the hill. From there, they could see every direction. How terrible! And were stocks really necessary? I felt any shred of compassion I had for the Magikas below leave me. On the boards above the heads of the prisoners, the brand of the Dusk Covenant was burnt deep in the wood.

My heart was racing now as I chanted the words, "Fly to the hill. Free the Purples."

Our formation tightened, so that now I could see my fellow riders chanting the same thing as we dove toward the hill together. We'd passed the confusion. We were going to make it!

I swear, it's been like herding cats. Did I say dragons were intelligent? You can scratch that. These fools couldn't find their way out of an egg.

Who could do that in the first place?

Dragons. Or at least the ones who leave the egg and make their way in the world.

One Magika in red robes waved a staff over his head and together they launched fireballs at our formation. All joking died as we rolled and dodged to escape the flames. Two of our dragons flamed back, but their flames came dangerously close to the prisoner formation at the center of the Magikas and the Magikas dodged aside from the flames.

Cynos was signaling vigorously and I could tell from the feeling of Raolcan's thoughts that he was concentrated on keeping the Reds focused. I needed to think of a way to get to the prisoners past those ranks of Magikas.

Two Reds dropped back and Raolcan snapped at one as it passed, flaming at the tail of the second. They spun back into line and we swept upward with the rest of the formation, following Cynos. He was signaling to swoop up, regroup, and then dive together toward the hill, all flaming at once.

It would be effective. Together, with our dragon's bellies shielding us from their fireballs as we flew in a tight formation, we could set the entire hill ablaze. But what about the prisoners? We needed to keep them safe and then we needed to get them out of those stocks! Was it a key that unlatched them? We'd need to find the key.

Not a key.

Oh, look! I saw it now, too. There was a lever that could be pulled to open up the entire mechanism and let a prisoner out. Simpler and more heavy-duty than a lock and key system. I supposed they never expected anyone but the Dusk Covenant to make it up that hill in the first place.

It was in that moment that I saw him. Leng! His head was twisted slightly upward, like he was struggling to look up at the sky.

He was there! He was really there! I needed to get down and get him out of those stocks. My hands itched to do it and my heart raced with excitement. If we could just fly close enough, we could swoop in while the others were fighting. We could-

Stop distracting me! We can't free him until the fight here is done. Focus!

Fire tore through our ranks and around me yells and grunts filled the air. Raolcan hissed as a fireball hit his tail and I gritted my teeth hard, apology filling my thoughts. I shouldn't have distracted him. The dragons on either end of our formation flamed and then each one in turn flamed in pairs at Cynos' sign. Even those with riders clearly burned by the Magika's flames kept in formation as we dove toward the hill.

Fire wreathed the top of the hill like a blazing orange crown. Three Magikas, lit like candles, stumbled out across the hillside and fell down the steep sides, rolling through the grass and trees, spreading fire as they went. Distracted by the fires around them, even those untouched by our flames could not focus to launch another attack.

I should have felt relief that we'd quelled their attack, or sadness for the Red Dragon Rider I saw fall from his saddle, his body a charred mass. Instead, I was filled with terror as I watched the flames rolling toward the prisoners at the center of the hill.

Chapter Eighteen

We had to get down there before the flames got to the prisoners. They were roaring across the grass, slowly eating up everything in their path, whether tents or flags or the clothing of the Magikas they touched.

Hold on.

I gripped the reins as our formation wheeled in a large loop together around the crown of the hill, but my eyes were on one small figure in the distance, held in place by cruel stocks. As we dove again, our formation burst apart, each individual dragon breaking off to chase the scattered Magikas. Raolcan dove straight toward the stocks. Would we make it in time? The flames were licking the base of them as three Magikas fought the blaze. If we dropped into that mess it would be one against three, but they would have the fire to distract them.

I'll drop you right onto the lever. Unstrap now so you are ready to leap off and throw it clear.

Leap off? Throw the lever in the middle of roaring flames? My heart hammered in my chest, but my clumsy fingers scrambled to obey, fighting against the leather straps to loosen them and work them off. We were already diving in closer, the air rushing around me. And we must have been getting close because it was feeling hot on my face. I was jolted as we landed hard on the ground.

Now.

I grabbed my crutch from its place and leapt down, stumbling over the uneven terrain. My lungs and heart raced with the intensity of the moment, but the hot air seared my lungs and I clutched my chest, coughing as I stumbled to the lever. Behind me, I heard Raolcan blast a gout of flame off. I glanced over my shoulder to see him dodge out of the way of one of the Magikas, searing another with his flames.

I grabbed the lever with both hands, but it wouldn't budge. Down the line, a scream erupted as the flames reached the prisoners in the stocks. No! This couldn't happen. I was here. All I needed to do was pull this lever - and it was stuck. I grabbed the top of it again, pulling down with all my weight. Nothing.

Help comes.

Maybe one of the other dragon riders was on their way? I spun around to see Raolcan battling three Magikas as they leapt and spun through the flames, firing balls of flame at him. Were they somehow immune to the fire? He worked hard to keep them all at bay so that their flames missed both him and me.

I scanned the sky for help, but the Reds were out of my line of vision. Had another enemy appeared, or were they still in battle against Magikas scattered across the hill? Where was this help coming from?

And then I saw it – a dark figure growing closer by the second, swooping toward the hill. Good. Hopefully whoever was riding him was faster than I was. I worked at the lever. Were the coughs I heard my own or someone else's? Would there be any Purples still alive by the time we freed them?

Stand aside. That wasn't Raolcan's voice! I'd heard that voice in my head before.

I leapt out of the way the second before Ahlskibi landed beside me, grabbed the tiny lever in his massive jaw and pulled it down. The gears creaked and squealed and then the locking mechanism freed. I rushed down the line to the first Dragon Rider. Not Leng. I hurried to help him out of the stocks and left him coughing and leaning against the wood as I moved to the next prisoner.

Almost done here. Something is happening in the river valley. Cynos rushed that way.

The next rider down the line was dead. A fireball must have hit her before we even reached the lever. I tried not to look as I skirted past her toward the next one. I couldn't see who it was around the curve of the strange structure. When I finally turned around the bend, I saw the Dragon Rider slumped in the stocks. A gleam from the fires around us reflected from his nearly-bald head. Leng!

I scrambled to his side, tugging at the stocks and freeing him. His head hung low and I shook him. Had he breathed in too much smoke?

He shook his head and then looked up at me.

"Dreaming," he muttered.

"You're not dreaming. It's me."

"Ahlskibi."

I looked behind me and nearly leapt at the huge head right behind my shoulder.

That's the last of the Magikas. They fought hard. I've rarely had a human put up such a fight, Raolcan said.

Ahlskibi leaned past me, nuzzling Leng with his huge head. Leng tried to straighten, but stumbled forward, and I quickly got an arm under him to help him stand. His body must be seized up from being stuck in place for so long. What would his mind be like after such suffering? I couldn't think about that now. I had to concentrate. There were other riders to save.

I flew around the others. They do not live. I'll get the one you saved. Get Leng ready to ride. I'll be there in a moment. We need to get back to the valley. I've lost track of what is happening there, but Cynos flew that way as soon as we removed this barrier. It must be serious. Cynos isn't the type to leave a job unfinished.

Ahlskibi would want to carry Leng.

Ahlskibi is in no condition to carry anyone right now.

Leng shook himself, caressed Ahlskibi with one hand and then pulled himself slowly straight, seeming to see me for the first time.

"Amel? Can it really be you?" His dark eyes were full of so much hope that I just wanted to reassure him.

"It's me, Leng."

I have him. Okay, get ready.

Leng reached up a shaking hand and caressed the side of my face. I winced – not from his touch but from the look of his raw, bleeding wrist. He needed help and care.

No time.

"It's really you." He gathered me in his arms, so tenderly, so gently that I could barely breathe from the affection that welled up in me. He was safe and living. He felt warm and strong against me, despite his injuries and suffering. I hugged him back, pulling him gently closer, reveling in the safe feeling of being in his arms.

"I was so worried," I said. How did you tell someone that they were slowly becoming a part of you? How did you keep from scaring them with how real it felt? Laying my cheek against his chest felt like coming home. I didn't want to move from this spot. What if I let him go and he was gone again? What if I lost my grip for a second and he was hanging by a thread over death one more time? He lived too dangerously. He loved things that were too dangerous.

The same things you love – adventure, truth, and doing good in an evil world. Can you hurry it up? We have a valley full of Ifrits to deal with.

Raolcan landed behind us, the flames licking at his feet.

Climb on.

"Wait," Leng said, before I could pull away from our embrace.

Gently, so gently, in the middle of flames, swooping dragons and the remains of a hard-fought battle, he took my face in his battered hands and gently kissed my lips. I leaned into his kiss, savoring his love and loyalty. I didn't want to ever stop kissing him.

You're going to have to. I can't keep these flames back anymore and we have big problems below. How many Ifrits do you think kisses kill? My guess is zero. Shall we place wagers on it?

Leng broke away, caressing my hair one last time, his eyes filled with love and pain. "I can hardly bear to part with you again so soon. You're all I've thought about these past days. You and Ahlskibi."

"Ride Raolcan with me?"

"I can't. Ahlskibi needs me, too. He's been through a lot."

Where had he been all this time?

It's an interesting story, but not one for right now.

Raolcan was practically hopping from foot to foot as we broke apart and walked in opposite directions to our two dragons.

"I have so much to tell you," I called to Leng as I mounted Raolcan. The other Dragon Rider we had saved made room for me. He sat crooked in the saddle, like he was struggling to straighten. "Stay safe until I can."

Leng smiled at me as he mounted Ahlskibi without a saddle or reins. "I've made it this far."

Barely. He'd barely made it this far. No wonder Dragon Riders had short lives. And I'd fallen head over heels for one of them. I didn't want to stop loving him, either. I'd take the risk and the potential pain just to be close to him in the moments that we could be.

Are you about done?

Yes, but only for now. No promises for later.

Chapter Nineteen

Raolcan launched into the air, kicking up high so we could see the whole valley laid out below. The rushing river threaded through the Feet of the River, but below us, a battle raged. Savette and Rakturan stood at the center of it on their rocky outcrop. Some of the men of Baojang must have joined Rakturn, because the Rock Eaters and Baojang fought, but between them, Ifrists fought, too. I watched Savette raise a hand as light shot out and took one of the Ifrits in the chest, evaporating him in an instant. Was she growing more powerful?

Cynos and the Red Dragons swooped among the earth-demons, flames, and weapons their only defense against the power of the earth. How many of those horrifying creatures lay beneath the water before they were summoned up? How many more lay there even now?

I clutched the saddle as Raolcan dove toward the battle, but I wasn't thinking about a strategy of any kind. I'd already seen the battle and what we were up against. Twenty-three dragons – if we were that many now that some of the Reds had been killed in the attack against the hill top – and a few men from Baojang - were not enough to win against an army of Ifrits. Not even with the Chosen One on our side. If Hubric was here, he would have had some prophecy to quote.

One like this?
Surrounded on every side, not overcome,
Light battles the depths, commands armies come,
Her battle not with mortal man, but earth and fire
Ancient ally returns in battle dire.
Did Raolcan know the prophecies, too?

Did I forget to mention it?

Yes. He definitely forgot to mention that.

I grew up with them.

Like a Castelan. Dragons taught their little ones a lot better than poor farmers did. I had no idea prophecies even existed before I met Hubric.

Below us, a wall of men in Baojang saffron crashed into the red-faced Rock Eaters. I cringed at the screams below as steel met flesh. This was so wrong. People shouldn't wreck each other's bodies like stomping through Fall leaves. Weren't we too precious for that? Wasn't life too precious to be poured out all over the river rock?

Cynos' wave of dragons flew between the Ifrits, swirling and flaming in intricate formations. If only it did much good. The earth creatures batted at them, roaring with mouths of open flame, but they were not slowed as they poured out from under the river and toward Savette and Rakturan.

Their ring of Baojang fighters was thinning as the larger army of Rock Eaters and traitorous Baojang warriors pressed against them, desperate to reach Savette and Rakturan on their tall rock. Dotted among them were Dominion Magikas. I'd never be able to trust one of them again, whether they claimed to serve the Dominion or not.

We dove toward the human battle, Raolcan and Ahlskibi flaming the men at the flanks of the Rock Eater side, rolling to take bursts of fire from the Magikas on their bellies.

The Purple Dragon Rider behind me held tight to my waist, his head lolling slightly. He needed medical care, but there wasn't time now. I reached behind me to tighten his straps. He'd better not fall off. Raolcan could only do so much at once.

I'm already a bit of a wizard doing this much.

What are you doing? Flaming a couple of enemies and flying in circles?

He needed teasing right now. This situation was too intense. Even from here, I could see we were losing. Whatever had happened to Ahlskibi had weakened his flame. It still worked, but his bursts were small compared to Raolcan's.

Savette and Rakturan fought in twin precision, but they were vulnerable up on that rock as the Ifrits pressed forward, despite Cynos' attack.

I'm doing more than you think. I promise you. Help comes.

We circled again to attack the rear of the Rock Eater's army, barely dodging the attacks of the Ifrits who were closing ranks with the rear of their army. Behind me, someone screamed. I spun to look behind my shoulder. Two Red dragons slammed against the ground, dragon and rider instantly dead and the very rocks shaking and rolling at their fall. Behind them, a third dragon was thrown by an Ifrit against one of the statues on the river bank. He hit it hard, sliding down the statue onto the rocks below where blood mixed with the turbulent waters of the Great Drake river.

My heart was in my throat. We were dying. There was no help coming. What was Raolcan even talking about when he said help could come? There must be thirty Ifrits now, and our army and dragons were fewer by the minute.

Raolcan rolled suddenly and I clung to his saddle, gritting my teeth. A cry of pain right behind me told me that our situation was serious. We plummeted toward the earth, rolling so quickly that I couldn't tell up from down. Raolcan pulled out of the roll at the last second, his belly skimming the earth as he swooped back up to the sky, gaining height slowly. Was he hurt?

A bit. I'll survive.

I turned to look at the man behind me. Where he had been only moments before, there was nothing but broken straps and a smear of blood.

We got too close to one of the Ifrits. We must take more care.

But could we? Below us, Savette screamed as she disintegrated an Ifrit right in front of her. Rakturan raised a hand, light shooting out of it to destroy a second Ifrit. But their army was gone, slain before them to a man. Enkenay crouched in front of them, flaming Rock Eaters as they pushed the assault over the bodies of the fallen. It wasn't enough. They'd be overrun in minutes.

I saw Ahlskibi land on their flank, swaying from the effort of his flight. Leng leapt off his back, drawing a short sword as the two prepared to defend Savette's flanks.

Where was Cynos? Was that him sprawled across the ground on the far side of the river? I couldn't tell from here. There were only two Reds still flying. The rest littered the rocky river banks, lumps of sacrifice and loyalty laid out on the ground they lived to defend.

We would join them soon. I was certain of that. There were too few of us. Good thing Cynos had sent Hubric away so that he wouldn't have to die here with us. I finally understood why he'd looked at me like he had when he left. He'd been sure that I wouldn't survive this.

I swallowed as I watched the Rock Eaters begin a chant, shaking their weapons on every beat. I was afraid of them. I could admit that now. As afraid as I was of the powerful Ifrits and the mindless damage they inflicted.

Now! Raolcan said. What was he so excited about?

We spun to land beside Ahlskibi, Raolcan joining his defense against the onslaught of the Rock Eaters. I held tightly to his saddle, not daring to dismount.

Don't dismount. Stay on.

No need to tell me twice. The earth shook, a terrible earthquake choosing the perfect time to shake us like kittens in the mouth of a strange dog. Leng stumbled, grabbing Ahlskibi for support. I looked anxiously to him, but his expression was determined.

Our enemies were not daunted by the shaking earth. They weren't daunted when – to my horror – the ground between us and the Ifrits burst open in a long rip, river water pouring into the gash as it lengthened across the course of the river. They paused, though, when the first figure flew out from the rent in the earth. Their faces filled with horror when a burst of twenty more poured through the gash, body upon body upon body rocketing from the tear in the earth up into the sky, wings unfurling, and arrow-like necks extended as they shot upward.

It couldn't be. They were dragons. More than I could possibly imagine in every color I'd ever seen and a few more.

I gasped, letting go of Raolcan's saddle to splay my hands out across his neck. I needed to feel him - alive under my hands - to remind me this was real and not some illusion.

It's real. I told you help comes.

The Ifrits understood what was happening first. They scattered, fleeing out from us in every direction, their only aim to put distance between themselves and the swell of dragons. Flames burst where the dragons found them before they could escape.

The Rock Eaters, as one person, dropped their weapons, falling to their knees in shock.

My shock was just as great as theirs. Where had these dragons come from? What were they doing here? I looked to Leng who was shaking his head in confusion. I looked to Savette and Rakturan, who spun - hands clasped together – in wonder, watching the dragons as they flew.

Raolcan? Do you know what is happening?

The voice in my head was not his. It was many dragons all at once – hundreds of them. I flinched at the force of it.

Prince of Dragons. We greet you.

I shook my head. Were they talking about Raolcan?

This time it was he who spoke to me, a note of chagrin in his mental voice. *Did I forget to mention that I was a prince?*

I was pretty sure he hadn't forgotten, and he was going to have a lot of explaining to do.

Gladly.

Soon. Once this mess was sorted out.

That's right. Focus on the problem before us and not on a tiny detail about my ancestry that I failed to mention.

I'd be irritated if I wasn't so ridiculously grateful.

Hold onto that feeling. It's exactly right for this moment in time.

Dragon School: Prince of Dragons

Chapter One

"Now what?" I asked.

Someone – Leng, I thought - had lit a fire after we bound up his cracked ribs - and we stood around it uncertainly. He favored them slightly, but they weren't preventing him from moving around almost as gracefully as usual.

The boy has amazing pain tolerance. I'm impressed, Raolcan said.

I put the kettle on the fire to brew caf because that's what Hubric would have done if he were here. I missed him. If he were here he could tell me how worried I should be about Leng's injuries.

Let him tough it out. It's how dragons do it. Definitely don't say anything. He wouldn't like that.

Around us, there were so many dragons that shadows blocked the sun. Dragons herded the Rock Eater warriors and defeated Magikas into a huddle nearby, while others stood guard around them. Dragons dotted the sky where they chased down Ifrits. Dragons gathered up the dead – both men and fallen dragons - for the funeral pyres. My heart ached for Cynos who had given his life and the lives of the other Red riders to fight off this invasion. It ached just as much for the Purple Dragon Rider who had been snatched from behind me by an Ifrit. His body lay among those ready to be shown our respect for the dead.

"They brought five ships," Rakturan said. He'd taken on a new life since he left us, like he had found a strong vision. He and Enkenay had flown out over the ocean to survey the ships as soon as the Ifrits scattered. "Three Rock Eater ships and two from Baojang. There are skeleton crews still aboard, but they won't sail with the dragons guarding them. Are these dragons truly loyal to your dragon?"

I looked at Raolcan. He could speak for himself.

I'd rather not. Go ahead and speak for me. Tell him that the dragons will help until we have this situation in hand.

"They're here to help. For now, at least," I said.

"It's my intention to take those ships and return to Baojang," Rakturan said.

Savette gasped and I felt my own mouth open in surprise. That was the last thing I'd expected him to say.

"And return valuable assets to our enemies?" Leng asked quietly. He stood with us, but he'd been tending to Ahlskibi as we dealt with other tasks. Ahlskibi was clearly injured, favoring his right side and occasionally coughing out black clouds of smoke.

"Baojang is no enemy of mine," Rakturan said. At Leng's sharp look he shifted uncomfortably and added, "And I do not want my great nation to be *your* enemy either. I will return to her and warn about what I have seen. We have our own enemies like the Dusk Covenant there and our own tales of the Hasa'leen – the bringer of light, your Chosen One. It's time that my people heard that she has come to us. We need to make peace between our nations to tackle this greater threat – the threat to peace that the Dusk Covenant brings."

"We don't dare risk Savette that way," I said quietly. After all, I was a Lightbringer now. She was ours to protect, as well as my friend. Leng gave me a curious look. "Hubric is certain that she is the Chosen One."

"He is?" Leng's eyes ran over her, his jaw clenching at her bright eyes, uncovered by their blindfold.

Savette pulled the scarf back up to cover her eyes, as if she felt uncomfortable under his gaze. "I am devoted to Truth. Beyond that, I don't know what I am."

Leng straightened his shoulders. "Then she can't go anywhere. Though that doesn't prevent this man from leaving. His plan is solid. If war can still be prevented - even after the sacking of Casaban and this invasion force - then peace must be pursued. We've all seen what war does."

He looked sadly around him at the bodies being laid out in a long line along the riverbank. Did he have friends among them? He certainly had suffered alongside some of them. He didn't notice Savette grab Rakturan's hand, clutching it tightly in hers.

"Were they your friends, Leng?" I asked gently.

"They were becoming my friends, although they would have died anyway - none of their dragons survived the attack on Casaban. Ahlskibi only lived because he was out hunting in the countryside. He was set upon by an Ifrit and escaped during the battle but was too injured to immediately follow me. We lost our connection for a time."

Leng caressed Ahlskibi's snout as he spoke. They were both still shaken by what they'd endured, and no wonder. I'd be gutted if anything ever happened to Raolcan.

Nothing will. I'm a tough dragon.

Behind us, Savette and Rakturan whispered intently together. She seemed distressed as their voices gradually grew louder. With the sun setting red over the dark sea and the dragons laying out the dead, their whispers made me shiver. It was a grim evening, despite my relief that my loved ones had survived.

"Because it isn't safe with me," Rakturan said.

"It's not safe apart from you! Together we are stronger, and I can't bear the thought of you being hurt or killed across the sea from me."

"I will be fine, Savette. I am a prince of Baojang. I will not be killed. We both are stronger than we were before." He was pleading with her, but I wasn't so sure he was right. After all, the diplomatic party he was with and even his own bodyguards had been willing to risk him before. This was a risky choice.

"When you are gone, they'll marry me off to someone else just like they were planning to do before."

His mouth was open to argue but he shut it at those words. A moment later he smiled.

"What if I married you before I left?"

She still looked uncertain, though more hopeful than before.

"There's a ship of Baojang drifting out there and a ship will have a captain and a Captain of a Baojang ship has the right to perform marriages. I'll marry you before I leave, right here where the Feet of the River meets the sea."

She stood on tip-toes to kiss him, their long hair intermingling in the breeze.

I guess that's a yes, then.

They were so sweet together. But wasn't this place supposed to be significant for their magic? Why hadn't we seen any of that happen in the battle?

You didn't notice dragons pouring out of the ground? That didn't seem significant to you?

Well, obviously I'd noticed that.

That's the magic of this place. Both Dragons and Ifrits can be called up here. Ifrits because this place has deep ties to the earth from which they are created, and dragons because Haz'drazen keeps the cavern system open and one outlet is here.

They came through caverns under the ground?

Yes. I started calling to them when you and Hubric first met with the Reds two hours north of here. Even with that much time, it was difficult for them to come so quickly.

But they came. They came for their prince. I was still trying to wrap my head around the idea of Raolcan as a Prince! Would he tell me more about it if I asked him?

I'll tell you something else, instead. My friends have found Findar with Hubric's messages.

Chapter Two

They're bringing Findar here. He's wounded from the battle.

Excitement filled me. If only Hubric were still here. He'd be relieved that the messages were safe. I turned to Leng.

"Is there some protocol about accepting Hubric's missing messages back?"

"So that's what brought you here. I wondered why Hubric would leave his duty." Leng nodded his head thoughtfully. "Protocol says that the highest-ranking member is always offered the messages unless there is some reason to do otherwise. Since you are Hubric's apprentice, that would mean that you should take them, even though I rank higher than you do." He glanced to where Rakturan and Savette were whispering together and cleared his throat. "I think we can recover the messages on our own."

Raolcan led the way down the rocky river banks, giving our prisoners a wide berth. Ahlskibi walked so close behind us that I was worried about being singed by his smoky black coughs.

"Can we do anything for Ahlskibi's injuries?" I asked Leng.

"Not really. They're magical. He needs time to heal. The medicine of the Whites would help, but there are none here and our own first aid practices are of little use to an injured dragon. He needs rest and time. He will survive this."

I hadn't even thought about him dying. Thinking of it now filled me with horror. He wasn't close to death now, was he? If he was that injured, we needed to get him help right away.

Listen to Leng. He knows what he's talking about. Ahlskibi is fine. He's a big complainer at the best of times.

The black sooty cough that burst past me was laced with flames. It scorched the right side of my leathers and I gritted my teeth in annoyance, chastising myself. It was wrong to be annoyed at a hurt dragon.

Even one who did it on purpose? He didn't like my dig at his irritability.

Maybe Raolcan could keep the teasing to a minimum. Especially since I was standing between the two of them. Leng snorted from beside me and I jumped. I wasn't used to anyone else except Hubric following along with our silent interactions.

Leng took my hand with care, like he was afraid I might pull it away but also like he was leaving room for me to do that if I wanted to. I felt my cheeks heat and I turned my gaze away, afraid to let him see what I was sure my eyes were showing. His callused palm felt hot and certain against mine. I had very little certainty in this life.

"I'm glad we came in time," I said. How did I tell him that my heart would have broken if we hadn't? How did I tell him that he filled my thoughts without sounding like I was pining for him?

You are pining for him. Why didn't you suggest that the boat captain marry the two of you? You're as far gone as Rakturan is.

How did I tell Leng that I didn't ever want to let go?

Oh, for pity's sake, tell him something before I start fake-coughing fires.

"I'm glad you rescued me, too, Amel. If you'd been any later, Ahlskibi would have tried on his own and I couldn't have borne his death." He stopped for a moment, his dark gaze meeting mine with warmth and affection, as if he was also holding in more than he could express with words.

Did you hear that? Ahlskibi the snappy-one owes me. I plan on reminding him of that.

I thought Raolcan was supposed to be a prince. Was it too much to ask for a little dignity?

Not you, too. I left to get away from all of that.

He did?

Well, technically I was sent, but I'm not getting into that.

Leng was still looking at me and I felt my cheeks heating.

It was impossible. I had to speak. "I couldn't have borne *your* death, Leng Shardson."

He leaned down and very gently kissed me. "I haven't received permission yet, Amel Leafbrought, but life feels like something that can't be promised from one day to the next – not anymore."

"Our futures were never certain, Leng." I fought to look into his dark grey eyes despite my galloping heartbeat. Did he see all the way in when I looked at him? What would he think if he knew how frail I was inside?

"I promise to use what days I have left making your days better." His voice was so deep and gentle when he spoke to me – like he had his own tone for me. "If you'll let me."

I swallowed. "I'd like that."

Why did I have to sound like such a fool? Why couldn't I have clever, romantic things to say back? Things like a character in a story? Why couldn't I sound like someone worth devoting yourself to? Instead, I was tongue-tied and blushing and my head felt too full to think.

"You're wearing my davari," he said. "And whose promise is this other one?"

"Hubric's." Was that relief I saw on his face? "He promised to come back for me."

He nodded and his smile grew. "We'll find him before he can look for us and return his messages and his honor." He leaned his forehead against mine in a gesture so tender that my heart fluttered like a trapped butterfly in my ribcage. "Remember, you have my heart in your palms."

This time it was me who kissed him. He held me very gently, like he was afraid of breaking me.

Here's Findar. Unless you plan on putting on a show for him, I think kissy-time is done.

A red dragon stepped out from behind one of the broken statues. In his mouth, a limp Findar hung like a fish dredged up from the river bank.

Chapter Three

This is Saifmid. He recovered Findar for us.

Saifmid – the red dragon – shook Findar like a puppy with a stick in its mouth. A rain of small objects fell from him, including a dozen message cylinders. I scrambled forward while Saifmid dropped Findar to the ground. Falling to my knee and propped against my crutch, I gathered up the precious messages as quickly as I could. Hubric would want them kept safe. He'd want them to be secure.

"Your Dragon Rider belt has slots for them. I don't know if Hubric told you that," Leng said, helping me up. My hands were full of messages, so he lifted me to my feet and helped me settle against my crutch. "Look."

On the inside of my belt was a cloth panel. I'd known that. What I hadn't realized was that the cloth could be pulled out slightly, revealing loops. Leng gently took a message from my hand and showed me how to slot it into the belt.

"They're uncomfortable there, but you know they're safe. Not everyone uses them, especially not for long journeys. They're just too uncomfortable, but until you have somewhere else to put them..."

"It's perfect." I smiled at him, slotting the messages into the loops in my belt. When I looked up again he was kneeling over Findar.

"He's alive but unconscious."

"Can we help him?" I asked.

Leng snorted. "He'll live. He has no obvious injuries to bind. He probably slipped – or was pushed in the battle - and hit his head. He can wait with the other prisoners until we decide what to do with them."

Leng hoisted Findar awkwardly into a half-drag, half-carry. He winced at the pain of his ribs, stumbling slightly under the other man's greater weight. Ahlskibi nudged him with his snout.

"You're not carrying anyone until you have time to heal."

Ahlskibi coughed, flame flashing across the rocks in a harmless direction. I agreed with the sentiment. Leng had no business carrying anyone, either.

"Fine. You can guard him. Will that make you feel better?"

It must have been satisfactory, because Leng put Findar down, leaning him against the feet of a stone statue and Ahlskibi settled himself gingerly on the rocks beside the unconscious man. We all liked to feel useful. I understood Alhskibi's frustration.

"What *are* we going to do about the prisoners?" I asked.

Leng pulled at his ear with one hand as he thought. "The closest city to here is Casaban and it's in enemy hands. There's a city north of here along the coast – Saldrin. We could go there for help. Or we could head northwest toward Leedris City and try there. Obviously, we can't take care of this ourselves. We simply don't have the manpower."

My brothers will stay and watch these prisoners until humans can come and take over their charge.

I hadn't even asked Raolcan if the dragons wanted to deal with the prisoners themselves. Hopefully, he wasn't offended.

Why would dragons want to deal with human problems? My brothers will stay and watch the prisoners until you can bring humans here, but we should leave soon. My brothers don't wish to stay too long.

"Ahlskibi told me what Raolcan says," Leng was nodding as he spoke. "I think we'll need to leave immediately."

After the wedding.

"To Saldrin or Leedris City?" I asked aloud.

Leedris. It's time we found out if Savette's family will support her as the Chosen One.

"I agree," Leng said. "Leedris makes sense. It's about two days flight from here."

"Do we bring the prisoners with us or fly alone?"

"That's a good question. We'll have to think about the logistics of it."

But right now, we need to fly to the ship or we'll be late for the wedding.

What?

You did want to see your friend get married, didn't you? Don't worry about the prisoner. Ahlskibi will guard him.

In the distance, a burst of fire shot up from the Baojang ship with a sharp 'crack.' I leapt, fear filling me. We were under attack of some kind. Rakturan and Savette had been heading out to that very ship! Could we get to them in time?

Ahlshibi's puff of flame and smoke looked more like a laugh than a cough and Raolcan was shaking, his own puff of flame flashing harmlessly over the river rock. What...?

"Have you ever seen a night flash before?" Leng asked me, smiling in a far too self-assured way. "They're a trick of Baojang for special occasions, like a fiery flower shot up into the sky. They guard the recipes for it closely, but I heard a rumor that it's made of some kind of earth."

My mouth fell open. So, we weren't under attack? That was on purpose? They shouldn't go terrifying people like that!

"I think it's to signal the wedding. Rakturan must be in a great hurry." Leng took my hand. That *did* sound like Rakturan. He had his own way of doing things. "Do you think Raolcan will let me ride with you? Ahlskibi is a bit busy right now."

As long as he doesn't get any ideas while we're there. I think I've seen all the romance I can handle for the next fortnight.

We climbed up and Raolcan swooped into the cobalt sky, twisting slightly as he turned toward the ship. It was probably just to remind us who was in charge of this flight, but the sudden twist left Leng grabbing my waist for stability and I didn't mind that at all.

You're welcome.

Chapter Four

We looped around the Baojang ship and I craned forward to look at every detail. The woodwork along the hull amazed me. Strange symbols cut into the rail all along the deck and intricate swirls and scrollwork were carved up the mast and across the deck, like the whole thing was a work of art. The sails – saffron in color - whipped in the bracing wind and were bright against the still charcoal sea as the last gold of the sun sank beneath the horizon.

I gasped at the beauty of it, whooping out loud as Raolcan zipped over the water, skimming so close to the dark waves that his belly slid along the crest of them. Leng was laughing behind me and all I felt through my bond with Raolcan was exhilaration.

Was he really a prince of dragons?

Really.

Even with this love of fun?

And a heavy load of responsibility. Why do you think I was sent to Dragon School as tribute? Even the Queen's own family is not exempt from the ancient pact. One of us had to come, and it was me who was ordered to go.

Ordered to an early death and bonding to a human he didn't know by his own family. It seemed cruel.

No more cruel than life has been to you. You'll find that no one's path is easy. Not if you look carefully enough.

Maybe that explained why he'd hinted that he was supposed to be someone else's dragon. Maybe Haz'drazen sent him there for a very specific purpose. I waited for him to answer my thought, but he stayed silent. In a way, the silence was telling me everything I needed to know. There had been a purpose for him and it hadn't been me.

On the contrary. I moment I heard your mind I knew you should be my rider. Sometimes people don't know what true value is until it's right in front of their faces.

Savette was waving to me from the ship deck and I waved back. That blindfold certainly never seemed to hinder her and now here we were, arriving for her wedding! When I first heard she was promised to the Dark Prince and I'd thought about her wedding, I'd expected pomp and lavish festivals for weeks. Instead, she'd marry the Dark Prince on a ship with only a skeleton crew, two dragons, and two Dragon Riders for wedding guests.

Behind her, Rakturan was in deep conversation with the men on the deck. The waving swords and guttural tones made me flinch, but Raolcan didn't seem worried.

It's just the way of Baojang. They speak loudly and carry big swords. I don't feel the need to brag like that despite being the best armed in any room, but some people just have to let everyone know they are in charge.

That was rich coming from him. Although it was true that he hadn't even let me know he was a prince.

Was I also supposed to mention that when I was a dragonlet my favorite color was yellow? I thought I'd let these insignificant things come up naturally.

I was laughing when he landed on the rear of the ship, causing massive waves to roll out on either side of the ship and a yell of worry from the sailors.

Fools. I'll only be a moment.

I noted that Enkenay was circling the ship in the sky. Perhaps he'd also elicited worry when he landed.

But definitely dismount quickly. I might be heavier than I thought.

Leng leapt down and reached a hand up to me, so I grasped it and slid from Raolcan's back. He leapt up the second I was off and took to the sky. The ship rocked boisterously at his departure and I was flung into Leng. He steadied us and laughed.

"Purples are an arrogant lot and Raolcan certainly fits in."

Hadn't Raolcan said that Leng was very Purple? Did that mean he was arrogant, too?

You should expect that – after all, he's trying to ignore those painful ribs like they don't even exist. If that's not Purple arrogance, then I don't know what is. Good Dragon Riders take on the traits of their dragons. Next time you land on a ship you might be the one teasing the sailors.

I doubted that would happen.

I'll keep working on your sense of humor.

Someone had given Savette a new dress – white, flowing sky-silk in filmy ripples that highlighted her slender curves. Gold embroidery traced the edges in the same type of pattern as the carvings on the ship. A wedding dress?

In Baojang they marry in purple clothing. This is probably a trade item that Rakturan has taken from the Captain of the ship. It suits her.

"You look lovely," I told her as she drew close to greet us. The scarf around her eyes had been replaced by a filmy white scarf made from the same sky-silk and her long blonde hair hung loose around her shoulders.

"Rakturan says we must hurry," she said. "The Captain says that if he wishes to reach Baojang this season then he must leave now before the winds change."

"Right now?" I asked. Were ships really so sensitive? Why didn't Rakturan just fly? Enkenay didn't need a certain type of wind.

No, but he needs somewhere to land or he'll fly himself to death. A ship is better for a long sea crossing. Enkenay could take a few rests riding on the ship so he doesn't tire out.

I hadn't thought of that. Could he just float on his belly in the water?

Would you want to sleep while floating on the sea?

I shivered.

"Join us!" Rakturan called to us, motioning for us to join him and the Captain. He looked exuberant, like he could hardly contain his excitement, though the Captain gave him the occasional side-long look, clearly still nervous about his glowing eyes. The rest of the crew rushed about, clearing tools and rope to the sides, arranging a string of red lanterns on either side of the ship and lighting them. They hung a golden cloth at the rear of the ship deck with lanterns in front of it, too.

The rear of the ship is called the 'aft.'

"You'll find the ceremony strange," Savette whispered to us as we followed her. "Rakturan warned me it would feel foreign to us. Please don't object. I want to marry Rakturan according to his people's traditions."

"Of course," I agreed, but Leng held onto my hand like he thought he'd need to protect me. That seemed extreme. After all, it was only a wedding.

I didn't know how nobles in the Dominion married, but it was relatively simple for commoners. Your families made an agreement oath – that they released their hold on their son or daughter and forgave all debts owed so they could be free and clear. The couple affirmed that they were entering the marriage without coercion and stated their names clearly for the town and then said their new family name together – usually the groom's family name, but it wasn't unheard of to take the bride's. Then we all ate a lot of food and those who could dance, danced until the night grew late and everyone left for home. Simple, but sufficient. Could a Baojang wedding be much different?

The night flashes were the main thing that was different. The sailors arranged themselves formally around the Captain and lit off a careful sequence of flashes that filled the sky. I tried not to flinch, but I must have still been nervous because Leng gripped my hand firmly, as if to steady me.

Seriously, they need to stop firing those things off. They could hit someone.

I wasn't paying attention to the Captain's speech, which was in a language I didn't speak. He read it out of a book, stumbling occasionally as if it were an unfamiliar task.

I didn't care, I was watching Savette's face. Even without seeing her eyes it was clear she was happy. Her smile grew when she and Rakturan joined hands and a sailor rushed forward to chain their hands together. Hopefully, they weren't planning to keep them chained together, or their lives would become complicated very quickly. Rakturan leaned down and whispered to her and his cheeks flushed at whatever she whispered back.

More words were said and Rakturan spoke as well. Could Savette understand any of this? Her confident smile didn't waver, though she blushed a pretty pink when he leaned in close to murmur something to her before finishing his speech.

When he was finished, another sailor presented a golden bowl to the Captain. He drew two golden loops and a long, thin golden chain from the dish. With a quick step forward, he drew a tiny knife and reached up to Rakturan's ear. I couldn't make out his precise movement, but when he was done the loop was in Rakturan's ear. Savette never flinched when he did the same to her, though a tiny drop of blood fell on the white shoulder of her filmy dress. They were linked now, by the loops in their ears and the long chain. A sailor rushed forward to unlock the chain around their hands and the bride and groom knelt on the ground, fingers of both hands interlaced and the Captain said a few words and Rakturan repeated them, and then the Captain spoke again and Savette tried her best – with help from Rakturan – to repeat them.

When they were done, the Captain made a pronouncement, Rakturan kissed Savette very formally, and the whole ship burst into a cheer. Night flares lit off by the dozens and Savette's smile was the only thing brighter.

That one almost hit me! Savages! You can tell they have never been civilized by dragons. That's a terribly backward nation your friend is marrying into. You should tell her that.

Chapter Five

"I think we should read the messages," I told Leng as we leaned against the ship railing. The sailors had prepared a feast on short notice and we were waiting for Savette to finish eating before we returned to shore. She'd have to come with us then, while Rakturan sailed for Baojang, and I wasn't looking forward to splitting them up. What were they going to do about those earrings with the chain?

"You can't. It goes against our traditions." He seemed tight and tense now that the wedding was over, like he expected something terrible to happen at any moment.

To be fair, we did just rescue him from a flaming hillside – a fire which my dragons put out, thank you for noticing – and then hauled him off to an impromptu wedding.

Now *I* felt tense. I needed to remember the messages and prisoners and Savette and Leng and the dragons and –

Enough. One thing at a time. The dragons are not your concern. They are my brothers and I will manage their actions. The prisoners can be dealt with once Rakturan is on his way. Findar still sleeps.

"They were lost before. They could be lost again," I argued. "The safest way to ensure they reach their intended destination is to read them ourselves. Then, if something happens to them, we can still relay the messages."

"Amel, these things are in place for a reason. Would you feel safe giving a Purple Dragon Rider a message if you knew they would read it?"

"I would if I knew the message was too important to lose."

"It doesn't work that way." He looked so tired. We both leaned against the rail, our backs to the festivities, looking out over the dark ocean. I let my shoulder nudge up against his. "We've been trusted with messages for hundreds of years because people know the messages are safe and secret in our care."

I shifted my weight irritably. So what if we'd done it this way for years? It clearly didn't work. Didn't he see that?

"Well, I think that with war on the horizon and cities collapsing, and the Dusk Covenant everywhere, we should find ways to make sure our messages reach their recipients. One way to do that is to read them so that they can't be destroyed by fire, water or theft."

"I'll think about it." He said it like he was ending the conversation, but he leaned his shoulder against mine to soften the blow.

But it wasn't really his decision, was it? I had the messages and it would be up to me if they were read. I'd give him until tomorrow to decide and if he didn't say anything, then I'd just go ahead and read the messages. Someone had to. What was the worst that would happen if I did?

"There's this place we could go on the way to Leedris - Backwater Manor," he said. "We could get help there instead of a nearby city."

I reached for his hand, wanting to offer comfort as I broke the news. "We were there two days ago. It was destroyed by Ifrits."

He cursed.

"Hubric said it was a Lightbringer safehouse."

"He told you that? And he told you about Savette too - that he thought she was the Chosen One." Leng looked stunned. He took my left hand in his gently and pulled my sleeve up to expose my wrist and then looked up at me with a puzzled expression.

"What did you expect to find there?" I asked, pulling my wrist back.

"This." He drew his own sleeve back, exposing a tattoo of a rising sun over a single hill. The sign of the Lightbringers.

"Well, I only agreed to join a few nights ago. He didn't exactly have time to demand body art."

He laughed. "So, you are one of us now?"

I nodded.

"Then I think I should tell you something." His tense look had returned. "When I was in the south I met with some of our informants there. The Dusk Covenant is spreading like wildfire. They feed on the discontent among us and twist the words of the prophecies. They have found a girl that they plan to bring to Dominion City and set up as the Chosen One of prophecy."

"Starie Atrelan," I said.

He went pale. "How do you know?"

"We were there when she arrived at the Garrison of Dominion City. One of the Generals in the room dropped dead under her gaze."

"This is worse than we feared. Things are coming to a head faster than I imagined." He ran a hand over his bald scalp, chewing his lip at the same time. "There was a rumor that they are trying to infiltrate the dragon's lands, too."

What rumor?

"What was the rumor?"

"It was very vague. Just a rumbling that they plan to strike at Haz'drazen. Our pact with the dragons has long been the strength of the Dominion but, like in all places, there are those who wish to disrupt the peace here and bring the Dominar down. They plan to strike at the heart of our strength – the dragons.

Stay where you are. I must leave for a time. Enkenay will bear you back to the shore by his promise to me.

Where was he going?

I'll be back soon.

That wasn't an answer.

Chapter Six

We were all quiet as we rode Enkenay through the night. I clutched Leng so tightly that I was afraid he'd get annoyed, but I wasn't used to riding a dragon I couldn't speak to. It felt weird. Savette rode at the front with me and Leng behind her. I could hear her sniffling.

Her first tears had come on the ship when Rakturan detached the golden chain from their earrings and kissed her goodbye. I tried not to watch – they needed their privacy – but it was hard not to be drawn by their sweet words and the way he kissed her tears.

Enkenay was being cranky about carrying us. It was a wonder that he would even do it – dragons didn't like carrying people who didn't belong to them – but he seemed very attached to Savette, and it wasn't very far. As soon as he dropped us off, he would be returning to Rakturan to sail across the sea with him. I was going to miss that white ghost of a dragon.

He set us down close to where Ahlskibi was watching Findar. Leng and I scrambled off and Savette stayed long enough to whisper in his ear before he launched back into the air to return to Rakturan. Despite the late hour, the skies were still busy with flying dragons. They guarded the prisoners and took care of whatever dragon-ly needs they had. The dead were all honored now, and the fires put out, so there was little else that needed to be done.

We trudged through the night, careful not to twist our ankles on river rocks. Leng picked up bits of driftwood as we walked.

"We'll want a fire," he said. "Ahlskibi says that Raolcan left your baggage and his saddle nearby. We can set up your tent and make some tea, perhaps."

"I could use some caf," I agreed. How had Raolcan removed his own saddle? I didn't realize he could do that.

You never give me enough credit.

He was nearby!

Not really. Our range grows.

Well, I was grateful that he'd left my gear. We were all tired and we needed our rest, though blankets would be scarce. Maybe Ahlskibi would let us curl up against him.

Unlikely. He's very irritable with all his injuries. Constant pain will do that to a person – even if that person is a dragon – as I'm sure you know.

I wished we could do something for him. He was standing when we arrived, teeth bared. Was he so irritable that he thought we were enemies? No. Findar was awake and sitting on the rocks before him.

"Findar," I said. Now that he was awake, we had questions to ask.

"Stay back," he said.

"Or what?" I leaned on my crutch and I knew I looked like an easy target – the same target he'd stolen a blanket from and tricked into trusting him. But I wasn't that. I was Sworn and I knew how to use this crutch as a weapon.

He looked around him, like he was searching for a way out.

"There's nowhere for you to go, Findar. We have taken your allies captive and they are under guard, you have no weapons, and Ahlskibi will flame you if you bother him. He's feeling irritable right now, so maybe you should sit down and talk to me."

"Do you have things covered over there?" Leng asked from where he was laying out driftwood for a fire. He was watching us tensely, like he wanted to step in and take over and was holding himself back. I swallowed. I wanted him to be proud of how I handled things and respect me as a fellow Dragon Rider.

"Findar doesn't worry me," I said. "He's the kind of person who hits old men from behind."

"We'll just make some caf and set up the tent, then," Leng said, feigning disinterest.

That's the nice thing about Leng. He lets people be independent even when he might want otherwise. You should try reading minds sometime. It would help you understand people better.

"And you're going to explain why you stole those messages and why you brought them here," I told Findar.

"I won't." He crossed his arms over his chest. His face was still swollen from his fight at Casaban, and there was a crusted lump on his head, probably from where he fell during the battle.

"You knew what was happening here. You brought these messages here in hopes that you could prevent them reaching their recipients and benefit the people you serve – the Dusk Covenant. Am I right?"

His eyes told me I was, though his lips narrowed as he pressed them firmly together.

"Did you expect to see the Rock Eaters here?"

"What do you think?"

"I think that it would be wise to answer me."

"Or what? You're a girl and a cripple! You won't torture me, and you won't let the dragon flame me. There's nothing you can do to me that would make me talk."

I wouldn't let his insults injure me. "You fought against us at Casaban, didn't you? You're a traitor."

"I told you I'm not talking. Why even ask questions if you can't back up your demands?"

"He did," Savette said from behind me. I glanced back at her, but she wasn't even looking at us. She was setting up the tent. I knew one thing Findar didn't. Savette could feel the truth.

"And you stole the messages to deliver them to the Dusk Covenant," I said.

He just shook his head in disbelief.

"He did," Savette said.

"You know what's in these messages?"

He stared past me, statue still.

"He knows. I think he read them," Savette said.

"Then I guess I'll need to read them, too."

"You can't." His answer was too quick. "It's against the law."

"Lie," Savette said. She was done with the tent and she was helping Leng brew the tea. When I glanced back at them, Leng's eyes shot me a warning look. He didn't want me to open those messages, but Findar had read them already. Was it really so bad if I read them, too?

I started to pull them from my waistband, one by one. I set them on the ground before me and noticed something I hadn't when I'd tucked them in. One of the cylinders was slightly different than the others. It bore a sign on it of a spiral with a line through it – the sign of the Dusk Covenant. I picked it up and examined it.

"I think I'll start with this one."

Chapter Seven

Findar crouched like he might attack me, but Ahlskibi coughed beside him, letting a gust of flame burst past. When the cough was past, Leng was suddenly at my side, a long knife in his hand, he favored his side, like his injury was finally tiring him out.

"I think you should stay put while the Dragon Rider reads your message, don't you, Findar?" Leng's eyes narrowed as he spoke.

I cracked open the seal on the end and slid the paper out of the cylinder. I moved to the small fire and held the slip of paper so I could make out the words.

I read it aloud. "We planted a snake with the crown. Finish capturing the coastal cities. Then send the sign of the boar to Lieutenant Iskaris of the Dominar's Dragoons. He will know what to do."

"All the Coastal cities are under threat?" Leng asked.

At the same time, I said, "Who is the snake in the Dominar's court?"

We looked at each other. I chewed my lip. Tension filled Leng's eyes. We thought we had a big decision ahead of us before when we thought all we had to do was figure out how to deal with these prisoners and deliver the messages. Now, we had twice the problem. The Dominar was in danger, and so was every city along the coast. I felt a stab of fear rip through me. What should we do?

Findar began to laugh, looking from one face to the next. "And you thought I was the one in trouble. You're on a losing side. Both of you."

"We could keep trying to question him," Leng said quietly to me, "but I don't think that's the best use of our time, not with this news. It's unlikely that someone like him knows any specifics."

I nodded and tucked away the other messages.

Leng strode forward, seized Findar by the back of the neck and pushed him ahead of him. The limp from his broken ribs was barely noticeable. "If you can't shed light on things here, you can join your Rock Eater allies under dragon guard."

I watched him escort Findar down the river bank to where dozens of dragons still swirled around the prisoners, occasionally using their flames to remind the prisoners where the boundaries of their imprisonment were.

I sank down on a rock next to the fire, staring into the flames. "What should we do."

"We'll need to split up," Savette said quietly.

I stole a glance at her. Her bright eyes looked forlorn without Rakturan's matching pair nearby. I noticed that she still had the gold loop in her ear, even though the chain was gone. She had to come with me no matter what. She needed protection and she had no dragon of her own.

I'm working on that, Raolcan said.

Really? That was what he was working on? I wouldn't have guessed that. It still didn't change our dilemma. Savette laid out cups and brewed the caf while I stared at the flames. I should read the other messages. That's what I should do. I arranged them in front of me on the rock. Savette handed me a cup of caf and I thanked her, taking my first sip just as Leng stepped out of the shadows and joined us. He took Savette's offered caf with a murmur of thanks and sat down awkwardly, cradling his ribs.

"We have decisions to make," he said grimly. If only Hubric was here. He would know what to do. "These are the top priorities in my mind - Savette's protection, warning the Dominar, warning the coastal cities, dealing with these prisoners. We have one dragon fit to ride – Raolcan." Ahlskibi snarled, his flames lighting up the night and Leng turned to him. "Don't grumble. I'm trying to look out for you. That's called love. Deal with it." He turned back to us. "We are going to have to choose."

Wait for me. I'm almost there.

"But every option is important," I said, sipping my caf slowly and staring into the fire. What if we made the wrong choice? What if it led to calamity.

"Life is all choices, Amel. The worst of it is that the things you want most are usually pushed aside by things more urgent ... but not nearly as important."

I met the burning intensity of his eyes by firelight. Beside me, Savette's tears slipped down her face, shining in the firelight. Was she thinking about Rakturan and his choices?

And here we are.

Raolcan landed beside the fire, flirting his wing dramatically at the last moment. As he drew his wings in, a second dragon stepped forward, a red dragon whose sleek scales were now covered in scars.

Eeamdor.

Chapter Eight

Savette gasped, dropping her caf with a clatter and leaping up to embrace her fierce dragon like he was a missing puppy returned to her.

I've been working on this for a while, Raolcan said proudly. *They were keeping him captive on the Ruby Isles. We arranged to break him out. I had hoped he'd join us sooner, but this is good timing.*

He was amazing! He'd been fighting for Eeamdor's freedom all this time? Who was this 'we' who helped him?

Dragons. We do have our own goals and plans, you know. Someone has to take care of Savette. She chose well with Eeamdor. He's boring, but noble.

Boring?

He can't take a joke.

Is he why you flew off so suddenly?

Among other things.

And are you going to tell me about those things?

Not all of them.

Of course. I didn't have any secrets left with him in my mind all the time, but he held on to his.

I'm a dragon of mystery.

"I'm not sure if this helps things or complicates them." The lines on Leng's forehead grew deeper. He pulled a map out from his pocket. "Do you know where Hubric is?"

"Oh!" I took the tiny cylinder from around my neck and pulled out the slip of paper within. I read it aloud. "The view is great from here. I can see the Grey Sea and Leedris Castel. Join me at dawn."

That made no sense to me at all. He said I could figure it out, but he seemed to forget that I wasn't as educated as I should me.

"Hmmm," Leng said. "Somewhere that can see Leedris Castel and the Eastern Sea – it usually looks grey - at the same time. You'd have to be on a mountain to do that..." His voice trailed off, but then he snapped his fingers. "Here, look." I moved in closer and he traced a line on the map. "'Join me at Dawn' he means the Peak of the Morning. It's one of the mountains in the nearby range. "

On the map, it was close to Leedris Castel, and also on the way toward Vanika where we'd last seen the Dominar.

"If I go that route, I can bring the messages to the Dominar and also bring Savette to Leedris Castel."

He nodded. "It won't be easy to bring these prisoners with you, though. Not only is it a long way to go without food, they will slow things down by being on foot without supplies."

"But where else can we take them?"

He pointed to Saldrin. "Here. Even if they walk it will not take long. If I load them on ships, I can sail them there in a day."

"Or they could seize control of the ships and try to escape."

"They could, but I'm hoping the dragons will come, too. Then I could warn a coastal city and take the prisoners somewhere safe."

"How will you sail three ships?"

"I'll make the crews sail them or risk being flamed by Ahlskibi and the other dragons."

I bit my lip. "That means splitting up again, doesn't it?"

I have reason to seek the Dominar. This would suit my plans perfectly.

"I would bring the prisoners to Saldrin and warn them of coming attacks. You would go to join Hubric again and together you could keep Savette safe and also deliver the messages to the Dominar."

"What about Ahlskibi? You said he wasn't fit to carry someone."

"He can rest on one of the ships when he needs a break. I'll be careful with him."

I bit my lip. I wasn't happy with us splitting up. I'd only just found him again and every time I lost track of him, something terrible happened.

He tucked the map back in his pocket and took my hands in his. "Listen, it's only for a while. It's the only way that makes sense."

I nodded. But his dragon was wounded. He was recovering from a trauma. Who was to say that Raolcan's dragons would listen to Leng and keep the prisoners together as the sailed to the city?

They will.

What if the prisoners overtook him and killed him?

"You wear my davari," Leng said, touching the ring on my finger. "It's as true now as when I first gave it to you. I will find a way to be yours. Until that time, you hold my heart in your palms." He kissed me. "But we both have responsibilities. We can't risk our Dominion just to keep close to each other. Wear my davari, and remember that I will return to you as quickly as I can."

I nodded, but I felt the tears tracing trails down my face. I hated that everyone I loved always had to go. I hated that it always meant risk and danger. If I had my way, there would be no more risks ever again.

And no more fun.

If that was what it took, then yes.

"Let's get some sleep. We'll need to leave as soon as dawn comes."

I found a place to sleep beside Raolcan, but I woke often through the night and glanced over at Leng sleeping against Ahlskibi. I felt safer just seeing him across the fire from me, but I would have liked it better if he were closer.

Seriously, can I just get some sleep? I'm starting to dream about bald-headed humans with all your pining going on in the back of my head - and that's something I've never wanted.

I closed my eyes and fell back asleep.

Chapter Nine

"Are you sure these dragons will work with Leng when you are gone?" I asked Raolcan the next morning. I was saddling him as we chatted and adjusting his load just right to keep him comfortable. Savette would have to fly without a saddle.

They are dragons just like me, Amel. Free, but not without an understanding of our shared responsibilities. They'll help him bring the prisoners to Saldrin.

I was just nervous about leaving. I didn't want to go.

You don't want to leave Leng, but what alternative is there?

I didn't want to be rational. I wanted to be *irrational* and get what I wanted.

Don't cinch those so tight. It's not my fault that you're in this situation.

Oops. I hadn't meant to hurt him. Savette was already on Eeamdor's back – saddleless, but content. I gave her Raolcan's reins - it wasn't like he actually needed them – but I kept the saddle. I needed a place to store my crutch while we flew. We'd have to be careful not to fly too dangerously. Savette's perch was tenuous, though Leng had rigged safety straps for her.

He walked around our dragons, looking nervous. "You know where you're going?"

"Raolcan does, and you drew me a map in the back of my book of Ibrenicus Prophecies."

He nodded, but he didn't step back so I could mount Raolcan. "Be careful, Amel. Take care who you trust and please keep yourself safe."

"I'll be okay, Leng. I'm worried about you with all the prisoners."

He shook his head, making a shooing motion with his hand. "They won't be a problem."

We were either both very confident or both trying to keep the other from worrying. Eventually, he gathered me up in his arms for a fierce hug and gave me a gentle kiss before helping me up on Raolcan.

"I'll be safe," I promised.

He stepped back, leaning against Ahlskibi to give us room to launch. I hated that I was going to leave. I didn't want to go. There must be something more I could say or do. I waved, then tapped the davari on my finger and he smiled.

Oh, for the love of the wind and sky...

Raolcan leapt into the air and I scrambled to hold on, waving as Leng grew smaller and smaller. The smaller he grew, the larger the ache in my heart.

Cheer up. He isn't dead or hurt, he's just taking care of his responsibilities, the same as you.

I twisted in the saddle to see Savette following behind us on Eeamdor. It was so strange to think that he'd been alive all this time and on his way to her and I hadn't even known. Which reminded me, Raolcan had a lot of explaining to do.

You can't possibly be angry with me. You know Savette is happy to see Eeamdor again. And he's happy to see her.

Well, I wasn't angry about that. I guess he didn't know for sure when they would be reunited, so he probably didn't want to get our hopes up.

Life is uncertain these days. I had no way of knowing that they'd ever really be reunited.

But he had kept that whole Prince of Dragons thing from me. And he still hadn't explained what he was really doing there or where he had been called off to.

I waited, but he didn't fill in the blanks. Irritated, I clenched my jaw. Well, I was done with people keeping secrets from me. The minute we stopped for a break, I was going to crack open those other messages and read them.

I thought you were only going to read them to keep them safe.

That was the original plan, but I felt like I was flying in the dark. I wanted them both to keep them safe and to start to shed some light on things.

I advise against it.

But as the hours passed, the messages seemed to grow heavier. I counted each cylinder where it dug into my midsection and the thought of opening them and reading them filled me with speculation. There were fourteen messages. Fourteen secrets waiting to be read.

Seriously, they are secret for a reason.

Like his secrets? Like whatever he was keeping from me? Why were you called away, Raolcan? Where did you go?

We flew northwest in silence, following the road, but staying far enough away to avoid sight and then moving north of it toward the Dragon Snout Mountains. They stood purple and foreboding ahead of us. Eventually, we stopped to take a break, eat some food and stretch our legs. I'd left half our food with Leng, so we had very little left. Hopefully, we'd find something to eat soon. I didn't have more than a few coins. It wouldn't take us far.

Savette and I got down from our dragons and ate our cold lunch in silence. The cylinders were a constant itch, drawing my mind to their presence. After a few minutes, Savette looked at me, her face crinkling in worried lines before she spoke.

"When we get to Leedris, we'll split up."

"What?" I almost dropped my waterskin.

"You have messages to deliver, and I have my own path to walk. I need to talk to my father, the High Castelan, and convince him to side with me in the coming conflict."

"Are you certain he'll be there?"

She shook her head.

"He wasn't very helpful when you were being given away as a tribute bride."

She pressed her lips together like she would say no more about it. My chest felt tight and my heart was racing. This was one thing I couldn't allow! Hubric would be furious if he knew I let the Chosen One slip away. Rakturan would be equally angry to hear his bride was undefended. What was I supposed to do?

"You can't," I said, spitting out the words over my thick tongue. I was so stunned that I felt like I could hardly talk at all.

She crossed her arms. "We all have our responsibilities, Amel, and I'm not a pet that will follow you all the rest of my life. I have my own path to walk. By nightfall, we'll reach the mountains and camp south of Leedris Castelan. The next day, we'll arrive. You can deliver your messages and you and I will part ways."

"But-"

"I've thought a long time about this, and I think it's best. I'm done hiding. It's time to show the world who I am."

Chapter Ten

This was a complete disaster! It was up to me to make sure that it didn't happen. But how did I do that? I didn't have any allies here except Raolcan. Who was going to help me convince her not to leave us? Maybe I should just follow her? She couldn't stop that, could she?

And your messages?

How important could they be, really? I pulled the first one from the slot and opened the seal, frustration filling me as I pulled out the tiny slip of paper detailing military logistics and the armies being sent north. Important, but in Leedris Castel I could find someone else to carry that message.

And will they tell the Dominar that the ground has burst open and Ifrits rage across his land? My dragons did not kill all of them.

They could do that. You could say the whole thing in a single sentence.

And will they tell him of the coastal invasion?

They could do that, too. It didn't have to be me bringing the messages.

Actually, it does.

It really didn't. Hot tears ran down my face. When had I started crying? But I was just so mad. Everyone left me.

That wasn't Hubric's fault. Or Leng's. Or mine. Or Rakturan's.

Everyone kept me in the dark.

That's unfair.

I pulled open a second message. It bore news of Starie's visit. I could tell the Dominar who Starie was and how much to trust her, but so could someone else. I shoved it back in its cylinder and into my belt. I grabbed a third message. Leng would be horrified. He would tell me to put them all back.

But he wasn't here, was he? It was only me here, all alone to deal with this mess.

Hey! That hurts! I'm here, too.

"Oh yeah?" I said, "Then if you're here, stop keeping secrets from me. Where did you go? Why were you sent to Dragon School and why am I the one who has to deliver the message to the Dominar?"

Calm down. Take a deep breath. You are not owed all the information in the world. But to satisfy your curiosity, I went to see a representative of Haz'drazen. She has given me a message for the Dominar that I am sworn to give to him directly. I may not share it with anyone else until that time.

"So you were being all mysterious because you didn't want to hurt my feelings?"

You have enough troubles of your own. Focus on them. But know that there are two things we must do. We must bring Haz'drazen's message to the Dominar, and we must keep Savette safe.

Because she was the Chosen One.

And because I owe it to my home and people to keep her safe. That was what I was charged with before I left for Dragon School.

I felt that knowledge click into place like a key in the correct lock, and as it turned in my mind I gasped. He'd said he'd gone against what he was supposed to do when he chose me. He'd said that he was sent to Dragon School to honor their pact. He said that Eeamdor had to step up when Raolcan chose me. Together, it seemed so obvious. Haz'drazen had sent Raolcan to Dragon School to choose Savette for his rider. Somehow, they'd known before the rest of us that she was the Chosen One and they'd sent their prince to be her dragon.

The knowledge knocked my breath out. My head spun with what it meant. If Raolcan had chosen Savette, *she* would have had his protection and strength. She wouldn't have been snatched at the Ruby Isles – I was certain he'd have found a way to be there to stop that. She wouldn't have needed to be saved by me. She wouldn't need protection now.

So why had he ruined all that by choosing me?

There are people who save the world in obvious ways, Amel, and there are people who save what's best about us in less obvious ways. One is not more important than the other. Remember that when you doubt your path.

Chapter Eleven

I blinked away moisture in my eyes and cleared my throat.

We needed to get flying again, but I had time to read one more message. I pulled out the next cylinder from my belt as I looked around the rocky dell we'd set down in. I couldn't see Savette anywhere. She may have slipped behind one of the rocks for a little privacy. She was still human, after all.

The mid-day sun was hot and both dragons were stretched completely out on the rocks, sunning themselves. I sat down and examined this next message. In the bright sunlight, the outer markings were easy to pick out. This cylinder had a boar on the outside and was addressed to Lieutenant Iskaris, Dominar's Dragoons. Wait. I knew that name.

I pulled out the message from the Dusk Covenant. Just as I'd remembered, Lieutenant Iskaris was listed as the man to send word to when their invasion was complete. I was carrying a message addressed to him. What would it say? I swallowed and cracked open the message.

Maybe reading these hadn't been the best idea. My hands fumbled with the cylinder and it took three tries to get the message out of its holder.

"Iskaris," it read. *"Continue as planned and watch for news from our invasion force. We have reason to believe that the Dark Prince escaped without suspicion during Baojang's attempt on the Dominar. He continues to be an asset we can rely on. When he surfaces again he may contact you. Watch for his message and send word as soon as you have any.*

There was nothing but an ink stamp of a boar as the signature. I reread the message. Could it be true?

That Rakturan is working for our enemies? Just because they think he is, doesn't mean that he really is.

I was still reading it when I heard a twig crack. I looked up quickly, hiding the message in my pocket.

"What do you have there?" Savette asked, stepping forward and putting out her hand. In the golden mid-day sun, her hair shone like gold. In the sky, a raven shrieked, making me jump.

"It's one of the messages I'm to deliver."

"You're reading them even though Leng asked you not to?" She tilted her head to the side, emphasizing both her question and criticism of me.

I felt my cheeks heat. What if she knew what was in the message I was holding? Would she worry that Rakturan was untrustworthy just like I was?

I don't think he's working for our enemies. Or at least, not anymore.

"You look upset," Savette said.

"I am upset." Why lie? Didn't she have a right to know what was in the message? I couldn't quite look at her, though. Instead, my eyes drifted over the rolling foothills we'd set down in. You could see a long way from here. Maybe as far as the Eastern Sea, though puffy white clouds hid the horizon right now.

"Let me see." She held her hand out and, reluctantly, I put the tiny slip of paper into it.

She read it and handed it back. "Let's get going. We're wasting time here."

"You're not worried about the note?"

"I know who Rakturan is. I married him for a reason." She was already on her dragon, strapping in. She looked like the goddess of dragons in her filmy white dress on the back of her serpentine red dragon. The flamboyant blue and white sky behind her only amplified the look.

I climbed up on Raolcan's back. Savette's gaze shone at my back and I felt awkward. Did she judge me for doubting her husband?

Raolcan launched into the sky, barrel rolling as he ascended.

Stop worrying. There's nothing you can do whether he is guilty or innocent.

But there had to be something. I should warn someone. Savette needed more protection than ever. I tucked the slip of paper back into its cylinder and into my message belt. I wouldn't deliver that one, but if we found Hubric, then I would show it to him. I hadn't felt this ... lost ... since I'd joined Dragon School. I wanted to go in so many different directions - with Leng, with Savette – and yet I was stuck flying to find the Dominar.

We flew through the clear skies and I watched as the forest faded to mountains. We flew higher, crossing over the arm of the mountains as we moved toward Leedris Castel. When we got there, Savette would leave on her own. That ate at me. I wasn't going to think about how angry I was with her for putting herself at risk. I wasn't going to spend all my time worrying about her safety.

I spun Hubric's davari on my finger. Was he near to here? Leng had said that I needed to find a mountain called "the Peak of the Morning" but there were dozens of different mountains here and rolling hills as well. How would I even find the right one? Did Raolcan know which one it was?

I'm not sure. We have different names for these mountains. It might be further up along the range.

Was Hubric there already, waiting for us? Watching for us to join him? I twisted the ring in my hand and tried not to think about how long it would take him to find the Dominar and return to that spot. Probably a lot longer than two days. Which meant that even if I found the place he meant, then it would be empty and Savette would want to keep on going to Leedris Castel.

Hold on. I feel a strong current in the wind approaching.

A few moments later it hit us, a powerful force of wind that filled my ears and made me deaf to anything else. Raolcan pushed into it snout first, angling deeper into the mountains to keep from being blown aside.

I'll try further up.

We flew upward, my breath growing more labored as we climbed. I was seeing spots.

Not good. You can't breathe here.

We plunged down again, jostled and jolted by invisible forces until Raolcan had us almost level with the peaks of the mountains. He dipped around their shoulders, moving closer to the ground. I looked behind me to make sure Savette was still following.

Nothing.

Where was she?

I scanned the sky behind and above us.

Was that her and Eeamdor tumbling toward that blunt-headed peak? Raolcan?

I see them. I'm twisting to follow, but this wind is unnatural. It's not like anything I've ever felt before. It must have knocked them off course.

I lost sight of them as they fell to the feet of the mountain. It rose like a tombstone, tall, flat and blunt, from the surrounding landscape. At least I wouldn't lose track of where we lost them.

Hold on tight. It's getting worse.

Chapter Twelve

It was at least another hour before we found them at the base of the mountain. Even on the ground, the wind was too powerful to hear words. Savette crouched under her dragon, the two of them tucked up against the mountainous cliff, trying to avoid the worst of the wind. I fought my pack open and pulled out my last blanket. Savette's dress wasn't warm enough for this wind.

Dismounting awkwardly, I stumbled to where she was and offered her the blanket. She mouthed a "thank you" but her words were lost in the wind.

She feels a great evil – like the Ifrit. She thinks the wind comes from it. I know there are other healing arches. Not all of them are on maps or even known to dragons. Perhaps the Dusk Covenant raises more Ifrits somewhere close.

This felt even worse. To cause winds so strong, what sort of ominous magic could they be creating? Was this what it was like when they made Starie into whatever she was now?

Maybe. I noticed an anomaly when we were landing here.

An anomaly?

Part of this mountain looks like it was carved out by the hands of man. If we investigate, there might be shelter there.

I motioned the Dragon Rider sign to follow to Savette and then stumbled forward, but the wind was too strong for me. I stumbled, falling hard on the rock and cutting my hand. I pulled myself up, only to lose my balance again.

You'll have to ride.

I climbed back on and clung to Raolcan as he struggled forward against the wind. Behind us, Savette and Eeamdor did the same. She shouldn't be

258

alone against an enemy who could affect the weather. Couldn't she understand that?

Look!

He was right. A crevice between two rising mountainous cliffs was in the rock we approached. It was clearly carved by humans. A large pillar it stood just outside the crevice, its shaft carved with swirling dragons. I'd never seen a pillar just left somewhere with nothing to support.

There are grips on one side. You could climb it and stand on there to look out over the horizon.

Or you could fly to the top of one of the mountains.

Not everyone has a handy all-purpose dragon, you know.

Point taken.

Behind the pillar was a crevice. It had seemed small from our angle until we drew closer. It was tucked between the rising mountains in such a way that you had to follow the curve of the land and really get in close to realize that there was more than enough room for a dragon to enter it.

We pushed against the wind – it was particularly powerful rolling over the mountain and through the narrow canyon between the mountains - and entered the crevice. Once we were inside, we immediately saw the door. It was along the mountain side of the crevice, a wide, yawning black hole, but with a carved-stone frame and steps leading into it. It was still wide enough for a dragon, so I stayed on Raolcan's back as we slipped inside.

The silence within was almost deafening.

There's no wind here.

My ears echoed with the sound as my eyes adjusted to the dimmer light. It wasn't dark like a cave. Long slits had been cut in the rock high above and through them, light filtered in to keep this outer room bright. A gust of flame lit up my vision and I flinched into Raolcan in surprise. A moment later the figure registered – Kyrowat!

I slid off Raolcan, but his warning was lightning fast.

Stay back. He's hurt and angry. Go further inside while I tend to him.

Inside? I looked around. Oh. Up a set of steps on a wide platform was another door – this one, human-sized. I hobbled forward, flicking my crutch into a weapon. What had hurt Kyrowat? Was there danger behind that door?

Behind me, I heard Savette and Eeamdor enter the room, a second puff of flame told me that Kyrowat wasn't excited to see yet another dragon.

You'd be irritated, too, if you were full of arrows.

Arrows? Where was Hubric? It wasn't like him to leave his hurt dragon's side.

Nausea filled me as I entered the inner room. I saw a dark footprint smeared across the stone and quickened my pace. This room was also carved from rock. There were tables, benches, shelves, water barrels and a wide stone fireplace all hewn from the rock and in front of the water barrels a bundle of rags had been left.

No. Wait. Those weren't rags. I rushed forward, dropping to my knees beside Hubric's fallen form. His eyes were closed, his teeth gritted, and in his hand, he held a metal ladle. He must have been trying to get water. Sweat poured from his face, mixing with the blood pooling beneath him. How long had he been here?

Since this morning. They made it almost as far as Leedris Castel, but war is upon us. They were shot out of the sky and managed to flee back to here.

Where was he hit? I pulled back his cloak, examining his leathers.

He groaned. "Knew you'd come. More on the way."

I was so relieved to hear his voice that I didn't know whether to laugh or cry. I settled for a muffled sob of relief.

Chapter Thirteen

"Hubric! Where are you hurt?" I drew back, looking him over. The pool of blood was sticky and crusted on the edges. Was he still bleeding?

"Caught my ribs. Can't get back up." He moaned.

"Savette!" I called, positioning myself to help him stand.

Savette's hurried footsteps echoed on the stone floor and then she was beside me helping me stand Hubric up. His head lolled against her shoulder as we half-helped, half-dragged him toward one of the benches.

"I saw a glimpse of beds behind that door," Savette said, nodding with her head to one of many doors that stood ajar around the room.

How could one old man be so heavy? We were already stumbling under his weight and I could barely manage to do my part while leaning heavily on the crutch. Carrying him the dozen steps to the door dragged for what felt like an hour. Savette was right. There were four beds in the dark room with a drain on one side of the rock floor and a rain catchment on the other. A trickle of water fed a large stone basin. At least we didn't need to worry about water.

"This place could withstand a siege," Savette said as we stumbled to the closest bed. "I found a storeroom off the outer sanctuary where the dragons are. It's stocked with wine and dried foods in barrels. There are clothes and blankets. Bandages and herbs."

I noticed she'd helped herself to a fur-lined red cloak. It looked a lot warmer than the wispy white dress beneath it. Would there be anything to help Hubric? Could he be helped?

Kyrowat can be, but he needs all my energy now. Eeamdor guards the entrance.

It was the best we had but I was still sweating with worry and fear as we laid Hubric on the nearest bed. Neither Savette or I were doctors.

"Here," Savette said, unlacing Hubric's leathers and stripping him to the waist. He moaned, but his eyes were shut in pain and he didn't speak. She pointed to a mass of bruises on his side. "Broken ribs."

Even I could see that. Worse, at the center of them was an angry wound, crusted, but oozing.

"Is there still some of the arrow in his wound?"

Savette's hands moved deftly around his back and her face went pale. "I think I feel something."

"Hubric?" I asked. "Do you know if the arrow is still in your back?"

There was no answer. I checked him carefully, but he was still breathing.

"He passed out," Savette said. "He probably feels safe enough now that he knows we're here for Kyrowat."

That made sense. "We should turn him over and look at the wound."

Savette nodded and gently, ever so gently, we turned him in his cot and looked at his back. The entry wound was obvious, but the arrow head had been broken off. I could just see splinters of the shaft peeking up through the wound. Sweat broke out on my forehead as I thought about digging that out. I gritted my teeth together.

"Maybe it can wait," Savette said. "Maybe we can find someone to help him. Leedris Castel is only a day away."

"Can you just heal him with magic?" I asked.

"You know I can't. I could just as easily kill him. Maybe if we were in healing arches..."

But we weren't, and the nearest arches probably had something bad happening there. I was certain the winds we felt were not from an act of good.

"So, we either dig it out or try to go for help, but that wind pushed us off course. I don't think you could fly against it all the way to Leedris Castel," I said.

"I don't think I could, either," Savette said, biting her lip.

"I'll go look for supplies."

What did you use to extract an arrowhead from someone's back? A knife, obviously. I had a vague feeling that there should be hot water and bandages and a salve of some kind. Maybe a sewing kit.

There was another store room off the main hall that had everything I needed. Like the other rooms, it was lit by holes in the rock far above and the supplies were laid out on long, fully-loaded shelves. Someone had created this place to endure through storms or even siege, like Savette said. I didn't have time to explore the rest of the room, so I gathered up what I had and returned to Hubric's side. Savette had lit a fire in a small grate nearby. There was wood in a stone box not far away.

She was already filling a kettle with water from the stone basin. "I can't believe how well this place is set up. Its like it's made to be a shelter. I wonder who it belongs to."

"It must be another Lightbringer refuge," I said. "I'm pretty certain it was the one Hubric told me to come to after Leng was saved."

"That makes sense," Savette said, putting the kettle on the pothook while I laid out the materials I'd found.

I washed my hands with water from the stone basin and then tried to feel for the stub of arrow in Hubric's back. Ugh. It felt terrible! I tried to grip it with my fingers, but I couldn't get a strong enough grip on it with all the blood making it so slick. He was still trickling blood all over the white sheets and woolen blanket beneath him. Good thing there were more in the store-house. Now, where were the pliers I'd grabbed from the supply room?

Savette rushed over with a smaller basin full of water and I cleaned the pliers in the bowl, wiping them carefully afterward with a cloth.

"This had better work," I muttered, easing them around the arrow, trying to just grab arrow and not flesh. I gripped the pliers hard and steeled myself to do what I needed to, gritting my teeth and ignoring the trickle of sweat running down my spine.

I pulled as hard as I could and Hubric half-moaned, half-yelled in pain. The first pull wasn't enough. I felt the arrowhead give, but It was stuck on something. Bone? I hoped not.

There are people here. This is a problem. I need a human here right away.

I looked up at Savette, but her mouth had already dropped open. Raolcan must have called to her, too. She leapt to her feet and raced from the room as I turned my attention back to the arrow stuck in my mentor's back.

Chapter Fourteen

I gripped as hard as I could with one hand, bracing my hip against Hubric's prone form as I worked at the arrowhead. I tried not to think about the fact that it was buried in bone and not wood, twisting and pulling just like I would to get an arrowhead out of a stump. It pulled free so suddenly that I heard a tearing sound as it ripped back through the flesh and out of Hubric's body.

I felt like I was going to be sick, but I fought the impulse to take a moment and gather my thoughts. There just wasn't time. I jammed a cloth into the wound, hoping I hadn't hit anything important when I dug it out of his rib. How did people recover from these things? How did they survive when their bodies were torn apart? It was almost miraculous that a person could suffer so much destruction and in a few years look like nothing had ever happened.

I cast the arrowhead and pliers to the side and took out the sewing kit, carefully threading the needle with red fingers. When that was ready, I dipped a cloth into the basin and tried my best to clean Hubric's wound before removing the cloth and beginning to stitch the skin closed. It was like stitching leather slippers, the tug and pull felt familiar and memories of sewing slippers by the fire of my own home came back as I made careful, tidy stitches, not too tight so that they pulled and puckered or too loose where they didn't hold together.

Hubric must have passed out from the pain. He wasn't moaning or yelling anymore, and although his breathing was ragged, it was steady and sure. When I was finished, the kettle was boiling. Maybe we should have waited to clean everything with hot water. Was that what you did in these situations?

My hands shook as I poured hot water into the basin and mixed it with more cold water before washing his back again, and then carefully bandaging it. Outside the room, voices drifted toward me, but I couldn't hear the exact words.

You're needed.

I hastily took a sheet and blanket from one of the other beds and laid it over Hubric, before rushing out of the room. Hopefully, he wouldn't wake while I was gone. The Great Hall looked different now that I wasn't focused on Hubric. It had a huge fireplace and high vaulted ceilings and seating for a hundred people. How many Lightbringers did they expect to come and seek shelter here? We'd need to investigate all the rooms very soon, so we could know if there were other ways in.

I hurried through the Great Hall into the anteroom where the dragons were. In the doorway, I stopped in my tracks. Savette stood right in front of me on the platform, hands raised in a placating motion. In front of the platform, a group of people stood with wary looks in their eyes. The ones in the front – burly men, some grizzled with age, others as young as I was – brandished weapons. Behind them were women and children. I heard one toddler crying. What were so many people doing traveling like this – with no horses that I could see and little in the way of luggage?

"Take off that blindfold if you want us to believe you're a Leedris," one of the men said to Savette. His face was grim, like he expected to strike her down.

"The Leedrises are the ones who put us in this mess in the first place," another man said. "If she is who she says she is, we'd do better without her."

"No," I said, quietly, and yet my voice rang in the enclosed room. I hobbled forward, watching as all eyes went to my crutch. Were they assessing it for whether it was a weapon? "Savette Leedris is the Chosen One of legend, and she is under my protection – mine and these dragons.'"

Always one for drama, Raolcan reared up so that his head scraped the ceiling, even though he hadn't fully straightened. He hissed, showing his teeth.

One for drama? That's unfair!

"Who are you people?" No one spoke. The men shifted in place like they were assessing whether they could kill a dragon. How desperate were these people? I pointed to a middle-aged woman toward the back of the crowd. "Speak up. What are you doing here with no horses and no baggage?"

"We're refugees fleeing the war, Dragon Rider."

Chapter Fifteen

"What war?"

They looked around at one another as if someone else might decide to speak. Finally, the middle-aged woman spoke again.

"Leedris City is under attack by the armies of Baojang. They swept down from the north and have laid waste to everything in their path. We're all that remains of our village. We fled before them like game birds before a dog."

There were barely fifty of them. I felt my heart sink and my belly roil inside me. So, it had started. The Dominion was in the grip of war, and if enemies had swept so far south already, we were in worse trouble than I ever would have imagined. I swallowed a gasp of fear before it started. Now was a poor time to choose to mourn or shake with fright. There was too much to do.

"Why did you come here?" I asked. Was this place so well known that we could expect to see droves of people arriving?

"Handas – an old man from our village – knew about this place," she said. "He helped construct it when he was a younger man. He was leading us to it when he died on the path."

"You were attacked?"

She shook her head. "His heart gave out. He had that symbol on his wrist."

She pointed to the wall and my eyes followed. The Lightbringer symbol was chiseled into the rock. I hadn't noticed it on the way in. So, this Handas was a Lightbringer and he'd led his people here.

I nodded in understanding. "If we're going to share the sanctuary of this place you'll need to stop blaming Savette for your problems. This war is not her fault."

"How do you know she's the Chosen One?" the man at the front asked. He and the others hadn't relaxed their stance. They still saw Savette and me as threats and only were listening to me because I wore Dragon Rider leathers.

"Show them your eyes," I said quietly.

Reluctantly, Savette drew the scarf down. The room flooded with light until tiny carvings on the walls and inscriptions sprang to life in the dim anteroom and I saw now how dirty and tired the people in front of me were. It was ridiculous for them to be squaring off with us when they needed rest and food.

"Have you seen enough?" I asked. "We want to help you. Savette can do that best right now. Please don't try to harm her. I have my own wounded to care for."

When their stances relaxed, I nodded to Savette and turned to leave.

Kyrowat is anxious about Hubric. He says he's feverish.

Hopefully, I'd find something for fever in the storeroom. Was Kyrowat as injured as Hubric?

Worse, but dragons heal more quickly than humans do. He's already burning infection away. With care, he will shake he worst of it by tomorrow morning. Fight for Hubric and I will continue to attend to him.

And Eeamdor? He'd clearly had the self-control to let the refugees pass.

I told him to watch but stay hidden.

Probably for the best. I'd go out and watch myself once I had Hubric's injuries under control. I was halfway out of the room when I heard Savette speaking.

"Come with me and I will show you where food and water are. Bring your little ones."

I shook off the worry of leaving her with so many armed men. Raolcan would warn us if there was a problem.

They are afraid and that makes them dangerous, but I think they are calming down. I'll keep half a mind on them. Hurry back to Hubric.

I hobbled back through the Great Hall and back to where I'd left Hubric. The supplies I'd left on the side of his bed had been knocked to the floor and his blankets tangled around his legs. He moaned, mumbling to himself, but his words were impossible to understand. I leaned over him, feeling his forehead. He was burning up with fever. If only one of the refugees had been a White Dragon Rider. Then I would have the help I needed.

I found one of the cloths, wet it from the large stone basin and put it over his forehead before turning to tidy the things he'd scattered on the floor. We might need them all again, and sooner rather than later. I washed out the cloths over the drain, using the hot water from the kettle and then hung them by the fire. Hubric's leather jacket and linen shirt and leather Dragon Rider boots and leggings received the same treatment and then I tucked his sheet back around him and changed the cloth on his forehead. He'd tangled the sheet again before I was finished. If he didn't stop moving he'd pull his stitches apart.

"Shhhh," I said, leaning over him. "Easy now, Hubric. You need your rest."

He thrashed against the blankets, blood oozing through his bandages.

"You need to rest, Hubric. You are safe here and so is Kyrowat. Rest." I laid a hand on his arm, trying to help him feel calm, but he didn't still.

What could I do to calm him? My voice wasn't helping, and Kyrowat was fighting his own fever. Was there some smell or sound that might be something he was in contact with every day?

Wait! I pulled the book of Ibrenicus Prophecies from my pocket and began to read. I watched as his thrashing stopped and he calmed. I paused for a moment to readjust his sheet, but even that tiny pause agitated him, so instead, I sat on the edge of his bed and read steadily, letting the words wash over both of us like cool rain in the heat of summer.

Hubric grew calm, his breathing regular and the blood on his bandage stopped it's constant leaking. Good. This was good. I'd just have to keep it up as long as I could. I could hear noise in the next room as Savette helped the refugees. Her calm voice carried over the anxious voices she spoke to. In my mind, I felt Raolcan, ever-present, ever-watching. He would keep us safe while I kept Hubric calm. I read on, trying not to worry about Leng delivering prisoners to Saldrin or what we were going to do once Hubric recovered. I needed to concentrate on this moment and on getting him better.

"For the Light will suffer when the dark grows strong. Many little ones will be lost and the strong oaks will bend and snap but the strong will stay firm to the end and shine light into the dark so that no one goes without hope. When the light is gone, hope dies with it and when the last memory of our foundations washes away, we will have nothing left but our word and truth. Hold fast to the truth, even when it may seem more ridiculous than the lie. Let your word be strong as the mountains, for our word and the truth is all we have, and it will keep us anchored to the end."

Had it kept Talsan anchored until he gave his life for me? Would it keep Leng anchored as he fought for the same purpose so far from here? Would it keep Rakturan anchored even when the evidence suggested that his heart was divided? Would it keep Savette anchored even though she was so bent on going her own way?

I bit my lip and read on. Savette came in when I was close to the end and brought me soup, but I let it grow cold as I read to the end and began again at the beginning.

Any time I stopped, Hubric stirred and I didn't dare let him grow wild. Savette changed his clothes and murmured that the refugees were settled and she had checked on the dragons. Still, I read.

The light faded from the room, except for the fire Savette had stoked and a candle she placed on a small bench near to where I sat. I read as she eventually took one of the three remaining beds in the room and fell asleep.

I read as the night rolled on and on in a seemingly endless stream of prophecy and darkness. And my fears and hopes and plans and aches seemed to roll up into the prophecy and find a new significance until I could hardly tell where one ended and the other began but both were sealed into my heart and seared across my imagination.

Chapter Sixteen

Y*ou're needed here.*

My eyes popped open at Raolcan's words. I must have drifted off. Hubric slept fitfully beside me. His hair caked with dried sweat and his face drawn and yellow. That wasn't a turn for the better. I needed to check his wound.

It will need to wait. You're needed here now.

I shook my head to clear it, took in a deep breath and fumbled for my crutch. How long had I been asleep?

Maybe half of an hour. No longer than that.

I tucked the Ibrenicus Prophecies back into my pocket and hobbled out of the room. The Great Hall was lit with a fire in the grate and one of the villagers was tending it. He nodded to me respectfully as I passed. They must have come to terms with Savette and me being here. Strange to think of a village man showing me respect when months ago I would have been ignored by someone like him. Back then I was a drain on the town – a cripple unable to work the fields or bear children. Raolcan had saved me from that when he chose me. I wouldn't have this life without him.

While I appreciate gratitude and praise, I really do need you to hurry.

I rushed through the door in the anteroom to find him standing shoulder to shoulder with Eeamdor, four purple dragons on the other side of the room from them, necks extended like they were challenging my dragons.

Eeamdor is not your dragon and neither is Kyrowat. That privilege is reserved for me.

Fine. They were challenging my dragon allies. Was that better? In front of them, stood four Dragon Riders all in black, their purple scarves and the random ornamented braids in their hair proclaiming them to be full Purple Dragon Riders. I'd never seen so many Purples in one place before.

Greet them, quickly, before they decide to flame!

Was he saying that the Prince of Dragons couldn't keep other dragons in line?

Of course not, but do you want me to have to show them who's boss?

I cleared my throat and eight heads swiveled to me.

"I'm Amel Leafbrought. Sworn of the Purple Dragon Riders." Was I supposed to give some sort of formal greeting? This would have to do, since I'd missed most of my training along the way.

"That's Kyrowat, Hubric Duneshifter's dragon," the woman in the middle said, her tone accusing and her finger pointing to where Kyrowat lay, still feverish. "Where is Hubric?"

"Hubric lies within, recovering from an arrow wound," I said. "Kyrowat is also recovering."

Her shoulders lowered in relief. Had she thought Hubric was dead?

They didn't believe me that Kyrowat's fever was from being shot. They feared I was hiding his rider's death.

"I'm Ashana Willowspring," the woman said. She was young-looking, though the fine lines around her eyes and mouth and the tiny silver threads in her hair told a different story. "Top Rider of the Purples. Where is your master, Sworn?"

"I'll take you to him," I said, keeping my voice calm. She wasn't giving anything away. Not fear or worry or happiness at Hubric's being alive. Without being able to tell what she was thinking it was hard to know how to react.

She's guarded. They've been through a lot. Seen too much. They fled to this place just like the villagers.

If they were all fleeing here, the war could not be too far behind them.

We will be able to defend this place.

But for how long?

Long enough.

I hoped he was right as I led the Top Rider to Hubric's bedside, but her calm, cool presence only made me more anxious. If a capable woman like this could be shaken by the coming war, it must be even worse than I imagined.

Chapter Seventeen

"The wound is clean, but infection set in before it was stitched. You're the one who stitched him, not the blind girl?" Ashana Willowspring asked as she examined Hubric. Two of the other Purples had followed us into the room to the terrified horror of the villager tending the fire outside in the Great Hall.

"Savette is not blind," I said, leaning over her to watch what she was doing. Was she suggesting that my stitching was so bad that it looked like someone blind had done it? "She is the Chosen One."

"Ridiculous. Say something like that again and I'll see you are never raised to our color. You can be Sworn for the rest of your life."

Like I cared about that. I shuffled nervously. What was she doing to Hubric's wound? She unwrapped his bandages and hissed at the angry red skin beneath.

"Danver," Ashana Willowspring gestured to one of the other Purples. He was slight and blond, with a small short beard. "Go check the storeroom for healing herbs. There must be something to cleanse a wound. You did well to pull the arrow out and stitch him." She glanced up at me. "But you did a lot of damage digging it out. I can see the marks. And you didn't clean it well enough. You're going to have to work on your ability to field dress wounds. This is completely unacceptable. How long have you been with Dragon School?"

"About a month." My relief that there was someone here who could help Hubric took the sting out of her obvious disdain for me.

She cursed. "Last wave before Dantriet disbanded the school and sent you all off in different directions?"

"Yes," I said.

"Get the kettle boiling. We have a lot to tend to here. Aliss." She turned to the other Purple – a willow-thin woman with red scars on her face and hands. "Survey our situation here and set up a watch with Rawlins, then report."

Aliss nodded and left as I scrambled to fill a kettle and place it back on the pot hook. The fire had burnt down and needed to be revived, so I set about it as Ashana continued to sort us out. Savette rose and carefully made her bed as we spoke. She had the air of someone who was being very quiet to avoid notice.

"Come here, girl," Ashana said to her. "Show me your eyes." Savette hesitated, so Ashana made an impatient noise and pulled Savette's scarf down herself. "Don't be shy."

Light flooded the room and Ashana took a step backward. Could I help the smug feeling at seeing her surprised look? It was hard enough not to laugh out loud. Savette sniffed loudly and pulled the scarf back up.

"I have work to do," she said and walked right past where Ashana stood frozen beside Hubric's bed. Her eyes were narrowed as if she were thinking very hard.

She looked to me. "Chosen One? Who said that first? Her or you?"

"Hubric did," I said, firmly. It was time for Ashana Willowspring to take us seriously. We weren't a couple of kids playing a game.

She nodded thoughtfully as Danver returned with herbs. "Thank you, Danver. These will do. Get some rest. We'll take turns."

He nodded and strode out of the room. Wherever he was resting it wouldn't be here.

Probably with us. Their dragons are twitchy and unsettled. Their journey was perilous. Rasipaer only needs rest, but Daieseo, Iasafae, and Drarjes are in shock. They need time.

What kind of horror could put a dragon in shock?

As much as it pains me to admit it, we are not the Almighty.

"Stop daydreaming girl, and bring that hot water here." Was Ashana always like this, or only after a trauma?

I scrambled up, crutch at my side and hobbled the kettle over to where she'd arranged the herbs in a small basin.

"We'll make a poultice with these herbs and hope there is time to draw the infection out of him. Now, tell me why Hubric thinks this girl is the Chosen One. Who is she?"

"She is Savette Leedris, a Red initiate. That's her dragon outside with Raolcan and Kyrowat. Hubric and I have seen her fulfill some of the Ibrenicus Prophecies."

"Hubric is a Lightbringer," Ashana said.

"You aren't?"

"Not all of us can give our lives to faith."

I felt the same way a few weeks ago. But did I feel like that now? A time was coming when we were going to need Savette and without the Lightbringers, she would be dead already. Without faith, we wouldn't have known to look for her. Without truth, people might choose to follow Starie instead and that would be a disaster. I was starting to think that these prophecies were the key to all of us surviving what was coming.

"I'm not sure that I agree."

"Well, then you're definitely Hubric's apprentice. Tell me about how he was injured and where you were last."

"I don't know how he was injured. We flew out of Dominion City three or four days ago with messages for the Dominar and those with him-"

"Three or four?"

"A lot has happened, and I was knocked on the head. It's hard to be specific."

She waved impatiently for me to continue.

"We were attacked by Ifrits along the Great Drake River, but in the aftermath, a man we saved stole Hubric's messages. We went after him - he took a boat heading to the ocean - and found Cynos Vineplanter along the way with twenty Reds. They agreed to help us recover the messages and help save a group of Purples we had heard were being held captive at the Feet of the River. Before we rescued the captives, Cynos sent Hubric with a message to the Dominar that Casaban had fallen and that we were invaded by Baojang and the Rock Eaters. Hubric left reluctantly and we attacked."

"He left without you?"

"Cynos was insistent that he would need every dragon available."

She nodded. "Continue."

"Cynos and his men perished along with the Purples we came to rescue, except for Leng Shardson. A group of free dragons helped us, and they have gone with Leng to deliver our captives to a nearby city while Savette and I came northwest with the messages."

Ashana Willowspring's eyebrows had risen steadily upward as I spoke and she cleared her throat, cutting me off when Aliss entered the room.

"There are supplies enough to keep the refugees already here for a month or more, but there is only one entrance," she said. "It could be held against a great force – even with as small a defense as what we have now – but not indefinitely. I'd say we could hold it for maybe a week. It's not a long-term solution."

Ashana nodded. "We need at least a day to rest the dragons. It will take longer than that if we try to save these refugees." What other option was there? Would she leave them to die? I felt sick at the thought. "The wave was at least a day behind us. We should have that long to rest."

It sounded like she was talking herself into something.

"It grows faster," Aliss objected. "We don't really know if we have a full day. Look how quickly it took Saldrin."

"Saldrin?" I asked. I had a sudden image in my mind of waving goodbye to Leng.

"Our enemies are like a black wave flowing over the land," Aliss said. Her expression was strained. "It washed over Saldrin two days ago and over Leedris City yesterday. It is on its way here."

I felt like someone had knocked the breath out of me.

"Why does Saldrin matter so much to you?" Ashana asked.

"Leng and the free dragons who helped us are taking the prisoners we captured to Saldrin."

Her expression became as grim as mine did. "Help me dress Hubric's wounds with that poultice, girl. It will be ready now. Don't go yet, Aliss. There will be time to rest, but before then, we'll induct this girl into the Purple. She's earned it, and if we get out of this alive we'll need her."

They were going to raise me to a Color? I was so surprised that I stopped stirring the herbs for a moment.

"Surprised?" Ashana asked me with a smirk. "When you're Top Rider you need to remember the long-term as well as the short-term. Your value to us is as important long-term as organizing our defenses here is for the short-term. So, stop gawking and put that poultice on your mentor's back so we can go to the anteroom together."

Chapter Eighteen

"What made you change your mind about me?" I asked Ashana as she helped me wrap the bandage around Hubric's poultice.

"Your account of events matches your dragon's and Rasipaer keeps telling me that your dragon is important. Raolcan the prince of something or another. Why the dragons sent us a prince is beyond me, but I can see a resource when it's flung in front of my face. We'll induct you to the Color, rest up and when we leave, you'll come with us."

"And the refugees?" I asked. We left Hubric's room together, Aliss leading the way and Ashana right at her heels. Savette looked up at me as we entered the Great Hall. She was serving some sort of food to a group of children. My heart twisted at the sight. I couldn't leave them here unprotected.

"We'll deal with that when the time comes," Ashana said, but I wasn't convinced. She clearly felt pity for them, but not the responsibility to keep them safe. How could someone be dedicated to truth and not see how we owed these little ones our protection?

Not everyone is you, Amel Leafbrought. Ashana Willowspring is a great and efficient leader, but she does not see as clearly as you do.

I felt my face heating. Raolcan shouldn't flatter me like that.

It's not flattery if it's true. I'm always telling you that.

We entered the anteroom. Raolcan nestled against Kyrowat who was fast asleep.

He's doing better, but he needs rest.

On the other side of the room, three of the visiting dragons curled together.

They're friends – used to being together. Eeamdor and Drarjes are outside keeping watch.

Was Eeamdor up to that?

Reds don't sit still if there's the smell of battle in the air – like there is right now.

At least Raolcan would be here for whatever they were going to do to raise me to their Color.

As if she had read my mind, Ashana spoke. "Usually there's a lot of pomp and formality to this. At least a dozen purples will stand and give testimony to who you are and why they think you're ready to be raised to a Color. Usually, there would be three days of trials and tests. We don't have time for any of that. Or for feasting or celebration. We'll do this quick and dirty because we need every competent recruit we can muster. If Hubric can get you this far in a few weeks, perhaps he can make a full Dragon Rider out of you by the end of the year and take on a new apprentice. We will need that. If we live to see the year out. So, all we'll do today is the last test – and only the most important part. To do that, three of our purple dragons will listen to your mind. This is a great sacrifice for them – both because they are tired right now and because Purples are reluctant to enter minds other than those they choose. It's more personal than they like and puts obligations on them that they do not appreciate. Do you understand?"

I turned to the dragons, who were regarding me with what felt like resentful yellow stares. "Thank you for this great honor."

One of them coughed, staining the wall black. I knew dragons well enough by now to know that was no accident. If he thought that would worry me, he hadn't been through what I had over the last few days.

"Traditionally, you fall backward off the cliffs of Dragon School and let your dragon catch you while other Purples listen to your mind. They will determine if you are fit to serve your color."

"There aren't any nearby cliffs here." I had butterflies in my belly at the idea of falling backward off a cliff, but I could trust Raolcan. I'd done things a lot more dangerous with him since we met.

I'm not allowed to talk to you about the ceremony or speak to you about it until afterward.

Typical. If only Hubric were here to watch. He would want to see this.

I can ask that Kyrowat be one of the ones who helps with your testing.
I'd like that.

"We'll use that pillar. Can you climb it without both legs?"

I remembered the stone ladder carved into the side of the pillar. Yes, I could climb that. I nodded.

"Then you climb it now – leave your winter cloak here, it's too bulky – and then you stand, facing out over the horizon and answer any questions the dragons have. When they are done, you fall backward and let your dragon catch you. You must be silent through the whole ritual. Simple enough?"

That was it? It almost sounded too simple.

Ashana's smile was predatory. "I've seen that look on a Sworn face a few times. Trust me when I tell you – simple is not the same as easy. Get going."

I gave her my cloak, took a deep breath, and left the anteroom through the crack in the stone wall. It was about time that I was considered a proper Purple, war or no war. It would get me that much closer to a free life with Raolcan. Who wouldn't want that?

Chapter Nineteen

Outside the anteroom, the wind had died down since yesterday, but green leaves were littered across the forest floor – evidence of the wind that had ripped through the trees. Rawlins nodded to me as I passed him. His eyes scanned the horizon constantly from his perch on the nearby rocks. I looked around me at the towering mountains on either side and the forest floor running down from where I was and spreading out into the valley below. From here, I could see the sea below and a black blip rising into the sky north of here. Leedris City? I'd ask Raolcan, but I knew he was supposed to be silent right now. Eeamdor sat on a peak up the side of one of the mountains, his red form obvious against the rock. I was glad he was watching out for us.

It was only a few steps from the door to the pillar and I took deep breaths to keep calm as I crossed them. I placed my crutch at the base of the pillar, gripped the ladder with determination, and began to climb. Ladders were almost as common as dragons in my new life as a student of Dragon School. So was falling from heights. I climbed carefully, but quickly. After all, Hubric needed me to return and care for him and the dragons needed to get their rest.

When I reached the top, I pulled myself into an awkward sitting position on the pillar. There was room all around me – enough that I could stand without any real worry of falling off, but not much more than that.

Stand and spread your arms out on either side.

That wasn't a dragon voice I recognized.

I am Rasipaer. Are you worthy to ride a dragon of the Purple?

I thought I was. Well, not worthy exactly, but I really wanted to keep doing it. Raolcan wanted me to be his rider, too. Didn't that count for something?

Brace yourself.

The torrent of thoughts that ripped through me left me gasping. I hadn't caught any of them, but I felt like I'd been pulled through a sieve, weighed and measured. Any secrets I'd had before were his now. Any sense of who I was had been inspected minutely. I felt very small.

I looked across the horizon before me. That didn't help. The vastness of the Dominion was more than I'd ever expected. Inside its borders, I was nothing but a small human who'd been given the chance to ride a dragon. There was nothing particularly spectacular about me. I let my eyes rove across the landscape beyond. What would happen to me if I failed this test?

Fail and you become a servant. Usually.

That was Kyrowat. I recognized his mental voice. He didn't like talking to humans.

Who does?

What was I seeing coming from Leedris City? Was that a pillar of smoke rising into the sky? And what was the dark shadow that crept across the ground toward us?

All of us have something at our core, Rasipaer's voice said in my mind as I tried to concentrate on the shadow. *"We are ambition or mercy or understanding or something else. What are you?*

What did it matter what I was when that shadow was creeping forward? Fear gripped my heart. Was that the "wave" that Ashana and Aliss had seen on its way?

What are you? he repeated.

What was I? When it came right down to it, I was a friend. A friend to Raolcan and to Savette and to Hubric and to whoever else needed me. Now, could we focus on something more urgent? Like what that shadow was and why it was creeping forward. How close was the edge?

I followed it over the landscape with my gaze, looking for the forward edge. It was hard to distinguish the exact point along the land that the shadow melded into the normal landscape. Close to us – probably closer than that shadow, I noticed something gleaming in the woods. I squinted my eyes.

It was close to the treeline. Close to where I stood on the pillar. What was that? I kept losing track through the canopy of trees. Wait. It was more than one thing...

Are you dedicated to truth above your own comfort and ambitions?

Obviously. If I wanted comfort or ambitions I'd be following Starie around letting everyone tell us how great we were instead of holed up in a cave with Savette, Hubric, and Raolcan.

Are you ready to pledge yourself to keeping your word, upholding truth and being loyal to your dragon in all things?

This time he didn't wait for an answer. He blasted me with his truth-sieve thing again, but this time I could feel three distinct minds combing through mine, Rasipaer, Kyrowat and one other.

Daieseo. Dragon to Aliss Landris, the fresh voice said.

What they did this time took far longer than last time and I fought to find that thing sparkling in the trees as they fought to sift through every random thought and impulse of my being. There. In the trees. It was hard to concentrate, but I'd found it. What was that? Oh! A glistening silver-skinned dragon.

Wait. What? Kyrowat was listening as he sieved.

A glistening silver-skinned dragon, crawling across the forest floor with another beside him. They carried something between them – some dark shape and there was something wrong with their wings. Were they broken? Around them, men with swords and armor stumbled. I'd seen them before. They looked exactly like the dragoons that surrounded the Dominar.

Enough. Now she swears the oath and we finish, Kyrowat's voice rang in my mind.

You aren't- Rasipaer's was cut off by a sharp thought from Kyrowat so fast and blade-like that I couldn't catch it with my mind.

Amel, swear that you will serve truth and Raolcan, for the honor of the Purple.

By my word and the truth which is all I have, I swear.

Was that...? It was! An Ifrit rose from the ground behind the silver dragons, harrying them as they fled towards us.

Fall backward and finish this.

Didn't he see how important that was? Those dragons and those warriors meant only one thing –

Fall! Quickly, now!

There was no time to keep looking and no more time for this ritual. Not now. The fastest way down was the way they already wanted me to go. I crossed my arms over my chest, closed my eyes and pitched backward. It was up to Raolcan to save me or I'd crack my head on the rocks below. But he'd never failed me.

The wind whipped around my hair as I tumbled backward but no strong back met mine. No powerful wing flap soared upward with me underneath.

I opened my eyes to see the ground rising to meet me.

Oh no.

Chapter Twenty

A claw snatched my foot seconds before I smashed across the rocks. *Gotcha.*

I couldn't breathe, couldn't think, couldn't speak. My heart raced, and black flecks danced across my vision.

Just breathe. You'll be fine.

Why did he wait so long to catch me?

It's a Purple thing. The longer I let you fall before I catch you, the more honor there is for you. It's considered a great thing if you trust me enough that I don't have to save you until the last minute. I did you a favor.

It hadn't felt like that! It felt like I'd been about to die!

But there was no time to dwell on that. Raolcan had to help me get Savette and save those people in the trees. He was moving before I finished the thought, racing us toward the anteroom. I stumbled off his back, grateful when Ashana shoved my crutch into my hand with a quick "Congratulations."

She was cinching the straps on Rasipaer tighter. On either side, her riders did the same. No one spoke, but it was obvious that this time they had the same priority that I did – the dragons in the trees.

"Savette!" I called. "Savette! You're needed!"

I raced into the hall, still calling her name. She nearly knocked me over as she barreled through the door.

"What is it?" she asked.

"Ifrits," I gasped as we rushed to Raolcan and scrambled onto his back. The last Purple dragon was already leaving the antechamber. No time to strap in properly before Raolcan was through the crack in the wall. I scrambled to tighten my straps as we plunged into the cold air beyond and took to the skies.

The silver dragons were closer, lumbering awkwardly over the ground toward our hideout. They were minutes away, warriors circling them. The warriors were flagging, their steps dragging, their arms slow to raise weapons and their shoulders bent with exhaustion. How long had they run like that?

The Ifrit reached their rear - lifting up one of the warriors and smashing him on the ground – as we gained our height and swooped toward them behind the other Purples. Savette reached out her hands, light filling her. If she lifted off Raolcan as her power filled her, where would that leave her? Hanging in mid-air? I grabbed her waist as she lifted off of Raolcan's back, hastily slinging a strap around her and tightening it.

Light surrounded us all – so bright and overwhelming that I struggled to see outside the brilliance. There was a feeling of shooting forward and then the light left us, bursting through the trees and surrounding the Ifrit. He crumbled to nothing in the act of wrenching one of the dragoons in half.

The other Purples swept behind the fleeing dragons and warriors and with horror, I realized four more Ifrits had joined the fray. With no more effort than a horse swatting a fly with its tail, one of the Ifrits slapped at Rawlins and Drarjes, shattering them against the ground. One look at the tangled mess of human and dragon was all I needed to know that I'd never get to properly meet the Purple or his dragon. The other Purples flamed energetically against the Ifrits, but Raolcan held back, letting Savette recover her strength and fill us with light again. We spun around, settling over the fleeing party of Silvers and warriors before Savette launched her second attack, evaporating a second Ifrit as it lunged at one of the Silver dragons. It burst into pale mist and was gone.

The other three Purple dragons swung around us, signing desperately about the way the Ifrits seemed invulnerable. Did I know enough sign to explain that their fires were not enough? Raolcan would have to tell them.

I am telling them, but they aren't listening.

Even to their prince?

They are arrogant. They think Haz'Drazen would not have assigned me to your care if I was in her favor. They haven't been south since they were given to humans and that means they don't know the heart of Haz'drazen.

Fools.

Exactly.

One of the last two Ifrits swatted at Aliss and Daieseo. Seconds before he hit them, Eeamdor swooped in from his perch, flaming angrily at the Ifrit and distracting him, drawing him away from the fight to chase after the moving target. Would he be able to outrun the Ifrit?

He's fast, even for a Red. He'll be fine. At least someone still knows how to show respect.

My eyebrows rose in my surprise. Had Raolcan called Eeamdor for help?

Even I know when to rely on allies.

We needed to get these new refugees into the fortress and find a way to hold out against the Ifrits.

There were still two left.

I glanced behind me, grateful to see the first Silver inching through our door, his warrior guards fanned out around him. We needed to get them inside, finish off the last two Ifrits, and then follow them within to safety. Raolcan rose up over the battle to give Savette a better view as she filled again with light. How many more times could she do that?

This one last time, and then she will need to rest.

But there were two Ifrits.

Yes.

I signed desperately to Ashana to bring her dragons in. This was our last shot at finishing off the Ifrits. She ignored me, wheeling to attack again, and this time Danver and Iasafae were too slow. The Ifrit snapped at them, biting dragon and rider in two with his gaping, fiery mouth. I flinched at the sight, horrified by the destruction.

The last Silver figure darted behind the pillar and into the cave and behind him. Eeamdor dove for safety. I signed desperately to Ashana to fall back, but I didn't see her response before Raolcan wheeled around again and Savette let loose her light. I was blinded by the blast, clinging to Raolcan as ripples of power spread out from us across the valley and consumed the last two Ifrits with a burst of power. They fragmented to dust and blew away on the wind. In the after-shadow of the burst of light I scanned the horizon. In every direction I saw Ifrits. The two who died must have been burnt on my vision.

No, they're not," Raolcan said as we followed Ashana who was finally diving for cover within our sanctuary. Aliss was right on her heels and Raolcan dove behind them. *Those are all real. And they come for us.*

We crowded in behind Aliss, fear filling me as we shoved into the crowded anteroom. Ashana pushed through the crowded people to the entrance to the Great Hall and felt up along the doorway until she found what she was looking for. A small stone door swung open beside the larger door, revealing a lever. She pulled it dramatically and looked at me.

No, not at me - behind me. I turned and watched as a stone wall slid across the entrance, blocking us from the world beyond just in time to seal us off from the Ifrits outside the door. We were trapped here with a month's worth of food for the humans and nothing for the Dragons and no other way out.

Ashana fell to her knees and my eyebrows knit together before they fell on the dark litter being carried between the two silver dragons. On it lay a bleeding man, missing one arm. His face was completely concealed by the mask and crown of the Dominar.

Dragon School: Dark Night

Chapter One

B*oom. Boom. Boom.*
I leapt at the sound of pounding on the rock wall behind me – it was more of a massive vibration than a sound. More of the feeling of a small earthquake than fists on a door – though that was what was causing it. Behind me – just behind the rock wall – dozens of Ifrits were pounding. If they found a single crack, they would slide in and rip us to pieces. I bit my lip and told my mind to calm itself, but my heart raced all on its own.

That's right, Raolcan reminded me. *Deep, easy breaths. Don't let it take your clear thought. We will not die here.*

How could he be so certain?

Dragon princes don't die in holes like rats.

Then where did they die? And could we avoid going there?

"Amel," Savette whispered urgently.

I followed her gaze to where everyone else in the room was kneeling and then hurriedly scrambled off of Raolcan to join them.

"Get up," a man beside the litter said. He was burly and encased in a shining metal breastplate and greaves, his dragon helm obscuring his face. "The Dominar – glory to his reign – is not conscious. He was gravely injured in our flight. I am Lieutenant Iskaris of the Dominar's Dragoons and I require your aid."

Fear like ice shot through me, chilling me to the core. This was Iskaris? The man that the Dusk Covenant was sending messages to? We must keep anything important from him.

Be careful with those messages you have. You haven't given them to the Top Rider, have you?

Why would I do that?

You'll have to wait until the Dominar is conscious and give them to him yourself, if you can. Or to Hubric if he comes around first.

I swallowed. It wouldn't be hard to keep them hidden, but the Dominar was missing a limb and his pallet was soaked with blood. Would he survive this?

"Amel Leafbrought," Ashana Willowspring said. "Lead the Dominar's dragoons to the area we set apart for Hubric. We can attend to the injured there, including the Dominar. I'll see to the defense of this entrance, Lieutenant."

"Actually," Iskaris said, overriding her. "I think real warriors should see to the defense. Tredwell, Curnan, see to it."

Two men saluted, moving tiredly toward the door, as if men in armor could do what dragons could not. Ashana stood to one side of the door to the great hall, one hand on her hip and a single eyebrow raised in a way that made me squirm even though it was directed at the Lieutenant.

Anyone who ignores the Top Rider is playing with fire.

Anyone who was dealing with the Dusk Covenant was playing with a lot worse things than fire. The Lieutenant was in league with the demons outside our door, whether anyone else realized that or not. With a grimace, I hobbled forward to lead him within our defenses. It felt wrong – like drinking poison on purpose.

When dragons drink poison, it burns up within us just like disease. It can't survive our fiery bellies.

Handy. Too bad I wasn't a dragon.

Be that fiery belly. Bring him in, then burn him up.

I clenched my jaw, determined to do just that if I saw the opportunity.

"This way," I murmured, gesturing for them to follow me through the door. The Dragoons already had the Dominar's litter unhooked from the Silver dragons and were shuffling forward with it. No one had told us about Silver Dragons in our Dragon School training.

No Silvers are given as Dragon School tribute. They are dedicated to the Dominar as a part of our treaty with Haz. The riders of the Silvers come from the ranks of the Dragoons and are powerful, dignified warriors.

It was surprising that Raolcan wasn't Silver then.

Are you suggesting that Silver is better than Purple?

Never.

Good. I don't need flashy scales to show my majesty. Which is good, because right now these two need help. They suffered grievous injuries as they fled and cannot fly.

"Were you hurt in the battle?" Iskaris asked, eyeing my bad leg as I led him through the Great Hall toward the room we were tending to Hubric in. Iskaris' eyes narrowed when he saw the refugees within and a second stab of ice went through me. I could sense his coldness toward them. Was I the only person here who thought life was important?

Don't be dramatic. There's Savette and Hubric and the Dominar, and I don't think that Ashana is nearly as cold as you have judged her to be. She won't leave them now that Ifrits are banging down the door.

We'd see about that.

"I'm a cripple," I said easily. Of all the threats that Iskaris posed, the threat to my dignity was the smallest. I led them within Hubric's room. "There's a bed here."

I watched as the lieutenant looked around the room and sniffed. "It will do. Clear this other man out of here."

"He's still recovering from an arrow wound and fever," I said, defensively.

"We'll keep this room clear for the Dominar," the lieutenant said. "Only those trusted by me may enter."

His dominant personality and thick muscles made me feel small and insignificant, but someone had to speak for the injured, and I was the only one here to do it.

"Hubric needs rest and a place to recover. So do the Dominar and your wounded men. It will be easier to tend them all in one place."

His glare made me want to take a step back, but I took a deep breath instead and kept my feet where they were.

"Did you tend that man's wounds?" he asked as two of the Dragoons laid the Dominar on the bed Savette had slept in the night before.

I had to swallow to make my mouth wet enough to speak. "Yes."

"Then tend to the Dominar, Dragon Rider. The next time I give an order and you speak back, you can learn what it is to feel my boot on your neck."

SARAH K. L. WILSON

I nodded, fear making my mouth dry again and my palms sweaty, but I'd kept Hubric safe for a while longer and maybe, just maybe, I'd be able to help both my mentor and my ruler recover.

Chapter Two

I was afraid to touch the Dominar. Were there rules about how to touch the ultimate authority of your land?

If I had to guess, I'd say the biggest rule is to keep him from dying.

Nervously, I unwound the cloak that draped his form. It stuck to the drying blood on the pallet underneath him and I had to rip it in places to detangle it. Someone had made the pallet by stretching tent cloth over two poles. When the dragoons set it down they had just laid the entire contraption on the narrow bed.

Behind me, I heard two of the dragoons tending a stab wound in a third man's leg, but I had to concentrate on this. It felt strange that they weren't doing it themselves. After all, did I look like a healer?

They're rattled and Iskaris is warring within. The Ifrits aren't behaving as he expected. He has ordered his men to tend their own wounds while you see to the Dominar. I can't tell if he wants you to fail or succeed in keeping him alive. I'm not sure that he knows either. Personally, I'd like the Dominar to live.

That made two of us. I gently unbuckled the clasps of the thick leather clothing on his torso, examining him for wounds. So far, his arm was the only severe wound. The sight of the blood-soaked bandaged stump where his arm had been made my mouth feel dry. I tried not to look as I checked for any other bleeding. I had to strip him down to his underclothes to look, but the rest of his body was fine – bruised and discolored, but not stabbed or shot with arrows. I replaced what clothing I could, spread a sheet over him, and gingerly lifted his crown to check his head for wounds.

"Don't," a voice said from behind me. Ashana was there, looking furtively around her. "Removing his crown is a death sentence. Look at the pallet. The blood isn't coming from his head."

"It can't be comfortable to lay with your head in a metal mask," I said. I followed her gaze to the dragoons behind her. They were talking in a close huddle as they stitched and bandaged wounds.

"I'll help you with the arm," she said in a tight voice. Her eyes were sharp and careful, but her tension wasn't directed at me.

"I'm sorry about Rawlins and Danver," I said as we unwrapped the bandage around his stump of an arm.

"So am I. We were friends for many years. They both were a great help to me in managing Color affairs and I will miss them every day now that they are gone." Her voice was sad, but firm, like she was both mourning and persevering all at once.

I enjoy her strength. A truly strong mind is rare in humans.

"Feed the fire. Then go to the storeroom and find us a small metal pot and some tar," she said, her voice clipped and tight. She was looking at the wound with a deep furrow in her brow.

I swallowed hard and moved to obey. It was good to have orders to follow.

"And Amel?" she said right before I left.

"Yes?"

"You did well out there. You are one of us now." She pulled one of her scarves off her arm and tossed it to me. "Wear our color with pride."

"Thank you."

The look in her eye made me feel a foot taller. I held the scarf reverently as I turned to leave the room, my face hot with pleasure. She'd given me her own scarf to wear.

It's traditionally given by your mentor. I suppose with Hubric ill it makes sense that she'd give you hers.

The scarf was a damask silk, embroidered with swirls and dragon claws. I tied it around my neck, just under my leather collar, as I walked. There would be more purple scarves, but none so precious as my first. I wanted to keep it where it was easily seen by anyone passing. It was the exact color of Raolcan's scales.

Wear your purple with pride. I certainly do.

I hobbled through the Great Hall, noticing that the refugees had cleared out of the hall, except for one older man who sat near the large fire but also near the door to their sleeping quarters. He was leaning back in a chair as if he were asleep, but his eyes glittered as he followed my movements, so I wasn't fooled. He was watching over his people. In the middle of the Great Hall, Iskaris spread out maps, his healthy warriors – ten of them – arranged around him. I hurried past them to the storeroom, keeping my eyes to myself. It would do me no good to draw more of his attention.

When I reached the storeroom, I closed the door and breathed a sigh of relief. Iskaris was pure trouble. He was a traitor. And we were walled up in here with him. What were we going to do?

"Is that you, Amel?" Savette whispered from the shadows.

"What are you doing in here?" I whispered back.

"I can feel them, Amel. The Ifrits. They are going to find a way in."

Chapter Three

"Soon?" I asked, my whisper strained.

"I don't know, but soon enough. I need a way to find more strength. It was all I could do to hold those few back before they drove us into this place and now their numbers grow by the second."

I swallowed, feeling lightheaded for a moment. Their numbers *grew?*

"Do you think some of these herbs might help you?" I asked, stepping behind some shelves as I scanned for a pot and tar. The pot was easy enough, but where would people put tar, and why had Ashana asked for it in the first place?

"I don't know. I just didn't know what else to do. I don't like the way that Iskaris is looking at me."

I clenched my teeth. That sounded even more ominous. Didn't he realize that she was our only defense if the Ifrits broke in? What we needed was more information. That and a way out.

"Do you think he knows that you know the truth about him?"

"No. I would be able to tell if he did." She shook her head, following me as I searched for tar. It wasn't with the herbs or the kitchen supplies. I moved to the back wall where the stone was rough like they hadn't finished carving out the storeroom. Had they planned to expand it someday? There was a rack of tools along that wall.

"Then how is he looking at you?"

"Like he's worried. I think that somehow... No. That's crazy."

"What's crazy?" I stopped by a rack of hand tools and Savette leaned in close so that her lips were only a hair's width from my ear.

"I think he's working with the Ifrits."

Ice shot through me, lingering afterward in a way that made my skin feel too tight. When she said it like that, it seemed obvious. After all, the Dusk Covenant had some sort of deal with the Ifrits, and Iskaris was definitely Dusk Covenant.

If there was ever a time that we needed more information, it was now. And where could we find information other than those messages I'd been given?

I pulled them out of my waistband and furtively slipped the first message out of my waistband. Savette nodded beside me.

"If there's anything else in there that could help, we need to know. Things have changed. What were you looking for back here?"

"Tar."

"I'll find it while you read. There's something about this storeroom. I keep feeling like I need to be here." She began to search the shelves while I skimmed one message after another. I'd read most of them before, but it felt necessary to re-read them in case there was something I'd missed before. Supply lists. News from Dominion City that seemed to have little importance. The last note I read was the only one that seemed significant.

Comard Eaglespring to the Dominar:

Glory to the Dominar,

I will lead your armies out, heading north at first light to assist in recovering your person and defending the north from threat of engagement. We will take the path of Haz in our advancement and suggest you meet us at the Maiden's Head if possible. I have left the city under the defensive guard of General Honorspur and Grandis Elfar of Dragon School who has brought to us the Chosen One of Legend. Perhaps this will finally placate Haz'drazen. Once again, she sent an emissary protesting our handling of Baojang and making demands regarding our disposition of resources. I remain concerned about the rumors reaching my ears of a traitor among your guard. I must reiterate the need for care in telling friend from foe and must remind you that if you are required to take a darker path you should remember the words of Ibrenicus.

In faith,

Comard Eaglespring

What in the world was that last part about?

"Tar," Savette said, handing me a small pot of tar. I jumped at her words, hurriedly stuffing the note back into my belt.

"Anything interesting?" she asked, but she seemed to already know.

"One thing, but I don't know what it is. I'd better hurry back with the tar. Are you safe here?"

"I don't know." She bit her lip. "I'm not seeing anything that will give me the energy I need."

"Go see Raolcan. Sometimes he has good ideas."

Sometimes? That's harsh.

She nodded and we slipped out of the storeroom, splitting up to head to our goals. As I hurried past the table of dragoons a hand wrenched my elbow, pulling me off balance. I fell, barely catching myself, the pot and tar clattering to the floor.

"I barely even touched you and you drop everything?" an annoyed voice asked.

"I walk with a crutch," I said, pulling myself back to my feet. I'd bruised my good knee. It throbbed under my leather pants.

Iskaris snorted. Of course, it would be him grabbing my arm. What did he want, and would he see in my eyes that I distrusted him? Would he realize why?

I avoided eye contact, using the excuse of recovering the tar and pot.

"What do you have there?" he asked.

"Supplies for the Dominar's wound."

"Did you or your master have any messages when you arrived here?"

I hadn't expected that. What did I say?

It would be unlikely that neither of you had messages.

"Yes," I said, trying to cover the flood of heat to my face by adjusting my load of tar and pot.

"You can deliver them to me," Iskaris said. "It's important that we have all the information available to plan our next move."

If I did that he'd know. I clenched my jaw. How did I tell him know without drawing suspicion?

"I'll check to see if there are any for you after I finish helping with the Dominar's wounds."

Nice.

He shook his head. "Bring all of them right away. It's essential to our planning to have them."

"I ... I... I..."

Maybe you don't remember this, since you didn't listen to me when I told you not to read them, but NO ONE is supposed to read those messages except for the recipient. You can tell him that.

I cleared my throat, but my voice still came out in a croak. "I can't do that."

"You can't?" There was an edge to his voice.

"It's our duty to keep our messages private." I was such a hypocrite.

Better a hypocrite than a traitor.

Wasn't a hypocrite a traitor to themselves?

Just hold the line. I'm sending help.

"It's your duty to help in the defense of the Dominar, glory to his reign. Or have you forgotten who is in that room beyond?"

I swallowed.

"Answer me."

What was I going to say?

"Amel?" Ashana Willowspring stepped out into the Great Hall with her arms over her chest. "What is keeping you? We need that tar hot or risk losing the Dominar's life to infection."

Iskaris straightened, but his whisper rang in my ears as I hurried to follow Ashana. "We're not done, Sworn."

Chapter Four

"Put the tar in the pot on the fire and heat it up," Ashana said briskly when I entered the room. The wounded dragoons were nowhere to be seen, leaving only Ashana, Hubric and the Dominar. They must be finished patching up the more minor wounds. I hurried to obey. "Then come over here and hold him down."

"Isn't he unconscious?" With the pot on the fire, I was free to hobble back to her, checking Hubric on my way past. His forehead was cool and his breathing easy.

"Don't worry about Hubric. I checked him not long ago. The poultice has leeched out his infection and his wound looks much better. He'll recover. Let's make sure the Dominar does, too." Her authoritative directions made me feel safe – like things couldn't really go wrong when she was near.

"What do I do next?"

"We're going to need privacy. Shut the door and lock it."

I hurried to obey. After all, I didn't want anyone else in here, either. I didn't trust Iskaris, and I needed to keep these messages from him.

"We should take off his mask," I said. "I know you said that we can't, but how can we watch his face for signs of pain with it covered up?"

Ashana bit her lip, worrying it between her teeth before looking up and meeting my eyes. "What we do here can never be talked about after this – even between us. Promise me."

"I promise." I shivered under the importance of the vow.

"Remove it carefully. There's a strap at the back to keep it on tight. You'll have to loosen that."

"What are you doing?"

She had a leather strap tied up on his arm near his shoulder. She worked to cinch it tighter, getting it so tight that I thought the leather might break. The Dominar's arm was missing at the elbow, and while Ashana had reduced the bleeding from the grizzly stump, angry red lines were crawling up from it on his bicep.

"The red lines are the infection," Ashana said as she worked. I gently lifted the Dominar's head, feeling for the strap and loosening it as she spoke. "If it gets into the rest of him, he'll die."

Gently, I eased the crown and mask up a little and laid his head down on the pillow. "So you're going to keep it out with the strap?"

"Not even close," Ashana said, drawing a massive knife from its sheath on her belt. She placed the knife in a steaming basin of water beside her as I carefully removed the Dominar's crown and mask. "When the tar is hot, I'll cut off the infected part of the arm and coat the stump with tar to seal the wound. It's his best chance to survive this."

I gasped at her words and at the face revealed when the mask was removed. The man under the mask was barely older than I was, his dark skin and hair slick with sweat and pale with blood loss. My breath stuck in my throat. If anyone had asked, I would have said he was at least twice my age and wise beyond his years.

Ashana coughed and I realized I'd been staring for too long. "The Dominar isn't the man. The Dominar is the crown and the weight of tradition and respect."

I nodded, soberly, setting down the mask and crown on the bed beside him. Ashana handed me a cool cloth.

"Wipe his brow while I fetch the tar."

With trembling hands, I obeyed, carefully wiping away the pain-sweat of the most powerful and significant man of the Dominion. What would we do if he died?

It would get very complicated very quickly. That must not be allowed to happen.

Hopefully, Ashana knew what she was doing. Had she done anything like it before?

You don't become Top Rider by sitting around plucking daisy petals. Ashana Willowspring has earned her place, her honor, and the fine lines on her face the hard way. Don't forget it.

If only she was a White.

And don't ever let me hear that come from you!

As Prince of Dragons, wasn't he supposed to care about all dragons and not just Purple ones? I was careful not to disturb the Dominar as I gently patted his face with the cloth, too.

I have a brother who is a White dragon. He can care about that color.

Maybe it was all a game, just like the thing about eating horses.

I keep telling you that's real.

Or how he was happy to be with me when he should have been with Savette.

Was that a growl I'd heard through our link?

"The trick to it," Ashana said as she sat down across from me on the narrow bed, the Dominar between us, "is to do it quickly. He'll likely wake from the pain. He'll jerk and thrash. That will be a problem. You're going to sit on his chest and hold his shoulders down while I cut the arm and tend the wound." My stomach lurched at her instructions. "Your role is important. Don't let me down. If you lose your lunch, I'll take that scarf right back and your Color with it." Could she do that? "Ready?"

I swallowed the rising bile and moved to sit on the Dominar's chest, my hands pinning his shoulders in place. I wasn't at all ready.

"Wait," I said. "What's his name. I feel like I should know that."

"It's 'Dominar' since the day he put on that mask and it will be until the day he lies cold in the ground – which won't be today if I have any say in the matter. Now, are you ready?"

He looked so young and vulnerable. I should be protecting him and not harming him.

This is protecting him. I'll be here with you all the way.

"Ready," I said hoarsely.

Chapter Five

The moment her knife bit into flesh his eyelids fluttered open and a moan escaped him.

"Shhh, easy now," I crooned. "It will only be for a moment."

He wailed, pushing up against my hands and I leaned all my weight on his shoulders, grimacing at the effort. He was strong – his muscles hard and thick. Would my full weight be enough to keep him down?

"Keep him still!" Ashana ordered.

Banging fists on the door distracted me for a moment.

"Still, Amel! Do you know what that means?"

I clenched my jaw and pressed my lips tight together, channeling every scrap of strength into holding him in place. His head thrashed from side to side, eyes shut, and features screwed into an expression of agony, but I had the feeling that he was trying his best to work with us. If he wasn't, my weight wouldn't be enough to keep him in place. Little whimpers escaped him, searing my heart with guilt.

He must live. He will die if Ashana doesn't treat his wounds.

"What's going on in there?" a muffled voice called through the door.

There was a thump and then Ashana murmured, "Almost done."

The Dominar hissed and fell limp, his mind must have shut off to ward against a flood of pain. I swallowed, but my mouth was too dry to even whisper. When I turned to watch Ashana, she was deftly bandaging the stump of his arm.

"Get his mask back on," she whispered.

I let go of his shoulders. Moving my weight off of him, and grabbed the heavy crown, carefully setting it over his face and on his head. It felt like a cruel thing to do.

Ashana sighed. "It's not ideal, but his guardians will be ... testy ... if they find him without it and now is not the time."

The banging continued on the door as Ashana removed the leather strap from the Dominar's upper arm and I worked to cinch the strap of his mask-crown.

"He's so young," I said. "Too young for all of this."

"Never speak a word of that. There are things surrounding this you know nothing of."

"What's his name?" I asked.

"He gave up the right to a name when he took the crown. I told you that."

So cruel. How did a person live like that? As a symbol rather than a person?

The banging on the door grew louder.

"Open this door! Open it now!"

"Remember," Ashana whispered. "You will never speak of what happened here. I have your oath on that."

I nodded, an acidic taste filling my mouth. The secrets I had to keep were piling up so high that soon I'd be restricted to talking only about the weather.

"Go sit with your master. We'll pretend that you have been tending to him. Hurry."

I scrambled to obey as Ashana picked up her tools and basin. Something large was wrapped in a bloody cloth in the basin. I shuddered when I realized what it was. Ashana seemed unconcerned, striding to the door and unlocking it quickly so she could step aside as Iskaris and the other dragoons barreled through the door.

"What happened here?" Iskaris demanded.

"I was merely tending the wounded," Ashana said. "Look for yourself."

Iskaris' eyes scanned the room, a frown on his face. "Keep this door unlocked. From now on my dragoons will guard the Dominar's bed."

Ashana nodded. "Have you devised a plan for the defense of this place?"

"Nothing is getting through that door. Concern yourself with your own business, message bearer. You're no warrior."

The grim set of Ashana's mouth told me that the insult had found its mark. "I'll just clean up, then."

Iskaris nodded. "When you're done, I'll speak with you in the Great Hall. We have things to discuss."

He was going to ask her for our messages. And when he did, he'd see the ones that incriminated him. Should I destroy them before he saw them? Or hide them somewhere?

No and no. That's not the Purple way. We own the truth as it comes to us.

Despite my worry, I couldn't help but feel a stab of disappointment. Here I was, with the Dominar. I would have hoped that he would wake up and set things right, but the ruler of this whole land was hardly older than I was, unimpressive in every way.

It's a mistake to judge by appearances or to judge a man by how he looks while he recovers from injury.

I mopped Hubric's forehead with a damp cloth as my thoughts rose into a flurry. I was just as disappointed with the Dominar's dragoons as I was with him. They were the elite force of the nation, and what? They were incompetent, broken down and small, cowering here in a cave.

We're cowering in a cave, too. And I'm a prince and Savette is the Chosen One. Everyone is human – even dragons. No one really rises above that no matter what kind of prestigious position they find themselves in.

Why was our Dominar out wandering in the woods with a tiny handful of guards?

After Vanika, they moved to a mountain fortress, but when Baojang swept down from the north, the fortress was overrun. They fled through a secret passage to the woods and flew - aboard the Silver dragons - south towards the capitol, but the Dusk Covenant was a step ahead of them. Ifrits came from all around and attacked the Dominar. He and his dragoons have been fighting and retreating for seven days, slowly moving mile by mile as they fight. The dragons were no match for so many Ifrits – but you know that. You've seen it in person. These men here are all that is left of more than a hundred dragoons, guards, and warriors. They are battered, broken men. Iskaris alone has any fight left, and we both know that he is a traitor.

I felt a chill creep into me. How did he know all of this?

I've been talking to Ayancig and Inrujee the Silver dragons. They watched their brothers perish and they are deeply wounded and battered. Neither can fly. They bear the honor of Haz'drazen, serving the Dominar as we have promised since the first pact.

If they had been overwhelmed, what chance did we stand?

I have an idea about that.

I almost jumped when Hubric's eyes sprang open. My hand froze where it held a cloth to his forehead.

"I'm back." His voice was hoarse, but his wink was firm and sure.

Chapter Six

"Hubric!" I couldn't contain my delight. Finally, some ray of hope in these dark caverns!

"I need to see Kyrowat," he whispered.

"Kyrowat is resting just like you should be. Here, drink something," I said, offering him a cup of water from the bedside.

He held out his hand and I helped to ease him up to a sitting position, propping him up against the headboard and offering him water.

"He survived." His tone held gratitude and relief.

"For now. We're in a bit of a situation here." I glanced around. Two dragoons sat silently on either side of the Dominar's bed. I couldn't tell him everything with them there.

Sending help.

Gently, but succinctly, I sketched out what had happened before we found him and then what happened after, glossing over the Dominar and Iskaris and leaving the messages out completely. Hopefully, the grave look on my face and the frequent glances at the dragoons were enough of a signal to him to show him that we couldn't speak freely.

He nodded, leaning his head back against the headboard like he was too weak to sit up straight. Just when I was considering helping him lie down again, Savette entered with a steaming tray. She spoke with the dragoons, offering them broth and flatbread and then brought a cup of broth to Hubric, offering it to him gravely.

"I hear that congratulations are in order," he said weakly.

"Thank you," even strained, her smile was lovely. I missed seeing her eyes, though.

"I also heard your blushing groom fled the moment he could."

"And I hear that you want to see your dragon," she replied when he'd finished sipping his cup of broth. "I was sent to help with that."

Hubric eyed her skeptically.

"Well, if you don't want Amel and me to help you, then you'll have to wait a long time. Those legs aren't going to hold you up until you have time to rest."

"Fine, fine," he grumbled, but he seemed too tired to be actually upset, allowing us to help him pull his dragon rider leathers back on and tie his scarves.

We were tying the last two when Ashana Willowspring walked in. She checked on the Dominar despite the wary glances and sudden straightening of his guards and then rounded on us.

"I see you're in your element, Hubric Duneshifter. It's not every day that you have two servants to help you dress." She made a conspicuous sign with her fingers that meant nothing to me. Was this yet another secret language. How many of these did Hubric know?

"Haven't you heard? I've come up in the world, Top. I have my own apprentice, an ally or two and I've really mastered the cards. Perhaps, you'll play a round." His own fingers tapped a rhythm on the bed that didn't fit with his words. Secrets within secrets – that was Hubric's way, and apparently Ashana was the same way.

"You know I'm always up for a game," Ashana said, pulling a stool and small table over and producing a deck. She was planning to play right now? She cocked her head slightly to the side. "Unless you were in a hurry to get up?"

"No, I'll stay for a round or two. Gather my strength." He sounded so casual about it when he'd been determined to leave only moments before.

"In that case, I have work to do," Savette said, gathering up the wooden bowls and cups.

"I could use some tea, my dear. Perhaps some with feverfew or comfrey?"

"I'll see what we have."

"Don't go running off now," he added in a warning voice. "I don't see any dark-haired princes to save you."

Oh! There was still some bitterness there! Savette set her mouth in a hard line and left, her white gown flowing in her haste.

"Well, your injuries haven't hurt your tongue, have they?" Ashana said, dealing the cards. "Have you taught your apprentice how to win at cards?"

The wary look she shot me made her question clear. Would I know what she was communicating through the card game?

"Hardly," Hubric said dryly. "You can't make a winner in only a few games."

Ashana's shoulders relaxed and she allowed herself a tense smile as she said, "You play first."

Hubric laid down two mountains and Ashana laid down three demons so quickly it was as if she knew what he would play.

He whistled. "I've been sick. You can't go easy on me?"

"I didn't take you for a weakling, Hubric." Her tone was light, but her eyes were grim as she laid down her next hand. Four warriors.

Hubric responded with seven dragons. How did he have so many in his hand?

"I'd call that a draw," she said running her hand over all the played cards and gathering them up. He went pale at her words but cleared his throat and took the deck to deal again. I thought that maybe I understood at least a little of that interaction. She was telling him that we were stuck here with the Ifrits outside and only four dragon riders and he was suggesting that the dragons might tip the balance in our favor. Then why had she cleared them all away? Did that mean what I thought it did? Was she saying we had no hope?

"Maybe we should raise the stakes," he said.

"I can't go any higher. Deal."

Hubric dealt the cards and Ashana placed the Dominar down.

"Risky move," Hubric said.

His tower card was laid beside her's and then she laid a hurricane. His counter was a gate. Was he suggesting that we find another way out? That was the obvious solution to the situation, wasn't it? But where would we find one? Her two knaves left him chewing his lip.

"Three might do better for you," he suggested.

"I doubt it."

"Can I offer a suggestion?" I asked him. His expression was confused as I reached into his fan of cards and pulled out a shadowy figure – the assassin – and laid it on the table.

"You shouldn't play a card like that without a good reason," Ashana said coolly. "Take it back."

I cleared my throat, worried. Did they understand what I was saying?

"I wish I could, but it was already played," I said, pushing it to the same place on the table that her knaves sat.

Wordlessly, she placed her white queen beside the Dominar card. The lines in her face looked deeper as casually, she dealt out five dragons surrounding them and with a questioning look at me, placed two more beside the assassin. I nodded, my breath in my throat and she laughed, suddenly.

"Well, I don't think I've ever lost so badly, Hubric. But I'd rather lose with you, I suppose." My mind corrected it to 'lose to you' but that wasn't what she meant, was it? She meant exactly what she said. We were playing a losing hand with a traitor in our midst, the Dominar at risk, and none of us knew how to get out of it alive.

Chapter Seven

"Cards?" Iskaris asked, entering the room as Hubric hurriedly gathered up the cards and tucked them into a neat pile. "At a time like this? I expected more from you, Dragon Riders. My men tell me that we are running out of time. I've instructed them to pack basic supplies into whatever we can find to carry them and to construct a litter for the Dominar. I don't have time for foolishness anymore. What messages were you carrying?"

We are running out of time. Savette is with me. She says the Ifrits are sapping the strength out of the door. It's three feet thick – but that isn't thick enough. It will crumble before the day is done.

His eyes were on Hubric, though I felt my own face heating.

"Only one," Hubric said. "From Cynos Vineplanter of the Red to the Dominar – a verbal message – five ships of Baojang and the far Rock Eaters have invaded our shores where the Feet of the River meets the Eastern Sea."

"Grim news." Iskaris frowned and turned to Ashana. "And you?"

"I don't answer to you, Iskaris," she said easily. "And my messages have nothing to do with you. As such, you don't need to know their contents."

My heart leapt. Perhaps if she could keep their contents a secret she could keep mine safe, too.

"I'll read them and determine that," he said.

Forget messages and concentrate on the door. It's coming down. What other alternative is there?

If the door, thick as it was, was not sufficient to keep the Ifrits out, then what could we do? We were no match for them. But there had been something in the message from Comard Eaglespring about remembering the words of Ibrenicus. Could that help us?

Savette has been feeling through this shelter and she thinks she knows a way. I told her how this mountain was made when the dragons built our underground warrens. One of those warrens is not far from here. She thinks she can punch through the rock and open a path.

Knowing what else Savette could do, I wasn't surprised.

If she isn't too weakened from the fight outside.

Ashana and Iskaris' voices were rising as they argued.

"–haven't even read them myself," Ashana was saying.

"All the more reason to check them and if there is no more information in there than we already have it won't have hurt anything."

"What information do you expect? A magical cord you pull and then a door spins into existence?"

I wouldn't want her mocking tone aimed at me. I should interrupt and tell them about the warrens.

No!

Hubric laid a hand on my arm with a small shake of his head at the same moment. Was he speaking to Raolcan, too?

He speaks to Kyrowat. Together we are finding a solution. We will drill a hole through the rock to the warrens, using Savette's power and our flames. Then, we take the refugees out that way and escape through the warrens with them to safety.

And how far away was safety?

Maybe close, maybe far. I will know more when we enter the warrens. The Silvers can carry the Dominar, and we will help guide the people through. It's better than the alternative.

It would also give the Ifrits access to the dragon warrens.

We'll have to take that chance.

And why shouldn't we tell Iskaris ourselves?

If he really is a traitor, he'll try to sabotage us. Wait until the way is made and the plan hatched before you tell him.

"I'm not such a fool as you think," Iskaris said to Ashana, putting his face in his hands for a moment. I shuffled backward. His men stood behind him, looking in that moment, as raw and desperate as he was. "I know what our options are right now. I'm just looking for something – anything – else. The Dominar's safety is my only concern."

It sounded like the truth. He really did care about the Dominar. And yet – he was Dusk Covenant, wasn't he?

"Anything other than *what?*" Ashana asked.

"As far as I can tell, we can either stay where we are and be slaughtered when the door breaks down in a few hours, or surrender now and beg for mercy," Iskaris said, grimly.

In the absolute silence that followed the whisper from the Dominar's bed was as plain as a bell.

"Mercy."

Chapter Eight

"Dominar?" Iskaris asked, rushing to his side, but the Dominar's head lolled to the side again, clearly no longer with us. "My liege?"

Ashana cleared her throat. "He'll be in and out as he recovers. He lost a lot of blood."

"I've seen the wounded before," Iskaris snapped. "I don't need a lecture."

He straightened, and I felt an urge to step backward from the intensity of his movement, but Ashana didn't flinch at all, she leaned forward as if she wanted to fight. Hubric yawned beside me.

"The Dominar – glory to his reign – has spoken," Iskaris said clearly and with a determined look on his face. "We will rest for one hour and hope he regains consciousness in that time. Whether he does or not, we will surrender and ask for mercy."

"Are you sure he was talking about that? Maybe he just wanted relief from the pain. The man does appear to be missing an arm," Hubric said casually.

"Enough." Iskaris glared at Ashana. "Keep your riders under control and make sure your dragons are ready to leave in one hour."

Ashana stared at him for a long moment, as if to prove that she couldn't be ordered around.

"Let's go check the dragons, Riders," she said eventually.

I helped Hubric stand and we hobbled along behind her as she left the room. I stole a glance back at the Dominar as we left the room. Would he be safe here without us? Even though these were his guards, they didn't seem to care about him as much as he deserved. And I didn't believe that he wanted us to surrender.

Neither do I. Think about what he said.

He had said a single word, "mercy." Yes, it could have been in response to what Iskaris was saying, but what if it meant something else? I couldn't think of what else it could mean, though.

When you wanted to warn Hubric and Ashana about Iskaris, you relied on the card game.

But mercy had nothing to do with cards.

But could it be a reference to something bigger that others would understand?

Why was that note from Comard Eaglespring bothering me? It was like my mind was trying to make a connection between the two and it just couldn't tie them together.

Hubric was oddly silent, as if his thoughts were preoccupied as we made our way to the dragons. As soon as I said that he looked at me and quirked a smile.

"Is that Ashana's purple scarf I see around your neck, Sworn? Have you been given your colors while I was recovering?"

I felt my cheeks heat with pride. He'd noticed.

"Keep up this pace and Ashana will have to worry about you taking *her* job. It's deserved but don't let it swell your head. You're still woefully undereducated for the role." Was that tenderness I heard under his harsh tone?

"I'm glad you survived," I said, affectionately. I was worried he wouldn't.

"I could say the same to you. I thought I'd lost you, Sworn. It made me feel my age – and no one wants that."

I stifled a laugh. We were almost through the Great Hall despite our slow pace. I didn't want to urge him to go faster when he was still so vulnerable.

"I have a foggy memory of you reading the Ibrenicus Prophecies to me," he said.

"You heard me?" And here I thought he was unconscious the entire time!

"Did you read them all?"

I laughed. "At least three times. I thought it was keeping you calm."

"The Prophecies have a purifying effect. And they stick in the mind. Tell me, do you remember one that starts, 'Behold, behold in the dark of the night?'"

The words sounded familiar. I wracked my brain to think of them as we entered the anteroom where the dragons shuffled nervously from foot to foot while shudders filled the room from the Ifrit's attack on the door. There were already too many dragons in the anteroom – packed in too tightly and smelling of something...

Fear. We smell of fear.

Behold, behold, in the dark of the night... something about a light emerging from the ground, right? Something about the dawn of hope and the mercy of the past. Was that right? Maybe this was what Comard Eaglespring meant about remembering the prophecies. Maybe they contained some hint to getting out of places like this.

The Silver dragon's scales were so sleek that it was hard to tell where one scale ended and the next one began. I paused for a moment when they came into view to look them over. Even Eeamdor's sleek red scales looked rough in comparison.

They're royal dragons – beautiful and poisonous.

Not as royal as Raolcan. And he didn't need poison – other than some of his words, of course.

I resemble that implication.

Hubric practically dragged me to Kyrowat's side in his excitement, finally releasing me when he was close enough to slump against his dragon. Kyrowat had better not flame me! It wasn't my fault I was standing so close. I quickly hobbled over to Raolcan. He dipped his head low, looking me eye-to-eye as he recited the prophecy I couldn't remember.

Behold, behold in the dark of the night,
Surrounded and harried to flight,
Up from the ground through the earth's veins
Light of light and he who reigns
Dawn of hope through mercy of the past
Arriving to shine over us at last.

Mercy of the past. Had he been referring to that? Perhaps that was too much of a stretch. After all, mercy was probably mentioned a lot in the Ibrenicus Prophecies.

So what? Do you think that's referring to another time that Savette and the Dominar will be buried under ground together?

What?

Well, who else would you call 'light of light' except Savette? And despite the fact that you took off his crown for a while, I think it's still safe to call the Dominar 'he who reigns,' don't you? I think it's time to find that mercy of the past.

I swallowed and looked to Hubric. His hoary eyebrows highlighted a stormy gaze.

"Do you believe, Sworn?"

Clearly, he and Kyrowat were having a similar conversation, and knowing Hubric, he was probably dead certain that the prophecy applied to this. Crazy as it was, I thought I might agree. After all, they had applied to Savette so far, and losing her to Ifrits now would be a terrible thing.

"I'm worried about your back. You aren't fit to be moving around like this." I was avoiding the question. I *did* think it was possible. I just wasn't sure where we'd find this "mercy of the past." Other than building this place, had anything ever happened around here? Even Savette hadn't found it and she'd been looking for a way out while I was occupied with the injured.

That hammering in the background was getting to me. It was like I could feel icy cold sapping my strength and making my belly roil.

"I'm fit enough," Hubric growled. "Now that I'm out of bed I don't want to hear anything more of it. I know you and Raolcan are talking. Do you have any ideas?"

I wonder if this place was built because it was close to the warrens. Perhaps it was a stop along the way. If that was the case, maybe the warrens were cut off by a shift in the earth. Is there somewhere in this hole where the rock face looks crumbled rather than smooth? Like it wasn't carved out so much as caved in?

"There's a place just like that in the storeroom," I said aloud with a sudden memory of staring at the wall while Savette helped me look for tar and a pot. There had been shelves set up in front of it, but it was definitely there. And hadn't she felt something pulling at her when we were there?

Chapter Nine

"I'll stay with the dragons, and tell Ashana," Hubric said. His eyes told me he had been following our discussion through Kyrowat. He turned, looking for her. She was somewhere near her own dragon. Whispering to Aliss who was tending wounds on her Daieseo. "You go and check that store-room."

"Hubric?" I whispered, waiting for him to look back at me before continuing. "We recovered your messages." I pulled them one by one from my belt and handed them to him. "You should read them while you wait."

Anger filled his face. "You read these, Sworn?"

I bit my lip. "Just read them."

"No."

"What they say is important to us."

He shook his head. "It troubles me that you broke our honor in this."

"I wouldn't know Iskaris is a traitor if I hadn't read them," I hissed.

His brow furrowed but he kept silent.

"Just think about it," I said as I left. Sure, he might be mad, but it was a good thing I read those notes. Maybe they would see that our policy of keeping them secret wasn't helping anything.

I think you underestimate how irritated he is with you right now. If we didn't have Ifrits on our back and so many people relying on us, I think you might be sorry you ever admitted that. Good timing, by the way. I need to try that. Admitting to something bad when something evil is after you is a great way to avoid being punished for what you did.

Was he just trying to rub my nose in it?

I hurried into the Great Hall, my crutch skidding on the hard floor in my hurry. Iskaris and his dragoons were eating at one of the tables and a few of the refugees were at the other end of the hall, quietly eating soup. I swallowed down a stab of fear. It wouldn't just be us who suffered if we didn't find a way out. Iskaris didn't mind sacrificing those innocent children to the Ifrits. That couldn't happen.

"I require those messages now that you aren't busy, Sworn," Iskaris said as I passed his table.

"I don't have any," I said, hurrying by. His eyes followed me. What if he asked me to stop and prove it? I didn't have them anymore, but I also didn't have time to waste. How much of his hour was left?

Fortunately, he didn't ask anything more and as I entered the storeroom, I breathed a sigh of relief, shutting the door behind me.

"Amel?" Savette was there already! "Lock the door behind you."

I carefully barred the door and hobbled to the back of the room. Savette was in the back of the room, pacing back and forth.

"I can feel something close – I'm just not exactly sure where. It's in this room, though. I have a feeling that there's a way out through here."

I hobbled to the back wall, gripping the tool-filled shelf. "Help me move this."

She strode over and helped me move the shelf. "You know your suspicions about Rakturan aren't true, right? I have never felt evil from him and his eyes are filled with white light."

"You're still thinking about that?"

It wasn't obvious that the wall had ever been a door. It just looked like a rough wall with seams of lighter rock running through the black.

"What else would I be thinking about? It bothers me that you trust Hubric unconditionally and now Ashana, but you doubted Rakturan. How are we supposed to be friends if you doubt my husband?"

"You know that there are Ifrits about to burst in here and slaughter us, right? And it's up to me and you to get out of here?"

"You think the way is through here?" she put her hands on the rock but turned to me. "It's just that it's very hard to concentrate knowing that I don't have your full support."

My mouth dropped open. She cared that much about my opinion?

"It was one thing when you acted like I was a child who couldn't be let out of your sight, but now this idea that you know everything, and I have to listen to your judgment on this is just too much. I just can't concentrate."

"Ummm ... Savette. You could have said something, you know."

"I'm saying something now."

"I hate to interrupt you when you're dressing me down, but do you think you can feel a way through that wall?"

She paused and frowned. "Do you know how hard it is to connect to the truth when you're full of doubts?"

"No." What was she talking about? Wait. Her magic ran on truth, right? So, was she saying that she couldn't operate it to its full potential unless she was being completely honest and so she was revealing her inner frustration to me?

That is exactly *what she's saying. Hear her out. Besides, she has a point. Rak is not our enemy.*

Says the guy who once carried him in his mouth.

I would have tasted it if he was evil. Evil tastes like lima beans.

Now, *that* had to be a joke.

"Well, it's difficult," Savette said, leaning her forehead against the wall.

I drew in a deep breath. I should have remembered this. I shouldn't have let it fester in her.

"Savette," I said. "I want you to know that if you are saying that Rakturan is beyond suspicion, then I believe you and I will trust your judgment. You have my full confidence."

"I want you to swear."

"Swear what?" I was practically bouncing in place. I needed *her* to concentrate and find a way out of here!

"Swear that no matter what happens you'll trust Rak and give him the benefit of the doubt."

I closed my eyes and took a deep breath. I didn't like making this promise. I was naturally wary of people. But I had much bigger things to worry about.

"I promise."

She smiled. Light filled the room and with it was the sound of rock scraping against rock as the glow around her hands became brighter and brighter and brighter until all I could see was white. I fell to my knees, my hands covering my ears against the screeching scrape.

As soon as the sound was gone, I opened my eyes. A tunnel – barely wider than a dragon – stretched out in front of us into the deep black of underground night.

"What did you do?" A tingle of awe ran across my arms as I spoke. Had she drilled a tunnel through the rock?

"It used to be here, but the ground shifted down at this fault. The entrance was below the floor, so it didn't line up anymore. I just reminded it that this was its place and that it belonged here. Just like Rak and I belong together."

Was it really that simple?

To her it is. Isn't that magical?

Chapter Ten

S houts and curses from outside the door were all it took for me to shake out of my stunned haze and pull myself back up on my feet. My crutch wobbled a little as I rushed toward the door. There were going to be some very concerned people on the other side of that door.

Yes, but not concerned about you.

What?

We've been busy, too.

I unbarred the door to chaos. The refugees huddled in the door to their sleeping quarters. In the center of the Great Hall, Iskaris and Ashana were nose to nose, faces red and spewing words at such an alarming volume and pace that they weren't worth trying to understand. Besides, the cause was obvious.

Across the room, the door to the anteroom had been transformed into something large enough to allow a dragon to enter. The raw edges of the newly-expanded doorway glowed red hot and the rock that was once carved in straight lines was now a rippled circle.

Dragons could melt stone?

When you convince seven of them at once to really concentrate...

I scanned the room for injuries. Surely someone was hurt from that.

Have a little faith in us. Ashana went into the room first and had everyone back up.

No time to discuss it. There was room for dragons to come through. There was an entrance to the warrens. We needed to start moving before the Ifrits burst through the door and got in here with us.

I thought I heard something crumbling behind us a moment ago.

Then we needed to move quickly. Across the room, Hubric hurried through the very center of the cooling door, his leathers and hair smoking slightly as he made his way through. Skies and Stars! That door would light anyone but a dragon on fire! Aliss was next, with Daieseo. They hurried towards the huge storeroom door. A door, I realized in retrospect, that was plenty large enough for a dragon. Perhaps this room had been designed to be entered from a different direction.

Okay, this is the plan. No objecting, anyone. Raolcan must have been talking to more people than just me. *While Ashana keeps Iskaris busy we need to move. Aliss and Daieso have volunteered to lead the way with Rasipaer. Ashana will catch up when she is ready. They will navigate the caverns as best as they can. The refugees must follow while the dragoons are still distracted. Savette, speak with them now. They have come to trust you. Impress upon them the need to hurry.*

Savette rushed off toward the refugees, leaving me standing in the doorway. I hustled to the side as Aliss and Daieseo barreled through. Aliss signed a greeting as the two headed into the storeroom. Had the dragoons missed what happened within?

Iskaris isn't budging on a surrender and that can't be allowed. We will all die if we surrender. No, no objections.

Clearly, someone wasn't seeing eye to eye with him on this.

I'm pulling rank for once and you'll follow my plan. Because I'm a Dragon Prince, that's why!

Someone had dared to challenge him! I wouldn't do that. It made me feel nervous just to think about it.

Back to the plan – Savette and Eeamdor are next after the refugees. Amel, go and prepare the Dominar to be transported. He will ride on my back. Because you're lightheaded and down a wing, Ayancig! I saw how you stumbled when we flamed. If you Silvers don't stop fighting me on this, I'll leave you here. Understood?

Ah. It was the Silvers who were objecting. I hurried across the hall, stunned that Iskaris had not yet noticed the stream of refugees running to the storeroom behind his back. He was shouting at Ashana about the hole in the wall, his face red and arms flailing while the guards on either side of him had their weapons drawn. They looked back and forth between their angry leader and the fleeing refugees, clearly uncertain whether to support his rage or find out what was going on.

I darted past them, ducking into the Dominar's room. The two dragoons stationed there leapt to their feet.

Kyrowat and Hubric will go next, then the Silvers and Dragoons. Because you are warriors, Ayancig, and you will want to bring up the rear. Even I know that much. Oh, yes, be my guest, complain away. When your master awakens he can reverse all of this, but while he is vulnerable, I'm taking the reins and yes that pun is intended!

Wow, I'd never heard Raolcan sound so intense! I rushed toward the Dominar but had to throw up my unoccupied hand and stop in my tracks when they crossed their blades in front of me.

"No one approaches the Dominar without our permission."

Chapter Eleven

"We need to go," I said. "The Ifrits are almost through the door. Whether we plan to run or surrender, the Dominar needs to be moved to a pallet for transport."

They looked at each other before nodding and stepping aside. They both looked worn and haunted, like there wasn't much life left in them.

"Lieutenant Iskaris has decided to surrender, then?" one of them asked.

I shrugged. "Can we use the pallet you brought him on?'

"No, but we can use the tick mattress on the bed if we use the rope lattice from the old pallet."

I followed him to the bloody, discarded pallet. He was right. The ropes were the only salvageable part of it. Together, we detached them from the rest of the makeshift rig, took Hubric's mattress off the narrow bed and laid it in the net of ropes and tied it in, rushing to cover it with the sheets and blankets of the bed. Would we have enough supplies with us, like bandages and water?

Savette packed up a few things for our saddlebags. Hurry.

"Have you seen Ifrits before?" the Dragoon asked me as we worked. "You looked like you knew how to fight them."

"We've been encountering them for the past few weeks," I said. No need to get into details while we hurried. "There. I think that will hold him. Can you two carry him from the bed to the pallet?"

They nodded and lifted him carefully from one to the other, his mask never shifting. We tied one of the ropes around him to keep him from falling and tried to make it as comfortable as possible.

"Have you seen anyone surrender to them before?" the Dragoon asked.

I paused. "No one really has time for that. They usually die before they have a chance."

He nodded grimly, as if he had expected that. Why was he willing to surrender, knowing what it meant?

No more time for chitter chatter. I'm outside the door. Bring the Dominar.

"Can you lift the pallet?" I asked the Dragoons. "Follow me."

We rushed out of the room to the chaos beyond.

"What are you doing? Return your liege to his room!" Iskaris yelled as we emerged, but Raolcan was already barrelling past him, skidding to a stop in front of us.

"Load the pallet on Raolcan," I said, ignoring Iskaris. "Try to balance it on the saddle between his shoulders."

"Not hanging from the side?" the Dragoon who had asked about the Ifrits asked. He looked nervously at Iskaris, but his mouth was set in a hard line and I knew he was with me on this. This was the only hope of saving the life of our ruler.

Jakvar. That's the Dragoon's name.

"It's too narrow where we are going. He needs to be up top, so we can squeeze through tight spaces."

"I said stop!" Iskaris said, shoving Ashana out of his path. She recovered her balance, drawing a long knife from her belt and lowering into a fighting stance.

"Surrender is death, Lieutenant," she called back. "We have only one option. We flee and possibly save the life of our Domianar, or we all die."

"Listen," Iskaris said. "I'm the Dominar's personal guard. Would I really put his life in danger if there were another alternative?"

"You would if you were Dusk Covenant," I said, quietly.

"What's the Dusk Covenant? I'm a dragoon lieutenant and nothing more."

"Then come with us," Ashana said. "Save your master. We've found a way out. Probably."

Iskaris' face twisted with indecision, but as he paused to consider, the Dragoons with me hurried to load the Dominar on Raolcan's back. Without waiting for a reply from Iskaris, Raolcan rushed toward the storeroom and I hobbled after him, the two Dragoons with me.

The Silver dragons waited for us to pass before following Raolcan into the storeroom. The moment we went through the door, I heard a cracking sound.

The door gives way. Run.

I wasn't much of a runner. Not with a bad leg and a crutch.

Grab the side of my saddle. Use me instead of a crutch.

I grabbed the side of his saddle with my left arm, letting the crutch dangle from its strap, and took long one-legged leaps, letting Raolcan bear most of my weight.

Just like that!

Ashana shouted from behind me, but it was no longer shouts of anger, but shouts of fear and urgency. Iskaris called out, too. Was he fleeing with us, then?

As the dark of the warrens swallowed us up, I realized belatedly that I had not thought to bring a light.

There is a lantern and flint in my saddlebags. When we stop, we can light it – if we have time.

A dim, shadowy light flickered occasionally in front of us.

The others have lanterns. Theirs are lit, but the passages twist and turn.

As we turned our first corner, a powerful boom shook the ground. I knew without having to be told that the door had been breached. There would be Ifrits behind us now, and dark earthy places were their natural territory.

Chapter Twelve

I wasn't sure how long we'd been running when Ashana passed us.

"The Dragoons came, too," she said between gasps of breath. "They're behind you as a vanguard. I'm going to catch up with Kyrowat. He says the path branches up ahead and decisions will need to be made. He'll keep Raolcan in the loop. You'll catch up to Hubric soon. He's just ahead of you."

The passage was too tight for a dragon to pass another dragon. Ashana barely squeezed by me. Whatever position we were in was where we were stuck. Behind us, there were only the Dragoons and Iskaris and the two Silvers to defend against the Ifrits. I swallowed, my lips thinning as I thought about how the man I trusted least was our rear-guard. None of the Dragoons had much drive left except for Iskaris – the possible traitor. Despite his denials, I didn't believe that he wasn't Dusk Covenant.

"Maybe the Ifrits are too large to fit in the passage," I said, gasping for breath. Raolcan's support was a huge help, but it was still effort to half-hobble, half-be carried.

The passage is still taller than it is wide. You can hop up on my back when we stop. It might be a better place to keep an eye on the Dominar from, anyway.

"Don't place any bets on that," Ashana said. "They didn't look very solid when we fought them. I think they could twist those smoke and dust forms into something slender enough to squeeze through these warrens."

I felt a spike of fear thinking of Ifrits pouring into the warrens like oil through a funnel, with nothing but a handful of half-hearted Dragoons and two broken Silver dragons between them and me.

"Hold steady," Ashana said.

Raolcan's silence in my mind only deepened my fears. After all, if he wasn't rushing to counter them and comfort me, then they must be accurate.

Hold steady, like Ashana said. Fear is the friend that makes us quick to respond and the enemy that makes our minds grow sluggish. Take the gift and reject the curse it carries.

Good advice. In the cloying darkness, my hearing felt like it was expanding outwards to fill the surrounding world. I could hear Raolcan's every breath and even the steady metronome of his heart. Behind us, scuffling, curses in the dark and the clink of metal against rock. What if they ran faster than us? What if one of them plunged his sword into my back, not knowing I was there?

From ahead of us, all I heard was the occasional echo of a voice. I wished I could see. I wished Raolcan would flame – just enough to see what was in front of us so we didn't fall into a hole.

Actually, I can see just fine in the dark. And if I flame right now, I'll torch Ashana and I don't think she'd like that.

Could he see how far behind us the Silvers and Dragoons were?

I don't have eyes in the back of my head, Amel.

Then they could be creeping up in this mineral-smelling cave, and they would never know I was here...

Except that I can read the Silvers' minds and I know they are still a little behind us. But the Ifrits are behind them. They follow us into the deep dark.

Did he have any idea how creepy that sounded? The idea of anyone following me in the dark was terrifying. When I added in the idea of horrific earth demons, I felt like I might need a rest stop soon.

Hold your nerve. We come to the first gateway.

Gateway?

These warrens were made by the Elders before Haz'draen birthed us, before she was an egg herself.

That must be old.

Older than you can imagine. They are so old that they are dangerous. We dragons maintain the ones we use often, but this is far from where we go. No one has been here for hundreds of years, but I sense the magic here.

Magic? He could somehow sense magic?

Dragon magic.

I didn't know dragons had magic.

Not many of us do, but in the old days there were many magical dragons and they were the ones who made these warrens in defiance of the laws of the world – held in stasis by their great power – a place to flee to when our enemies gather. A way to reach one another when the skies are inhospitable.

It seemed strange that dragons would build cave systems when they were creatures of the air.

Stranger than how we moved rivers and mountains?

Their world was one I'd never suspected.

Humans always assume they are the pinnacle and just live like it's true. It isn't true. You are only a small part of the world, though you matter a great deal to me.

Ahead, I thought I saw a faint glow of light. The glow grew stronger.

Hold tight to me now.

I gripped his saddle tightly. Ahead, the light called to me. I leaned out from Raolcan to try to see it.

No, tuck in tight. I don't want you falling off the ledge.

Ledge? I looked down. We were emerging from a tight tunnel to a wide open space. As the cave opened up, the floor became a stone bridge with nothing but a black drop in either side of the narrow rock. Thank goodness for the glow! Someone must have lit a torch ahead. I strained my eyes to see, hugging close to Raolcan and when we finally took a small turn in the path, I gasped.

In the center of the massive cavern was an island-like hub and out from it, a variety of bridge-paths branched out. The center of the hub was a massive statue of a rearing dragon. It was not the lanterns in the hands of the refugees or Savette's eyes that lit my path now, but the faint glow that surrounded the dragon statue. At his feet, purple swirls and dips of a regular size and similar shapes glowed like glyphs.

They are glyphs carved by a dragon claw. They channel the power of the gateway, but see how faint the glow is? The power here is faint. There will not be enough to transport all of us.

He wasn't making any sense. Transport? Wasn't it just a sign that told us which path led where?

It does that, too. Raolcan said as we stepped onto the center island. I felt a tension within me ease as soon as my feet hit the more solid rock of that center hub. In the ghost-like light, I searched for familiar faces, sighing with relief at each one. Savette and Eeamdor. Hubric and Kyrowat. Ashana and Rasipaer. The huddled refugees, silent in either awe or terror.

Under the feet of the huddled refugees a glowing sigil in a ring faintly pulsed. The pattern of it moved as if it were alive. It was almost as if it were welcoming them, since they stood within the ring, but there wasn't room for a single body more in that swirling, moving sigil.

See the sigil they stand on? It can take them far from here with a single word from me. I think there remains enough power to do that. Usually, you can do it often with only a small break between transports. Right now, with the glow so dull and the power so drained? We will be lucky if it moves them once. It will certainly not have the power to move all of us.

Were there more of these?

Undoubtedly, but where they are along the path and whether they, too, are stripped of power ... that is the question.

So, we were faced with a decision. Some of us could flee the terror of this living grave – but not all of us. I already could guess who Iskaris would nominate to go once he got here.

Chapter Thirteen

Fortunately, Ashana was the one barking orders when we arrived. "Yes, all of you. Every villager, every child, every bag you carry has to fit in that circle and room for a dragon and rider, too."

As she spoke, children wailed as their mothers hushed them and the quavering voices of the elderly asked for clarification. My belly flipped with queasiness. What if those were my children sobbing? My grandparents confused in the dark? If there was a way – any way – to get them out of here we had to take it.

"Unload the Dominar and bring his pallet here," Ashana said.

I scrambled to obey, Hubric immediately at my side. "The Ifrits aren't far behind. We must hurry."

Would we wait for the Dominar to be transferred to the circle if they came around the corner? Wouldn't it be better to get the innocents as far away from the clutches of the earth demons as possible? My heart was racing, my brain swirling round and round so quickly that I couldn't catch a thought.

Calmly now. Don't fear. I won't let those little ones perish no matter what comes next. You have my word.

If I had Raolcan's word, then it was as good as done. I felt my breathing slow as I climbed up on his back and began to unfasten the pallet. Behind us, Iskaris and his men arrived, the Silver dragons with them.

"What manner of place is this?" Iskaris breathed.

"A gateway." Hubric's words were clipped but steady. "We can get some of these people out of here."

"To where?" Beside Iskaris, his Dragoons formed a line, blades out toward the darkness, their dragons anchoring the ends of the line, despite their injuries.

"The Dragon Lands. Don't ask me where it leads to there. Kyrowat says that the gateways can be manipulated, but this one is low on magic and he says that if we try to change the destination it might sap the last of the strength of it. We'll just have to risk sending them to Haz'drazen wherever they end up in her lands. Ashana is trying to fit a dragon in with them to help with communication. Here, help us with the Dominar."

I had the last strap unfastened and was already shuffling the pallet toward Hubric's reaching arms. Behind him, Aliss and Ashana had Daieseo in the ring, lying down. People sat on his back, tail, and neck, crowding in so that they could all fit in the circle with the big Purple dragon. Aliss was wedged against his face, hers bent in close, clearly trying her best to keep him from complete claustrophobia. We'd better hurry before he panicked and flamed someone.

A real possibility. Hurry.

"I'm not going to send the Dominar to an unfamiliar location without a proper guard. Particularly not when he's injured," Iskaris said. "What do we know about how the dragons will receive him. They could flame the lot of them as soon as they arrive."

The closest faces of the refugees registered terror at his words and I shook my head vigorously to them. Savette slipped off Eeamdor and rushed to calm the fearful among them, her white dress and blindfold glowing in the faint light. Iskaris was going to cause a revolt.

"We need to hurry."

Hubric nodded, taking the pallet in a strong grip as I lowered one end towards him.

"Stop," Iskaris said. "Put the Dominar back on that dragon and then clear these people off. We'll get him to safety first – with a proper force of guards."

"No time," Hubric said gruffly.

I scanned the area looking for support. Could Hubric and I stand up to Iskaris on our own? These people needed protection – more even than the Dominar, though I was worried for him, vulnerable as he is. But there were babies and tiny children in that crowd of people. Tiny, desperate souls who were being chased by the things of nightmares. One little boy's panicked eyes met mine – wet with tears. His little lashes blinked and another tear rolled down his smooth cheeks. I would do anything to prevent these children seeing more terrors.

Aliss was busy keeping her dragon steady. Ashana paced the circumference of the circle, kicking feet and bags back into the circle with harsh reminders that only what was inside the circle would be transported and that included limbs. And Savette... where was Savette?

There. She was standing beside the glowing stone pillar, her hands wrapping around it and the glow of her eyes piercing through the bandage.

"There's plenty of time, Dragon Rider," Iskaris said. "The Dominar is my top priority. No one else matters more, not filthy villagers and not you. He goes through that gateway and he goes with a proper guard."

"Do you want him to go or not?" Hubric asked. "Because if you want him to go, then lend me a hand and let's carry him over there before it's too late."

From the darkness, I heard a howling like a strong wind. I whipped around, staring into the darkness, but it didn't take long to see the flickering fires that glowed in the eyes and mouths of the Ifrits as they rushed towards us. I bit off a scream, but the people in the circle didn't bother to stop the cries of terror welling up from their throats. The only thing louder than their screams was the voice of Ashana.

"Stay inside the circle! No matter what, stay inside!" She grabbed a small girl who darted out of the circle, throwing her over her shoulder and stepping within the glowing glyph. "Whose girl is this?"

Before I could hear the answer, the people in the circle seemed to stretch and then vanish before my eyes, Ashana with them.

Chapter Fourteen

"Oops," Savette said from her place by the pillar.

"Get him back on Raolcan!" Hubric yelled urgently, pushing the Dominar's pallet back up. From the pallet came a moan, but I ignored it, clawing it back into place and scrambling for straps to fasten around his pallet. There would be none left for me, but I could cling to Raolcan without them.

I told you they wouldn't be harmed.

I felt a swell of pride at that, but there was no time to respond to his smugness. Hubric was already half-running, half-stumbling back to Kyrowat as Raolcan whipped around to face the incoming Ifrits. Savette left the pillar, leaping onto Eeamdor's back. The glowing glyph was gone, the last embers of the pillar's power drained from use. There would be no escape there.

There may be other gateways in here somewhere.

Hopefully, those little children were safe with Ashana and Aliss and Daieseo.

Daieseo will make sure the dragons on the other end know what has occurred here. They will guard the innocent. Do not fear.

I wasn't worried. These days I trusted dragons more than humans. What I *was* worried about was Rasipaer. When Ashana had entered the glyph with that child, they'd been separated.

He's a big boy. He'll be fine. If it were me, I'd be grateful to see you out of harm's way.

But he hadn't tried to get me into that circle.

You're a Dragon Rider, not a porcelain doll. It is our honor to defend the weak – even if that means staring down a dozen Ifrits in the pitch black with the ruler of the Dominion tied to an old mattress on my back.

I swallowed and cinched the straps around the Dominar tighter. Was it lighter in here? I thought I could see his chest moving up and down as he breathed. He moved like he was trying to sit up using his missing arm. I placed a hand on his chest as yells and screams around us told me the Ifrits were almost here.

"Dominar?" I said. "If you can hear me, you need to lie still. You lost an arm and are gravely injured. You are on the back of a dragon as we flee for our lives, but if you squirm too much these straps will get loose and you'll fall off. So, please stay still until it's safe to move."

I couldn't tell if his moan was pain or acknowledgment.

Raolcan left the ground with a burst of speed, launching us into the air. Beside us, Eeamdor launched, too. That's where the light was coming from! Savette had removed her blindfold and in the presence of the Ifrits, the glow was growing brighter and brighter.

"Hold the line!" Iskaris yelled, bracing himself, sword in hand. On either side of him, his Dragoons followed, the Silvers rearing up, ready to flame.

Was holding the line the right move? There was still time to flee. I scanned the other bridges. Which way would we go?

Rasipaer read the signpost. He said the way is not obvious, but it is between two likely paths.

And if we chose the wrong one?

There's no way to tell what would happen. We'll just have to play the hand we've been dealt.

The Ifrits closed in, but the first in line evaporated in a soundless boom.

Hold on tight. It's about to get interesting.

Hubric flew by so close that I held my breath, ducking low over the Dominar.

"Hold back, Amel!" Hubric called. "The Dominar is too important to lose."

Raolcan cursed in my mind. Knowing him, he'd been just about to dive into the ranks of Ifrits the way Kyrowat just did. Instead, Raolcan reared back, spinning to arc around to the back of the group.

Kyrowat flamed in steady bursts, Rasipaer following him in formation, filling in the gaps. Both dragons were cunning, and they seemed to avoid the grasp of the Ifrits with ease.

The problem was, we couldn't afford to lose any of them. We needed to fall back to where we could flee again. In the bottleneck of a tunnel, we would only face one Ifrit at a time.

Not much of a consolation if you're last in line.

A scream came from the Dragoons, but I was too distracted to look. Raolcan's turn was too tight and I almost slipped from his back in my awkward position over the Dominar's pallet. With a grimace I found a baggage strap and wound it around my waist, buckling it tight and then finding two more to make make-shift thigh straps. Heat blew back at me as Raolcan flamed at an Ifrit.

They're overwhelming us. We must retreat. Rasipaer leads the way.

I looked up to see Rasipaer barrel past, his belly inches from the top of my head. I ducked, instinctively. Raolcan lunged in front of Eeamdor who was trying to spin for another attack. He shoved him towards Rasipaer instead.

Reds! Hotheads, all of them!

We were right behind Eeamdor and Hubric was behind us. He was screaming for the Dragoons to follow.

"Belay that!" Iskaris yelled. "We stand for our Dominar!"

"They're too much for you! Flee!" Hubric called back as one of the Silver dragons was swept off the rock island by an Ifrit. He plunged with a flaming scream over the side. With his broken wings, he could not fly.

I'd never heard a dragon scream before. It seared me to the core. I bit my lip and held on tight to Raolcan, as if, somehow, I could keep him safe.

The world filled with light again as Savette launched a second attack, wiping out three Ifrits in a single moment. They exploded in clouds of dust, but a dozen more were pouring through the warrens toward us. If we stayed here, we would be overrun despite her efforts.

Through the clash and shouts of battle, a voice deep and heavy as an iron hammer smashed through to all our minds.

"Retreat."

I didn't need to look to know it was the Dominar.

Chapter Fifteen

When I joined Dragon School, I knew that riding a dragon wasn't for the faint of heart, but I could barely keep my eyes open now as we corkscrewed through the warren passage. Raolcan was half flying, half scrambling like a worm through a garden bed. He was using wings and legs indiscriminately and after just a few moments I'd lost any sense of up or down as we climbed along walls, vaulted off ceilings, and soared anywhere there was enough room for his wings to get lift.

The second we'd hit the warrens, I'd had to double over top of the Dominar – body to body – to avoid being scraped off Raolcan's back in our passage. I gripped my straps and his pallet to keep myself wedged that way, fear and adrenaline thundering through me so that I was a wash of intensity and anxiety. The world beyond was only something I saw in flashes and any sense of where our companions were, was completely lost.

I'm keeping track.

I didn't want to think about the dragoons on foot. What had happened to them?

In situations like this – when running for your life – it's best for each person to keep their mind on their own business.

But I couldn't do that. Especially not with my body pressed up against the Dominar's in a far-too-familiar way. His crown-mask dug into my shoulder and I bit my lip as every jostle of Raolcan's movement brought pain from where the metal hit my bone and added pain where straps dug suddenly into waist or belly or thighs. Comfort was not our priority. Survival was.

"Where are we?" the Dominar asked. His voice was quiet, but whether that was because he was speaking softly or because the rush of my own heartbeat was too loud in my ears, I didn't know.

"Dragon warrens under the Dragon Snout Mountains," I said.

"We fled here," he acknowledged. "After that grizzly run from the stronghold. How many of my men survived?"

I tried to remember how many people I saw standing when we fled the Ifrits.

"Five, I think, and one Silver dragon." I fought against the memory of the other one falling off the edge of the rock island. I didn't dare let my imagination dwell on what happened after he fell from view.

"We started with three hundred."

Three hundred? That couldn't be possible!

"Treachery from within our ranks and armies of demons set upon us. I lost track of what was happening sometime during the fall of Leedris City. My arm..."

"Is gone. We had to amputate it to stop the infection," I said. I knew there was no use in trying to make it sound nice. There was nothing nice or pleasant about losing something as precious as half your physical capability.

"An acceptable loss."

He clearly hadn't been trying to live his whole life with a useless limb if he found the loss 'acceptable.' But I supposed that compared to losing two hundred and ninety-five friends it might not be that big of a deal. I wasn't even sure if that number included dragons.

It doesn't. Rasipaer has made an exception to our usual rules about communicating with humans and is filling the Dominar in on our situation. As the dragon of the Top Rider, it is his right.

None of us might live to see the day out, so usual rules probably didn't matter too much.

Purples have stayed hidden this long because we don't advertise. We have rules for a reason. Hold tight!

We squeezed through a tight space and I felt Raolcan fighting to get his legs through without crushing us on his back.

If the Dominar can make it without that pallet, we need to set it loose. See if you can move him when we get into this open area.

We'd arrived at another hub, but there was no light in this wide area except for the light of Savette's eyes near the front of the group. The only way I realized it was open was when we stopped pinwheeling through the warren and soared straight and level.

"Can you ride without being strapped onto a pallet?" My tone matched my emotions – urgent.

"Yes." His tone impressed me. If I had been answering, there would have been less surety in my voice.

"Okay, I'm going to unstrap you. You'll have to hold on to me so that you don't fall when the straps are off."

"Agreed."

I swallowed a lump in my throat, my mind completely filled with the task of loosening his straps without losing him over the side of Raolcan.

I unfastened the first one that was keeping his chest tight to the pallet and as soon as he was free he sat up, wrapping his arm good arm around my waist as I worked the second set of straps that held his waist to the pallet. Together, we shuffled off of the mattress as we loosened each strap. The straps had gone around both the Dominar and the mattress, so as I freed them, the mattress caught the air, whipping in the wind. I fought against the last strap, finally loosening it and the mattress flapped hard, pulling free and flying toward the chasm below.

I refastened the first strap around the Dominar's waist in the proper, dragon rider manner. My breath hitched in my throat as I realized suddenly what I was doing. I'd been so focused on the task that I hadn't realized how close I was sitting to the ruler of our entire Dominion. Too close. I froze, fearful of treating him too personally. It was different now that he was conscious of what was happening than it had been when he was ill.

"Can you help me?" He asked. "I've never strapped in with just one hand, and I'm not sure that I can put the shoulder straps on by myself – or any of the others for that matter. I will need to learn to fasten buckles with one hand."

I swallowed, uncertain about where to start.

"I promise, I won't bite," he said.

Nervously, I strapped him in the rest of the way and helped him turn to face the right direction before fastening myself in properly. Now that the pallet was gone, there were more straps to work with and I'd better use them or Raolcan would be furious. Besides, it took my mind off the fact that I'd practically hugged the ruler of our lands.

Not practically, Amel, actually. He had his arm around you. That's quite the honor, I hear, although to be fair his thoughts were entirely on how to fight the agonizing pain in his arm, not in how close he was to the Dragon Rider helping him.

Chapter Sixteen

We didn't stop, though Rasipaer dove around us, heading back the way we came. What was he doing?

He's swooping down to gather up any dragoons that survived our flight.

Raolcan's mental tone was grim. Were there any who survived? I craned my neck to look for survivors, but it was too dark to see.

Iskaris and two others live. Inrujee perished in our retreat. There was no chance for all of them to live – on foot and wounded as they were.

We should have gone back for them and loaded them on our dragons.

Then we would all be dead.

It felt too cold to think that way.

We saved as many as we could at the first gateway. What were the chances that all the refugees would fit within the glyph? I would have liked to send the Dominar and Savette with them, but we had no time. Even so, the light shone on us when we were able to get them safely away. I mourn the deaths of my brothers, but we are close to our own end, Amel. We can not spare energy second-guessing, we can only make the best choices we can in each moment, remembering that one false dive could be our last.

I shivered and placed my palms flat against his back to feel his warmth and remember we were still alive.

Savette is recovering from our last battle. Perhaps she will find the energy to use one of these fading gateways.

Now that was an idea with some weight to it!

Hubric's idea. He is five steps ahead of the rest of us – it helps that he truly believes in her and the Ibrenicus prophecies. Rasipaer continues to explain our situation to the Dominar. He is taking it well, considering what is happening.

Maybe Savette could use the dead gateway at the center of this hub. We were almost there - the black statue outlined by Savette's gaze.

No, not this one. She needs one that has a little energy of its own, so she can see how it works. She's never done this before.

Would she be able to do it now? She wasn't a Magika. Her power worked differently.

She also isn't a dragon and this is dragon magic, not Magika magic.

What was the difference?

Our magic is the magic of roots pulling water from the ground. We draw on life from within the earth. The magikas do this also, but more like finding wells here and there, where we siphon it out. Savette does none of those things. She reminds things of the truth of what they are.

Details aside, we'd need to find a lit gateway to do that. Raolcan dove suddenly, and my arms wrapped around the Dominar without thinking as we corkscrewed through the air in a downward barrel roll and then shot out of it like an arrow, zipping in an unpredictable pattern. My eyes shut of their own accord and all I could do was hold on and fight down the nausea and spinning headache that accompanied this insanity. It felt like a full minute before we climbed again, leveling off and slowing down. I opened my eyes, taking great, heaving breaths and screamed as a hand made of wind and dust snatched toward me. Raolcan spun away, seconds before it plucked me from his back.

They're too fast. They're everywhere. They led us into a trap.

Chapter Seventeen

H ow had they arrived here before us?
There are many ways in!

I scanned the area looking through the darkness for everyone else. Gouts of flame were all I could see of the dragons. Perhaps I could have seen them in the light of the flames, but Raolcan was maneuvering too erratically for me to keep my eyes fixed on any one point.

They're faster than me.

Things must be bad if he was admitting weakness. The Dominar slumped against my chest. The erratic ride must have been too much for his weak body. I wrapped both arms around him, keeping him from injury as best as I could. Raolcan spat flames and then spun himself to the side. Why did he bother?

It hurts them. Just not enough. There need to be more of us – at least four or five for each Ifrit.

Then why do it at all?

It slows them. Distracts them while Savette works.

If she spent all her energy fighting Ifrits, she'd burn it all away and we would never be able to use a gateway to get out of here.

If she doesn't, then we have no offensive weapon.

And then we die, one by one in the velvet dark of the warrens. I swallowed down bile, clutched the Dominar close and bit my lip. There was nothing I could add right now except hope and faith in Raolcan. He had to know that I trusted him and believed he could get us out of this alive. I fed my confidence and faith into him through our mental bond, thinking hard about how much I loved him, about how amazing his strength and faithfulness were. It was all I had to give him.

The dank smell of moisture in a closed space filled my nose and I shut my eyes against the nausea-inducing sight of flames and light flashing at sudden unexpected moments while we rolled and wove around enemies I couldn't make out in the dark. Something hit me – not hard enough to injure me badly, but enough that I was knocked mostly off of Raolcan's back and had to scramble to straighten myself. The Dominar hung from his safety straps.

If only I knew his name so that I could call to him and tell him I was helping. Instead, I worked silently, hauling him back up, inch by inch, sweat forming across my brow and my mouth dry from effort and fear.

Work faster. We are going to be in a tight place again in a moment.

I'd need to tighten the play on those safety straps so he didn't jar loose the next time we were attacked.

That wasn't an attack. Kyrowat flew too close avoiding an Ifrit.

I finally had the Dominar in place, his safety straps tightened so he wouldn't be able to move more than an inch in any direction.

We missed our chance at the warren. It's blocked. We're trying a different arm.

How would we know which one to take? No one had been able to read the center hub this time.

It won't make a difference. We aren't heading anywhere in particular except for away from these Ifrits – if we can get away. They might be at the next hub, too.

I heard a cry from behind us and Raolcan made a nasty noise like a cross between a hiss and a bark. Savette lit up like a torch ahead of us, Eeamdor somersaulting upward in a loop, and then she was facing the space behind us. I closed my eyes tight, but the flare of her light still left purple after-images across my vision.

Lean down over the Dominar and get as flat as you can. She's bought us enough time to make it into these tunnels.

I obeyed, pushing the Dominar flat and lying over top of him, arms spread out around us and clinging to the saddle, my teeth gritted, breathing fast, and nerves tingling. Something scraped across my back and I clenched my jaw hard to keep from screaming. I was bumped and jarred from every direction, like a rock tumbling down a hill, but I had the impression that I – we – were being squeezed.

It's very tight. We are going in first. Skies and stars, if I never see you again, at least let me not get stuck!

The rock scraped across my cheek and I squeezed my eyes tight. Nothing else could move. The breath seemed to press out of my lungs, each breath more shallow than the last. I half-sobbed – more in panic than in pain. Beneath me, I heard the Dominar moan.

Just as I was beginning to fear we were going to die like that, there was a sudden thrashing push and we were free. I eased my weight off the Dominar, pushing my hair out of my face. My hands came away wet and sticky, but Raolcan wasn't stopping. He corkscrewed through the warren like a dragon with his tail on fire, though I felt exhaustion in his movements. They were clumsier than usual, lacking his usual effortless grace.

I'm afraid I used up a lot of energy kicking through that tight space.

How would Rasipaer do with three men on his back?

Two men. One died at the last hub. Maybe more. They would have had to wait for us to push through that tight space.

I wrapped my arms around the Dominar again. Judging by the way his body slumped and rolled with every one of Raolcan's movements, he was out cold. The minutes drew out long, leaving a taste of acid and iron in my mouth. The taste of fear turned my stomach and made each second ring with importance.

I choked back a sob of relief when fresh air hit my face and Raolcan burst from the tight warren into a wide hub in a gentle soar. This time, there was a faint flicker of light at the hub. As we sped towards it, I risked a look behind my back, relieved to see Kyrowat pushing through the warren behind us. We hadn't lost my mentor yet. I fixed my eyes on the hub, anticipation building. Maybe this time there would be a way out.

It grew closer and closer and then suddenly, Raolcan spun back towards the warren. What happened? Was there an Ifrit I hadn't seen?

Savette and Eeamdor need help.

Chapter Eighteen

E eamdor crawled out of the warren to the wide bridge on the other side – were these bridges wider? – lit in the other-worldly blue light of the central hub. One of his wings was crumpled at his side and the other was completely gone. Savette was nowhere to be seen. I looked at his back a second time, certain I must be wrong, my breath speeding in panic.

Calm. Look beside Eeamdor.

She was walking beside her dragon on the wider bridge and for the first time since the healing arches, her eyes were dark. No, no, no! She turned her face toward me as if she could still see me, but there was not a flicker of light behind her blindfold. I had thought it was hard to hope before. Now, I felt only ice where hope had been. I'd counted on her magic to get us out of this hole in the ground. I'd been counting on a miracle. And what about Eeamdor? What did a dragon do if he lost a wing?

Underneath me, Raolan shuddered, giving me my answer. There was no coming back from losing a wing when you were a dragon. It was as bad – maybe worse than my leg and the Dominar's arm.

I swallowed hard, trying to think of what to say or do. Raolcan was circling as if he was watching Savette's back for trouble, and Kyrowat swooped in and landed beside them, quickly loading Savette up with Hubric on his own back. That made sense. Eeamdor could not carry her now, and now – more than ever – we had to hurry. Where was Rasipaer?

Stuck. Fortunately, the Ifrits are also stuck. They can squeeze more than we can – shape their body to fit the tunnel – but it takes time to adjust their corporeal forms.

Good. We needed time. Eeamdor limped toward the hub with Kyrowat flying beside him. Hubric signed encouragement to me – an 'all's well' sign and a 'keep it up' sign. He didn't bother to sign instructions. At this point, our dragons were the ones making the strategy decisions and I knew that while Hubric might have something to offer to them, there was no way I could help.

Raolcan circled near the entrance and I could tell from the way his body moved that he was tense.

I don't want to get too close. If an Ifrit comes out next ... I have you and the Dominar to worry about. But I don't want to leave yet, either. Rasipaer and his riders have yet to emerge. They might need help – like Savette did.

Wise. Raolcan was surprisingly wise about everything. Eeamdor and Kyrowat had just reached the hub when Rasipaer's gnarled snout shoved through the warren and out into the light beyond. He flamed irritably and shoved off from the ground in a weary soar. On his back sat a single figure – Iskaris. This journey had not been easy on the Dominar's guardians. We took up a spot on his flank, winging our way to the center hub. Iskaris drooped in the saddle, shaking his head occasionally like he was having trouble staying awake. He favored his right side and clutched the saddle desperately, like he might fall off at any time. Maybe he might. I didn't know how he'd lost his companions and just thinking of it made me shudder.

One was killed by an Ifrit. The other didn't survive the squeeze through the narrow part of the tunnel.

Unbidden, a memory of that journey rose to my mind, only this time I envisioned what it would have felt like to be smashed against the rock instead of merely battered by it. My own face and shoulder throbbed painfully at the memory, but I couldn't dwell on that now. If we survived this we could take a count of our injuries. Until then, we had to press on.

Raolcan was the last to land beside the pillar. He set down wearily next to Kyrowat, their massive chests heaving in synchronized deep breathing as they caught their breath from the long retreat.

Hubric had his hands on the central pillar, studying it with Savette as Iskaris slid off Rasipaer and joined them.

"Get us out of here," Iskaris said. "As quickly as you can."

Chapter Nineteen

I f I dismounted, I would have to leave the Dominar slumped over Raolcan, whereas this way I could hold him up, his head leaning against me. That had to be better for an injured man, right? They should have taught me this better in Dragon School. If Ashana was here she would have had a few sharp words about that.

She's probably got all the refugees to safety and is fretting for Rasipaer now.

I liked that thought. Could Rasipaer feel her so far away?

No. Our range is incredible, Amel. Few riders can feel their dragons from so far as you can feel me.

I felt a warmth at that despite the cold darkness around us, but there was a crackling feeling when I tried to smile. Blood must have dried across my cheek. At least we'd made it through that rock wringer alive.

"We're trying to see if we can get it to work on its own," Hubric said from the pillar. "The last time it had plenty of energy and Ashana knew what she was doing. This time, I'm not sure it has enough."

"It doesn't," Savette said, wearily, placing her head in her hands. "And neither do I."

"You can't give up now, girl." Hubric's words were gentle, but his steel core was closer to the surface than usual. We were all worn down.

"Well, don't just sit there! Do something!" Iskaris barked. "We have the Dominar to protect! Let's get that girl down to help you."

I had misjudged him. He must not be Dusk Covenant or why would he care so much about the Dominar? Why would the Ifrits be attacking him?

The Dominar is more important to the Dusk Covenant alive than dead. Don't mistake a desire to keep him alive for loyalty to the Dominion. The Dusk

Covenant wants the Dominion for themselves. They will use any tool necessary – including the Dominar.

But then he could just leave with the Dominar and the Ifrits, couldn't he?

It's possible that they have turned on him. I doubt the Dusk Covenant can control them like they think they can. Ifrits have their own goals and desires that no mere humans can dictate. Iskaris has his own goals, too, though they are murky to me.

It made a lot of logical sense.

Just don't trust him. We don't know for sure who he is.

"Calm yourself," Hubric said. He didn't even bother to look up at Iskaris. He was conserving his energy. "Savette, do you know why the power is so dim?"

"I've used up too much." Her voice was small.

"It's the power of truth, isn't it? The power to make things true again?"

She nodded her head.

"So, you need help thinking of the truth and bringing it back."

"This isn't helping," Iskaris fumed. "We need to set up a defense."

"Shut up. I'm working." I'd never heard Hubric so terse. "Amel, come here, please."

Gently, I leaned the Dominar over onto Raolcan's back, grabbed my crutch from its spot and slid down to the ground, hurrying to his side. Hubric must have a plan.

"Savette needs help. Come here. Sit beside her and take her hand, and I'll take the other."

"What are we going to do?" I hurried to obey, but I couldn't see what he had in mind yet.

"We're going to give her our minds."

Chapter Twenty

"I don't understand," Savette said.

"You're out of truth and the healing that comes from it," Hubric said. "Or rather, you're out of hope so you can't hold the truth of it in your mind anymore. Amel and I are Purples. We are dedicated to truth. Our dragons are Purples. They love the truth and guard it carefully, too. Kyrowat and Raolcan are going to channel our minds to you and you're going to take all the truth, and hope, and power that you need to fire up this gateway and get us all somewhere else. Rasipaer will tune it as best as he can, but honestly, anywhere is better than here right now. Remember the words of the prophecy: 'For in the day of darkness the Chosen One will find hope in our hearts, and from hope truth, and from truth, light that opens doors.'"

I licked my lips. Did I trust Savette enough to let her in my head like that? To offer up hope and truth? What if she took all of it and I had nothing left. I'd never heard of anything like this, but I'd seen what she did to the Ifrits. What if she couldn't help doing that to me, too?

I'm not big on trust, either, but don't worry, she has to go through me to get to you. I'll stop the access if it starts to harm you.

That's all I could ask for. I pushed an encouraging smile onto my face and gripped Savette and Hubric's hands in mine.

"Begin when you're ready," Hubric said.

"This is nonsense," Iskaris said, leaping off of Rasipaer to the ground beside us. "The Ifrits will be here at any moment. If you can't make this gateway thing work, then we need to flee."

His fears only reinforced my own. I tried to think about something other than Iskaris. Somewhere out there, Leng was either in hiding or fleeing for his life. Somewhere, Rakturan sailed across the Eastern Sea to his homeland to convince them war was not the answer. Somewhere Ashana was worrying about Rasipaer. Somewhere Lenora and Ephretti fought the Dusk Covenant. All those things made me more nervous than hopeful. I felt Raolcan reach out to me and I leaned into the comfort of his vast mind. *That* was hope. In the middle of terror and desperation, there was one person who was always there for me, who put me ahead of himself, who wanted nothing but good for me, who had risked himself and his own honor to choose me in the first place.

I leaned into that sense of Raolcan and that gratitude for his friendship, treasuring the hope of it, remembering the truth of it. I didn't know when Savette began to draw on that, but I felt a tug in me as if she were drawing on our hopes.

In the background, I watched as Iskaris slid the Dominar off Raolcan, carrying him to the center of the sigil beside us. My mind grew thick, but I held onto that feeling of hope. It was a good thing that he was bringing the Dominar close. Maybe even Iskaris was not who I thought he was. Maybe he really did care only about the Dominar.

A roar met my ears. At first, I thought it was from the light springing up in Savette's eyes, but Iskaris's battle cry rang out just after it. The Ifrits were here. I tried to turn my head to look, but I was frozen in place. I saw Hubric's eyes shift, but his head was locked in place, just like mine. The glow around Savette grew as orange glowing light burst over the center statue and heat flared at my back. Behind us, dragons fought Ifrits for our lives. The roar of lizard anger met the hiss of angry earth demons.

I lost track of time as my emotions and thoughts swirled within me, dragged out for Savette's use. Everything melded into screams, shouts and horrifying cries but at the center, I held on to that thread of hope inside me. I couldn't let it go.

Savette's light was blinding, filling not just the area around the signpost, but the whole hub. As if a dam broke loose, I could suddenly move again. Hubric tugged us to the sigil in the floor, around the Dominar. I stole a glance at Raolcan, gasping when I saw him joining Rasipaer in a deadly battle with an Ifrit. How would we get the dragons out of here if we had to get them all into the sigil at once?

There were three Ifrits attacking them, and as they fought, I saw one more squeezing out of the warren and into the open space. With each moment it took us to gather the power to leave, our foes grew in number. I bit my lip, gripping Savette's hand tighter, wishing she could hurry things.

And then the unthinkable happened. I was staring urgently at Savette's face when Hubric cried out, his eyes looking past me. I turned just in time to be knocked off my feet and thrown into the air. The world tumbled. Nothing felt real, not the glimpse of Savette and Hubric flying through the air beside me, or the view of Eeamdor's massive body skidding past along the rock. I realized in a flash that his tail had hit us, knocking us into the air, but as I began to fall back I saw him continue his skid, claws scrambling desperately as he disappeared over the edge of the hub. Savette screamed.

I didn't have time to see more before the earth came up out of nowhere and smacked me in the face. Everything went black.

Chapter Twenty-One

U*p, up, up!* Raolcan was screaming in my head.

I blinked my eyes open. I was on the ground. Everything hurt. My head ... oh, my head ... every blink sent shattering pain through my skull. I just needed to rest here a moment. I let my eyes close.

No time. Up.

A claw grabbed me, scooping me up. Should I be fighting? I opened my eyes just a slit. Savette sat in the middle of the sigil, hands pressed to the ground, but white light surrounded her. Kyrowat dropped Hubric in front of her, wheeling to flame an Ifrit hand that snatched out at him. Where were Iskaris and Rasipaer? Where was the Dominar? What about Eeamdor?

Eeamdor is dead.

Raolcan! Where was he?

Who do you think is carrying you?

We entered the circle, and everything went dark again.

Darkness.

I opened my eyes.

"Get in the circle now, or you'll be left behind!" Hubric was shouting. Who did he mean? Me? Not me. I saw Iskaris running across the ground, the Dominar in his arms. He stumbled, falling to the ground.

I reached awkwardly for my crutch. Yes, it was still there! Pulled myself up on wobbly legs. The world tilted wildly, making me dizzy, but I fought through it, dragging myself to their side and bending down to help Iskaris drag the Dominar over the line to the sigil. The look he shot my way was so strange that I didn't know what to think about it until I looked down. One of his arms was missing, blood dripping from the stump – the exact arm that the Dominar had lost fleeing these same enemies. I opened my mouth to ask him if he needed help, but felt my knees buckle beneath me.

Darkness. Something cold was pressed against my face.

I opened my eyes. We – the humans – were all in the circle, though someone was keening with sobs. Was that Savette? I didn't see Raolcan, but Kyrowat streaked by, flaming at an enemy and the Dominar was conscious, he was pushing a slumped person over the edge of the sigil. Iskaris? If he succeeded, the man would be left here.

Stop passing out. We need you conscious.

Like a person could control that. I crawled towards Iskaris. No man should be left here. The Dominar left him, stumbling back to the center of the sigil, blood leaking from his wounded shoulder. Pain seared into me and the bright light white became thicker until it filled me and everything around me. I grabbed Iskaris, rolling us both back into the sigil and holding on tight to him. He felt smaller in person than he'd looked when I first met him.

I felt a sensation like stretching and then darkness.

I opened my eyes.

I was falling, air rushing around me. Or was I? Was this a dream?

Nope. It's just you falling to your death. Here, let me save you again.

Strong claws snatched me from the air as everything went dark again.

This time I felt like I was out for a lot longer before my eyes snapped open. I was being carried in Raolcan's strong hands, but something felt very wrong with my body.

You're gravely injured. Don't fear. I will get you help in time.

Savette? Hubric? I'd saved someone at the last minute. Iskaris. Had he made it?

We are scattered. I don't know where everyone is. We fly like the wind to the heart of my homeland.

The Dominion?

The Lands of Haz'drazen.

I felt light, like I was going to fly off all on my own and go visit those clouds over there.

Stay with me.

Beneath us the land was black, but on the horizon, a sliver of pink light glinted over the horizon.

I won't leave you. I'm here, spider.

Was Raolcan okay? He sounded strange.

We'll get you to safety. Please, stay strong.

Everything went black again.

Read the rest of Amel's story in "Dragon School: Bright Hopes" or "Dragon School: Episodes 11-15".

Behind the Scenes:

USA Today bestselling author, Sarah K. L. Wilson loves spinning a yarn and if it paints a magical new world, twists something old into something reborn, or makes your heart pound with excitement ... all the better! Sarah hails from the rocky Canadian Shield in Northern Ontario -

learning patience and tenacity from the long months of icy cold - where she lives with her husband and two small boys. You might find her building fires in her woodstove and wishing she had a dragon handy to light them for her.

Sarah would like to thank **Harold Trammel, Eugenia Kollia,** and **Sarah Brown** for their incredible work in beta reading and proofreading this book. Without their big hearts and passion for stories, this book would not be the same

Visit Sarah's website for a complete list of available titles.
www.sarahklwilson.com